THE CIGAR SONG

A Story of Passion

EMIR LOPEZ

Based on an original story by Emir Lopez
and
An Original Screenplay by Emir Lopez and Doug Klozzner

Trilogy Christian Publishers
A Wholly Owned Subsidiary of Trinity Broadcasting Network
2442 Michelle Drive
Tustin, CA 92780

Cover design by: Cornerstone Creative Solutions

For information, address Trilogy Christian Publishing
Rights Department, 2442 Michelle Drive, Tustin, Ca 92780.

For information about special discounts for bulk purchases, please contact Trilogy Christian Publishing.

Manufactured in the United States of America

10 9 8 7 6 5 4 3 2 1

Library of Congress Cataloging-in-Publication Data is available.

ISBN 978-1-63769-068-0 (Print Book)
ISBN 978-1-63769-069-7 (ebook)

THE CIGAR SONG IS more than a story about cigars and baseball, it is a story about obtaining the unobtainable. Every day people are faced with obstacles that seem impossible to overcome, whether in school, work, in sports, or just life itself every single day. Emir tells a story of faith, of believing in yourself and your dreams, and of redemption. No matter what happens in your life, remember to always believe in yourself. Through my own experiences, I have always believed in myself. If you have forgotten how just read Emir's book, you will soon be reminded!

Dan Opperman is the 1987 1st round draft pick of the Los Angeles Dodgers who endured 5 elbow operations (3 Tommy John surgeries) and was forced to retire at the age of 25. He is now the Chief Legal Officer for the New Mexico Finance Authority.

Dedicated to you, Dear Reader… I only pray these words make you a better, happier person, and may your faith be strengthened by it.

I also dedicate this book to my friends, family, and anyone hungry for a little inspiration, for a little push! This story may change lives! Don't say I didn't warn you; you are in for a wild ride!

Contents

Foreword

By Carlos Fuente Jr.

As many of you may know, the tobacco business is my world, and it has been for my family since 1912. This business runs through my veins, it is my life. Needless to say, when Emir said he would be honored if I wrote the foreword for his book, I immediately accepted. I say this not just because *The Cigar Song* is nothing short of an amazing story everyone should read, but mainly because of the passion he conveys while telling the story. I felt it in his voice and in his desire to share a life-changing story with the world.

I am too extremely passionate about cigars and my cigar business, and I'm a firm believer that without passion, the world just comes to a halt. Passion can move mountains. I would say that whenever there's authentic passion behind anything you do in life, the end result is an undeniable success. Whether it is producing a great cigar, running a successful business, raising a family, staying true to your faith in God, or writing the next best-seller, without true passion, it is impossible to do.

True passion is what the world needs more of today, and as you read this book, you will realize passion is woven in the words herein as you turn each page while leaving the reader with a hunger and a desire to pursue their own dreams and God-given purpose.

The Cigar Song is a must-read, inspiring and moving, to say the least!

Introduction

"The world breaks everyone and afterward many are strong at the broken places."
Ernest Hemingway

I HAVE SPENT COUNTLESS hours thinking of how to make this story appealing to anyone who dares to read it, although I am not a well-known writer, and I consider myself a novice and inexperienced writer at best and someone who is just flattered and delighted to have anyone read my uncelebrated words. And while I sit here scratching my head, contemplating the idea that my story may be read by hundreds and even thousands, it is truly mind-blowing to me. Then I ask, "How do I complete the difficult task of keeping you engaged as you flip through these pages?" My only guess is I could start by giving you something you have never read before in a story so appealing you will not be able to stop once you start reading. Well, let us give it a shot! Shall we? First, *The Cigar Song* is a story of great passion. It is a story of the journey to achieve unfulfilled dreams through clear determination and a man driven by his search to bring about his deepest life's desires at all costs. Now, if this sounds familiar to you, it is because most of us want the exact same, but unfortunately, life is so full of obstacles and difficulties, many times it ends up derailing us in the end. Unless, of course, our conviction is so strong, we learn to overcome by finding joy even in the toughest of times. The good news is we get to choose…as the desire to want to live life to its fullest is built in our DNA, putting aside the hiccups and speed bumps we face along the way in exchange for that possible joy we may find in the end. The choice is ours! I can only hope you'll find this story has the kind of plot that inspires, and I will go as far as saying that I'm not going to write about what pleases audiences most according to today's popular demands, which is violence, sex, nudity, and perverse themes, and though I must agree these topics may be captivating, I choose to write from a different angle in an effort to keep you committed and wanting anxiously to read more as you turn the pages. So, I choose instead to write about real-life events, real-life circumstances, and about issues and occurrences, which haunt us all. I will also add a few cool ingredients I find most people out there believe to be interesting, for example, history, baseball, politics, love, and why not, *cigars*. In addition, I will mix in faith. "Faith?" you may ask. "And how does faith fit in with all those other ingredients, which apparently seem a bit distant and usually controversial?" Well, that is the hook, and as you continue reading, you'll find how it all ties together in a mind-twisting manner that's both appealing and puzzling; and honestly, if you're not a better person by the time you finish reading, I simply didn't do my job. See, I wanted to write a story where a story matters, not just topics of interest with a mysterious ending but about an alluring turn of events that captivate the curiosity and interest of the reader, you. Now, we mix all these different elements into one big mix, and what do we get? Well, you are still here, aren't you? *The Cigar Song*, it is just that…a unique and original story that may sound familiar to us all in many ways yet distant and abstracted because of where it takes place and where it takes us, even weaving in and out to a distant time and place far from today. Perhaps it is not just a rags-to-riches story filled with inspiration and core values for human life but also a reminder that where we are today in life, it is never permanent as everything can change in an instant, either for better or worse. In addition, this story may touch a few nerves with regards to this great nation of ours, the United States of America. I know, and what better time for a rags-to-riches story than now? These are fickle times where we may be realizing for the first time in our lives that even though things can be far from perfect in this country, why then isn't anybody leaving? Instead, it seems more than ever as if the whole world wants a piece of the American dream. The time is certainly ripe for a story about appreciation for this nation as these are times in our history when many people are finding out for the first time the true value of freedom and what it is like to manage and appreciate "one single dollar." Moreover, throw in the fact that these days many people are learning to appreciate a good job or just a job period, and I feel we need to become more aware of our surroundings and be more mindful, thankful, and grateful to live in a free country and in a place where we get to enjoy not just having freedom of speech and certain liberties negated to many around the world, but also the freedom to dream. We couldn't even begin to think what it would look like if we were to open our eyes to the possibility of losing this freedom we enjoy as Americans today, which is very possible if we do not take care of it, and I really do feel we have to become more zealous of the things that make us, according to most, the greatest nation in the world and the one place everyone wants to come to and be a part of. The US flag says it all as it waves freely in the open air... and when we look at it, no words are ever needed to express its true symbolism of its gift, which is liberty. *The Cigar Song* is not just the story of an underdog and a tale of a man of passion and unrevealed dreams who defies the odds, but also a parable of survival and refusal to accept mediocracy. It is more of a memoir in search of the true meaning of that beautiful flag; the red, white, and blue from the eyes of an outsider, an immigrant, and, of course, a life-long fan. This fascinating story, which also touches on the captivating world of cigars, should remind us of how much the make-up of a fine cigar resembles how most of us are made in so many ways, including the way life takes us, peeling through our many layers like onions only to find our true selves and purpose underneath the process of being planted and uprooted, shaped, and crafted by our surroundings and the uncertainty our lives pave along the way. These are just a few similarities between us and cigars as "...the tobacco plant comes from the ground, from the dust, and like us, it eventually returns back to the ground, to the dust...here today and gone tomorrow." The life of Jaime Colon becomes his very own melody and what I call "The Cigar Song," a title that suddenly came to me after listening to the lyrics by singer Matthew West where he voices, "Well, your life is the song that you sing / And the whole wide world is listening," which is exactly how Jaime feels as he is constantly monitored and supervised, always sensing he is singing the song of his life with his every move, surrounded by bright lights and in front of an audience with many critical expectations. I can only hope *The Cigar Song* serves as an inspiration to anyone who dares to receive it, perhaps allowing it to ignite the fire within in pursuit of fulfilling your own dreams. And, finally, I want to say that if one single life is changed by this written message, then I guess I did my job, and I am a happier man for it.

How It All Started. A Forgotten Piece of History

As the entire village rests in the dead of night, every little sound from the wilderness is mildly heard. From the endless buzz of crickets to the nocturnal birds and what sounds like maybe monkeys mimicking each other from a distance. It all collides, blending in delicate musical harmony. These are the sounds of the night serenading a tired West African village after a long day of festivity, and to them, however, it is relatively almost silent, being so used to it. This time of the night is when the jungle comes alive; when the big cats and large animals hunt while the others take cover in trying to stay alive, but tonight, and in this village, the people of Sierra Leone sleep peacefully.

The night sky is covered by a sea of bright stars, which from the village look like the reflection of millions of tiny sparkling seashells. The bright full moon shines upon the land like a lighthouse guiding merchant ships returning from a long voyage at sea, and a group of scattered clouds attempts to slide in front of the potent lunar presence to cover its silvery light. Eventually, they do. Much darker now, the full moon is hidden by the passing clouds in the late hours of the night, and Princess Ijaba and her family sleep comfortably in the relaxing confines of the royal palace. The night is tranquil...peaceful...quiet... And then suddenly, the calm is shattered by a group of men, white pirate-like European men led by several African guides, who storm the village with muskets and metal swords. They look like hunters, but this time they are not hunting wild animals for a trophy, they are hunting people to make them slaves. These men are holding torches in their hands as they begin setting the entire village on fire. The palace guards are the first ones to go when the intruders methodically take them down one by one. Some of the villagers are shot, others slashed by swords and machetes, while a few others are being strangled with ropes. It is a sickening sight as screams of panic fill the air and a historic moment unfolds. Villagers flee from their huts, seeing the calm of the night suddenly turn into echoes of terror. Those who try to escape run without any direction amid desperation, seeking survival. There is chaos and confusion everywhere. The ones who are captured are brutally beaten, some shot and slashed outright, killed in cold blood. The intruders continue to torch the huts, and in no time, the entire village is ablaze.

Ahh...Of course, I am dreaming. Have we landed yet? I jolted as I awoke from my dream...well, it was more like a dark and ominous nightmare, but as the sudden thumping sound of the wheels of the plane touching the landing strip abruptly interrupted my bad dream, I was glad it was over. Still shaken, I watched as the plane finally came to a stop at the end of the runway. Suddenly, a cool breeze struck my face the minute I stepped out of the airplane, followed by a thick wall of humidity that could have penetrated a concrete fortress, but I was glad to be home after almost thirty years. The year was 2005.

Cuba is my homeland and the home I left along with my family almost three decades prior, but I certainly was not sure I was prepared to face all the changes I would encounter. I was skeptical, to say the least, and to tell you the truth, a bit scared too. Not scared for myself as I later confirmed how safe it was for tourists there, especially those coming from the US, because the Cuban government could be in serious trouble if anything were to happen to one of us, but I felt emotional fear for what I was about to face there. Then out of the blue, I took a deep breath in trying to compose myself, and I think it worked as I felt more relieved.

Just minutes prior, as the plane descended, came a hasty sadness, which instantly collided within me at the grotesque site of what appeared to be an airport tarmac down below at the Jose Marti International Airport located about nine miles southwest of Havana. It was the appearance of the tarmac that should have been changed fifty years ago, but this was only the beginning. A sign read, "Welcome to Cuba," but somehow, I felt the complete opposite as I immediately sensed an unwelcome feeling, almost as if everything within me rejected my presence there. And what a sad comparison with any of the previous airports I had just seen on my way there, starting with when I first departed from McCarran Airport in Las Vegas, a modern airport where you could not find a piece of trash on the floor if you tried. Then in route to Cuba, I had a stop in Phoenix, another contemporary airport, and finally, in Mexico City; this one, sprawling with people and congested inside and out but still up to date, and now this. What a shame and what a pity to find this airport in Cuba in the condition I did. I certainly did not expect such abandonment and neglect on behalf of the Cuban government, but there I was. They say first impressions are everything, and if this airport was only the tip of the iceberg of what I would eventually see in Cuba, then I should have jumped on the very next plane and returned back to the US, but I did not. Everything looked as if it were stuck in time, deteriorated, and rotted, old and battered down by Father Time and, of course, neglect. Never in my wildest imagination did I think the portrayal of the present condition of Cuba told to me by people who had previously visited would be this real. I always believed they were exaggerating, *just rumors*, I thought. Well, I guess not, and at first, I was quite impressed by the lack of luxury in comparison with the other airports I had just passed through as it gave me a sense of calm and peace, it was different. I like different.

I felt like I could relax and enjoy a different way of life, but I quickly adapted, and my curiosity suddenly took me over. Now, I wanted more, I wanted to see the rest. The lack of every basic need and so-called normal things we are exposed to here in the US was quite alarming to me, and again, my disappointment was just getting started, but aside from the poor maintenance and lack of luxury I would see upon my arrival there, which was impossible to ignore moving away from the airport, at the same time I experienced something beautiful and mesmerizing. The island was just astonishing, the culture incredibly rich and the entire place warm and captivating, but most impressive were the people. These people, my people, left an incredible and almost unforgettable scar within me as I immediately learned to admire their perseverance, their survival abilities and skills, their love for life and resiliency, which I find sort of difficult to express with just words. This alone helped me cope with the harsh economic reality they live in, and I could not help feeling bad for them, but I chose to feel compassion and admiration instead. I guess I was intimidated by their capacity to do so much with so little and, on top of that, to have enough energy left to simply continue living, smiling, playing their internal music, and singing their sad song, which to me was quite remarkable. I asked myself a simple question, *Would I be able to do it?* And this threw my mind for a spin. Would I be able to survive one single year there if I were to trade places with them? And my answer was simple…*No!* "What is going on? Why can't things be different here?" I continued to ask over and over, but no one around me dared to answer these questions in order to help satisfy my curious persistence. I know my intellect was being tested, so was my soul. My heart ached; it was as if they were all hypnotized. Now, I knew they were obviously scared as they were constantly being followed and listened to, but then I finally concluded that this was the correct term for what I saw in their eyes, fear; then I understood. Now I was the one who was afraid. I felt a strong conviction that I needed to do something during my visit, but what could I do? It seemed to me like I could perhaps provide a little piece of heaven during my stay and possibly get away with certain things while I was there only because I was a foreign visitor, a tourist, and someone who, of course, played by a different set of standards and rules. I knew for one that I was able to buy my family much-needed items in stores where only tourists shopped, exposing them to some of what they were missing because, for the most part, Cubans are not allowed to partake in many of the activities tourists can or shop in certain stores where only foreign visitors shop. It was ironic to see that even in their own home, so many things were prohibited, and this I was not aware of, but what I really did not know was that the minute I would step on the plane coming back home, it would all go back to normal for them, and they would again return to their hell, their misery. It was as if they were given a short break and a tiny recess to impress me so that I would leave Cuba with a good impression of what life truly is there. Luckily, I was able to read between the lines and grasp the truth, and it sucked. I tried to pretend I was there to check out the old neighborhood and to visit my family after all those years, but I just could not hide it well enough, and the ugliness of such a beautiful place haunted me. Many times, bringing me to tears. Their forced smiles and half-truths tortured me, and nothing but frustration defined that moment and time. I wanted to scream, but that was not an option, and I really felt like Moses in the book of Exodus in the Bible when he first realized he was a Hebrew only after living his entire life believing he was an Egyptian and part of the royal family. Then suddenly, after learning the truth, he felt in his own skin something he had never felt before, the pain of the Hebrew slaves building the pyramids, his people. Like Moses, I was too wounded at the sight of my people aching, and the bubble of innocence within me had just burst as I began to comprehend that this place was a true nightmare and no different from Egypt back in the days of Moses. I was heartbroken and feeling quite nostalgic when, to make matters worse, a sign hanging from a wall quickly caught my attention, reminding me to just be and to try to enjoy my time there since I knew I just could not change a thing. The sign read, "Cuba, sunny today, tomorrow and always, just try ignoring the obvious clouds." It was a handmade sign in Spanish and one with no explanation needed, as I immediately understood! Yes, I clearly accepted that the beautiful beaches and the rolling mountains were only an illusion and much like putting makeup on a pig or falling into a mud pit then trying to clean yourself with baby wipes. Now, when I mentioned earlier that I was scared, I was simply implying afraid for what my eyes would see and what I was about to experience, and not necessarily physical fear, for walking in the streets of

Havana, I felt much safer than walking in some of the streets in the US, and besides, if anything were to happen to a tourist, especially an American while visiting Cuba, this would be trouble for them, so, for the most part, I always felt safe there.

I jumped up and stopped a private car in the middle of traffic and asked the man how much he would charge to drive me the whole time I was there. To my surprise, the man, who happened to be a well-known doctor of over thirty years, informed me that he made more money driving tourists around than he did as a practicing doctor in Cuba, a surgeon. Then he continued with a huge smile, telling me he would be delighted to drive me anywhere I wanted to go for just one hundred US dollars the time I was there if we had a deal right there and then. He mentioned it had been a bad week for him. His last customers, a group of tourists from Spain, were asked to get out of his car by the authorities and quickly escorted into a different car that would take them back. He was never paid. The doctor then proceeded to tell me he had been fined by the Cuban government too for attempting to show them the real Cuba outside of the restricted areas, which was a big no-no, but he claimed he was simply trying to do his job. You know, customers first, right? I believe that is a universal thing, but in Cuba, the rules do not always apply, only the ones they make. By "They" I mean the Cuban government, and so to all this, I was stunned and a bit impressed by the old guy, so I hired him on the spot. I immediately said to myself, *how can a lifelong doctor make less than a taxi driver? Who would want to be a doctor then?* I asked again. So, after hiring him for the ten days I was there, I had him take me to the middle of the city of Havana so I could walk around and see the sites. Still stunned, I asked what his name was, and he amiably replied, "Armando. Dr. Armando to those outside of this car, but to you, I am just a friend!" The man replied with witty, gracious laughter, and we departed the Jose Marti airport and headed towards the center of the Cuban capital. I, too, introduced myself, and we took off down the street in the classic car. The place was amazing, and as I looked to my right and to my left only to see old buildings, some from centuries ago, cars from the '40s and '50s everywhere, and people walking and riding bikes as far as I could see, people flooded the streets and sidewalks like in New York City. Only it all appeared to be in black and white, so to speak. Yes, even the rusty metal water drainages on the street gutters were nothing standard, like those on the streets of old Paris. The old streetlights with the fancy lamps, half of them off, only seen all over Europe seemed out of place here, and the dull unpainted buildings reassembling decades of economic injustice at the hand of the failed Cuban revolution all seemed to notice me, and if they could talk, they would probably be welcoming me to Cuba with what appeared to be a smiley face. All I could do was smile back.

Huge trees to provide much-needed shade on both sides of the main street stood tall in rare ageless form like guardians. I really felt as if I were in a time capsule, a bit sketchy but fascinated. The Cuban women parading the sidewalks were all beautiful. The men were as gracious and friendly as my driver, very sociable and eager to install a conversation in a heartbeat. A good-looking crowd for sure, and it made all the difference to me as an outsider, making me feel welcome for the first time. It was interesting to see the clashing outer appearance of so many different ethnicities in one place, only they were all the same today's Cuban. Except for the occasional tourist that could be easily mistaken as they liked to blend in to not be a target of harassment. No, not that kind of harassment, of course, but the kind of constantly being sold different items as they walked through, which is how the street vendors make their living, usually targeting tourists. One thing that really caught my eye was the apparent truth to the lack of racial division there. In Cuba, and at least to the naked eye, in my opinion, it appeared as if they are all one people in the same predicament, survival. These are people who live the constant suffering of a slowly dying system, which takes many of them with it, and who do not have time to be bickering over racial differences. So, they learn to live together and get along in order to survive. Maybe we should take a page from their book and apply it here in the US. The women there are as plain as can be but still gorgeous. Natural beauty. Nothing too fancy, even though they try to emulate to the best of their abilities American fashion and designer lifestyle. The working girls that are known there as jineteras, or "horse jockeys," these girls stick out like sore thumbs, though they would rather be called "tourists' girlfriends" to better blend in and to not call too much attention to themselves. For the most part, the women there do not really wear expensive makeup, nor do they use fancy hair products, but the little they do use makes them look alright. However, there was a certain look in their eyes that instantly caught my attention, as if they were all screaming for help in desperation, and this is the reason they will marry the first foreign visitor who proposes as a way to escape and as a way to get out of Cuba to have an opportunity at a normal life. Many times, just to be able to help their family back home once they leave Cuba. But what is normal anyway? Is what we have here in the States normal? The stress, the constant wants and need to accumulate more stuff, things; the rat race we live daily? What is it? Or is their world more of the norm? Can there ever be a balance, a middle ground in this life? If you have nothing, then you want what you see in the movies, the glamour, the lifestyle...and for the most part, once you have it all, it is usually too much, and it ends up killing you in the end. Isn't that right?

As I looked around the old city, I was taken by the beautiful palm trees decorating the streets in every direction. Huge, thick trees with Tarzan-like branches hanging down almost to the ground, maybe a hundred years old, and providing a unique atmosphere under the hot tropical sun. Some of the streets made of colonial brick as old as the city itself, along with the usual city noise and the smog from the busy traffic blended with the difficult-to-ignore streets full of cracks and in much-needed ill repair, as if abandoned and forgotten. All the surroundings were probably built by the grandparents and the great grandparents of these people who made it the glorious place Cuba once was. Sadly, unable to maintain it by providing the required upkeep after decades without resources, the result of it is the Cuba we see today, decayed and on the verge of a total debacle. For anyone coming from a place like the US, a visit to Cuba is nothing short of gripping. It can easily be described as an immediate culture shock with a quick invitation to want to see more as it was for me upon my arrival, but Havana is indeed a splendid city, and to not see it with a sense of empathy is impossible. This lost city cries in desperation as I cried, unable to process the thought of what it would look like if it were ever renovated the likes of Miami Beach today. It would be just grand, but Old Havana was just that, old and only grand in its own way. Beautiful in more ways than one and especially to someone like me coming from the City of Lights, the contrast was just fascinating. I could really appreciate its relic glow and distinctive appearance, and I, for one, appreciated the lack of paint and the shutters on most of their windows but without glass. I can easily see how this would not be of any attraction to them who see it all as life as usual, but for me, even the absence of a central air conditioner was refreshing. I kept thinking the old buildings could be sold for millions of dollars and converted to various commercial uses in a thriving real estate market if Cuba were to ever open, but to them, the people there, which they use as homes and probably pray daily they do not collapse while they sleep, these epic structures are just old ruins where they bury their sorrows daily. Between every beautiful building and colonial structure, a pile of garbage and litter lay, and though to me it seemed out of place, to them, it was just routine. *Do they even have city garbage trucks or a sanitation system here?* I thought...but maybe it is not in Castro's government budget to clean the place up... What a joke! More of the things they exchange for free education.

Cuba is a mystical place, to say the least, mysterious in so many ways to us here in the States because of the embargo, extremely rich in culture and in history, but completely forgotten. Stuck in time! More like abandoned! This is quite a striking land and a remarkable people, but in ill need of restoration, and not just structurally but also socially. The obvious contrast of the streets filled with countless potholes, untrimmed bushes growing along the sidewalks, and garbage-littered street corners almost seem out of place when just a block or so away we find five-star hotels lining up in the tourists' area that reminds us of those in Miami Beach and Cancun. The buildings all around Old Havana where the Cubans live, not the ones used for the tourists to stay in, not the hotels but the people's homes, are gray and dull, unpainted, and unkempt while other parts of the city are quite a site to see. The entire place is disheveled, and it very much looks like some of these old buildings may come down at any moment, as I mentioned earlier. Many of them are not even in livable condition and outright unsafe, but all I can think of is how much money these buildings would go for here in the States? These are irreplaceable colonial buildings; they are not replicas, but the real thing left there to rot by time and yet another unkept and forgotten piece of Cuba. The entire country filled with priceless vehicles from the 1940s and '50s is a tourist delight, and the cathedrals from centuries ago are nothing short of admirable. They even have a very distinctive replica of the Capitol Building in Washington DC, also mentioned earlier, which sits in the center of Old Havana, making it hard to miss. Yes, an almost identical but smaller version of the Capitol Building can be found in Cuba, constructed early in the twentieth century, and I can proudly say that right across from it is the Monserrate building, which is where I was born. I lived there with mom and dad for the first two years of my life until we moved to Jaimanitas, a small town just a couple blocks from the beach. The Capitolio is yet another structure from years ago, which accents this momentous city, and, like this building, the entire island is filled with a certain beauty of its own, but I repeat, to me, the most impressive thing there was the people. *What strong people*, I thought, and my hat went off to them for enduring over six decades now of this mess. They are a people melted into one true kind, the repressed and oppressed people of Cuba who have suffered over sixty years of what appears to be an endless dictatorship, and yet, they endure. The Cuban people are dying slowly, and they have been dying since the late 1950s when one dictator overthrew another, and I knew this was happening because I still have family there, but I had to see with my own eyes. I had to see for me, it had been almost thirty years since my dad, my mom, my sister, and I departed from there; I was ten.

This trip, however, impacted me so deeply I began to write the minute I sat on the plane coming back to the US. I am not even a writer, but I just was stunned by my enduring experience. I was in shock, and I was deeply wounded. I hurt for them, and I ached for their pain, their despair, their lack of desire to live another day in such dire-straight conditions in my eyes, and on top of all that their soul-searching ambition to one day be free. This quickly became apparent to be probably the fuel that keeps their fire burning, but just barely. I like to compare it to the last of a tank of gas in a vehicle where all that filth sits, and why they tell us not to run the car on an empty gas tank to avoid that filth at the bottom of the tank from getting into the engine causing it to clog it while ruining it.

It is a true miracle how over eleven million people live on that island today. Ironically, many of them seem to live forever, and I, for one, had never seen so many men and women well in their 80s and even 90s just walking around like they have no clue of what their age is and without an idea that they are supposed to be in a nursing home in bed resting and waiting to die. A seventy-year-old in Cuba acts as if they are forty-five, while the same forty-five-year-old here in the States looks twice their age because of all the stress, the bad foods we eat, the overeating, and the fast-paced life we lead as Americans. So, physically they appear to be in much better shape but weathered and beat by the sun and the lack of fancy lotion and sunblock creams. They do not get to have all the comfort we so lavishly enjoy here in the States, but it keeps them active. The fact that most people do not own cars gives them no choice but to walk everywhere, and the exercise alone helps expand their days. We do not get to see much of that here in America where a man in his 40s will die while golfing of a massive heart attack after receiving notification from his advisor telling him that his Merrill Lynch account has depleted to almost nothing due to a hiccup in the stock market the night before. Not there, not in Cuba, and maybe this is something we can learn from this seemingly Third World country. Perhaps we stress too much! The rat race alone is enough to kill us here in the US, along with the constant competition with the guy next door. Some say the credit can be given to the island's climate, which makes it so soothing, perhaps the weather, the ocean's cool breeze, and the mountains' dew have a lot to do with it, while others acknowledge their diet and involuntary exercise routines. Neither by choice, of course, but due to food rationing and the absence of fast-food restaurants, as earlier mentioned, having to walk or ride a bike because of not having a vehicle compared to families in the US where it seems like each family member must have their own car. Then we wonder how we got to be number one in the world in obesity here in the US? What happened to a vehicle per household like back in the 70s? Things have changed for sure, both here in the United States and in Cuba.

Based on my observation, and I am no expert in this matter, by not having fast-food restaurants there and by not eating out constantly because it is way too expensive for their miserable salaries to afford, most people in Cuba eat at home. So, people walking everywhere and eating mostly homemade meals, it must have something to do with why they live longer and why they are in much better shape. Also, since all the talk about how great their socialized/free medicine is a complete lie, meaning it does not apply to their citizens as they so proudly advertise, the people there find other natural means instead of dying taking an array of prescription drugs. They choose to just live instead of depending on doctors to prescribe them expensive pharmaceutical poison to alleviate their pain. I also believe the absence of cheap buffets and value meals filled with saturated fats and a million preservatives that only clutter the arteries of an entire nation here in the US gives them literally much more time to enjoy their miserable lives, which can also be viewed as some form of apparent punishment and torture. Sad but true!

I honestly believe the lack of stress helps but living too long in those conditions must be awful too. On the one hand, they do not have to stress about monthly bills piling up, but on the other hand, they have nothing, but they want nothing because they do not know what they are missing, so go figure. Their anticipation of a sudden political change is all they look forward to still after all this time. A change that could bring the winds of transformation back and the return of freedom to Cuba is what may bring a legitimate smile to their faces; this is what keeps them all alive. I think!

The waiting is their hope to live another day and possibly be a step closer to seeing a new Cuba one day soon. So, they try to live long enough to see that miracle come to fruition. A free Cuba at last!

I clearly remember weeping repeatedly upon my arrival on the island, mainly at the sight of their bare existence, and that feeling never really went away even after I came back home. It literally broke my heart, and though I wanted to help, I just could not. Maybe I just did not know how. I wanted to save them all, but I did not know where to even start, and it took me some time to get over it if I ever did at all. So, I found refuge behind my writing once I left, and I wrote as my way of expressing my pain, as my way of venting out my disappointment, and this is what I came up with to expose America and the world to my heart-ripping experience of what really goes on there.

I desperately tried to listen to my driver Armando when he said to try to just enjoy my time there and to try to make memories since I was not going to be able to change a thing. I can literally say I left part of me back there.

This experience touched me so profoundly that it literally scarred me to the point where I asked myself these questions, *what if these were my children living in those conditions? What if I had to stay there for good and be another one of them? What about you? Do you see yourself giving up everything you have today and embarking on a life of hopelessness? Could you do it?*

This is a story that needed to be told, and for the sake of humanity, I hope the world is listening. As you read these lines, would you ever be able to look or think of this small island the same? This is certainly not a political-maneuver attempt against Castro's dictatorship on my behalf or against his communist party of over sixty years, nor is it a piece of attention-getting literature or propaganda in order to attain sympathy. I simply want the world to know how it feels to return to a place I left as a child, along with childish memories, only to find a piece of hell there. How traumatizing must my experience have been when it inspired me enough to want to write a book?

Now, this was something I had never done before, and I was quite impressed with my endeavor because, outside of my basic college and high school English classes, I had never been properly instructed on how to write a book or anything for that matter, but here it is! When a person is truly driven by passion…watch out, world! Stuff happens!

Now, I would like to ask you to take a moment and to walk in front of the mirror. Then to close your eyes for a split second and slowly open them back up. Now, what do you see? That reflection is "you," and wouldn't you agree that the image you see before you has been and will always be the closest companion you will have your entire life? In some cases, your very own worst enemy, all depending on how you live your life, but it could also be your best friend! Whatever the situation, it is the image, which accompanies "you," "us," "me"; every time we celebrate, every time we smile, cry, or suffer. If we live long enough, we begin to learn that the image of us in the mirror is and will always be along for the ride because that is simply who we are, the body, that is. This is the person we have allowed circumstances to shape us into, and, like it or not, we will have to live with the result of what we have molded it to be. The actions and decisions we make for the rest of our days, as well as carrying on our backs what our past drags along in nothing but a conscious display of the heavy burden of our mistakes and the guilt of our wrongdoings. Also, the spoils gained and the satisfaction received as a result of our good deeds. The admiration and respect we receive by doing the right thing also live well within us, and that is a good feeling. The material things we accumulate are nice too, but they are temporary. Those are typically for someone else to enjoy since we cannot take any of it with us when our day comes. Bummer! Ever seen a U-Haul truck behind a hearse? Exactly!

I have thought about it, and I now realize that we do not have to accept mediocrity. It is a choice, and we have the power to shape that image in the mirror and all that comes with it any which way we choose. Yes, including our circumstances, we have been given control like the potter who works on a shapeless piece of clay in turning a chunk of nothing into a masterpiece if we so desire, but many people do not know this little ancient secret, and they go through life believing they must take life as it comes, and in believing so, they do nothing to help their circumstances. Some people even tend to lie down defeated, and they bury their heads in the sand while slowly dying in disappointment and misery, thinking this is a normal instinct for human beings, when in all honesty, we have been given all the tools to triumph over every obstacle in the way to accomplishing our dreams and living the life we were meant to live. But it takes work, and it is not always easy. Sometimes life is hard, and that is why many quit, they give up. Look around, we are surrounded by winners, champions, and accomplishers. We live in a world of finishers, doers, and dreamers. There are people who stop at nothing because they are aware of these words… Think about it! We are already winners the minute we are conceived and born because out of those millions of sperms going after the egg, we are the ones who made it. Just something to consider! So, remember this: "If what you are doing is not producing any resistance, then what you are doing is not worth doing at all," Jaime's uncle announces proudly…and he concludes by saying, "If it were easy…it is never appreciated!"

Throughout history, all the great ones have left their mark in the world, their footprints. A mark often measured by victories and accomplishments, all of which may have been the predecessor to many shortcomings and pitfalls. Yes, many if not all the great ones of the past have stumbled time after time on the way to reaching their goals and to creating and inventing new revolutionary ways. Believe it or not, falling on your face can be a good thing at times.

If it weren't for this, we would have never walked as infants, and we would have continued crawling on our hands and knees the entire time to avoid the painful stumbles and the awkwardness of having to learn the difficult task of walking. Think about it, if as small children we would have given up the first time we fell in trying to walk, then we would have never walked at all, but children are resilient, they do not allow one, or two, or a dozen falls to stop them. They persevere because they do not know any better. They know not to quit; they do not know there is this option, and so unknowingly, they simply burn the ships. Ironically, as we grow up, we lose that drive and determination. We become complicit with life, often settling for less and forgetting about the dreams we had as children. Do you ever remember saying, "Yeah, I am either going to be a pilot or a doctor," but somewhere along the way, someone told you could not, and they said you were not smart enough or good enough or simply said, "Oh, you will never do that! No one in your family has ever done that. None of your family members have ever left this town." It has been proven that only perseverance can lead a person to their true destination, to their triumphs, to personal fulfillment and success. "Determination is often the first chapter in the book of excellence," they say, but somehow along the way we learn about fear, and we become comfortable with that mediocrity word I mentioned earlier, and we suddenly forget about all the goals we set growing up. We stop believing, we stop dreaming. We begin to listen to those who tell us we cannot do something, and as adults, all the dreams just die. As "big people," we neglect our plans once all the noise of life becomes turbulent and impossible to control. I did not want this to be one of those things that get buried under the rug, and that is why I felt compelled to tell this story. I felt the need to place you, the reader, in the unique position of perhaps having some type of compassion towards those who do not have the same opportunities as we do or simply those who squander the good breaks in life for their lack of knowledge and understanding. Sometimes because of their inexperience and other times simply because of plain old stupidity created by both the external and internal voices! So, to express my sentiment about what I experienced in this fateful trip to my homeland after so many years and about what I witnessed and what I lived, I created a story based upon true-life events to capture the moment, space, and time and to generate a clear picture of what life really is in today's Cuba. A place I left an exceedingly long time ago but where I was transported right back into the second the plane landed. Cuba is my natal home and a place I will always love, but what is happening there, even as we speak, tore me up. People outside of Cuba do not know and possibly will never know unless stories like this are told since all we know about Cuba in the US is how close to Florida it is.

We know about their beautiful beaches, their world-renowned baseball, their famous music, their boxing, their extravagant cigars, and, of course, the mystical sixty-year-old embargo, which has accomplished absolutely nothing, and in addition, because a magical veil has been placed over Cuba for way too long, making it taboo to even talk about in the US. So, here it goes… The easiest way for me to breach that gap was to write a story about a fictitious character, a man who may very well represent anyone of us. Now, in my story, he is a person almost like Dracula, someone who may have been seriously misunderstood and possibly, in the wrong place at the wrong time for most of his existence, never quite fitted in his role in life. A person lost in the confusion of a fake identity, a man hungry for answers and thirsty for freedom. At this, we come to the story of Jaime Colon, our protagonist. Jaime is a man determined to live his dream, steadfast and firm to sing his very own song, the song of his life, but he is disturbed by the turmoil that surrounds him as his entire existence is one of uncertainty and confusion in which he is forced to live a double life. See, Jaime is just another government puppet in Cuba; he is constantly under a watchful eye, always monitored as he tries to perform his job; like a caged animal, even though others may not see it this way. He is always told what to do, and his thoughts and ideas can never be exercised without approval. Like most Cubans living under Castro's communist regime, he does not control his own life, and he lives buried in his sorrow and distress day in and day out. "You know, every good cigar has a story, a history. The tobacco plant comes from the ground, from the dust, and eventually it returns to the dust, but in between, making a fine cigar is a complicated and fascinating process. Just when you think the tobacco leaf is all dried up and left for dead, some old man at a cigar shop makes a beautiful cigar."

These are the words of Jaime's old and wise uncle as he tells stories as usual, who at his old age still masters the art of cigar-making. Yes, the old man can manufacture one of the finest hand-rolled cigars in all of Cuba and maybe in the world. Jaime's uncle, El Tio, is part of a long lineage of tabaqueros (cigar makers) dating all the way back to Columbus' first arrival in the island, but wait, let us back up a bit though and allow us to close our eyes for a moment and let us imagine an *aerial overview* of Cuba…a thin and long island surrounded by the blue ocean of the Caribbean.

We then move to explore the colorful land, the majestic mountains, the crystal-clear rivers, and we suddenly end up over the almost perfectly arranged green tobacco fields. Ahh! The famous tobacco fields in the Vuelta Abajo region where rows and rows of tobacco plants all dressed elegantly under the hot sun fervently dance along the mild island wind that carries from the ocean onto the hills of the province of Pinar del Rio, "Home of the Cigar."

Cuba is the largest of the islands in the Caribbean, a beautiful thin strip of land in the shape of a crocodile resting upon the crystallized, warm blue waters right at the tip of the Gulf of Mexico and just ninety miles south of Florida. Cuba the island and its people have endured hurricanes, natural and political disasters, almost total extinction at the hands of the Spanish upon their arrival in the island back in 1492, and, to top it off, attacks from almost every pirate empire we can think of. Throughout the centuries, there has been a mixing of multiple races to make a people, the Cuban people that is a blend of many different races all in one, from the original Taino Indians and other indigenous tribes, the Spanish, the French, the English, African slaves, a great Jewish influence as well, and even the Chinese making this conglomerate and assorted mixing into my people. Talk about a melting pot! Cuba is no different from the United States in that sense; it is a fusion that unifies all the above-mentioned races and backgrounds to form one people, and over the years, it has worked. When African slaves were forced across the Atlantic, enduring abuse, torture, torment and having to adapt to living in a new country and in a new world. But as they say, every coin has two sides, and aside from some of the ugliest episodes in history taking place during the whole slavery era, Cuba became known for its great architectural advancements in the New World, all built by slaves and thus setting the platform for receiving the name of "The Pearl of the Caribbean" and even "The Paris of the Caribbean" for such modern architectural, technological and even medical advancements throughout the years. During the 1930s, 40s, and 50s, Cuba flourished greatly in many different areas, including economically, and with World War II in full swing in Europe and around the world, it became home to many running away from the war and settling in a place where work and business thrived. Through it all, African slaves were the workforce to build the island for centuries. The slaves built the foundation of the perennial place Cuba became, and the same slaves also influenced music and tradition there. Today, a great deal of the music we listen to on the radio can be accredited to Cuban musicians who created many different genres from salsa to cha-cha-cha, danzon, guaguanco, mambo, and the world-famous "El Son," which is pretty much the foundation for most of the Latin rhythms today, influencing the world of music as we know it. Cuban baseball and boxing, among other sports, also became internationally renowned, and to this day, many Cuban baseball players have greatly affected the major leagues as well as international baseball. Cuba also became well known for its early technological and political advances and sophistication. In addition, the year-round perfect weather and the island's unmatched beauty called the attention of many around the world for centuries, and it made Cuba a targeted vacation spot for people from all over the globe. Today, Cuba's reef is known to be one of the last untapped natural resources on the planet and one widely appreciated by divers all around. During the 1950s, because of its ideal geographical location, hotels began to sprout all over

Cuba, where gambling was legal, attracting many visitors from around the world. The glamour and unique setting of the tropical island became an epic theme, which also attracted the mob's involvement in an extremely lucrative enterprise until Castro's takeover in 1959, when the new regime went on to nationalize everything, eventually becoming a communist nation. That is when every American and foreign business was taken over by Castro while basically bankrupting the island over the next fifty to sixty years. As a matter of fact, tourism has been Cuba's number one resource, closely followed by the tobacco industry as Cuban cigars have been known to be among the best in the world for many, many years, and its well-deserved fame has been accredited to a unique tradition in mastering the art of cigar-making. Much of it due to the fertile soil of the island, its climate, and generations of people specialized in the mastery of the art. Although Cuba's location is ideal for commerce, as a tropical island it equals having some of the most beautiful beaches on the whole planet, and its white-sand beaches, the warm, clear water, and the perfect temperatures blend right in with the high humidity to create a wonderful habitat for its unique vegetation, which includes tobacco, coffee, and sugar cane. Also, with no poisonous or dangerous animals in the island, Cuba is a heaven for hikers from all over the world as well. In providing a bit of a history class and in a mild braggadocious way to help pique your interest even more, upon Columbus' discovery of the New World and his arrival in Cuba in 1492, he was quoted by saying, "This is the most beautiful land human eyes have ever seen." Columbus then proceeded to try changing the name of the island to Juana after a member of the Spanish court, but apparently, this did not stick as it is still called Cuba to this day, and thank God, because instead of Cuban, I would've been called a "Juananese." Not cool! Hah! Now, Cuba's beautiful landscape of green tropical forest and the smooth sea breeze welcomed the uninvited European visitors with open arms. This place was an absolute paradise, unlike anything they had ever seen before, which instinctively must have left the tired sailors out of breath seeing the tall coconut trees along the beachfront and the comfortable, peaceful environment, which immediately made Columbus and his crew believe they had arrived somewhere near India. The Spanish proceeded to call the islands "The West Indies" only shortly after, realizing they had landed in another continent altogether, and according to them, "they had suddenly discovered America." History tells us and has done over the years that the name of America came from one Amerigo Vespucci, a Florentine transatlantic explorer, who was a navigator with Christopher Columbus in 1499 and the first geographer to realize that the Americas were separate continents, but in all honesty, where the name America comes from has many different versions, and we will leave it at just that, besides, this is not a real history class and like Jaime's uncle always said when a conversation about Cuba's discovery would arise, "And who cares who named it, what matters is we are stuck here today, and that is that." The old and all-wise uncle has a reputation for both being a great tabaquero but also for being a eat storyteller. The always sun-browned uncle from the many hours he spends out working on the fields and whose face resembles one of a man who has worked hard his whole life. He is a man who has never been seen without his straw hat and his guayabera shirt, never carrying less than two cigars in his right shirt pocket. He is tall, prudent, and a man of few words. El Tio is often observant of his surroundings with a critical eye but very few critics. The old man stands proud as he looks around at the land. His eyes almost shut, staring into the sun, and as if waiting for something to come down from heaven, he barely blinks. Maybe he waits for the winds of change as most people in Cuba have for over sixty years now. He stares…and he stares at the land as time slowly dissolves before him in appreciation of what his eyes see. He takes it all in with every breath. El Tio always talks about life in the island before Castro, and he makes comparisons reminiscing about the not-so-distant past of over six decades. He talks about the food in the old days, and his mouth waters, his eyes grow misty as he remembers, "Oh, Cuba was just glorious; you should have seen her. She was the most beautiful place in the world." But I also once heard someone add, "Yes, she was a beautiful place alright, but we should have known she would be a heartbreaker in the end," this reference regarding the last sixty years under communist dictatorship, but back to Cuba now.

What a contrast of beauty, innocence, and despair, need, want, and hopelessness all in one place. The faces of the people tell it all with the all-so-common blank look they carry. It is almost as if one could film a silent movie where no words would ever be needed to expose the dialogue.

"Sometimes silence can be the loudest of voices!" Like they say, "A picture is worth a thousand words," and today's Cuba is a perfect example of that. It has become a forgotten item in the basement of the world. Its resources run dry. Even though tourists from all over the world continue to visit the island and talks of the embargo finally being lifted one day soon continue, but the people keep just hanging on to their small glimpse of hope and singing their sad song. The children of Cuba head in the same direction as their elderly, hopelessness. Hmm? Hello! Is anybody listening? Jaime's old uncle goes on to say with an awkward smile that, as a matter of fact, the Spanish did indeed try to change the name of the island from Cuba to *Juana* as I already mentioned. "Yes, they tried to rename the island after a member of the Spanish royal family but never succeeded. They came too far, stayed too long, and we ended up kicking their butts out in the end anyway. Yeah!" El Tio mutters proudly, puffing on his cigar stub, and continues saying that to too many people, this was a glorious find, a grand discovery, but I think history shows us otherwise. Instead of being called "the grand discovery of a new continent," it should have been called "the massacre of an entire race and the extermination of a people." All done for greed, just like it has been done throughout history *in an effort to expand, conquer and accumulate more*. Today, many experts anticipate the stock market to hit rock bottom again possibly around 2020 and beyond after crashing in 2000 and in 2008, and this next one could very well be "the *big* one" they have been prognosticating many times in the past. With housing prices skyrocketing to almost an all-time high after hitting a record low about ten years prior and causing a great economical demise, the next crash may be even bigger, some experts say, possibly driving the world economy to shambles, bringing in new unknown diseases, global unrest and eventually *war*. People have been trusting their retirement accounts and 401ks to a volatile market, which is unpredictable, uncontrollable, and almost impossible to understand. We tend to trust our financial advisors and money managers, who all work for the very same financial institutions we place our money into. They tell us we must invest our money in a limited menu of products all belonging within the same investment firms. Does that even make any sense? They tell us we have to diversify our investment portfolio, but since they only invest it all within the same line of investment options, it is very much like placing all of our eggs into many different baskets to lower our risk, but in all reality, all we are doing is placing all those baskets on top of a three-legged table. And what happens when you place anything on top of a three-legged table? Exactly! *Boom!* In 2008, when the market crashed last and where everyone lost money and much of the equity in their homes, sending many into financial ruin and bankruptcy, did any of our financial advisors tell us to pull our money out before, since they were the all-knowing experts? No way, not a chance in the world, because this is how they make their money. They are supposed to work for us and on our behalf, but these are all employed advisors representing only the best interest of the financial firms and institutions they represent. What fools we have become! We have become a herd of sheep, the dumbest animal in the animal kingdom. We are a society of followers where the blind lead the blind. We as a people, humanity, have managed to suck dry every single natural resource, and we are doing away with many animal species worldwide almost to the brink of extinction. Yes, greed is an ugly thing, but since not knowing what the heck we are doing has proved to be fatal, we continue to destroy everything we put our hands on until the day we finally annihilate our entire human race and the world with it. We are headed that way, we are doomed to one day vanish and seize to exist altogether because of our own greed and gluttony, but back to our story… The Taino Indians were the dominant natives of the island and other aborigines in Cuba, approximately 250,000 in number at the time of the discovery in 1492, but less than fifty years later, the Indian population in Cuba was almost wiped out completely. Yes, just fifty years later, only a few Indians had survived illness, diseases, massacres, and harsh treatment under the Spanish conquistadores. This is far-fetched from the glorious stories told by historians about Columbus' grand discovery, but as always, everything happens for a reason, and all the brutality and inhumane treatment brought upon the Indians gave way to a new race of people when the Spanish began raping the women. The offspring of the mixing between the Spanish and Caribbean natives was called a "mestizo," and a new race was created. The Taino Indians were beautiful people physically; tall, tan-skinned, with straight black hair, and extremely passive, but they were almost exterminated in a matter of years. You can still see a small trace of their mark in the people of Cuba by some unique features like the nose, skin color, and a welcoming smile, but this is seen less and less as races continue to mix and remix with time. As construction began to expand throughout Cuba, the native Indians initially became the workforce behind building towns and developing the island after the arrival of the Spanish. Many were forced to dig for gold as well and began to rapidly die because of the hard labor. These were passive people, not warriors, not soldiers, and not slaves. The Taino Indians were proud and not at all interested in digging for gold in their own home and for someone holding a whip. Shortly after the arrival of the white man in the island, the inevitable revolting started to spread, and the refusal to work, which led to almost total genocide. They would rather die than work for an outsider, not in their own home, and it did not take the conquistadores long to figure out there was extraordinarily little gold in the island. The mountains were green, and the rivers were clear, not the mountains of gold the Spanish envisioned upon their arrival in the New World, which were later found in Mexico and in South America, but not in Cuba. Cuba quickly became Milton's *Paradise Lost* of some sort as blood covered the innocence and purity of the natives until their unavoidable disappearance. Many were burnt alive, tortured, hunted with dogs, and killed. The grand discovery of the New World was nothing but a cruel deception behind a glorious finding; just another cover-up, another masquerade, and another governmental scheme in keeping the people blind. Spain received the glory and all the credit at the expense of a dying race, and what a compliment to history that was!

Still taught in classrooms today as an awe-inspiring discovery, when in all reality, it was the complete opposite. Columbus was not just a visionary and a great sailor, but he should have also been given credit for the murderer he was and an accomplice in the disappearance of a people. Shortly after doing away with most of the Indians in Cuba, the Spanish began bringing African slaves to the island to do the unfinished work since they were stronger, less stubborn, and much more durable under the burning sun. The severe humidity, the hot sun, and the punishing whip on their backs were all synonyms with barbaric and cannibalistic treatment and an unforgivable piece in time, which ultimately led to a new wave of trading goods, *slaves.* Treated as if they were not human beings, the slaves were taken away from their land, from their home, their loved ones and brought to a strange faraway world to work and to die. It must have been an unspeakable site, but why am I telling you all this history? Because our story, the story of Jaime Colon today, is nothing short of what happened 500 years prior, as Jaime is a direct descendant of one of these African slaves. *Ijaba* was her name, and she was Jaime's great grandmother to the tenth power. As most of us today may very well be directly connected to one of those slaves from many years ago in one way or another. Maybe not through direct ancestry by blood per se, which was true in Jaime's case, but perhaps many people today may have been related to slave owners or just simply related to a merchant whose job was to deliver the precious cargo from Africa to America. In one way or another, though, all Cubans became related to the slave trade, whether by choice or not. The slave trade, an unfortunate incident and ugly part of our history, as cruel and grotesque as it was, also gave way to a new breed of people, a new race known as "the mulatto." This was a mix between a Spanish man and an African slave, mainly in the form of rape, just like with the Indians. Jaime's great-grandmother, Ijaba, was one of those slaves. Born a beautiful African princess and later brought to the island against her will and as part of the precious cargo in the slave ships. Ijaba means "a wish fulfilled."

The Spanish were amazed at the many wonders the New World had to offer upon their arrival, beauty unlike anything they had ever seen and wholesomeness that was unparalleled. Today we are still amazed at the grotesque ugliness left behind by the slave trade because aside from the cruelty, this was the biggest involuntary mass migration in the history of the world.

There have been many large migrations of people in the past where people left their homes and families behind, like the Irish, Italians, Germans, Russians, Cubans, and more, but none to the extent of this one where for hundreds of years, men, women, and children were taken from their homes against their will and brought to a foreign land to work and to die, to Europe, the Caribbean, and North and South America among other places, these people were ripped from their homes, ripped away from their traditions and their dreams to become part of a business. They became "trading goods," no different from corn or wheat. They were part of an enterprise where they were the merchandise, the stock that was being exported, sold, and exploited, and behind all the pain, suffering, and tears, laid a hard road ahead, hundreds of years of anguish and inequality to this day. Columbus, however, is less and less remembered for his grand discovery in recent years, and perhaps when I was a child, he was one of the greatest navigators and explorers in history, supposedly discovering America and the New World; a statement, which to too many speculators is overrated and perhaps wrong, but we now see him as who he really was…another disturber of harmony and another spreader of cruelty.

If you really think about it, America may have very well already been discovered by the Vikings many years before, just maybe. Why not? Analyze this, how could they, who were tremendous navigators and explorers, have come all the way to Canada and not gone a little farther down to the northern coasts of the United States? Strange, huh? And in the case of Columbus, how can someone be given credit for discovering a place where people already lived? You can discover treasures, cures for new diseases, and even buried artifacts, but not an entire continent where people already lived and a place previously already discovered and occupied by the Native Americans and the Indians of the Caribbean. Makes me wonder where the credit is... Columbus Day is not even celebrated as a national holiday anymore. Maybe they know something we do not know. History tells us that Columbus arranged a deal with the Spanish monarchs before setting sail, proving he was a shrewd negotiator; however, he died poor, bitter, and forsaken in the city of Valladolid. Some people will even argue that this was his curse for disrupting and corrupting a way of life. Some say the gain of some may very well be the demise of others, as it was in his case. Columbus received credit for discovering the New World as we know it, and though he was an amazing man of the sea and a visionary well fitted for the quest, like many conquerors, he was eventually conquered by that which he had conquered.

I personally believe he died of a broken heart. He died of guilt and shame for the irreparable damage caused by his own grand discovery and his collaboration in the extermination and massacre of an entire race, of a people, because soon after his arrival, other expeditions began to take place, such as Cortez to Mexico conquering the Aztecs and Pizarro to Peru where the entire Inca empire was exterminated, and all their gold taken in very little time and with very little resistance. The Spanish brought disease, firearms, steel swords, and horses, enabling the natives to match them and thus overtaking them though they were greatly outnumbered. Now I must ask...if the Aztecs and Incas were so sophisticated and, in many ways, extremely advanced for their time, why wasn't it that they were the ones to conquer Europe instead of the other way around? Some historians give credit to the superior vessels used to sail across the ocean, all which is debatable and left to open argument, but that is only my take on the matter, and why do I keep going all the way back in history and what does this have to do with our story? Let us just keep going a little further, and we will see how everything ties together.

What Influence Did the African Slaves Have in Cuba?

The Story of Jaime's Ancestor, Ijaba

Western Africa, the year is 1697, and we find ourselves on a beautiful beach in Sierra Leone, north of what we know today as the Ivory Coast. We explore a land full of matured trees of all different sizes along the seacoast and down at the beach, pleasant-sounding waves crash into the break, splashing water high in the air and bathing the coast. The fresh water sends a clean scent into the air, it resembles tranquility and certain peace as if nature smiles upon this land; a sign that God is pleased with His creation. This is all-natural beauty untarnished by civilization, or should I say un-civilization? Why is it that everything *man* touches, he ruins? The joyful contrast of the crystal blue water of the Atlantic and an immense beach of white sand plays forefront to a thick wall of mangroves serving as a protective fence and separating the coast from the jungle right behind it. Files of coconut trees of all different sizes to the north line up perfectly, almost purposely planted the same distance apart; it is truly a stunning site and beauty beyond words. Gorgeous curtains of green rolling mountains can be seen from the beach, accenting the already picturesque view. If there is a place on this earth called paradise, this is probably it. As we slowly move away from the coast and towards the land, we now capture idyllic scenes of nature as inexplicable colors come together all in one stage. A sparkling, skyscraping three-hundred-foot waterfall appears in the center of a thick mountain range, all carpeted by a profound green jungle. Antelope and gazelle graze the grassy fields in the background, and hundreds of colorful birds accent the sky. Moving deeper inland and away from the ocean, we spot the first sign of human life as a young girl wearing a colorful outfit fitted for a princess picks a flower. This young girl is Ijaba, Jaime's royal ancestor. She is indeed the fourteen-year-old princess of one of the main villages of Sierra Leone and the rightful heir to the throne. Ijaba gracefully moves between the bushes, selecting the prettiest and most delicate of flowers for her mother, the queen. Not far behind, several members of the royal court chaperone the young girl. An elegant horse carriage awaits a short distance away, but Ijaba innocently continues to play without a worry in her mind.

Ijaba is thin, delicate, and her braided hair is adorned with all kinds of precious stones. A gold necklace is fitted perfectly around her neck, and several gold rings are around her wrists and ankles. She wears silky slippers-like socks while all her servants are barefoot. The young girl carries on picking flowers throughout the garden, and the more ground she covers, the more we are exposed to the beauty of this place. It is absolutely astonishing here. As she looks to her left and to the right, high and low, it is nature at its best; there are no flaws in this perfect masterpiece. Ijaba does not know time, nor does she worry about tomorrow because there is no doubt in her mind, she will inherit a royal world as she becomes a woman and the future queen. Then, in the same magnificent African kingdom, she will raise her royal children and her children's children in the comfortable atmosphere of the royal palace. What goes on inside the head of a little princess? What can she possibly think about? Perhaps, what dress will she wear for the dinner gala tonight as new gifts are being presented to the royal family from leaders of neighboring tribes? Maybe she is contemplating what she will name her new baby elephant? Kids think about these things and especially royalty, they do not have a worry in the world. Worry? What is that? Ijaba often stops to feed the many peacocks that roam the garden at the royal confines, and she skips around as the chaperones follow. Can she possibly be thinking why peacocks are such beautiful birds but make such horrible noise? Why can't they sing beautifully? Everything is so naïve and unclever at that age and on that stage, but this is what life is supposed to be like for a little princess. Little princesses do not worry, they do not fear, nor do they have to plan for tomorrow because life is supposed to be all perfect… After Ijaba leaves the garden, she holds in her hands the flowers she has personally picked for her mother, the queen. The elegant horse carriage moves unhurriedly through the garden, and Ijaba and one of the royal ladies ride in it, spotting villagers who pass by carrying baskets and jugs on their heads. They call out and wave happily to young Ijaba in their native language; they stop and salute her with respect. One of the men almost drops his jug as he attempts to bow to the princess. Ijaba laughs. Her royal companion keeps a stern look, but as soon as they move past them, she also laughs. Ijaba and her royal lady share a humorous look, and as the horse carriage advances, Ijaba reaches for the lady's hand. The two ladies hold hands, and the lady chaperone looks to one side while Ijaba looks the other way.

Wild animals roam in the background, which would be a strange occurrence here in our world, but this is typical for the village, after all, they do live in Africa. I keep referring to the unusual sights and sounds, but this is home to them, this is everyday life. At the royal palace, her mother the queen and her father the king, each sitting on their own hand-carved throne, are there, waiting for her with anticipation. Both dressed in their royal garb, beautifully decorated silk robes with golden stitching and all sorts of precious stones on them. They both wear luxurious necklaces suited for a king and a queen. As they emerge from the largest, most elaborate structure in the village, they smile, hug, and kiss their royal-blooded daughter with loving affection. Other villagers defer to them with great respect and stop to admire the presence of their loyal leaders. Armed guards with shields and long spears surround them. I imagine in our time, in this present day and age, all kinds of people would have been taking pictures left and right, paparazzi, television crews, and every front of the media would have swarmed the place, and let us not forget "secret service." But not here, these people love and respect their leaders, and no one would even dare to approach them without first taking the rightful protocol to do so. Besides, the royal guards are all on their toes, they are always armed and ready. A few moments later, we find ourselves in a celebration of some sort as they usually have when the royal family parade about the palace. The sound of loud drums play, and people chant loud pre-rehearsed remarks at the king. He waves back at his people with admiration, and Ijaba proudly accepts her father's approval of the citizens of Sierra Leone.

As the celebration winds down and the sun has now set behind the ocean, night comes. Bright torches outside the palace are the only source of light as the entire village now sleeps. It is quiet, and now in the late hours of the night, everyone sleeps except for the palace guards who never do. As the entire village rests, every little sound from the wilderness is mildly heard, from crickets to the nocturnal birds and what sounds like maybe monkeys mimicking each other from a distance. The sounds of the night serenade a tired village after a long day of festivity. To them, it is relatively almost silent, and this time of the night is when the jungle comes alive; the big cats and other large animals hunt while others take cover and try to stay alive, but most of the people of Sierra Leone sleep now peacefully.

The night sky is covered by a sea of bright stars, which from down here in the village look like millions of tiny sparkling seashells. The full moon shines upon the land like a lighthouse guiding merchant ships returning from a long voyage, and a group of scattered clouds attempts to slide in front of the lunar presence to cover its bright light, and eventually they do. It is much darker now in the village as the full moon is hidden by the passing clouds in the late hours of the night as Ijaba and her family sleep comfortably in the relaxing confines of the royal palace, the night is tranquil...peaceful...quiet! And suddenly, the calm is shattered as a group of men, white pirate-like European men led by several African guides, storms the village with muskets and metal swords. They look like hunters. These men are holding torches in their hands as they begin setting the entire village on fire. The palace guards are the first ones to go as the intruders methodically take them down one by one. Some are shot, others slashed by swords and machetes, and others are even strangled with ropes. It is a sickening sight. Screams of panic fill the air as a historic moment unfolds. Villagers flee from their huts as the calm of the night suddenly turns into echoes of terror. Some try to escape from being captured and run without any direction amid desperation, just seeking survival. There is chaos and confusion everywhere. All those who are captured are beaten, some shot and slashed outright, killed in cold blood. The intruders torch the huts, and within extraordinarily little time, the entire village is ablaze. These men are mercenaries, hunters, only they are not hunting wild animals; they are hunting people, and they go from village to village, taking people prisoners to sell them into slavery.

From inside the royal palace, young Ijaba watches, horrified, and she screams at the top of her lungs as her struggling mother is wrestled down by several men. She screams in horror, and tears flood her face in disbelief and confusion. The king is dragged away by three men, his royal outfit is ripped from his body, and he is left there almost naked. All his jewelry is ripped off, his crown removed as they mock him. He tries to defend himself, but it is all in vain. And finally, he is repeatedly smashed in the face with a musket butt, and his almost naked body dragged outside unconscious. Ijaba has seen enough, with all the courage in the world, she storms behind the men to try to save her father, but she is knocked down, and repeatedly, she is kicked in her face. In much pain, Ijaba tries to stand back to her feet, but she cannot. She lays there watching and unable to contain herself, she storms back after the men, this time crawling desperately on the ground towards them. She is caught and held back by one of these monsters. The man pushes her down with his foot, and with diabolic laughter, he encourages two others who are wrestling with a woman a short distance away. Ijaba fixes her eyes on the woman who is none other than her mother the queen and whose royal attire has been completely ripped off her body, leaving her now fully naked. Ijaba, screaming loudly, claws the backs of the men raping her mother, but she is grabbed and dragged off once again. There is just enough time for her to glimpse a large knife slitting her mother's throat, Ijaba screams in horror. The young girl has no energy left after struggling with grown men to try to save her mother from the hands of these monsters.

After a few moments of sitting on the hard, wet mud in a state of shock, she is grabbed and thrown onto a pile of children who have been taken away from their parents as well. She continues to contemplate the scenario in a state of alarm. She lays there motionless as hysterical tears stream down her face, and she watches the other children cry uncontrollably in fear and desperation. Moments later, Ijaba and the others are carted off among the flaming and severed bodies of her fellow villagers, and the squirming, suffocating pile of men, women, and children is an unspeakable sight. The wooden cart being pulled by two large oxen with long horns in which Ijaba and the others are being carted off is filled with children. As the large wooden wheels begin to turn, Ijaba looks up to see her dead, bloodied father the king strung up and hung from the tallest tree for all to see. She screams, but nothing but silence sneaks out of her mouth. The horrific image lingers in her mind even though she tightens her eyes to forget. She trembles with fear, and her little body sits among the other frightened children, unaware of what the next stop will be, unaware of their future, and tortured by the disturbing sights surrounding them. She closes her eyes to try to ignore it all, to get away from this inferno, but the loud screams and the crying of the children riding with her do not allow her to do so. Ijaba is in disbelief, in awe. Unexpectedly, in one fateful bang, the entire side of the overloaded cart collapses, and at least ten of the children aboard fall off the wagon. Princess Ijaba is among them. Suddenly, panic sets in among the children, and the loud screaming becomes even louder. But in the middle of all the commotion and massive clutter and dust, Ijaba is suddenly taken and dragged away by a man wearing mud all over his face to camouflage himself. The man places his giant hand over the young princess' mouth to keep her from screaming, and he proceeds to tell her he is one of her father's royal servants who has miraculously survived the massacre, and this brings much comfort to the already scared young girl as she realizes she is now safe with him. Placing her over his shoulder, he carries her off and takes young Ijaba into hiding in nearby bushes, and before anyone realizes, they are gone. Ijaba stares at the man with a lost look as he carries her in his arms like precious cargo. She looks at him to try to remember his identity, but she can vaguely recognize him. After a few moments, her mind begins to cooperate, and she now recalls this is a man who she had seen many times before attending to her father at the palace, and she recalls him being one of the food testers for the royal family and someone close to her dad. The man carrying the young princess in his arms trots through the tall bushes on the side of the royal palace like a raging bull and finally disappears into the wilderness as his grass-colored outfit matches the surroundings and no one can spot him.

After they have covered enough ground to see the royal palace well behind them from a distance, the man finally stops running, and he lies on the ground for a moment with young Ijaba next to him. He takes a quick breather before they continue, then he quickly jumps up and keeps on running with Ijaba still in his arms. The man tries to recollect his thoughts to figure out what to do next in trying to escape the horrific scene for good, making his main objective the safety and protection of the young princess. He is somewhat confused and unsure, but all he can think of is to continue in a direction that will not put his princess in any danger. The safest way is forward and away from the madness, and as he makes a run far from the village, he peers back at the sickening scene behind them of his entire village on fire, and his eyes grim with pain and tears of fury swell inside a stern look within his eyes. He says nothing as he holds anger and pain inside, and as his body sweats profusely after the long run, he trembles with uncertainty, holding Ijaba close to him. One thing he knows is he has kept an oath he made many moons ago to protect his royal highness, as he has done just that in saving the young princess's life. After a long run, they finally stop to rest for a moment before they continue. He looks back at the giant flames that now cover many of the structures surrounding the royal palace at a distance, and "the man with no name" tells Ijaba it is time to go, afraid that someone might have followed, "Princess, we must go now! I must take you as far away from this place as possible." They stand up, and the man picks the young girl up onto his arms. As they get ready to continue moving deeper into the jungle, a herd of terrified horses runs wildly past them, and it barely misses Ijaba and the man. As they watch the herd disappear at a distance, they can see it go on to trample several villagers along the way who also attempted to escape the madness as the scared animals race through away from the burning inferno at high speeds in the blink of an eye. Ijaba looks at the man with a sigh of relief after seeing the others who had not been so lucky and who were trampled by the crazed animals. Several people lie on the ground in pain after being run over by the horses, and there is nothing Ijaba can do to save them. She reaches with an outstretched arm and offers her hand, telling the man she wants to walk the rest of the way; she knows the man is dead tired and his legs are about to give. She knows he has done enough. They begin to walk slowly now, and they get closer to a hilltop where they can clearly see all the chaos down below. The man places his hand over Ijaba's eyes to keep her from witnessing the grotesque sight of villagers who fight capture and the village itself, which is now completely ablaze. The ones who fight being captured are slashed, dismembered, torched, and burned alive with savage disregard for human life. These are villagers whom Ijaba knows, and many are children no older than she. Ijaba continues to weep. The hero with no name, a man maybe thirty years old, cries silently at par with his young princess as they walk together like two lost toddlers in desperation after being separated from their mother. The man, feeling paralyzed and unable to help his own people, gnashes his teeth in anger, and Ijaba hangs on to his bare and sweaty body, almost pleading for her life. The shaken little girl is almost convulsing with fear, but the hero picks her up again and slowly continues to walk away from the village deeper and deeper into the wilderness, often looking back from the hilltop. The man manages to pull Ijaba far enough from the chaos and into a nearby field where he feels it is finally safe to stop for a short rest. There is a tranquil pond there. They drink from it and cool their worn-out bodies. Ijaba sinks in the pond, and she runs water through her hair and her face. The man splashes water onto his chest and takes a few sips into his mouth as if not wanting to waste too much time and continuously looking to his right and to his left like a scared deer drinking water from a pond. After a short stoppage and the much-needed break, he tells her it is time to go, and they continue to move slowly and further away from the burning village now way below them.

"Come on, Your Highness, we must go!" After walking for a good hour, they have finally reached a resting place far enough from all the madness, Ijaba and her guardian sit against a blooming tree along a gently flowing river, and the young girl notices the man is perspiring hard. Unable to control his nerves and tired from the long journey, the man begins to weep. Sobbing. Ijaba watches him, and unable to control her emotions, she too begins to weep. He turns to her and whispers, "My children are gone! Everything and everyone are gone!" She puts her arms around him to comfort the man. They pause here for a few minutes. Moments later, Ijaba has fallen asleep. She sleeps in the arms of the man as he continues to weep in silence to try not to wake up the young girl, his eyes are closed shut, but tears go on flowing down his face as he just stands there holding on to his princess.

It is nighttime, and the man has placed young Ijaba underneath a small bush, and even though tired and weary, he stays up all night protecting the young princess with the fear someone may have followed them. Ijaba rests peacefully, often tossing and turning. The man catches her every move like a police-trained watchdog. Finally, the morning comes. The sky is still dark from a cloud of smoke, which covers any shade of blue above. Ijaba is comfortably resting on a soft pile of banana leaves the man has prepared for her as a bed. She sleeps, and the man watches closely over his future queen like a jealous lion, almost with the same fatherly fervor he would have watched over any of his own children; children he has no idea of their whereabouts and no idea he will ever see again. "The man with no name" stares at young Ijaba's face as she sleeps a short distance away.

Her eyes twitch rapidly as if she is having a nightmare of some sort, and assumingly so after the night they have just had. The man gently pulls away from Princess Ijaba and fixes his eyes on the village from afar, which is still smoking from the deadly fire. All the villagers who were captured the night before are roped and chained together. Some are knocked unconscious and thrown into a pile to be taken away like lifeless human garbage. The man looks heavenward and mumbles in his native tongue with his eyes closed in prayer as a lonely tear rolls down his slick cheekbone.

The tear continues to slide down his smooth, dark skin almost in slow motion and then drips onto his neck, then down his chest, and it finally ends on the ground underneath him. The single tear is quickly absorbed by the hot earth beneath his feet, and it feels almost at home, especially since the entire continent of Africa is crying and the land bleeds as it hears the cry of its dying children. This fateful night, over five hundred men, women, and children were either killed or taken away in chains from their homes to never return and to be sold into slavery. Hundreds of African prisoners are taken from the village down to the coast to be shipped to either Europe or America. The bad guys use long, thick *bamboo*-like sticks to bind the necks of the slaves together in pairs and to keep them in single rows. Their hands and feet are tied. Some are crying, some bleeding, and some moaning and complaining from the tight ropes that almost cut their circulation. One thing for sure, all of them are scared, from the youngest to the oldest and even the tough and strong hunters from the village sob like babies as now captured men. In files of bamboo rows, they are guided through the jungle and out onto the coast by their capturers, often hitting and whipping the slaves to make them march on. When they finally arrive at the beach, the native men from the neighboring tribes who have served as guides for the Europeans stand there awaiting their pay as promised, but what they receive instead is death as their hearts are pierced by the sharp blades of the intruder's swords one by one. Their lifeless bodies roll down the sand staining the beach with their blood. Not one of them is left alive.

The guides received no payment after betraying their countrymen, and this is the price they pay for being disloyal to fellow Africans. Once again, a curse is unleashed at the end. Karma...perhaps. Half-dozen giant sailboats await several hundred yards away for the small boats filled with slaves to arrive. To then be taken across the Atlantic to America or towards coastal Europe and unto the slave auctions. Small boats are loaded with slaves and taken aboard the giant crafts a short distance away, which these African men, women, and children to this point have never seen before. The ships, which are anchored a short distance from the beach, are a sore eye for the slaves who have never seen such monstrous vessels. The men aboard are also curious to see the merchandise, some have never seen a colored person before, but what really catches the eye of these men who have been out at sea for such a long time is the almost naked bodies of the African women. These ruthless and hungry seamen practically drool as the women begin to come on board, but they are instructed by their superiors to stay away from them. They are not to be touched. Really? How long until disaster strikes? When a bunch of women-hungry, nasty bearded men, who have been out at sea for many months, are all alone at sea with these women? The slaves are amazed by the size of the large ships, and they inspect them carefully in amazement as they get closer and closer, but little do they know that these magnificent large vessels will soon become a graveyard to many of them. As the first group of slaves comes aboard the ships, they are inspected and separated by an intimidating assembly of men who specialize in selecting only the best merchandise. The tight ropes are removed from their hands, and the long bamboo sticks are dropped onto the sand, but before the slaves can get too comfortable, heavy chains are placed on their wrists and ankles instead. Yes, chains, thick and rusty chains made of metal. Jaime's ancestor Ijaba and all the other slaves are then branded with hot iron like cattle to mark their destination. A red-hot letter "C" is branded on the side of their necks to let them know this group is headed towards Cuba. Loud screams can be heard from a distance as the torturous incident takes place, and the horrific screaming seems to echo into eternity as the defenseless slaves' necks are branded with the hot iron markers.

Desperation and panic set in among the slaves, and then suddenly, one of the slaves has had it, and he decides to take a stand as he refuses to stick his hands inside the shackles attached to the chains. The white men are startled for a moment as in disbelief, and the slaves witnessing the brave stand are too in a state of surprise at the sight of this courageous man simply refusing to give in. The man trembling with fear keeps his firm position. The white men stare the heroic slave down with anger and in apparent disbelief, and for a moment, they sense perhaps a bit of remorse at their cruel actions and possibly even fear realizing they are outnumbered by these much more physically gifted men, who if organized could really put up a resistance…but this is just a minor obstacle, and it does not prevent them from getting their way because they do have muskets and much more superior weapons. Guns and powder! However, this one brave act, though, is the first of many rebellious stands by the slaves. A noticeably short-lived and almost irrelevant stand, but one rebellious act against the intruders letting them know what they are doing is wrong. Everyone watches as the daring slave begins to walk backwards, pleading his case in his native language but refusing to stick his hands in the shackles and waving his hands in the air, apparently declining, expressing disgust in rebellion. But before he can get too far, three of the white European men on board unleash hell upon him, beating him severely. Following a short scuffle, the men eventually end up stabbing the African slave to death in cold blood, and as big and strong as the man is, his resistance is all in vain. After being stabbed several times in the neck, he is left there bleeding at the mercy of the waves thumping the beach. The lifeless body belongs to none other than "the man with no name," and the same man who saved Ijaba's life earlier now lies dead before her and all the others to watch. His name was Inugu.

These savages, these ignorant and spineless beasts, do not feel the smallest hint of remorse as they purposely perform these brutal acts of violence openly to set an example to the other slaves as to what will happen to them if they do not comply. Ijaba watches quietly and weeps. Others weep as well. Suddenly, she asks another slave if anyone knew his name, but no one knew. After a few moments, one of her fellow slaves mumbles his name quietly. "His name was *Inugu*," the young lady whispers. Ijaba shakes her head as tears roll down her face, maybe realizing she never got to thank him for saving her life, and she begins to mumble his name repeatedly, "Inugu... Inugu...Inugu!" And all this is far worse than any kind of brutality these people have ever seen done before at the hands of neighboring tribes during disputes in the past and far worse than internal wars or anything they have ever seen before, period. Thomas Jefferson called the English in the Declaration of Independence "The disturbers of harmony" during the war of independence from England. Now can we imagine what the African slaves must have called these Spaniard monsters as they talked among themselves during this ugly episode in history? I wonder what they thought of these beasts as they ended many of their lives by pulling them away from their home. What must have gone through their heads as they watched all this unfold?

Aboard the ships, the women cry hysterically, and the men groan in pain. The slaves, who are systematically placed in rows, almost one on top of the other, to make more room to fit as many as possible inside the large boats, lie piled below the decks in the dark, dank, stinking cargo hold. These African men, women, and children are jammed and chained together like wild animals. There is no food or water. Some of them are bleeding, some vomiting, and others are just in shock. Half-naked, dirty, and frightened young Ijaba is now among them. Her eyes are fixed on "the man with no name," who lies dead on the beach as the waves have pushed his body onto the sand, and several crabs now begin to crawl and nibble on his flesh. All she can think of is she is alive because of him; the man who saved her life is now dead, and she only wishes she could trade places with him.

It is now early morning, and the large white sails are finally dropped all the way down and almost touching the precious human cargo. The slaves stare at the waving giant sails as the wind picks up and the ships begin to slowly move towards the sea. After several hours of staring at the African coast from afar, the land slowly begins to disappear behind them, and the hundreds of men, women, and children aboard the giant wooden ships sail away from the African continent to never see their home again. Night draws near, and the last few shades of the sun set behind the ocean, the painful weeping of the slaves covers the air.

The world of civilized man as we know it has now aboard some of their ships a new wave of trading goods from Sierra Leone to distribute to the other side of the world…young, strong, valuable *African slaves*. The voyage across the ocean is a long one, but immediately after setting sail towards the New World, they are hit by a storm, unlike anything they have ever seen before. Just hours after departing from Africa, it almost feels as if God is angry at them as huge waves come crashing against the boat with the strength of a million angry bulls. The waves make thunderous pounding noise as they collide with the ships, and everyone is afraid, including the white men in charge. Panic sets among the slaves as the motion of the ocean has most of them vomiting and dizzily hanging on for their dear lives. They are all wrestled one on top of the other with every pounding wave, and as they swim in their own bodily waste, the slaves beg for their lives and pray to the heavens for mercy, chanting loudly in their own language. The storm lasts several hours, and by the time the morning arrives, they all sleep on top of one another like a pile of dead dogs. The sunlight begins to sneak between the cracks in the wood, and as the slaves now begin to wake up, they can look at the aftermath of the fateful first night at sea. Words cannot express the disgusting site. The entire cargo hold is flooded with salty seawater, and several dead bodies float among them. As more and more of them begin to wake up from the nightmare, reality hits. The sea is now calm, and there is not one ounce of wind, but as more of them begin to open their eyes and realize it was not just a bad dream, all hell breaks loose among the terrified slaves, and their cry can be heard miles away as they mourn their dead. Others just cry in desperation, especially the children. The name of the slave ship in which Ijaba sails is *Agonia*, which means "agony" in Spanish, and it seems like a perfect fit now. They could not have found a better name for it. The ship is now all alone in the immense ocean that is so enormous the seemingly large vessel now looks like a small straw floating in a large pond. The smaller boats containing food, water, and other supplies that accompanied Ijaba's ship when they left Africa have all vanished in the storm from the night before, and they now sail smoothly towards the land. After hours of calm, their second night at sea suddenly draws near as the sun begins to set. The smell of death is now overwhelming. Many lifeless bodies are among them, and some of the slaves continue to vomit while others find comfort resting on top of one another to try to sleep off the hunger and thirst. Their lips are dry, their eyes lost, and their bodies are filthy. Suddenly, an old woman begins to hum a song. Others join in humming what sounds like an incredibly sad folk song. It is apparently a song of mourning for their dead, or perhaps this is a song about the new lives they now lead as slaves.

After days of sailing amidst the blue ocean, finally, the first signs of land appear on the horizon. From the top of the mast, one of the crewmen yells, "Tierra!" which means "land" in Spanish as they have finally arrived in the island of Cuba. The crew quickly began preparing for their arrival in the island, which includes getting rid of all the dead. The slaves down below hear all the commotion but are not sure of what is happening. They look at each other with curiosity and nervously wait. The dead are simply too many to count, many children are among them, and roughly a quarter of the slave population on board did not make the long voyage. When the ship is only a short distance from the beach, the cargo doors open, and a dozen armed men walk down below the deck to begin preparations to unload the merchandise. The smell is intolerable. One of the men drops his musket on the ground and begins to vomit uncontrollably. Some of the slaves look up to see what is happening, but most of them are still lying down motionless and weak. The men in charge sort through the slaves to see who is dead and who is alive and begin tossing all the dead ones overboard. The sharks that have been escorting the boat have a feast as the corpses begin to fall left and right from the slow-moving wooden vessel as it enters the bay before it comes to a complete stop. A few of the slaves that are still alive are so weak and dehydrated from the voyage they appear to be dead. Some look so bad they are thrown overboard anyway as their new masters find them useless and unsellable; "These slaves just take space," the men would say, and they are of no value whatsoever at the auction. After this, they are tossed into the water along with the dead ones and eaten alive by the hungry sharks. Once all the dead are removed from the boat, the slave masters rinse the slaves off by pouring buckets of saltwater on them in order to make them look like a more appealing product, to clean them up. The boat has finally found a resting place in the small bay, and by now, all the sails have been rolled. They have entered a seaport in Havana harbor, and the anchor has been dropped. The boat finally comes to a halt, and moments later, for the first time in weeks, the sunlight finally hits directly inside the cargo hold. As they open the lids leading below the decks where the slaves are held, they become blinded by the bright sunlight, and at this, they are finally introduced to their new home. The unloading process begins, and as expected, the slaves are treated in the same brutal manner used to load them onto the boat back in Africa. Like chained animals, they are bunched together and removed from the ship like cattle. The surviving men, women, and children are guided down a side road and straight to a slave auction. Ijaba and her fellow Africans all chained together are roughly probed and displayed to a courtly group of Spanish noblemen. The slaves are lined up in a single file on top of a wooden platform in which they take turns, going in front of well-dressed noblemen who crudely examine their dark-skinned bodies, teeth, and genitalia in choosing their merchandise.

Jaime's uncle remembers this story all too well. His grandmother told it to his mother, and his mother told it to him and his brothers many times before, and he now tells it to everyone he can. He says, "And it took many years after the Spanish arrived, years of bedding the exotic Caribbean natives and the African women and many years of giving birth to mulattos. Years of English and French and even Chinese influence, until finally the Cuban people found our identity... We became the result of a bunch of different races and cultures mixed into one, just like in the United States. We became what we are, we became what they were, and we learned to acquire their trends and traditions, and here we are today." Jaime's old uncle lights up another cigar with the same easy and relaxed manner he is used to, and he continues to tell the story in front of a handful of family members and friends inside the Colon home. His grandma, well in her late 80s, is there as well. She fans herself with an old colorful homemade fan made of cloth and wooden sticks as she sweats slightly on this hot and humid day. The uncle continues to speak inside the little house, and everyone listens attentively. The old grandmother calmly takes her eyes away from the old man, and she looks out the window as if telling Jaime's uncle she has heard this story too many times before. She then proceeds to slowly stretch her old bones by attempting to stand up from the old chair, and a young cousin helps her to her feet. The Colon home is small and humble but cozy. The house is clean and made from wood, with varnished wood floors and painted all white with blue trimmings around the doors and windows. The paint is somewhat faded from being painted last over twenty years ago, and the roof is made of colonial orange tile to keep the house cool. Several tiles are missing. There is no central air conditioning, of course, as it is in most of Cuba, but there are a few spinning fans throughout the house. All the windows are kept wide open, allowing the summer breeze to circulate and at the same time keeping the house cool. Just bare essentials adorn the inside of the small house. An old couch still in good condition from probably before the revolution, and two unpainted wooden handmade rocking chairs occupy the living room area. Several mismatching frames with colorful paintings of nature hang from the walls along with many family pictures, taking the attention away from the dull interior walls inside the house. "Who needs fancy paint anyway? Food is much more important. Paint does not nourish you, food does," sarcastically voices the old grandmother as she continues to slowly fan herself. In America, people pay outrageous money to have painters come out with unique patterns to imitate these old walls and give it a vintage look, while here in Cuba, this is as natural as the sun rising in the morning, and they pay nothing for it, and it's not called vintage but real, maybe time-warped and desolate. In the kitchen, an old 1950s' G.E. refrigerator, which makes more noise than it makes ice, sits on top of several pieces of 4×4 to make it a bit taller, but this is a necessary luxury here. If you do not believe me, just place an old broken fridge outside on the sidewalk and count to three. I guarantee you; it will not be there by the time you say "four." While here in the US, all you must do is drive to any Walmart; even without money, you pay with a credit card, and minutes later, your fridge is being delivered. What an irony. On top of the dining room table sits a large bowl with several avocados almost the size of oversized papayas and a few ripe bananas. The fresh smell of the organic fruit covers the entire house, and the pleasant aroma gives the home a unique and familiar essence. The dining room table is covered with a clean long white tablecloth to protect it from scratches even though it is not nicely painted, but that is how they make things last around here. The chairs are too unpainted but in good shape, and it all goes well with the old country ambiance. What we call a "rustic look" in America is simply not having any paint to touch it up at all here in Cuba, a norm. There are no Home Depot stores, but this all adds to its uniqueness. In Cuba, there are no furniture stores either, so if or when something breaks, they fix it. Things are passed down from one generation to the next, and it makes them appreciate the little they do have. The windows have natural wood shutters and no glass. They are usually wide open unless it rains, exposing the outside of the house and the beautiful country around. There is nothing but banana trees and colorful flowers on each side of the house. The backyard is full of tall mango trees full of colorful fruit, tons of them, with branches almost touching the ground filled with small, round, sweet yellow mangoes, which they call "manguitas." An old rusty tractor sits there beside the house, missing one of the front wheels just as it has for the last fifteen years and leaning on its side like it is about to tip over. The leather on the seat is now gone because of the sun and the rain, and the springs are exposed. Leading to the main highway is a thin dirt road, which takes us to the front of the Colon home. The dirt road, wide enough for a vehicle to drive through, has Mar Pacifico (Hibiscus) plants on both sides leading all the way to the highway. Green grass, which needs no sprinklers because of the constant rain, compliments the rest of the already explicit landscape as if intentionally landscaped by a professional crew. Behind all the fruit trees in the backyard, a huge tobacco plantation can be spotted. It goes as far as the eye can see in every direction. This is the Colon family plantation, which has been a fixture with the family for many generations. A light breeze weaves in and out, cooling the hot, humid day and often swaying the plants in unison rhythm as if moving in rehearsed motion. A wooden porch wraps around the house, and two old wooden rocking chairs sit in the front porch next to the door. A heavy iron ashtray is spotted lying over a fragile rusty metal table beside the rocking chairs, and there are several chewed-up cigar stubs in it. An old newspaper on the table is ruffled by the breeze making the distinctive sound of turning pages as the old man continues his speech before the other family members, who so attentively listen. Suddenly, Jaime walks in from behind him, kisses the old grandma on the cheek, and sits next to one of the children listening to the story. He motions to everyone to keep quiet, placing his index finger over his lip and trying not to interrupt El Tio. Jaime now sits like a child at storytime at his uncle's side and listens like everyone else. The old uncle goes on…

"And after all that, it took practically overnight for us to again become chained here in Cuba. Castro took over, and he took possession of everything, and that is that. Se acabo (It is over)!"

Members of the family mutter in agreement while some of the small children giggle at Jaime, making faces… Finally, he speaks, "Tio, so many times you have told the story of Ijaba. I love to hear you tell it."

The uncle checks his throat and replies, "Ahh, my know-it-all nephew from Havana! What a surprise. Would you have it forgotten? After all, Ijaba means 'a wish fulfilled.' And by the way, youngster… I knew you were there all along. Cannot fool an old man full of knowledge. I have eyes in the back of my head, too," concludes Jaime's uncle with a smirk. At this, Jaime smiles and respectfully stands up to give his uncle a kiss on the cheek, as it is all so customary in their

Cuban culture. El Tio smiles and blows a smoke ring in the air like a swirling portent, and the old grandma speaks with an almost rusty voice:

"Amen, and she looks down on us today. She watches over us. Not over Castro, not the revolution, but Ijaba, your ancestor, watches over us." Jaime rolls his eyes and stands up, sensing it is time to leave the room after hearing the smart remarks by both his uncle and the old grandmother, but as he gets ready to walk away, an idealistic cousin quickly takes the uncle's litany with the fervor of youth and respectfully approaches Jaime.

"So, Jaime, if you do not agree, answer this...where do we find happiness in our beloved island anymore? In the perfect year-round weather? The pretty beaches? Because we have nothing else, we hardly see the outside world, if at all. Most of us anyway. Our government floods the island with an invisible wall of lies, and we are being crushed by an embargo from a giant that is only ninety miles away, and we..."

"Basta (Enough)! You are not helping," yells the old grandmother, stepping in and disrupting what was beginning to turn into an argument between Jaime and the young cousin. The cousin, maybe in his late teens, obediently shuts up and sits back down while Jaime grabs his things to walk out back. Leaving the house, Jaime reaches into his pocket, takes out an envelope, and with the familiarity of routine, he wordlessly sets it on the table as he walks out. Family members awkwardly look away. As he walks off, one of the young children checks inside the envelope, and it is stuffed with money. He runs over to the old grandma without delay and gives her the familiar envelope, which never seems to end its delivery month after month, guaranteeing all their monetary needs are met at the Colon home, even in Cuba where so many people struggle to meet simply basic financial needs. Where so many people struggle to feed their children and where there is so much uncertainty and necessity. Jaime jumps into his car and drives off without saying anything.

Being a government puppet sure has its benefits and definite advantages, but Jaime hates his place in the world, and he knows he is not sought-after as the man his grandma and uncle raised him to be. He swims against a raging river like a wild salmon on his way upstream from the ocean. He is aware he is despised by many for the role he plays, and he hopes one day he can finally express his position. He wishes there will come a day when he can tell everyone how he really feels, but for now, he must continue to play the game; he must continue to wear his mask.

Who is Jaime Colon?

So, who is Jaime? What kind of man is he? What is he like? Earlier in our story, it was established our protagonist is a simple man who lives a life of routine, habits, and schedules. Like most Cubans living under Castro's regime, he does not control his own life. He does what he is told just to get by and to preserve everything he has worked so hard for, but his dreams continue to be buried behind a masquerade he wears only to please those who call the shots around him. Jaime is a government employee, a puppet of the Castro system, and a government official of some sort who has secured a rather comfortable position for himself, unlike that of most Cubans today, but he knows he is far from the person he would like to be as he has betrayed every ounce of integrity just to stay afloat, he has denounced his own honor like most people do over there in order to survive a totalitarian system where if you're not with them, then sadly you are against them. You either dance, or they make you dance... You are either part of the system or against the same corrupt and hypocritical lawless regime. Jaime truly hates what he has become, but what are his alternatives? In a place like modern-day Cuba, if one does not dance to the sound of their drum and the rules of the government, then one does not dance at all. Jaime has learned to play this game, and this has made them believe he is one of them, that he is another one of their followers and part of their crooked ideology. Thus, allowing Jaime to put himself in a position of great respect and glamour among his peers, and in comparison, with most of the people who live there, he has been able to separate himself. Jaime, unlike most of his countrymen, can travel outside of Cuba, he owns a vehicle, well, he drives a government-sponsored car, and he is very seldom questioned or harassed by the police and the authorities. Jaime is an educated man who holds a bachelor's degree in psychology, and he works on his master's degree by taking night classes. His education had been put on hold during the years he played baseball, and immediately after his retirement, he returned to school to receive the degree he always promised his grandmother he would bring home one day. He speaks several languages, including Italian, French, and good enough English to hold a solid conversation. He used the books as a vehicle to put out of sight the shame of no longer being able to play the game he loved when his career was cut short by injuries. He then returned to the classroom, where he excelled as one of the top of his class and graduated with honors from the University of Havana. Jaime claims his reason for choosing this subject of study (psychology) was to learn to understand why people do the things they do, beginning with himself and eventually understanding completely why people like Castro get away with the things they do, his motives, his agenda, and his government. What kind of sick mind would push a man to do what Castro has done in Cuba for over five decades? he continues to ask himself after a short pause…in deep thought, of course. Jaime was always a studious individual who loved to read and to figure out the mysteries of life on his own but often confused about his place in the world. He always knew he did not belong there, and he would often retrieve to his old uncle for plain old, good man talk, advice, and counseling. His old uncle was his best friend, his teacher, mentor, hero, and the father he never had. The only man he trusted and one he respected very much. Jaime's confusion is no different than the confusion many Cubans today suffer from, and it comes from the lack of explanation of why life is lived the way it is in their homeland and the inability to do anything about it. See, whether you are a Cuban living in exile or those living back home, life is not easy because either you suffer in your own skin or you suffer for those left behind, but either way, you suffer.

Before Castro's takeover in 1959, there was little migration of Cubans to any part of the world, but soon after his self-proclaimed dictatorship, now Cubans have been spread throughout the world like cockroaches, especially to the United States. The lack of information there is horrendous as Cuba has been placed inside an imaginary wall, which does not allow outside media, free press, or even any type of literature not approved by the government to infiltrate its demonic oppression of over fifty years. Everything that is read in Cuba is controlled by the government, any talk radio, the music they listen to, and, of course, the internet is prohibited to the public, it is illegal there. But that would make too much sense. There is no satellite television either, no cable, no pay-per-view. Castro always said, "Imperialism is the enemy," and they bought it, or should I say…they were forced to buy it. Yet why is there so much need and despair in a place without imperialism? So much necessity, so much want, and why so much ignorance in a country that prides itself on having 100 percent literacy and where education is free? My question is… Why is there such lack of abundance in comparison with the rest of the world? Especially the United States! Furthermore, there was always the constant reminder and a desperate desire for a better life in Jaime's mind. He always knew there had to be a way! But some of his countrymen would even argue that he was just ungrateful and unappreciative of the grand opportunity he had been given. His position, which was lavished and one envied by most, allowed him a much better life, but in Jaime's case, his shackles were just a tad loose. What people around him didn't know was the fact that and perhaps what no one else knows…like many people in his position, he was threatened, his family at risk, and the constant reminder of him losing everything if he didn't comply with every command from this corrupt government he worked for. Most of the people in Jaime's life were not aware of the ongoing harassment towards him, the many threats, and the pressure of keeping the boys in line. The harassment I am referring to is one many in Cuba understand, but unfortunately, the rest of the world does not. The fact that he was often followed, interrogated and his loyalty to the government questioned because of his lack of brown-nosing was always intolerable. Therefore, I say that deep inside, Jaime was dying, empty and needy. He craved many of the simple things we enjoy here in America, which to most of the people living in Cuba today are all extravagant luxuries, and what he wanted more than anything else was to live without being controlled. He wanted to be free. One thing that always worried him was the possibility of the government taking over his family's tobacco plantation simply because he did not walk the line, and this is one of the main reasons Jaime so diligently tried to comply in his own rebellious way. This was, of course, something he had never mentioned to them, not even to his beloved Tio, and to too many, he might have appeared to be somewhat hypocritical and even two-faced. Many times, he had been threatened by the Cuban government officials that if he or any of the players ever defected while playing abroad, his family would suffer. That if he did not follow the rules, he would be removed from his position, and that if he were not a member of the Communist Party, which he despised, his life as he knew would be over. With time Jaime learned to hide his true feelings in order to maintain his job and his position as a respected representative for the Cuban national baseball team. "Swallow your pride," they say, "if you want to live another day. Play the game!" This was the advice of his Tio, and for the longest time, Jaime felt like he did not have any other choice. In more ways than one, doesn't Jaime resemble all of us? We each have different problems and circumstances, and we are all stuck in our own world for different reasons, but we learn to camouflage our true feelings behind the many masks we wear in order to get through life. It all boils down to decision-making. Yes, our lives are shaped by those decisions we make daily. Every single day we can make choices, which determine whether we go right or left, whether we stay or go, whether we speak or stay quiet, and evidently, the results of such decisions become a pile of calendar days we call *life*, our lives. Lives, which can be empty or full, meaningless, or filled with purpose and desire, full of written and imaginary goals and aspirations, and I ask… Are we really in control? Good question… Until one day, a desperate burst of anxiety explodes within, and a certain burning desire and an inexplicable warmth inside our hearts gets more and more real as it gets warmer and warmer; hotter and hotter as the intensity of the fire inside our souls disrupts our thoughts and needs daily. Especially those who dare to dream what seems like an impossible dream. A dream that will never come to fruition in Cuba because dreaming is not allowed, it is prohibited, and so we are told… Jaime says, "The people of Cuba are sick and tired of a tyranny that for over fifty years has engraved in their minds that the simple act of dreaming of a better future is a selfish and egotistic thought. And this is what creates confusion in Cuba, this creates mystification and finally enables them to do anything, and they find it simpler to just go along and die slowly. Or they suddenly grow inexplicable courage and come up with desperate and creative ways to try to escape that nightmare of a life they live day in and day out. Whether in a homemade raft with tied-up inner tubes, inside the wheels of an airplane, while working abroad for the Cuban government, or by marrying a foreigner in a desperate attempt to leave Cuba, they create the means to escape and possibly never to see their home and loved ones again. That is why they do anything and go anywhere in desperation, 'anywhere but there,' they say, and many are those who succeed. But the anonymous list of so many who have perished in their unsuccessful attempt remains, and sadly, so we will never really know their number!"

Jaime is an attractive and charming man in his early 50s; he is tall, slim, and well fit. He has the appearance of someone who loves life, therefore he enjoys it to the fullest, and he takes care of the only vehicle he has been given to navigate through it, his body. Now, his mind is a different story; he has been an old man since he was a little boy. He worries too much; he thinks too much and is now accustomed to his mind racing constantly at one hundred miles per hour. Psychologists say children who are *not* raised by mom and dad usually develop this complex, always feeling they have something to prove to the world. I like to call it the "I want to show everyone I can do it myself" complex. I am not Sigmund Freud, but it only seems natural for a person who has never had the warmth of a mother to want to seek it from the one person they feel they can trust the most, the one who has always been there, themselves, and so being selfish comes naturally. Jaime is a light-skinned mulatto with a natural golden tan, light eyes, and dark wavy hair. A chiseled jawline, broad shoulders, and a radiant smile are also part of Jaime's seemingly perfect outer appearance, but inside, he is torn, worn out, and he is slowly dying like many of his countrymen. So ironic to think that in a place where it is not unusual to see people well in their 80s and even their 90s walking around as if they were twenty-year-old, but it all comes with the same zombie song and dance. Are they alive? These people are breathing, but the question is, are they living? My guess is…they are not! Some say it is the island's pleasant weather and the ocean's clean air. Others will argue it is all due to the absence of fast-food restaurants, which continue to poison us here in America today and lead to having the highest obesity rate in the world and a population plagued by heart disease and other health problems. In Cuba, every meal is a home meal and organic. There are no fancy meat markets, all the food comes straight from the ground or the ocean next door, and even cooking oil is so rationed, this is a good thing. Funny to think of Cuban food as a healthy diet in food that requires plenty of fried items, roasted pork, and other meats, all of which are over seasoned for their unmistakable flavors. But still, people there seem to live forever. Maybe the secret lies in the lack of stress that comes from the American way of life. They have no credit cards, no car payments, insurance payments, and no expensive Christmas at the end of the year. Well, they do not have Christmas at all, and they have not since Castro took over, so, since Christmas is not celebrated there because communism prohibits it, think of all the money and stress they save! Perhaps because they are forced to do plenty of walking as very few people own a vehicle there. Jaime is one of the lucky ones who do, and he knows this.

Jaime is a direct descendant of an African slave, as we now well know, and yet he and another ten million people have fallen victims of Castro's filthy communist system making them all slaves today. Castro was the only person in the world who owned his own country as everything in Cuba belonged to him, and no one else owned anything. This system he and his cronies established in Cuba upon his takeover in 1959 pushes equality of race and color to its citizens and in the eyes of the world may seem like the answer to racism, like a noble idea of some sort, but this is only a way of putting themselves above all other governments where racial differences still exist today, but it is not so. Not true! This is a game, a lie and a trick, a dirty deception to control the people, and though initially it may sound like a good thing, its true agenda is quickly revealed as it is obvious that people come together and forget all about their personal and social differences when famine or difficult times strike. Castro was no genius, he only happened to be in the right place at the right time, and the people have no choice but to come together in order to survive now. In Cuba, blacks, whites, and any other background type are all in the same predicament, and all economic issues overshadow social ones. Who has time to think about racial differences when there is nothing to eat, right? Castro took advantage of a time where the people of Cuba were in desperate need of a change because the previous Batista regime was too led by a criminal and a corrupted man who ran a filthy government, leading to much-needed change at the time. This was when Castro organized his plot to overthrow him, filled with many false promises and political manipulation, and it was not until about a year or two into his presidency that he declared his true agenda of full-blown "communism." Everyone remembers that in 1961, an attempt to overthrow Castro was made with the Bay of Pigs Invasion, but it failed miserably for many reasons, and this brought the people together even more, giving Castro a sense of god-like complex and power, which to this day still reigns. Castro convinced them that the United States was trying to take over Cuba and warned the people of the many difficulties that would come about as a result, and they bought it. Bad guys vs. good guys! Him being the good guy, of course. The guy who gave Cuba back to the people, free education, free health care, and total and complete equality. Throughout the years, evident signs of discontent on behalf of the people of Cuba have emerged all too obvious to the world, and giving Castro's revolution a black eye here and there, and even though it endures, it is evident it was nothing but a lost cause and a failure. The evidence lies on the many mass boat lifts, which seem to occur every other decade since Castro took power, the Peruvian Embassy in 1980, and all the public protests from political prisoners and their relatives expressing a desperate cry for change and freedom.

The damage has been done, though, and it isn't about trying to reveal the true colors of a cruel and imperfect system anymore, but about panic, desperation, and about a need for change, which is as inevitable today as when Castro overthrew Batista back in 1959. The people are tired of lies, and they are drained by not seeing any results after all this time. It only seems reminiscent that they are always moving backwards instead. What happened to all the promises? What happened to democracy? What they got instead was misery, hunger, and being deprived of a decent life. Remember 9/11 here in the States? When everyone was covered by ashes and dust and horrified by fear in the City of New York? Well, for several days, we were all the same color, and we were all in the same desperate predicament, then suddenly the smoke cleared, and life as we know it returned. Then the look of hatred revisited the faces of those who despised their neighbor for being different, the lower class, the wealthy, the immigrant, the white, the black, the sick, the gays, the many different religions, the Conservative, the Liberal, and on and on we go on this roller coaster called "real life." Cuba is no different, Castro never ended racism and especially not poverty, but because of the ongoing oppression, everyone seems to come together as one in order to survive. Only there it has lasted over sixty years now, and no one seems to care, except for those who dare to live and take a chance at escaping. I do not see CNN, Fox News, or MSNBC making a big deal out of that either. I do not see documentaries about how desperate life is in Cuba and how a schoolteacher gets by on twenty-five dollars per month in salary. I wonder if there were large amounts of oil in Cuba like there is in Iraq, would things be the same? Would there be intervention to free the people from a dictator who sucks them dry? They certainly can't do it themselves, not in a place where everything and everyone is controlled day and night, where owning a gun is not permitted and where even disagreeing with the government can be viewed as treason, landing you in jail without any due process whatsoever. And to think it all started with an idea is mind-blowing. It began with a popular idea, and once this idea penetrated the minds of those willing to absorb it, it spread like a wildfire so wide it became lethal and deadly enough to endure over sixty years while wiping out an entire generation. Yes, I'm referring to Cuba, where it proved that once the deadly poison of these extremely dangerous ideas spread, it is immensely difficult to stop as history has proved this to be true in not only Cuba, but also in China, Venezuela, North Korea, and more... But today, with only seven communist countries left in the world, it is apparent that communism doesn't work, and looking back at all the countries around the world who attempted to install this system only to see it fail miserably, especially in Eastern Europe, one can't help but ask, "Now tell me, how well did that work out?" It is simple... There are certain natural freedoms a person cannot be separated from, and once those freedoms are threatened or taken away, people react. They rebelled then, and they will rebel now. It is an instinct that mankind cannot deny. They say the deadliest parasite known to men is an idea because it has no limits and no telling how far it will go. What happens is once these ideas, which are nothing but a cover-up for many false guarantees, lies, and deceit, become exposed, draining those receiving the information while believing the message to the point of complete defeat and leaving them exhausted and enabling them to fight back. Sometimes they believe it for long, denouncing it becomes even more painful. In Cuba, for example, for those who do not have a choice, who are either too old to flee or who don't know any better, the idea of Castro's agenda, as bad as it may sound, is all they have left, and if they denounce all they have believed all these years, then they are denouncing their entire lives. They would be denouncing all they have become and all they are. So, they live on instead, but as this double-edged sword continues to slice through lives there in Cuba, nothing is more dangerous.

These arousing and convincing schemes have destroyed lives, divided families, and pulverized dreams and hope for decades. They only lead to destruction in the end, as history has proven. Just look back over the past six decades there. Castro's deceptive agenda that criticizes capitalism to its very core but oppresses its people to the brink of extinction is no different than when the Spanish drove the Indians to almost complete extinction or what the Nazis did with the Jews during World War II. Castro may not have used concentration camps like Hitler did back in the 1940s, but the methods he uses to exterminate the people of Cuba who oppose him come in the form of mental concentration camps, food rationing, and imprisoning and torturing anyone who dares to disagree with his political views are no different. In addition, the treatment of political prisoners in Cuba is shameful and shocking, to say the least. These are people who simply oppose a dictatorship and who publicly express their opinion and discontent. People who have tried to save their country and countrymen from what it has become, and it is truly synonymous with disgrace, shame and inhumane for those who dare to rebel and speak up. They say prison conditions for political prisoners in Cuba are completely an alarming sight, to say the least, and what can we say about the dangerous and untimely escapes of men, women, and children of all ages in the middle of the night and into an ocean filled with hungry sharks in nothing but homemade wooden rafts to avoid a lifeless life and in search of a brighter future?

Think for a moment of how desperate the situation must be in Cuba when people feel they have no other choice but to throw themselves at the mercy of the sea, risking it all with just one hope, one goal: *freedom!* And though we all think that freedom is a cause worth dying for, the people of Cuba are a perfect example of this, as shown by their remarkable will to live, whether abroad once they leave Cuba or at home where they struggle to survive. Jaime often thinks of his ancestor Ijaba, the brave young girl his grandmother and uncle told him about his whole life. The same African princess who later became a slave and whose life was changed in the blink of an eye against her will when she was just a child; while throwing his head for a wild spin every time, he remembers her story.

Although retired from playing the game of baseball for many years now, Jaime's muscular forearms express details of his former profession, as previously mentioned. His eyes, sadden and tired, are almost a replica of this old uncle's eyes, which gloom with pain and sorrow and a never-ending thirst for the American way of life even though he keeps it all hidden deep inside with the fear that those around him may see through him. However, Jaime still looks ahead, and he hopes for an uncertain brighter future every single day of his life, but to no avail thus far. He does not seem to find the key to happiness in his vague existence, and his restless soul wonders in agony day in and day out in search of it. As a child, Jaime had always been very much loved by his grandmother ever since the day she took him to live with her. He was loved by his old uncle and the rest of the Colon family as well. The family was always quite close, where love and good manners were abundant, even in a place where the word "abundance" is as scarce as the freedom they share, but inside the Colon family, at the very least, love was always present. Good etiquette and education are a mandate in the Colon household, it is demanded and enforced. Discipline, integrity, and character thrive, and it helps ensure a proud heritage in one of the last, true, great tabaquero families in the island. Odd to say, though, in a place where so many things are limited and restricted, the Colon family sticks to their core values as if knowing these ideas are slowly vanishing from this world of ours. "Castro's dreams of communism, dictatorship, and a totalitarian system…they will all pass. This day will soon become tomorrow and on and on, but values and integrity will leave a scar in the lives of those we touch as we journey through this life." These are more words of wisdom Jaime remembers his old uncle voicing as he stares at nothing as if talking to the wind.

The Colon family takes care of the tobacco fields, and they all work nonstop in their trade with much pride, although the government takes most of the profit and they are not at liberty to run their operation as their own business. Everyone from the youngest to the oldest participates. Many of the field workers are of Haitian descent whose ancestors had come to Cuba to work in the tobacco or sugar fields and simply never left. For these Haitian field workers, work is all they know in an industry they love, and Jaime's family has embraced their hard work making them part of the family as well. Being an ex-member of the Cuban baseball national team, Jaime now acts as a representative for young ball players, as already mentioned. He scouts for talent throughout the island and monitors and follows the boys closely. Part of Jaime's job involves preparing these young hopefuls for the next level, mentally as well as physically. He follows the boys from the time they enter the youth leagues until they qualify for the big-time squad, the national team. He, against his will, reminds these young men, all well-known national hopefuls and the best in all of Cuba, that they owe their lives to a government that has made it possible for them to concentrate on playing baseball instead of having to pay their way through school by working endless jobs or having to worry about recruiting, scholarships and paying back student loans. He tells them all their other needs are being met. Really? By whom? By a government who cares…? No, not really, not at all, it is all part of a dishonest way a corrupted government injects into their minds to continue keeping these talented, brilliant, and gifted athletes drugged, blindfolded, and brainwashed. It literally seems as if these young men are being fed poison through a tiny imaginary straw called." An attempt to hang on to them just a little bit longer" with the hope that they do not open their eyes and see all they are missing outside of Cuba. Castro's revolution is desperately trying to hang on to a system that does not work and has not worked for years, if at all, and it is obvious that it is hanging by a thread and on its last leg. Liberty of choosing, freedom of speech, and freedom of preference is a must for every human being. Everyone needs it, everyone seeks it, and everyone desires it. Of course, unless you are a "slave" or simply someone who belongs by law to another person as their property and someone who has to obey them and work for them, which is the rightful dictionary definition of the word "slave…" Now, how many people feel this way in Cuba today? Most of them, I would say. The oppression of people by means of threats, manipulation, force, and mental and psychological abuse is a crime, and it should lead to capital punishment. The Cuban government should be sanctioned and penalized for their evil deeds. It is inhuman to rob people of their dreams and hopes as they have done all these years and to incarcerate, persecute and punish individuals for simply expressing their minds and speaking against an unjust system. Apparently, the embargo by the US on Cuba is not doing it. So, in order to make something out of nothing, some of the people of Cuba do whatever is necessary to survive. And I cannot say that I blame them. Some will marry a tourist and leave Cuba on a spousal visa. Others defect while working or playing sports abroad. Some will attempt to escape the island in whatever means possible, even if it means perishing at sea, but the truth is, their pain and despair are obvious, as demonstrated by these heroic acts knowing that if caught, hell awaits them. Jaime is not in love with the Cuban government, and, as a matter of fact, he could care less for their politics, but what he has done and what most people do in a place like Cuba, which is, they play the game. And I do not mean just baseball, but a mind game in which one pretends to go along in order to survive the wrath that comes with the opposite, which is what athletes, musicians, artists, professors, doctors, scientists, engineers, and other Cuban professionals have had to do in order get by. This is a dictatorship indeed and no different than Hitler's Germany, Stalin's Russia, or any other failed totalitarian dictatorship. I say again. "They own you, and that free education they offer is never free!" exclaims Jaime's uncle, and what a conflict, what a dilemma, huh? To not be able to be yourself, to have to live a double life with the fear that at any given moment anyone can identify the obvious fact that one does not agree with things the way they are, and they can snitch you out, and you end up in jail, just because… Imagine if, in America, people were to be persecuted for expressing their desire to be Democrats or Republican openly? Imagine not being able to pray to the god of your choice with fear of being incarcerated the following day simply because someone said they saw you doing so? Imagine there is no due process like in Cuba? No free speech? Imagine not being able to wear certain clothes because of where the clothes are manufactured or because of what the writing on a shirt contains? Imagine not being able to listen to certain music? For example, jazz. Yes, listening to or playing jazz is forbidden in Cuba. How is that so? How can music be dangerous to a governmental system? But as unreal as it seems, it is true in Cuba. At any given time, the Cuban government can dictate what is a danger to their revolution and take it away without any reason whatsoever other than 'just because.' To them, any idea that is not theirs is a dangerous idea, and immediately it becomes restricted and outlawed. It is amazing and mind-blowing, but real and true.

Does that make any sense currently? It does not make any sense to Jaime either, and neither does it to a few million other Cubans, even if at one point they were sympathizers of the so-called Castro movement only because they were tricked and lied to. It gets old very quickly as they become bored with all the false promises that never come to fruition and the empty propaganda and fear-inflicting threats that consume the hopes and dreams of the people. And no matter how loyal of a follower a person may be in Cuba, it comes to a point where their tolerance level to all the BS is so low, they simply lose hope and fade away; they simply fall off the wagon. Yes, in the words of Jaime's uncle, "and eventually, they all fall off the wagon." Meaning they throw the towel, and they give up, regardless of the consequences.

Jaime has seen it with his very own eyes as he has now too fallen off the wagon. The ideas that once made sense following as a young man are now displeasing to the core, fast-draining, and a pure mockery. He was once blind, but now he can see. He has learned how the system works, and now that he is exposed to the truth, he sees how it buries individuals in useless responsibilities and how mind manipulation and brainwashing has turned father against son, son against mother, friend against friend, and brother against brother. This is a system where one must whisper because saying the wrong thing can land a person in jail and where everyone has to wear a mask to survive because truth can be seen as threatening, as a conspiracy against a shattered government and its very own shaky foundation. Jaime began playing baseball when he was noticeably young in the streets of Havana before moving with his grandmother to the province of Pinar del Rio after his mother died. We do not really know much about Jaime's mom other than she was noticeably young when she passed away from complications following a routine appendix removal. As far as his father, he never met him, and he was never part of his life. Initially, like most kids in Cuba, Jaime played outside in the streets every day without any shoes and without a mitt when he was just seven or eight years old. He and the boys from the neighborhood used a broomstick for a bat, and if they were lucky enough to find an old tennis ball in someone's grandfather's junk, they would use that to play with. Many times, though, these kids round up a bunch of rubber bands and electrical tape, and they elaborately make a homemade baseball to play with. A far-fetched reality from modern video games, the latest cellular phones, and computerized gadgets that keep our youth glued to the television screens and away from physical activities here in America, huh? See, for most Cuban boys playing baseball is a way of life, being that baseball is the national sport and pastime there. So, baseball is in their blood, and making the national team is the ultimate dream. Also, the beach, an almost instant for Cuban kids because first, it is free, and second, because of its proximity to about anywhere in Cuba, where just minutes away a beach is found. You do not have to have any money to go to the beach either, and all you need is a bathing suit and a couple of friends. Outside of the beaches, there are the mountains, filled with all kinds of tropical trees, delicious fruit, and the rivers, which also play a huge part in playful youth life, and so, life can be quite simple growing up in Cuba until they grow up. Then reality hits, and a cruel reality full of restrictions, prohibitions and made-up rules that do not make any sense at all appear. It gets injected in their DNA, making it feel almost natural not to be able to travel outside of Cuba, so they do not miss what they never had, which is completely ironic to us in the US.

These kids never dream about playing professional baseball when they grow up because the Cuban government tells them they are not supposed to play for money but for the mere love of the game. "Money is the root of all evil," they tell them. Not the love of money, but money in general, which is completely idiotic and erroneous. The Cuban government engraves inside their heads these mind-polluting mantras until it is imprinted and making money feel like a negative thing, hoping they learn to associate money as being bad and making it useless to dream big. At the same time killing their ambition and desire to obtain a better life. They learn to become complicit and to settle for less, accepting their current situation as normal, settling for mediocrity. These exceptional athletes in Cuba's baseball play for national pride and to show the rest of the world the kind of baseball Cuba can produce without the millions of dollars in salaries and endorsements. They settle for an average life, and afterward, they become buried alive in the shadows of a decaying society just like the old buildings in Cuba. After years of standing in line to buy a loaf of bread, peddling to work or school on a bicycle, unable to travel the world freely, and accustomed to food rationings, it sucks them dry, and they just give up! True story! "When Cuban athletes do television interviews, you can sense these are all rehearsed speeches, and this is obvious by the sound of their forced and unnatural responses," explains Jaime. And these interviews sound something like this: "You do it all to represent your country, money is the devil, but national pride is a way of life. You can be a hero to an entire nation and become immortal where your name can too echo in eternity with the names of those who will live forever in the world of baseball." They are told to talk like this, to refer to the greats of the past, the pioneers, and the ones who have broken all the records in Cuban baseball as heroes. These guys will be remembered in history for all the ages, they are told to say. Instructed to say. Forced to say. While threatening them with keeping them from traveling abroad, kicking them off the team, and even intimidating them to harass their family back home if they try the unimaginable, defecting.

Jaime once too believed in the communist propaganda since he had been born after the revolution and did not know any better, but his blindfold was finally removed, and he sees the reality of what things have become, he sees the truth now. He clearly sees what a communist government tells their young athletes from the time they are in grade school and how they gouge the eyes out of the kids to try to curve their vision, making them practically "modern-day kamikaze pilots" just like during World War II, when the Japanese Air Force brainwashed their pilots into flying their planes into US Navy ships, immediately making themselves heroes of the war and martyrs in the eyes of the Japanese people. Cuban baseball, as instructed by their government, threatens and intimidates their players if they were to do the unthinkable but nevertheless, an array of Cuban hopefuls and established players manages to jump ship in pursuit of a professional career in the US and anywhere around the world where they are granted political asylum. In some cases, the other side prevails in keeping these superb athletes loyal to their cause, and years later, they wake up way past their prime realizing they blew a great opportunity, and now they live the rest of their lives buried in poverty and regret.

Baseball can easily help these guys make a great living playing abroad, and they know it, but so does the same government which sends them out to fetch them money and glory. For this reason, they try at all costs to prevent their athletes from defecting and seeking asylum outside of Cuba. Many times, the ones who do stay in Cuba become so heartbroken after their careers are over, realizing the window of opportunity has now been closed. In many cases, they are already too old and washed up to play once they defect, so they know it is a very tight window before they become buried alive in the slums of Havana, along with many world-renowned musicians, doctors, and scientists who once made a great contribution to Cuba. Of course, if any of these players were ever able to escape their misery? And I say "escape" because there is no travel outside of the island for pleasure, and only by escaping or defecting while playing abroad can one see the world outside of Cuba. Those that have gotten out past their prime still have been able to make a great living outside of Cuba simply by becoming advisors and trainers in many fields, not just playing baseball or boxing, but in many different areas. Yes, that is right, applying for an exit visa and passport to go see the world is forbidden in Cuba and not possible for regular everyday folks. Only the Cuban delegation of athletes, doctors, and government officials paid and financed by the government who collects any money paid to them for their services outside of the island have the pleasure of peeking outside of Cuba's imaginary wall. Now this, only after a thorough background check and many conditions, which are established by an irrational way of thinking and unspecific rules and guidelines that constantly change to fit a fraudulent program that only they understand. Terrible!

So, most Cuban boys hope that one day they can wear the uniform of the Cuban national team in any sport, but especially in baseball, which is the national pastime like in the US, and this way have an opportunity to travel, represent their country and see the world, the only way. Jaime had enjoyed an extremely short career as a player. He was an above-average baseball player for the Pinar del Rio team, who was the biggest foe of and presented the main threat to the popular team from Havana, the Industriales. He had been plagued by injuries early in his short career, and after only three years as the starting third baseman for the Pinar del Rio squad, his baseball days came to an end. Soon after retiring from playing the game he loved, he was named the youngest trainer for the team from Pinar del Rio and one of the youngest in the entire country. Jaime is an extremely pleasant man with a colorful personality and natural charm. He carries an extremely soft demeanor about himself, and he is well-liked, always making everyone feel good around him. Jaime is one of those guys who walks into a room, and the whole place lights up, even in Cuba, where they have so many power outages. Yes, sir, the Cuban government has made a habit of shutting off the power in the inner-city neighborhoods for several hours a day to save on energy. I guess this is all part of the sacrifices Castro talked about in his four-hour speeches where he always gave the people a mouth full of illogical propaganda filled with empty Marxist rhetoric. In addition, food rationing, lack of everything, and abundance of nothing, and this has been the story of Cuba for the last fifty years plus. Castro's fundamentalist government only came to destroy a beautiful island and a people and, after over fifty years, has added nothing. All the beautiful hotels and world-renowned resorts in Cuba today have been built by foreign hotel chains like the Melia corporation out of Spain and other European companies. The sugar cane industry, once considered one of the best in the world, has diminished to a point it is not even mentioned anymore. All the factories are five to six decades old or older, and the same goes with the coffee and mining industry, it is all gone. They have robbed the place dry. Literally!

The tobacco industry in Cuba, however, has been able to withstand the winds of time, and Cuban cigars are still recognized as some of the best in the world. Over the years, though, one of the most prestigious products to come out of Cuba, cigars, "the pride of Cuba," has faced stiff competition at the hand of rival cigar manufacturers outside of there; many of whom are owned and operated by Cuban cigar experts now living in exile and the same people who were once in charge of the cigar business in the island. These folks are the ones now producing a remarkably similar product to that of the authentic Cuban stogies, and as we speak, many of the cigars currently being perfected back home today, according to some experts, have either lost some of their lusters in recent years or their emulators are finally catching up and perhaps passing the once lavished and incomparable classic commodity.

For many decades Cuba raised the bar so high they became the undisputed heavyweight champion of the cigar world, but now Nicaragua, Honduras, and the Dominican Republic, among other countries, are right there neck and neck with Cuba, and this may have a lot to do with the known fact that most, if not all of the tobacco business in Cuba, is now at least partly owned by other countries. Cuba's rum is another delicacy to come out of there, with Havana Club probably being the most recognized brand, just as Cohiba may be the best-known when it comes to cigars. Many people may not know that Bacardi Rum first originated in Cuba before moving their factories to Puerto Rico when "the Beast" (Castro) arrived. Remarkably so, to be completely honest, basically, only tourism thrives there anymore, and just barely!

Thinking back, how the tobacco industry managed to stay relevant in Cuba after all these years is well beyond me, knowing that once Russia stopped supporting Cuba, they hit extremely difficult economic times and, as earlier mentioned, were then forced to involve different foreign interests to provide much-needed financial support to the island's economy the likes of Italy, China, and Spain, among others. Over the years, all Castro and his peeps have done is ruin Cuba and everything inside. They have pulverized what took so many years to build and turned it into a den of thieves in front of the world stage, but for some reason, Cuban cigars endured. It is well known that once Castro arrived, the people of Cuba could not own their business anymore, and for the longest time, they used the black market as the only way to conduct any kind of business. Only recently that knot has been loosened up a bit. Initially, everything was being controlled and run by the government, where the establishment owned it all, and no one was free to buy or sell without government authorization first, and this is the truth regardless of what anyone may say. Even when they finally began to allow small businesses to slowly operate, there was always a threat that at any given time, they could come in and for no reason at all close a business down in the blink of an eye. That is why so many were always hesitant to buy a beachfront property there, even as tempting as it may sound. You just cannot trust them, even now that Fidel is gone. That corrupted and lawless system in Cuba will continue until there is nothing left. A musician in Cuba, for example, cannot play whatever music he desires because the lyrics can be misinterpreted and categorized as counterrevolutionary by those in charge and automatically banned at any given time, especially if the musician happens to become popular, because in Cuba, no one can be too popular. Then that musician would be immediately shot down and unable to play or sell any of his music. See, there can only be one hero in Cuba, him… Castro. His clones have made this very clear from the beginning, and unless you're dead, of course, then you can be as popular as you want because if you are dead, then you are not a threat to their agenda. Interesting, huh? Jaime had been brainwashed like many Cubans born after the revolution to believe Castro's fairy tale had a purpose and a perfect design with a happy ending. An ideology that became words in the wind rather quickly. The people of Cuba were always told since the beginning of their charade that there would be a grand prize in the end, but it required uncommon sacrifice and a blind eye to the things that did not seem right or fair, and they bought it, believing it to be true, just like Jaime once did. Oddly enough, none of this went along with the things Jaime was taught by his uncle and his grandma at home. He always felt, however, like he had no choice and just like his ancestors had no choice when they were brought from Africa many years before. His uncle was right when he said Castro could not be trusted. He routinely lived with the constant fear that his farm and plantation could be taken from him at any time, just like it had happened to so many fellow countrymen that once owned land. Now, allow me to explain something in case you may be thinking, *Well, how bad was it really for Jaime's family when they were allowed to keep their tobacco plantation?* See, the truth is, in Cuba, no one is exempt as there is only one voice, one vote...the government. First, 75 percent of the land was taken from their rightful owners the minute Castro took over through a law passed called "The agrarian reform." They would walk in and seize the properties from the farmers and landowners with the pretest to redistribute it supposedly equally among the people, which never took place, and not one single acre of land was ever given to any of the Cuban farmers, but instead divided among those closest to Castro and especially the ones who were truly loyal to him and his cause. Second, farmers in Cuba do not own their harvest outright. His uncle, for example, upon collecting the harvest from the Colon tobacco plantation; the government had to be informed of the official production and given an accurate accounting of it all before taking their unfair share. Then to top it off, all the workers were paid and hired by them and not by El Tio, who was the rightful individual to do so. Especially since he knew exactly who did what, who had the most experience and had to have been paid more, but instead, the Cuban government would pay them miserable equal wages while they collected the bulk of all the profits. How is that for fair?

So, the next time you hear someone say that Castro did some good things in Cuba, you can politely respond with an extremely educated answer, "What good things and at what cost did he do them? A free education in exchange for their soul is no bargain."

Okay, but back to the baseball talk. For those that do not know, Cuba is divided into fourteen provinces and not states because the island is so small. Each province has a major baseball team. Now, unless Cuba is invited to participate in international events or tournaments like the Olympics, the Caribbean, or the Pan American Games, that is the only time Cuba forms a national team made of the best players from the entire island; an all-star team of some sort where only the best of the best will be recognized, but there is no voting by the fans like in Major League Baseball All-Star Game here in the States. These guys are chosen by government officials like Jaime, and it is not always about numbers and performance since only those who walk the line and those who follow the rules and kiss butts are the ones who make it, and that is when we realize there is more politics in baseball than you know, especially in a corrupted place like Cuba. For the last five decades or so, many people in Cuba have claimed to be on the side of the government just to be on good terms with them, and that is because over there and under that system, "you are either with them or you are against them."

Therefore, so many pretend to follow this autocratic and nonsense system and not because they want to but because they must if they want to live in peace. Anyone who disagrees with the system the Cuban government runs is automatically an enemy of the state, and at that point, their lives become a nightmare, instantly becoming traitors, worms, and enemies of the revolution simply for not agreeing or sympathizing with a non-pluralistic government, and therefore they become unwanted, many are thrown in jail and persecuted simply for showing any type of disagreement with the Castro regime, and a large number of Cubans are left with no choice but to try to escape from the island in search of freedom. Initially, all those who saw the disaster coming shortly after Castro's takeover, the ones who were smart enough to recognize his masquerade, fled the island immediately and were the lucky ones, those were the ones who didn't witness the cruel transition period that took place following the introduction of what would be a dark cloud of over fifty years. The new Castro government gave exit visas to anyone who wanted to leave in the early 1960s as a strategy to get rid of any opposition and to anyone who had been jailed for political reasons or for simply opposing the new system, who were categorized as "political prisoners" and, of course, did not have any place there and were quickly deposed. Looking back, those brave men and women who disagreed with the new Castro-led totalitarian movement that violated all aspects of the Cuban constitution and who stood up to it deserve much praise and recognition. Unfortunately, a lot of good it did as they all ended up either incarcerated, exiled, or worse, and from professionals to entertainers, university professors, and anyone who opposed paid the price one way or another.

Many were told to leave the island to never again be allowed back in. And just like that...shortly after, the government shut its doors, and Castro announced his communist preference. After that, no one could either leave or come back to the island, and the self-proclaimed Christ ruled with an iron fist for the next five decades. Consequently, only a selected few could travel. Musicians, athletes representing Cuba in international competition, diplomats, and a few other special cases would be the lucky ones to see the outside world. Cuban doctors and those in the medical field, whom Castro began sending out to other countries in exchange for money and much-needed resources, were some of the privileged individuals with no hope of traveling whatsoever. Since Cuban boxing, baseball, track and field, and other sports had become world-renowned, this was a great way to get out of Cuba and see the world. Therefore, sports immediately became every child's dream in Cuba. Many aspiring baseball hopefuls would aim high at the golden opportunity by training nonstop and preparing themselves for a shot at being one of the lucky ones to be selected. Baseball players in Cuba begin playing at the national level incredibly young, and the government wastes no time dictating what is the prime of their careers. They take advantage of these young players, sometimes still just boys, who will never have a chance to hire an agent or someone to represent their best interest. Many never make it because of injuries and end up ruined for life, both physically and emotionally afterwards. These boys, or should I say some of these boys, find themselves maturing prematurely and quickly turn into fine ball players; however, there are those who are ruined for life, almost like picking fruit from the tree too early or delivering a baby before its due date. They are rushed into stardom way too soon on many occasions, and it backfires often as the boys become plagued by injuries and some never recover, like Jaime. Since all sports in Cuba are amateur sports, these athletes can play if they are capable of being the best at their position and so long as they go along with the system. The government runs their lives, and they pretty much own them. Everyone lives in an "earn-your-points system." If you want a telephone line in your apartment, you must earn it. A color television, you must earn it, and I do not mean doing well on the baseball field and show up to meetings on time. I mean, volunteer work on a sugar cane field and civil watch for the local neighborhood, snitching on anyone not going along with the program. Who bought what illegally? Where did they get the money to buy it? Who is planning on leaving the country in a raft in the middle of the night because they are simply fed up? Who does not agree with everything Castro says? And more…See, communism is a hopeless cause and a system where a political party led by one man rules everyone else, a dictatorship, which for Castro and his clan has worked over the years to a T mainly because Cuba is a small island about the size of Florida, with no borders and a small population, which is much easier to control than a larger country. But nevertheless, they have outlasted the Soviet Union that was the founder of the going-nowhere system, so something must be working. Or has it really worked? The so-called Cuban revolution has stayed afloat all this time at the expense of eleven million people starving and having nothing, which to me says it has failed miserably, but they continue to claim victory while people, my people, continue to suffer and die in shark-infested waters trying to escape the food rationing, the power outages, the lack of freedom, the persecution and more. Now, tell me something, and try to pretend it refers to you.

How desperate must a person be to throw themselves into pitch-black ocean water in the middle of the night and aboard a homemade floating device with the idea of leaving their homeland for good and in a desperate attempt to make a better life for them and their family? How scary would it be? And I repeat...on many occasions, there are women and children and even elderly people along for the ride in these fateful journeys. Yet, so many people around the world view old Fidel Castro as a hero and as a great leader. Yeah, tell that to the people of Cuba! Tell that to the families of those he has sent to the firing squads and incarcerated without due process to never be seen again. Tell that to those who are still missing in the ocean. Tell it to the relatives of the thousands of political prisoners still being held without any hope inside inadequate jail cells and without any idea of how long they will remain in there. Tell it to the families separated by so many years of exile and anguish. Tell it to anyone, tell it to everyone, but just tell it. It needs to be told, it must be told because there are so many people out there who truly see it as the complete and total opposite.

Jaime was born in Havana, and after his mother died, he was brought to live with his grandmother and the rest of the Colon family in Pinar del Rio when he was just an infant. He never knew his father, so his old uncle El Tio was the only father figure he ever knew, and a good one he was. El Tio, whose real name was Andres, is a good man. A man of powerful integrity and strong character, a man of principles and conviction, and, of course, a great tabaquero too. El Tio is what they call "a Gallego" in Cuba, which is common slang for people from Spain, but the real term is for Spaniards from Galicia in the northern part of the old country and next to the French border. When El Tio was just seventeen when his father forced him on a boat and sent him to Cuba so that he would not have to enlist in the Spanish army, this was during the time of World War II.

The old man is tall and thin but strong and fit. A man who spent much of his time working out on the tobacco fields and making sure the work was being done right. He is hardly ever seen without his traditional Cuban straw hat. His dark skin from being in the sun is quite the contrast with his grey hair and bright blue eyes along with a mouth full of pearly white teeth, which he proudly accredits to drinking fresh milk and eating raw garlic daily. Go figure! Impressive, I would say, for a man who has smoked cigars his whole life and now in his 70s. He has a very calm demeanor and is a man of few words. He is observant and of little opinions. He keeps to himself but is extremely affectionate, often bathing those around him with hugs and kisses, especially the children in the family. He is a master cigar maker and an inheritor of the Colon family cigar mastery secret tradition. He really knows how to make some of the best cigars in the world from beginning to end, and he knows how to run the show the right way. From treating the soil to planting and caring for the tobacco plants, selecting the absolute best leaves that would make a top-notch cigar, to packing the cigars perfectly aligned in their rightful wooden, mahogany boxes, he is a true craftsman in his trade no different than a master chef in a world-renown five-star French restaurant. El Tio is not just an expert but a perfectionist who demands quality, class, and excellence, and, as a matter of fact, the entire Colon family work in the cigar business, and from the time the kids are in diapers, they are already crawling on tobacco leaves.

The old grandma is a strong woman, rough around the edges and short-tempered. She is not formally educated, never stepping into a classroom her entire life, and her reading skills are all self-taught. She loves the kids, though, especially Jaime. To her, Jaime is still the same little boy she brought home many moons ago. Her gray hair, light eyes, and tanned, wrinkled face express a combination of many traits. First, the obvious multiracial mixture of African, French, Spanish, and who knows what else heritage, and second, the sadness inside from the many years of waiting for a political change to bring life back. The grandmother's frail body has lived through and tolerated an entire life of agony and suffering, but there is also the sense of satisfaction for raising all the Colon kids herself and injecting them all with good manners and decency. She is firm in character but loving and affectionate in her very own way.

The old grandma oversees the inside of the Colon household, which relates to all the kitchen duties, cleaning, and making sure all the laundry is done. She also assigns all the work to the three practically adopted Haitian girls who help around the house. These girls are as much part of the family as any of the Colon children and are never treated as servants or help, but like family. Her tiny stature is in no way indicative of her real strength, as it is proven by her continuous chopping of wood using an axe for a firepit where they do all the cooking or by her incredible ability to kill any of the animals on the farm. Her relationship with Jaime is somewhat strange but in a good way. All the love and affection can be often interrupted by a scolding remark about why he has not settled down yet and found a wife, which drives Jaime crazy, but he tolerates it only because it comes from her. Jaime's grandmother's name is Abuela Yarina. Jaime is a trusted and respected government official whose job is to discover and recruit new talent for the Pinar del Rio baseball team in the off-season. During the baseball season, he travels with the team to all the games, tournaments, and to any kind of competition. He plays an extremely important role in the lives of the players; he is like a father figure to many of them, especially the younger ones. Jaime is the guy they run to when important decisions have to be made, and he is also the one they talk to when they need any favors or help of any kind. Jaime is well connected, let us just say he has all the contacts, and he knows people in high places to get his hands on anything and everything. His affiliation with his family's cigar business also puts him in a rare position to spoil anyone he desires with glamorous gifts in the form of exclusive cigars, which even there where he is surrounded by stellar competition; the Colon cigars are still considered a delicacy. Jaime's job allows him to come and go freely, and he literally works throughout the entire island. He is also an attractive man and a bachelor who does not have much time for serious relationships. Jaime is a smooth communicator, a great negotiator, and the most passionate person anyone could ever meet, especially about that which he is the most dedicated to, which is baseball, his cigars, and his family. He also loves the women…yes, Jaime has a soft spot for the females, and Cuba is not known for having the ugliest women in the world, so let us say Jaime does not suffer much in this department. As a matter of fact, this may very well be his downfall and his demise as in his personal life, women can be considered a weakness, but also a major fault as he shuffles them around like rag dolls with no regard for their feelings or emotions. He moves from one to the next without hesitation and never with any intention of a real relationship. Jaime's faithfulness only applies to his work and his family, but never to the women.

Call it the dark side of a man who, to this point, may have appeared to be spotless in many ways, but we all have to carry our own crosses of shame, and this seems to be his. Perhaps the fear of being tied down and controlled by a woman may resemble too much the stronghold the Cuban government has on him. Maybe his busy schedule is just too complicated for a serious relationship. No one really knows but him what the reality is behind it all but even his family wonders if he is ever going to settle down and get married, especially his grandmother Yarina. Jaime has taken advantage of his looks, his position, and his surroundings to enjoy the opposite sex to the fullest by having them at his disposal and at his begging call as needed. Never lonely but always alone as women weave in and out of his apartment like a parade of auditioning wannabe models constantly, and he calmly plays a no-strings-attached game. Almost as if they are just merchandise. He keeps his distance from any emotional attachment, and the minute he notices his leniency towards any type of affection other than just physical, he quickly pulls away. Often by simply disappearing without a trace and not showing his face around as his way of ending things without using any words and without the controversy of a break-up. Jaime likes to play the role of a roving bachelor and modern-day Romeo but in a very private way. He keeps his life confidential and does not bring any of the women around the family either. No one gets too close, and this worries the old grandma as she hopes he one day settles down and brings her a Jaime-seed in the form of a great-grandbaby, but Jaime has other plans, he dodges the questions and insists on having his personal life just that personal, often using the excuse that he is constantly traveling, and this makes it difficult to keep a steady relationship with any woman. At least, this is what he tells them, but in all reality, he dislikes the idea of being controlled, plus the fact that his mom left him when he was just a baby may still linger in the back of his mind, and it touches an overly sensitive spot, so he shields his emotions by showing very little empathy towards women in some internal way, but he hides it well. He hides it all behind a charming attitude and a fake smile half the time. He is great at portraying Mr. Cool, Mr. Friendly, and Mr. Charming…but never the real Mr. Lost, Confused, and Vulnerable.

Jaime is more cynical about it than anything else, and his critical thinking doesn't allow him to jeopardize or detour his chances of pursuing his dream, and so he plays with their feelings and emotions, and he could care less if anyone gets hurt if it isn't him. It is obvious how he clearly pushes women away as a method of not allowing anyone to get inside and trying at all costs to keep everyone at a comfortable distance while at the same time protecting himself from having to open and become exposed. Yet, he is never alone. Jaime knows the last thing he needs in his life is for some woman to waltz in and steal his heart, capturing not only his attention but, more importantly, detouring his dreams and ambitions.

So, he has decided to take it one day at a time while mastering the "no plan" plan to perfection. He knows what he wants, he knows where he is going, and a serious relationship with a woman is not his idea of heaven at this point and time. To him, women are awesome, great, wonderful, and beautiful, but he sees them as just companions and somewhere in between fun and games, friends and acquaintances, lovers, and strangers, but at no time does he plan on getting serious with anyone. He is certain this will put a restraint on his plans, and he is just too selfish and too serious about his dream to let this happen. Jaime does not even allow himself to develop deep friendships with any woman, regardless of how beautiful, smart, or talented she may be. He has developed a cold and systematic way of keeping them in the loop if he wants them and needs them but then turning them loose in a heartbeat the minute they get too close. Like a lion sometimes toys around with its prey before he devours it, Jaime too toys with these women in a no-strings-attached approach; none whatsoever, no exceptions, and no compromising.

Now, does this make Jaime the classic bad boy type in thc eyes of women, and is he just a calculating and manipulating Don Juan on a vengeance rampage against the opposite sex for not having his mother around? Maybe, I see how this could be the case, or is this just an angry attempt to take advantage of the ladies simply because he is a man and because he is able to do so? Or maybe he is just the typical pig or dog in the eyes of the women he dates for not manning up to a position of faithfulness and respect most people would expect following an episode of hot, intimate sex and after a few heated dates. Whatever the situation, for Jaime, it was just the way it would be and perhaps making this his downfall and his demise, in any case, far from a perfect man for sure as he would just not allow for anyone to destroy or derail his plan. He just knows the day will come when he simply has to spread his wings and fly into some unknown future that awaits him. This is his fate, he knows this life just does not belong to him, there must be more as he is not content and willing to accept his present situation as the standard. He knows in his heart that everything he is now missing and all his frustrations he unleashes on the way he handles his romantic relationships as if his only way to exhale, and he carries about a careless attitude towards the women in his life with no regard whatsoever for anybody else but him. Not feeling the smallest bit of remorse as these women who enter his life, perhaps thinking there may be a future, and they are forced to quickly exit out the door of indifference just a short time later. He uses beautiful women to cover his sorrow and pain as if filling a void, a gap. He does it to forget how miserable he is living a life where he is constantly trapped like a caged animal, followed, and expected to obey all the rules diligently, and so he uses them to fill an abyss of emptiness and desolation deep inside his very core. Again, the absence of his mother has proven to be a crucial direct hit to his heart, leaving a wide-open wound difficult to heal, often reminiscing about the day she left. He often thinks about how she left when he was just an infant, and he works hard to try to block how this untimely departure made him feel then and how it haunts even today. He knows her name was Marianela and that her nickname was Mimi, but nothing else. The grandma and the old uncle never talk about her. Physically, he remembers her having long black hair and big, brown eyes flowing with shiny tears as Jaime was taken from her to go live with his grandma right before she died. She had been ill for quite some time and could not take care of young Jaime anymore, and that is when his grandma finally stepped in and took the boy to live with her. In one last fateful visit to the hospital, Jaime was able to say goodbye to his mother before she finally died. She had asked the old grandma to bring the boy to see her following a series of medical tests, which proved she was not going to live exceedingly long, and as soon as Jaime left the hospital, she passed away almost immediately. They say it was heart-related, but since they do not talk much about her, Jaime had also decided not to bring up a subject that wounded him so deeply over the years. Good or bad, mom will always be a mom. A boy will always have a certain sentiment of attachment to his mother and a special place in his heart for her, and especially if there is not a father around. Mom is like a delicate flower in the eyes of a boy, a goddess of some sort, a hero perhaps for simply giving birth and for carrying us in her belly for nine months. I feel that way about my mother, and I believe most men do too. Jaime is grateful to have had his loving grandmother who made sure he lacked nothing as far as love, care, and affection, and he loved her very much, but she was not the woman who gave birth to him; she was not *mom*.

We now find ourselves in the middle of Old Havana. It is warm, humid, and on this tropical evening, the nightlife is festive with lights and music. It is late, right around two in the morning, but the old city does not sleep. Havana is a city stuck in time and always festive. The entire town and, as a matter of fact, all of Cuba is an ongoing party where the people use music and any type of festivity to try to ignore their constant struggle. Havana is full of buildings from centuries ago and priceless artifacts the whole world would salivate for, but to the Cuban people, these are just old statues and buildings recording their miserable injustice. All sorts of beautifully designed structures from long ago adorn the city, some almost in ruins but still standing. The architecture alone makes this place mystical. Too bad we (Americans) were the only people in the world who could not travel to Cuba freely and could not enjoy its long and well-preserved beauty not yet ruined by a McDonald's restaurant in every street corner and Marlboro cigarettes billboards. Almost an exact reversal of them we became because of the embargo, and nothing against McDonald's or Marlboro, I am just trying to explain Cuba's uniqueness in comparison with America as there is not much if any at all advertising other than the traditional communist propaganda hanging from billboards and street posts, but I'm just trying to make a point of contrast, that's all. Unique and untarnished beauty is found all around Cuba, only accented by poverty and need. What a strange combination, what a calamity. What a shame! In the '40s and '50s, Cuba was America's playground and seen by many as America's little sister, then suddenly it became forbidden fruit to us here in the United States once the bearded clown took over and suddenly any product of Cuba became illegal in the US. Yes, from cigars to rum, anything made in Cuba was illegal here because of the embargo placed over the island to squeeze them to the brink of throwing the towel and giving in to US political pressure.

I guess someone thought an embargo on the island would be the best way to get rid of Castro, but a lot of good it did, and after over fifty years, even after his death, his ideology still runs the country, and ten million people still suffer. When is it going to end? Now, this has not stopped any other country from traveling there, and it has not stopped Cuban Americans from returning to see their loved ones left behind while putting millions of dollars annually in the pocket of the same dictatorship we try to censor. It does not make any sense at all. Even American boats enter the Hemingway Marina and other seaports daily supposedly to gas up for a round of golf or simply for lunch in Havana.

This historical and nonsense embargo is simply absurd, it has not worked, and it never will. I say we lift it and allow the people to see what they are missing. I can almost guarantee it will very possibly cause a rebellion that ends it all once they are able to see firsthand what they have been missing this whole time, but until then, know that without military intervention, those guys who are holding Cuba hostage for six decades are not going to want to release their golden ticket. It is illogical to think otherwise.

So, what is the purpose of this embargo, this political strategy, and why isn't it continuously revised? Perhaps the embargo should be placed around Castro and his clan themselves and not over the entire country. Look, I do not know much about politics, but what I do know is Castro, and his players laugh at the embargo while the people of Cuba suffer even after his death. The embargo was supposed to have squeezed them to the point of exhaustion while suffocating their cruel tyranny, but it was not so. It never really affected them as they continued to eat well and live like royalty, so go figure! And all the while our amazing politicians smoke the same cigars no one else can enjoy in America because the embargo makes it illegal, and I bet you if they wanted one of those beautiful and exotic Cuban beauties, they could have her in their country club by noon tomorrow because the rules do not quite apply to everyone equally. Pure hypocrisy! I would say… Embargo equals a few smart dudes lining their pockets at the expense of too many lives, but welcome to the unfair game of politics!

Meanwhile, the city of Havana does a great job in disguising their daily struggle, and when night falls, it comes alive, packed with both locals and visitors. The nightclubs thrive. The vintage 1950s' automobiles are a tourist's delight as you look around it is all you see. The streets are flooded with happy tourists, most of them European and Canadians, especially men seeking a lusty time as hot-blooded Cuban women hang on their arms, smelling the green they will never be able to make in Cuba working regular jobs, all government-sanctioned jobs, because in Cuba, everyone works for the government, and I repeat again and again in an effort to make this a point very clear to those that don't know how it works there. There is no free enterprise like here in the US, and if they are lucky enough to have the opportunity to open a little shop or one of the famous "Cuban Paladares," a small private restaurant inside the people's houses, they can only do so by agreeing to a fifty-fifty split with the Cuban government. What a bargain, huh? There is only one other way to make money in Cuba, but not everyone is qualified. There is no formal education required, and even though the government knows it exists, they tend to turn a blind eye to it as this helps their deceptive agenda, and that would be the oldest profession in the world, yes, prostitution, which they will never admit to it, but it is all too obvious. "These Cuban working girls are not shy at all about their favors either. They must make that buck; they must survive. These are girls anywhere from as early as thirteen years old, and all the way up to, well, necessity has no time limit and no age, and there seems to be a market for everyone in the island," Jaime thinks out loud as he tells his story. He continues to sing the song of his life, narrating his pain as his heart continues to throb because of it. Jaime talks out loud as if he were having a conversation with his uncle and feels he has something to explain to the world, "Tio, you are not so wrong about me. There is so much you do not know, and so much I cannot say. I live every day with the fear of losing the little bit I do have, which is more than most here in Cuba. I live with the fear that they could harm my family if I do not walk the line. If I do anything stupid, like allow any of my players to jump ship while playing abroad, and I know this could bring trouble on my family."

Jaime takes a deep breath and continues his monologue as he walks down the street, just airing out his frustrations. "People have no clue what I really feel inside because I do such a good job hiding my personal storms. If they only knew, they would be amazed at the fact I have not had a nervous breakdown by now," Jaime mumbles as he emerges from one of the many nightclubs lining up the three-century-old Havana street. After a few drinks, he bids goodnight to his friends at the bar and makes his way out of the club, cutting a strikingly handsome figure. Tonight, Jaime is a well-dressed man about town who keeps two cigars in his right shirt pocket, just like his old uncle.

After having his drinks to bring the uneventful evening to an end, he feels a bit loose now, and he continues to talk out loud, slowly strolling down the street. "Well, I am indeed a respected representative for Cuban athletes…" he adds… Checking himself in a mirror outside an empty store. A couple of young Cuban women immediately latch onto him as he turns the corner, and they try to flirt aggressively with him, sending his ego for a spin, but Jaime politely avoids them and walks off alone.

"Not tonight, girls, have a good night. Buenas Noches!"

He then walks off and carries on, talking to himself, "I am entrusted with ensuring that no one dares to attempt the unthinkable and defect, seeking political asylum as we travel out of the country like it has happened so many times before, but not under my watch. I am assigned to prevent any of this from happening because it hurts the image of Castro's big lie."

"When athletes defect from Cuba or any other dictator-led totalitarian government, it tarnishes their image and the idea that everyone is so happy there. It gives a black eye to their agenda, their morale, and reputation, plus it gives others hope. See, the foundation of Castro's Cuban revolution was based upon a rock of lies and false promises, so it looks extremely bad when a defection takes place, and that is why we try to prevent it at all costs," Jaime adds as he walks off alone. After a few moments, he reaches his car, the same 1977 Alfa Romeo earlier discussed, which in America would have been anyone's first car at the age of sixteen, but to him and another ten million Cubans, this old car feels like a brand-new Rolls-Royce as having a car in Cuba is a luxury. Are you kidding me? In a country where a doctor makes three hundred dollars and a schoolteacher twenty-five dollars per month? Forget it!

All those fancy relics from the '50s we so often see in Cuba are usually passed down from generation to generation and are quite expensive even there. Many people around the world try to get their hands on them, but since the Cuban government takes such pride in having such a large collection of them, it is not allowed to ship them out.

"I was trained to engrave in their heads that they need nothing else. I would tell them that even millions of dollars will never replace what we have here in Cuba. And what do we have?" Jaime whispers…

He finally makes it home; his head is spinning. He either has had too much to drink, or he has been working too hard lately. He knows he needs rest. He enters his apartment, turns on the lights placing his keys on the table by the kitchen window, and continues with his mumbling, "That is right, it is my job to make sure they do not break the chains like my ancestors back in the days of Ijaba."

He looks around his home, at his possessions, which by American standards are lower-middle-class at best, but luxury compared to his family's home in Pinar del Rio and most of the people living in Cuba today. A single piece of lingerie lies on the edge of his bed belonging to Marisol, his visitor from a few nights before. Jaime picks it up and drops it inside one of the drawers in his dresser. He looks right at the mirror and continues his rambling…

"And not even because I care, but because I am afraid to lose what I do have; my government-sanctioned car, my nineteen-inch color TV, my wardrobe, an electric blender, and even a woman from time to time. I feel I am compensated well for being a hypocrite and a snitch. Oh, man…I am a disgrace." He then looks back at his image in the mirror, worried and ashamed. "So, am I free? Have I fulfilled Ijaba's wish? What or who have I become?" Moments later. Jaime, in his bedroom late at night, lying on his back in the dark, staring at the spinning fan, and with no one to talk to, continues, "My life is nothing but a lie. What does my future hold?" He lies uncomfortably on his back, rolling back and forth, tossing, and turning and unable to sleep. Then, a moment later, he suddenly jumps onto his feet and goes into the kitchen agitated. He pours himself a glass of water from the faucet, and he downs it. He then returns to his bedroom; he sits at the edge of his bed, more relaxed now. Turning off the light, he lies back down and finally rests for a minute, and after finally closing his eyes, he immediately drifts asleep.

For the next few minutes, there is nothing but dead silence inside the room.

Suddenly, Jaime begins to dream... His eyes move precipitously, and almost twitching, he snores lightly. As he goes deep into a comfortable dream, Jaime finds himself in complete silence in the middle of a dark, dense, and thick fog all around him. He sees himself as a little boy, maybe seven or eight years old, moving slowly through the impenetrable shadow mist... He is lost. Jaime, wearing only white cotton pants, barefooted and shirtless, with his pants rolled up almost to his knees, reaches with outstretched arms into the endless fog... Scared, lost, and unsure, he feels blindly for guidance, but there is none. He places one bare foot in front of the other as he moves slowly and proceeds into the dense unknown with caution. Suddenly, a figure appears in the midst. A short distance away and in the center of the foggy, cloudy mist, Jaime thinks he sees something, someone. He winks rapidly in trying to refocus his eyes, and while staring into the strange apparition, trying to make out what his eyes intend to catch not too far away, young Jaime is confused. Who is that? Was it ever there? And as the image slowly begins to fade away, Jaime tries to keep his eyes fixed on the warm and seductive figure, which pulls him towards it, but it quickly dissolves before his eyes. He tries making out the identity of the strange figure but to no avail. Jaime continues to sleep soundly. It is now morning, and Jaime is suddenly shaken up by the ringing of his telephone. He brings the phone to his ear, and it is none other than one of the trainers from the stadium. "Hello?" answers Jaime with a rusty voice. A man on the other end replies almost out of breath, "Oye, Jaime, where are you, mi hermano (my brother)? It is almost 9 a.m. Don't tell me you're still in Havana!"

At this, Jaime jumps out of bed and begins to get ready. He takes a quick shower, gets dressed, and immediately jumps in his car and drives back to the baseball stadium in Pinar del Rio, right outside of Havana. It is a long but pleasant drive all the way up the coast through rural countryside. Nothing but gorgeous country untarnished by massive construction and beachfront condos. He passes several different groups of migrating birds flying low, just barely over his head as he drives besides the blue waters of the Cuban coast. He sees many people walking and riding their bikes on the side of the road. There is barely any traffic. Old buses, trucks, and classic cars make up the only vehicles seen on the road. Every now and then, a newer car drives by, and these are usually rentals from the nearby hotels, which only tourists can rent, of course. Occasionally, wooden carts pulled by horses appear along the way, and he passes a few old tractors driven by local peasants, guajiros. When Jaime finally arrives at the Cuban national league modest, single-tier baseball stadium, without delay, he pulls right in, driving his baby-blue '77 Alfa Romeo, honking the horn, and kicking up dust to get the attention of those outside the stadium. He drives past Cuban boys playing baseball outside the stadium, and Jaime knows these young hopefuls are the future of Cuban baseball. Jaime quickly spots their bicycles parked by the bushes, which reminds him that this is what he did as a young boy with his friends too, and he smiles. The boys wave at Jaime as he is a full-blown celebrity around here, and he honks his horn again for their amusement. They wave back and attempt to run behind his car. He then pulls in one of the parking spaces and leaves his car right in the front of the stadium, and goes inside, where the practice takes place. From the dugout, Jaime watches the Pinar del Rio team practice out on the field in full uniforms, catching, throwing, and hitting. From the looks of it, these guys are having more fun than the kids outside the stadium. Jaime looks up, the sunny blue sky up above shows no clouds and not an ounce of wind as the Cuban flag hanging from the flagpole nearby lies motionless against it. Jaime takes a deep breath of the fresh air and gracefully pulls out a cigar from his shirt pocket. He does not light up, but instead, he moistens the cigar with his lips and places it in his mouth just for show. He then mimics at one of the coaches out on the field with his cigar in hand and puts it right back in his mouth. The coach nods his head and smiles back at Jaime, knowing well that this gesture means "Jaime is here."

Jaime has always been known for being the face of advertisement for his family's popular cigars since there are no television commercials in Cuba to promote any products other than communism. A sign at the stadium wall near the scoreboard proclaims in Spanish, "Pinar del Rio / Home of the Cigar."

With practice now in full swing, we take a moment to introduce the four baseball players in our story. Frank Aguilar, nickname *Chuchi*, is the first. Wearing his batting helmet featuring the team small tobacco leaf/cigar logo. He swings mightily and cracks the ball high into the outfield. Then cries out with exuberance as he takes off like a bullet towards first base. Base hit! He goes around first base; he turns and looks at his coach and then quickly goes back to the bag. One thing about Cuban baseball it is all about fundamentals. The basic strategies of the game. Baserunning, stealing bases, hitting to the opposite field, and they do not just live off the home run. It is beautiful and tactical baseball they play there.

The second is *Panchi*, playing center field, who lopes back to make a spectacular catch in the outfield and immediately throws the ball to…

Papo is the third baseman, and as a runner attempts to steal a base, the ball smacks into the pocket of the glove, making a loud noise, and he tags out one of the trainers dressed in street clothes clowning around and immediately whips it to… *Tito*, at shortstop, who catches the ball in one hop, laughs, and does a little dance. Two things are apparent here, these guys love playing the game of baseball, and they are exceptional athletes. All four players have similar built bodies, and it is obvious they are true competitors who take the game of baseball extremely seriously. They all share a physical resemblance but are not related, simply good friends. Chuchi, who looks like a younger version of Jaime, trots back to home plate, and as he spots Jaime, he smiles. He then calls out, "Oye, Papa, you ready to play ball?" The young player picks up a baseball and tosses it to Jaime, who, in a suit and tie, catches it. The other players see Jaime, and they too wave and call out.

"Oye, Viejo (old man), good catch, you still have good reflexes," yells one of the players to Jaime, who winks at him as he leaves the field and walks inside one of the offices in the stadium where a big-bellied Cuban official sit across a desk filled with what seems to be important papers. They both smoke cigars in the cramped, hot office where an electric fan whirls on the desk. The humidity is intense. Jaime looks around the small office and notices pictures of Fidel, Che Guevara, and other so-called heroes of the Cuban revolution hanging from the wall in mismatching picture frames. Jaime looks back at the man across the desk and takes a deep breath, a sign of boredom without being all too obvious.

"Hola, Hector. Como estas (How are you)?" The man looks at Jaime over his reading glasses, and as he reads from several documents, he informs Jaime, "The fifteenth Pan Latin Games are just around the corner. Over fifty-two hundred athletes from thirty-two countries will participate."

He then puffs proudly his cigar and points to an official poster of the "XV Juegos Deportivos Pan Latinos Rio de Janeiro/07," which is taped to the wall behind him and reminding him this is a big deal. The man proceeds, "Look, we took the gold medal in those games. There is no reason to come home empty-handed this time."

Jaime looks at the man and replies, "I know. I was there."

The man continues, "I have not officially told your boys yet, but it's no surprise they made it. Yes, your four favorite boys from the Pinar del Rio team will be part of this team. Look at Chuchi alone, more than thirty stolen bases per year in his first three seasons. Ninety-eight out of a hundred and five attempted bunts. This kid is a bullet to boot. Superstar written all over." Then the man gives Jaime a thinly veiled look of suspicion and continues with the conversation, "Jaime, I am sure they have been thinking of nothing else, correct?" Jaime frowns.

"Of course not," replies Jaime. Then the weighty official eyes him carefully.

"They have got to be ready to fly to Panama City in two weeks. Your boys and the others will train there for several weeks before the games begin."

"That is highly unusual, is it not? Just two weeks?" Jaime asks with suspicion as he peers at the weighty official from head to toe, trying to measure the man's intentions. The man is nothing but another one of these faithful communist comrades blinded by sixty years of darkness and mental pollution at the hand of the regime.

"It was not my idea…" replies the official back to Jaime, who sets his cigar inside an ashtray and turns to the irritated man.

"It makes sense, Hector. A politically neutral site, so there are no distractions, and they still have training facilities from the games twenty years ago. Right?" Jaime fires at the man.

"Right! But Jaime, this is their first trip abroad as a team, and perhaps some of the boys may have heard idle talk that they could have a bright future in the majors. Would you agree with me?" He continues, "Jaime, I don't need to tell you this is the youngest team Cuba has ever sent out, and celebrity endorsements, multimillion-dollar contracts, cars, and women are just too many distractions. Or should I say attractions that may be clouding these boys' minds… and honestly, I'm worried." And as he finishes his statement, the official, who now sweats profusely, stares closely at Jaime, and looking him right in the eye, he waits for a response.

Jaime then puffs on his cigar and calmly responds, "Like you said, Hector, idle talk. How am I to know what is inside their heads?

Boys will be boys, and by the way, they know better! I don't think these guys are the type anyway."

The official, now more aggravated, gets into it with Jaime, talking in a much higher tone of voice and so agitated his face has turned completely red, "You know what? That is right. America does not love baseball like we do. Her national past time is greed. Use and abuse, man… These kids know how much they are appreciated here at home. Take Felix, our catcher, for example, his mother just died, and to show our sympathy, we have promised to install his first telephone line and to give his entire family cellular phones too when he returns from this trip. Jaime, we still have not forgotten about the trip five years ago… That was a total disaster." Jaime gives him a stern look.

"How can I forget, Hector? You won't let me…" Jaime responds, and the man fires right back, looking Jaime in the eye and about six inches from his face now:

"We lost seven of our best ball players in one single trip, seven, Jaime. Not one or two, but seven. I will not let this happen again. Do you understand? It could mean my job this time. Is that clear?" Jaime gathers his thoughts before responding.

"No, it will not happen again, and I understand clearly," Jaime answers, taking a deep breath.

The man then walks around the desk with his arms behind his back, and as he turns to Jaime, he changes the tone of his voice, and now calmer, in an almost apologetic tone, he now whispers in Jaime's ear, ending their conversation: "They know it is not worth it. You go on about your day and do not you worry about a thing. Okay? It will all be fine. I have faith in you, Jaime," replies the man as he squeezes Jaime's hand looking him square in the eye, he continues much calmer now, "to these boys, you are like a father, Jaime, you are a hero to the community too. You were once a great player with a lot of talent. Set them straight, do not allow them to make any dumb mistakes. Get in their heads and make them see the big picture. Besides, if it happens again…it is you that must be worried!" The official sarcastically lectures Jaime, but sarcasm sounds too much like a threat, and Jaime does not like it, but he swallows his pride, and feeling more like a complete coward, Jaime nods and leaves.

All the talk without being too explicit simply means that if they attempted to defect like the others had done a few years prior, Jaime would be held accountable. It would also mean their families would pay the price for their actions dearly, just like the families of the previous defectors who lost their jobs, who were ridiculed and harassed by their neighbors and peers, and who were blackballed from ever being able to apply for an exit visa to leave the country. They were done! Finished! Jaime walks down the hall and exits the building towards the stadium where the boys practice. As he walks onto the practice field, he calls a quick meeting with the guys. In the middle of the baseball diamond, the players jostle around with joy as Jaime gives them the news of the upcoming trip. These excited young men, acting more like five-year-old boys, leap and horse around, climbing on each other's shoulders and hugging one another as if the greatest news has just arrived without any jealousy or envy even though not all of them will be making the trip.

After the four boys are congratulated by the rest of the team, they are revered with much admiration and sincere respect by their fellow players, knowing they could be next in line to travel outside of Cuba, and this gives them hope. Jaime, who rehearses a well-prepared speech inside his head, checks his throat several times before he finally speaks out, "Listen here, boys…even if only four of you have been selected this time to a roster of twenty-seven players, it was a tough thing to do, and you better well know that if I had my way, all of you would have been on that plane with me." They all nod their heads, and Jaime clears his throat and continues, looking around at their faces, "They just informed me that the four of you chosen are allotted 200 dollars to buy souvenirs for you and your families on this trip, plus a few incentives here and there. Do I need to remind you that in Cuba, a doctor barely makes that in a month? And some doctors may have to pedal a bike to work too. So, I really do not think that kind of money is too bad for just playing some silly game. Baseball may be the game you love, but it is just a game, so be grateful and thankful."

Immediately after, Jaime is lifted in the air by the team. Feeling like a fake conquering hero and a total impostor, he really wants to puke. Deep inside, he is dying and rotting away by the hypocrisy that consumes him after giving them that pathetic speech. The boys do not notice his pain as he covers it all too well with his perfectly fitted mask, that so familiar phony smile, and cool demeanor, but Jaime wants the ground beneath him to open and swallow him whole at this very moment. He knows he is duping and conning these young men, but he is also doing his job. "Not bad for playing a game? Be grateful? Be thankful? What am I saying? Who am I? Who have I become?" Jaime thinks out loud in front of the mirror inside the locker room.

A little later, Jaime heads back to Havana following a meeting to prepare for the trip. He has met with the boys and all the officials in charge of the Cuban delegation assigned to these amateur games to go over rules and regulations and over what is to be expected during the trip. Nothing but pure scare tactics that the players and coaches must agree to follow in order to make the trip. They must sign many forms, which include punishment for those who do not follow them. Plain and simple manipulation and control!

Going over the ridiculous protocol and setting all the strict regulations involved in international events for the Cuban team can literally give anybody an ulcer, but Jaime has it all down as he is aware of it all. In these meetings, they remind the guys of the importance of their flawless status as representatives of the entire country while filling their heads with guilt and culpability ahead of time in the event they do not win it all. "We must win! Must represent well!" Jaime reminds them. Again, he feels deeply disgusted about the role he plays. He hates his life at this moment, and his conscience is killing him. Jaime then drives back home immediately after, and his solemn demeanor says it all. The expression on Jaime's face shows the same despair and anguish his fellow Cubans appear to have on theirs while he drives through the country he loves, often looking at the steep cliffs along the coast. Strange feelings enter his mind, but Jaime is not suicidal, just critically wounded by hopelessness and fatigue. It is not a good feeling to be in his position; it overwhelms the soul and kills the spirit. We may have that same sentiment here in America too, when things do not go our way, we are not exempt, but it does not last long. I mean, we will never forget times like Pearl Harbor, 9/11, Hurricane Katrina, and other mind-scarring incidents, but we move on with our lives even though the memories remain. In Cuba, though, and for over fifty years, they live those moments daily, and that agony is part of a daily routine and not just a one-time occurrence. When Jaime finally arrives at home, it is already nighttime. He pulls up to a gas station to pump gas and finds himself in the middle of the old capital city and with no plans, his mind is overwhelmed, and all he can think of is he needs a little relaxation time. He leaves the car at the gas station after buying a cold drink from a street vendor and gives the man a few bucks to look after it, and he goes out for a much-needed walk.

He ends up in one of the many nightclubs in the city, a club where hot couples dance to sexy *salsa music* amidst vibrant colored lights and overdone tropical-themed décor. The dancers execute unique sensual patterns on the dance floor only found in Cuba. These dancers become so transfixed in their performances as if auditioning before a panel of world-renowned judges. Their passion for their dancing is all too obvious, and it shows! They use dancing here as a way of unleashing frustration or expressing what they hold inside. A certain fire can be seen at a distance as these attractive couples maneuver their well-rehearsed dance moves like professionals. What an art, what a talent, what an ability…and that's why dance students from all over the world come here to learn from them and to witness this explicit display of uniqueness. At the bar, Jaime finishes a bottle of Bucanero beer. He shows little interest in the two short-skirted *Cuban women* competing for his attention next to him, but a few moments later, one of the girls finally approaches Jaime. "Oye, Papi, look at you, all handsome and serious. You are going to need a wife to take away that midlife crisis you got on your face."

"Or a mistress…" replies the second woman with a smile and eying Jaime from head to toe, but he politely stands up to leave. The young woman becomes a little more explicit about her interest…and unbuttoning her blouse a few buttons and showing a little more cleavage now, she insists, "Oye, Chico, buy me a mojito, would you?" Jaime politely declines the young woman's obvious intentions by shaking his head and without making any direct eye contact. He then takes off, and the two girls are left there looking stupid and miserably unsuccessful. In baseball terms… Strike three, you are out! He leaves the club and walks towards his car, navigating the party crowd now in full swing, drifting in and out of the hot and crowded nightclubs lining the street. It is humid, it is hot, and loud music continues to pour out from every open doorway where people are having a good time, many of them tourists. Up ahead, he sees a couple of plain schoolgirls, maybe fifteen, standing near a club entrance. A man in a Disneyland shirt propositions them. The girls are not promiscuous, simply young practical survivors like most of these women. Jaime slows down and whispers to the big-bellied tourist, a man maybe in his 50s, "Amazing how these girls sell their bodies for almost nothing and still manage to wake up early the next morning to take an advanced chemistry exam so they can graduate with honors, huh?" The man stares at him with a dubious look, and Jaime sarcastically wishes him a good night…nodding his head. "Buenas Noches." It would not be too difficult to find one of these street hustlers or so-called tourists' girlfriends, teaching at a school the next morning or wearing a nurse's gown as they do this to survive. One good night with a tourist could very well be the equivalent to an entire month's earnings. So, do the math! As Jaime trudges away after making his smart remark to the stranger, the man is left there initially feeling a bit stupid but sensing this opportunity is too good to pass, he looks at the girls, back at Jaime, shakes his head, and proceeds to close the deal with the jineteras. And unable to do anything but watch, Jaime slowly walks back to his car and then drives towards his empty apartment, putting an end to the night. Inside his apartment home, the lights are dim, and the ceiling fan in his room is still on. The ceiling of the hundred-year-old apartment building is cracked, and if one did not know any better, it has the appearance of a ceiling that may collapse any minute.

Tired and ready for a well-deserved break, Jaime walks in, removes his shirt, and throws it on top of the TV in the living room. The window in front of the TV with a view of the Havana harbor is wide open, and the cool breeze enters the tiny apartment through colorful worn-out cloth drapes. A black and white poster of a box of Partagas cigars is hung next to the window in an unpainted picture frame. The glass in the picture frame is cracked, and a small postcard of the Statue of Liberty is clipped to one of the corners of the frame. Jaime removes his shoes and immediately goes to his bedroom, and lies down on his bed, wide awake in the dark. With both his hands resting behind his head, he takes a deep breath, with his tired eyes staring up at the spinning ceiling fan, he reminisces about his life.

Jaime suddenly has a brief flash…recalling the stories told by his grandmother. He sees his ancestor Ijaba as she is being torn from her burning village. He sees a wriggling pile of captured men, women, and children, and everyone is screaming… Continuing to watch, Jaime dives deeper into the troublesome flashback, Ijaba is now being sold in a slave auction to a Spanish nobleman in Havana. The nobleman, a well-dressed man maybe in his 40s, notices there is an iron-branded mark on Ijaba's neck, and he shakes his head with disgust. Immediately he takes the young girl with him after paying the auctioneer and away from the plaza where the slave auction was being held.

Ironically, the man does not treat Ijaba like the other slaves are treated, but he, who happens to have two daughters about Ijaba's age waiting at home, takes the frightened little girl and removes the rope from her wrists, untying her at once. He then asks that Ijaba sits inside the horse carriage with him and not walk beside it as all the other newly purchased slaves do. Ijaba is frozen, scared, and confused. She does not understand why he is doing this unusual act of compassion and may have even been wondering what his true intentions are, his motives, but the man humbly insists that she rides with him inside the carriage by repeatedly motioning with his hand for her to come inside until she finally accepts out of fear alone, but extremely skeptical. At this, other auctioneers who see what is happening look at the nobleman like he has lost his mind, and they laugh and mock him. The man simply ignores the crowd and tells the man steering his carriage to move away from the slave auction and towards their home at once. Ijaba, still frightened, barefoot, and cold, does not dare look at the man's face as she rides beside him inside a carriage the equivalent of a modern-day limousine. To this point, the young princess has no idea of what the man with the heart of gold looks like because she had never seen his face before as slaves were instructed through a translator at the plaza where the auction took place to always keep their eyes on the ground and to never look their masters in the eye. This proves as a sign of respect and acknowledgement of their rightful place in the world of slaves, where they are viewed as property of those who now own them. After a few moments of complete silence, the man suddenly places his hand on Ijaba's shoulder and pats her gently, and then he speaks to her softly in Spanish, "Esta bien (It is okay)!" She does not understand what he is saying but what the man says sounds much more different from the way the others in the boat had spoken to her and the other slaves. Also, much different from what the scary men at the slave auction were saying even though they were all speaking the same language as the man who now owns her. He speaks softly and gently, and at this, Ijaba breaks down in silent tears of relief. Perhaps the man's soft words are the first sign of kindness she has experienced since before being ripped away from her home back in Africa. His tone allows her a sense of relief, and whatever he is saying, even though in an unknown language, comforts her. He then places his index finger underneath her chin and lifts her face towards his, and smiles. He again says a few words to her in Spanish, which somehow make her feel not so scared as they make eye contact for the very first time. The nobleman notices the young slave girl is still trembling with fear, and he leans over, placing over her a soft cloth mantle. The securing gesture somehow makes her feel, for the very first time since this whole nightmare began, that she is going to be fine. Ijaba does not understand any of what the man has said to her to this point, and she does not understand what is happening or where they are headed, but it certainly does not sound threatening. She now begins to sense a glimpse of calm and security like she had not felt since she was home with mom and dad before the intruders arrived in her village.

Ijaba, now more relaxed, has fallen asleep in the comfort of the carriage as they move slowly through a country road. The nobleman watches her sleep as she snores lightly. He glances at the young girl from head to toe, examining her body, and he notices the marking on her neck again from the hot iron branded on her dark skin, and tears begin to slowly flow down his face. Her little body is full of bruises, and the markings from the tight ropes previously binding her wrists have now turned dark blue. The man wonders, *what is this?* as he imagines this horrible thing happening to one of his daughters back home. The nobleman covers his mouth with both his hands to not wake young Ijaba or let the man steering the carriage hear his weeping as he suddenly breaks into a hysterical cry at the horrible sight of the beaten African princess. This goes on for a few minutes as the carriage slowly moves towards his home. Upon arriving at the hacienda, Ijaba awakes to the sound of voices. The nobleman immediately asks his servants to handle the young girl with care. He instructs them to attend to her and to feed her, to bathe her, and to give her clean clothes. Now, little does the man know he is dealing with true royalty and a rightful heir to the throne back at her homeland, and as horrible as the marking on her neck is, and as bad as the treatment Ijaba received at the hands of the monsters who sold her was, so is the act of him buying her though with good intentions. People are not merchandise, items to be bought and sold; you just do not buy people. It is a repugnant act of disrespect for human life, and even though we have seen it happen throughout history, it is wrong. In this case, however, he saved Ijaba's life, and it is obvious he has different intents for Ijaba, but slavery and the buying and selling of human beings have always been one of the most appalling acts in history. Ijaba was Jaime's ancestor, an African princess who went on to become a common slave in a faraway land while paving the way for Jaime's family lineage.

Jaime finally returns from his flashback after he is awakened by the noise made by neighbors outside on the street. He looks over at his 19" RCA color TV, which is playing on mute, and unable to keep his eyes open for too long, he drifts right back to sleep.

A few days later, Jaime visits his family in Pinar del Rio, just about two hours from Havana. Back at the Colon home, he finds himself in the middle of beautiful tobacco fields and surrounded by giant hills of gorgeous green vegetation. The sun is hot and the humidity high as always. He hears joyful voices singing nearby. Then he notices straw-hatted field workers squatting along rows of small tobacco plants inspecting the leaves and working the field. Some of the workers use spray bottles to spritz the leaves, just like they have been shown by Jaime's uncle, who insists on keeping alive this old family tradition of spraying the tobacco leaves with different and unusual flavors. Jaime takes notice of all that goes on inside the heavenly compounds of the Colon tobacco farm, and he puffs on his cigar proudly as he walks away towards the village to try not interrupting the workers. At the village, Jaime strolls along with his sun-browned uncle, and they both are smoking cigars. The old man throws his arm over Jaime's shoulder, and they walk together under the midday sun. "Tio, my plane leaves in two days for Panama City, and I received a bonus for the trip," Jaime tells the old man. He then takes out an envelope from his shirt pocket, and the uncle pushes it away, fearing someone will see, as in Cuba, somebody is always watching…

Then the old uncle turns to Jaime and lectures him, "First of all, I will not accept any charity from you or anybody. I have all I need right here. We have all we need. Number two, you know if anyone sees you giving me money, I could lose the right to run the farm. They will shut me down, Jaime."

Jaime looks at the old man and begins to laugh. He quickly walks a few steps in front and bows to the old uncle as a sign of understanding but says nothing. He then looks away as they walk past children fetching water from a rusty pump on the side of the road, and an old woman tends to a goat in front of her wooden shack. *All this poverty and destitution in sharp contrast to the backdrop of beautiful purple mountains just do not make any sense, it should not be like this*, Jaime thinks. Jaime stops and looks at the old uncle straight in the eye. "Better take it, Tio. When I get back, I may quit my job and come work for you, okay."

His uncle peers at him, laughs, and proceeds. "Oh really? You, come work for me here? That is a laugh. Jaime, if you are so unhappy and confused, perhaps you should go visit one of those santeros around here that spend their entire lives lying to people and taking their hard-earned money," the old uncle intones behind a blur of sarcasm, and Jaime quickly fires back:

"Tio, a santero? Come on, you know I do not believe in any of that voodoo. The only burden that magic has ever relieved anybody of is their wallets, but it seems as if there is more of them out there than ever these days, just about one for every other block. It's a new trend around here," replies Jaime, almost furious at how some of these santeros just take their own countrymen for a ride, and the old uncle defends himself:

"Shhh! Remember, the walls have ears around here, my dear nephew. I don't believe any of that mumbo jumbo either, but we are the minority here in Cuba. I saw this movie once, and there is a line in it regarding this that says, 'When our ancestors came here, they brought their religion and traditions with them, and it is alive in Cuba today. They say the heart of Africa still beats here!'" To this, Jaime agrees by bobbing his head with a firm look while puffing on his cigar, and the Tio continues, "Five hundred years of ignorance and the guy with the beard and his clan continue to take advantage of it. Castro saw this, and he loved that most of us stayed buried in the ignorance behind the Santeria, and he liked the fact that many of the people in Cuba are ill-mannered, stuck behind the whole Afro-

Caribbean traditions passed down from generation to generation because they do not know any better, and it makes them an easy target. God forbid these people in Cuba open their eyes one day and are finally able to see. Imagine that? It would be devastating to their cause and their circus of over fifty years, but it is true, most of the people here in Cuba would rather go see a santero and pay them a month's wages than go see a medical doctor because it is all they know. The majority anyway," finishes the old uncle as he glances around the village, and Jaime discreetly slips the envelope in his pocket, unnoticed.

"I don't see a santero around here, do you?" wittingly Jaime asks as he pats the old uncle on his back.

"Oh, they are around…believe me, son, they are around. It is a big business nowadays, about one for every few blocks or so," replies the old man with a big grin and again taking a puff at his wet and chewed-up cigar. Jaime smiles and puffs on his cigar, also relishing the tasty "puro," and he follows by exhaling a smoke ring into the air.

The two men continue talking together in the sun, enjoying their colorful conversation, often laughing and giggling like children. El Tio keeps his arm around Jaime the entire time as a sign of love, affection, and trust. Jaime pays close attention to his old uncle while he speaks as if recording the wise words, uttering the man's mouth in his mind. When the old man speaks, he looks away without a care in the world as if wanting everyone to hear. Like a proud preacher or one of those famous orators back in ancient Greece. Jaime listens attentively, soaking it all in.

As the night approaches, the two men now sit in wooden rocking chairs on the front porch of the humble country home. They slowly rock back and forth and take delight in each other's company. Jaime does more listening than talking, but he throws in his two cents every now and then. The old man carries most of the conversation, and Jaime enjoys this. Time passes slowly as they cherish each other's company in pleasant opulence. Now in the late hours of the night, Jaime goes for a walk alone. He is curious about the earlier conversation with his uncle and approaches one of the locals walking by. "Oye, brother, do you know where I can find a santero around here?" Jaime asks, and the man quickly responds by pointing him in the right direction:

"Right there, the house with the busted door frame. Just walk right in and straight to the back… His name is Willy, he is there."

Jaime thinks for a moment, and frowning, he intones, "Gracias!" Not sure and somewhat nervous, he proceeds to the santero's house. He looks around as he crosses the street carefully and not wanting anyone to see him, then he enters the old house following a brief pause. He walks in and immediately notices the busted door frame. Jaime's body becomes chilled from head to toe, maybe a sign that he should not be there, but he continues through an unpainted hallway and towards the back as directed by the young man outside in the street. "Hello! Hey, hey!" Jaime calls softly… And in the back of the small ramshackle house, the curtains are drawn, the place is lit only by dingy candles, and many makeshift altars clutter the stained floor with photographs, fruit offerings, bowls, and gourds. Several four-foot plaster statues of catholic saints seem out of place, and cheap religious items hang on the cracked walls of the house. Flowers and dessert offerings are everywhere. The place stinks with an assortment of cheap fragrances covering the air. It is spooky and cold. Jaime's body shivers and goosebumps crawl up his spine. Suddenly, from the dark comes a little old, black man dressed in all white and wearing many colorful necklaces. With a chewed-up cigar stub in his mouth, he is barefoot, and his piercing eyes immediately find Jaime as he comes to the light. Jaime notices the man is missing several teeth as he gives him a half-smile, and he seems to be missing one of his eyes too. The missing eye is like that of a dead fish, just white, but he quickly covers it with an eye patch, just like those the pirates wear in movies. Wearing an untrimmed beard, much of it gray, the santero points at a dirty wooden chair with his index finger.

"Sientate (sit down)…" the man tells Jaime in Spanish with a creepy smile.

Jaime sits on the floor instead, unsure of the next move, frowning. He is in the abode of a priest of the traditional Afro-Caribbean religion, Santeria. Now, to give you a brief history behind Santeria, this is a religion founded by African slaves upon their arrival in the New World. The slaves, who were mostly part of the Yoruba tribes in West Africa, Nigeria, and Sierra Leone, were forced to convert to Catholicism by the Spanish and forced to leave their traditional religions. The Spanish used many brutal tactics and forms of abuse to convert the slaves, and throughout the centuries, many slaves were brutally beaten, tortured, and even killed as the Spanish attempted to convert the non-believers. Eventually, many of the slaves realized the only way to stop the brutality was to either convert or pretend to have already converted to the new religion forced upon them, and this is when the African slaves began hiding their traditional gods behind every known catholic saint, virgin, and statue to make their enforcers believe they had finally converted and given in to the ways of the law accepting Catholicism as their new religion. The slaves suddenly began showering the catholic statues with gifts and food offerings, and the Spanish loved it, believing they had finally succeeded in their mission, but the slaves were truly idolizing their own African gods now hidden behind every catholic statue imaginable, giving their gods a face behind the image of their favorite catholic entity to convince the Spanish of their conversion. In this way, they were able to continue worshiping their gods in celebration at the bayous without any interference from their masters. Clever, right? The Spanish idolized, served, and revered their many traditional catholic statues constantly as part of their religious practices in showing respect and admiration. Now that the slaves started doing the same, the Spanish believed they had finally become new believers of the faith they inflicted upon them, only they were bowing and worshiping their own African gods. It was also a tradition to light up candles to honor the catholic patrons in faith, and the slaves also proceeded to do the same.

Unlike Catholicism, in the African religions, it required animal sacrifice as part of the custom. Santeria has been around for hundreds of years in places like Cuba, Haiti, all the Caribbean, and even here in the US, among other Latin American countries and the world. This religion under Cuba's political system has gained much recognition in recent times and especially after the Cuban government almost immediately disallowed Christianity upon their takeover in 1959. Even reading the Bible became prohibited as taught by their Marxist-Leninist mentors in Russia, who dictated once upon a time that "religion is the poison of the masses," and they decided to follow this to a T by punishing and imprisoning anyone who did not obey. Maybe they thought faith would give the people hope and it could lead to bringing revolts and uprisings against the oppressive system, and so, any kind of religion became immediately regarded as anti-revolutionary and a danger to the communist agenda being hard-pressed to the people, except for Santeria and other African practices, which could be practiced at will in the island as the only form of belief system outside of the atheism Castro's government pushed. Maybe because this kept the eyes of those who practiced it bandaged and slaved in ignorance throughout the centuries, still with the ball and chain attached to their ankles as were their African ancestors. Unlike in years past, however, instead of shackles and a whip on their backs, they are now faced with a modern-day totalitarian dictatorship that dominates their every move and thought...communism. Now sitting across from Jaime is this unshaven, fat, dark-skin man, wearing pants that look like he has not changed them in weeks. His matching white cotton button-up shirt fits the same description as the pants, and he wears many colorful handmade necklaces. Barefoot, he reveals long, dirty toenails; the santero begins to mumble a tongue-twisting unknown language barely loud enough for Jaime to hear. The man then tosses several broken pieces of coconut shells onto a matt. He concentrates as if reading the future... Jaime wrinkles his nose. "This place smells rotten," Jaime utters as he glances at his watch. "How much longer?" Jaime asks...and at this, the santero places his hand over Jaime's lip to silence him.

"Shhhhhh! Be quiet!" the man replies. Jaime tolerates this just barely, and the santero finally speaks as Jaime removes the man's hand away, "Tell me about yourself. Why are you here?"

Jaime peers at him with a look of confusion and fires right back, "You tell me why I'm here. Isn't that why I pay you?"

With his head still down, the santero whispers, "Shh…it doesn't work like that! But I have good news for you. Enlightenment awaits you," the santero adds in a creepy voice.

"I'm listening," Jaime replies.

"Your turmoil can be calmed, your mind eased at last," slowly mumbles the santero. "But first, you must bring me a single living chicken… Oh, and twenty dollars, to begin your consultation," says the man, slowly raising his eyes to Jaime with a stern and demonic look all of a sudden, Jaime has already heard enough.

"Really, just one live chicken, huh? It will have to be one smart chicken… Tell me this, what am I doing here? What did I come here for? If you can answer that, we may be in business," Jaime explodes, ignoring the man's intimidating flare.

The santero leans closer to Jaime and responds, "Like I said, it doesn't work like that. I ask you some things. You answer, and then we go back and forth as I consult with the dead for answers, but yes, the chicken…its blood will wash away anything evil tossed against you. Cleansing you of all…all the bad deeds in your past too. For the ritual, another two hundred pesos…does that sound good to you?" continues the santero, and Jaime answers sarcastically:

"I would have to be crazy to pay for this." Jaime yells in frustration.

"Wait, you get a discount for the consultation," nervously replies the little man and waits as silence follows. Jaime stares hard as something behind the man catches his attention. He realizes that, on the table amongst various herbs and ashes, there are bits of animal guts and remains, and a dirty knife sits next to it with flies on it.

"Ay, Dios Mío (Oh my God)! Do you eat out of that table? Never mind, I do not want to know," says Jaime with regard to the mess behind the man, and he quickly stands disgusted and tries to walk away, but the man, now speaking in a higher tone of voice, attempts to convince Jaime to stay:

"Where are you going? Please, don't make irrational decisions; bad things could happen to you. Let us finish here..." says the santero, almost uncertain and hoping Jaime doesn't leave.

"But bad things have already been happening, look around. I could bring you a herd of goats and give you half my salary for five years, and it still would not get me anywhere here in Cuba. You are crazy!" firmly replies Jaime, and the little man refusing to give up fires right back:

"Come on, your relatives have been coming to me for years... What is your name again?" follows the santero.

"Yeah, and who do you think pays for it all? And by the way, aren't you supposed to know all sorts of things? Why then do you need me to tell you my name? You are supposed to know that aren't you? Ask your coconut shells," Jaime replies, and now angry and disgusted with the man, he walks towards the door to leave.

The santero tries to reason with him, "Please think about what you are doing. You could lose your mind. Yes, you could go crazy if you turn your back on the Orishas. You must know your life is not in your hands." At this, Jaime whirls around and points at the man, almost as if wanting to drag him outside to denounce him and his fake magic in front of everyone.

"I have news for you, little man; none of us are free here, not even you and your twisted voodoo. So, tell it to the man with the beard, and I don't mean *Jesus*. Wake up! Because it is obvious everyone is asleep in this place. You take their money by lying, inflicting fear, and brainwashing them, and they come to you because it is all they know...and you have no idea the kind of trouble you are bringing upon yourself for cheating these people of their money. Wake up!" Jaime screams at the top of his lungs, and he glares at the frightened man, who is sure Jaime is about to finish him with one punch for trying to rip him off. Jaime then storms away, leaving the front door wide open, and his words hang in the air as the santero is left there in shock. Defeated! And lights begin to turn on inside the homes of all the neighbors who have apparently heard the yelling and screaming of Jaime telling the santero he is a phony and a fraud. Now, this single incident may prove to be somewhat costly to the santero's once profitable business, and hopefully so. Jaime leaves the santero's house, and he is running. His heart beats like a steam engine, and his mind races both with joy and disbelief. He smiles with poise, happy beyond words because he did not fall victim to another scam by one of these wannabe witch doctors knowing these people basically make a living taking advantage of an entire country's ignorance and desperate people searching for answers inside years of tradition at the hands of divination and so-called interpreters of the future, mediums, and sorcerers. One day soon, hopefully, they will all open their eyes and see, but for now, at least Jaime is saved from the trap of lies these brainwashing manipulators set before the people. As a matter of fact, the popularity of Santeria has been on the decline in recent years in Cuba. What was once just rumors of the demise of the old religion is finally proving to be true as more and more people walk away from santeros every day, accepting traditional beliefs such as plain old Christianity, which is immensely growing in the island as of recent and partially after the visit by the Pope several years ago and the Cuban government loosening their grip. Today the government has begun allowing missionaries to enter Cuba and for Bibles to once again be read by the people, a practice also once forbidden for an exceedingly long time by the communist party.

After running for several blocks, Jaime arrives at his car. Almost out of breath, he gets in and drives back to Havana. A smile comes to his face as he drives away, remembering the look on the face of the old santero, who probably never had anyone stand up to him in defiance of his lies and scare tactics. Lies he uses to drain people of their hard-earned money, especially in a place where things are so tough, and yet these santeros continue to prey on their desperate situation and ignorance.

I wonder if they would listen if I could tell them how badly they are being played and manipulated by these santeros, these con men and women who take advantage of desperate and ignorant people, but after years of mind-controlling communism, which goes hand in hand with some religious practices in brainwashing their followers, they probably just don't have the resistance or immunity to fight it, so they accept it as normal instead. Some call this folklore, traditional beliefs, popular myths, and customs, while a few opportunistic individuals use it to clearly take advantage of their countrymen and profit from it. Upon arriving back in the city, Jaime finds himself at the Malecon Wall. The famous ten-mile stone embankment known as "El Malecon," which borders the north coast of Havana and was built to protect the city from pirate attacks back in the day. Quite impressive and almost like a miniature Great Wall of China, which became known as a popular hangout for locals and tourists for its idealistic location and panoramic views. This place is always alive with people. This part of town never sleeps, and it has not for centuries, and this is exactly where the famous Havana Carnivals were held before Castro began diminishing the festivities until they became almost extinct like everything else in Cuba. It is strikingly beautiful out here. The views, the ocean breeze, the city of Havana right behind it, and always sprawling with crowds of people. This part of the city has remained unchanged for several centuries, and from right here, you can see the Morro Castle. The same castle built several centuries ago with its lighthouse and where they still fire a cannonball every night at 9 p.m. to announce the closing of the city walls in case of pirate attacks just like they did almost 400 years ago.

El Morro is Havana's richest historical landmark and another custom here in the old city; this place is like an inviting ghost town full of tradition but also full of pain and sorrow because it has witnessed it all from the beginning. El Morro was not just a lighthouse but also a fortress constructed between 1589 and 1630 at the very tip of a peninsula across the bay from where the city of Havana was founded. The Morro was built to guard the city entrance against pirates and other colonist powers eager to gain control of this central transit hub between Europe and the New World. El Morro has been tested throughout time, the elements, and even foreign attacks, and in 1762, unable to withstand an attack from the British, who ended up taking control of the castle and the entire city of Havana for about a year. The city was later returned to Spain, and that's when King

Carlos III immediately ordered the construction of the La Cabana Fortress to ensure an event like this would never repeat itself.

The construction started a year after, becoming the largest Spanish colonial fortress in the Americas and covering the expanse of twenty-five acres of land. The Cabana was named after the Spanish king, originally called the San Carlos de la Cabana Fortress, and today it can be reached by ferry or by driving around the bay over the land around its unusual shape, which hugs the rocky cliffs of the Havana Bay with thick, imposing stone walls, a moat and, of course, the historic lighthouse, which can be seen miles away. The almost five-century-old lighthouse, whose light as dim as the brightness of a dying flashlight, was once and will always be a historical monument, but these days all it represents is the suffering of the people here in Cuba, and so atrocious is the condition; one can't help but pity them, and this is exactly what many tourists say when they leave Cuba, even though no visit to Cuba is complete without a visit across the bay to see this expansive historical complex. La Cabana, under different dictatorships, has been used as a military prison over the years and one that the infamous criminal Che Guevara, one of Castro's right-hand men, oversaw, and where many tortures and firing squads occurred without due process during his time there. Do not believe everything you hear, and the next time you see anyone wearing a Che Guevara T-shirt, know that they have no idea who he really was and the many atrocities he committed. I tell you, the world is full of ignorance, and I see this as the equivalent to someone wearing a Hitler T-shirt, in my opinion.

After learning all this, I keep asking… This beautiful place, along with its beautiful people, but how much longer must they suffer? The Morro Castle, the pride and joy of Havana and historical landmark, watches the injustice of a people daily. It cries louder than the crushing waves beneath it, just like Africa wept over its children during the slave trade hundreds of years before. Cuba also weeps over its dying children today.

"Today's Cuba has turned into a place where one single tyrant and his many puppets and followers control the fate of over ten million people. It has become a place where more and more men, women, and children lose their lives at sea almost daily trying to escape their misery and anguish in search of a better life and the curse of the slave-trade days lives on," recalls the old uncle as he continues narrating. "And it appears to me the curse of slavery has never been lifted over Cuba as we are still slaves today. Castro's party is the slave owner, and communism the whip on our backs. Perhaps, some of the Holy Scriptures from the ancient books of the Bible also apply to Cuba and its people for the worshiping of false gods and for idolizing man-made statues. For continuing to practice of all sorts of magic and divination over the years that God, according to the book of Psalms, became angry with the people of Israel for worshiping foreign gods...found in Psalm 81:9: 'You shall have no foreign god among you; you shall not bow down to an alien god.' And following this in Psalm 83:11-12, it reads, 'But my people would not listen to me; Israel would not submit to me. So, I gave them over to their stubborn hearts to follow their own devices.' It is biblical...and then God turned his back on them, allowing other nations, the Babylonians, Assyrians, and neighboring countries, to conquer them and to take them into captivity, almost at the brink of exterminating them several different times over. For their disobedience, for practicing witchcraft, sorcery, and for abandoning their loyalty to the one true God of the universe, the creator of it all and the God of Abraham, Isaac, and Jacob. In Cuba today, the same thing is happening, and the people and the land maybe are under the same dilemma in the eyes of God as the people of Israel. God may have become angry at the Cuban people for their rebellious acts and maybe, just maybe, may have allowed for Castro to have ruled this long; just like Pharaoh in Egypt for over 400 years. I have a reason to believe Castro may have been placed here by God to demonstrate his discontent over the people and their rebellious acts. Just my thoughts...if anyone cares."

The old uncle continues his long speech with his eyes now full of tears, but he quickly pulls out his cloth hankie, drying his eyes as he continues…

"It just doesn't make any sense for this man to have ruled this long and to have caused so much harm to our people and our island." El Tio suddenly keeps going, even more inspired now, "Throughout the Holy Scriptures God expressed many times he was a jealous God, and he gave his chosen people specific instructions, but they did not listen. Sounds familiar? 'Do not have other gods. Do not make any idols in the form of anything in heaven above or on the earth beneath or in the waters below,'" he says as if giving a speech in front of a huge crowd and in a higher tone of voice…

> You shall not bow down to them or worship them; for I, the Lord your God, am a jealous God, punishing the children for the sin of the fathers to the third and fourth generation of those who hate me, but showing love to a thousand generations of those who love me and keep my commandments.
>
> Exodus 20:5-6

"Now, that is in the book of Exodus, chapter 20…but no one listened, and how could they when Castro himself prohibited them from reading it? The children of Israel were instructed by God through Moses during their exodus out of Egypt not to worship anything that remotely resembled other gods, but they rebelled against God, and in Cuba, the same thing has happened over the years. It is all they have done for centuries since the arrival of the African slaves, obviously making them slaves themselves. Just my input… I mean if anyone cares to know what an old man thinks…" the old man, almost out of breath, concludes as he now sweats profusely, a bit agitated. He wipes his forehead with a white cloth handkerchief that he gently removes from his back pocket. He wipes again and puts it away, taking a deep breath and puffing on his cigar, which is now down to a tiny stub. He blows a smoke ring into the air…

Moments later… To ease his mind, Jaime now trudges along the Malecon Wall all alone. He sees two poor Cuban men fishing a short distance away, and there is a juice vendor selling cold drinks to three foreign college students in Harvard shirts.

The young students take pictures with the man, mocking him but little do they know that this apparent poor juice vendor could very well be none other than one of the professors at the University of Havana, which is just around the corner. As many people in Cuba today must work side jobs to be able to survive simply because the government's pay is not good enough to provide a decent standard of living there. Anyone from doctors, professors, and even physicists and all kinds of professionals can be seen driving cabs to make ends meet and to be able to buy most of their much-needed essentials in the black market where in today's Cuba, everything can be bought and sold because if you have cash and especially dollars, you can do okay, but this means risking it all if you are caught. So, in Cuba, all business deals must be done in the black market and under the table, or they do not get done at all. Crazy, huh! Jaime continues moving slowly down the old city, watching his surroundings. He takes notice of two Cuban girls who smile hopefully at the Ivy League guys from earlier who stop to buy from another street vendor on the crowded sidewalk, this one is selling "Fritas," a sort of Cuban hamburger and a delight to eat back in the day. But today, God knows what kind of meat these are made of because red meat is illegal in Cuba. So, I seriously doubt it is real hamburger meat. Only tourists who can afford to eat in restaurants where the locals would not dare to enter, and high government officials have the luxury or pleasure to see a steak around here. What a joke! And how sad is that? Something we take so lightly here in the States, a piece of meat, a steak. A dish many of the restaurants in the casinos in Las Vegas make part of the daily specials advertising on the city billboards for as little as 4.99 dollars and including a side dish and a free ticket to lose all your money too.

"But really, the situation here in Cuba turns people into just POS, which means 'Plain Old Survivors,' and no one, I repeat, no one has ever died from eating a 'whatever' burger around here, not yet anyway and not that I know of," clarifies the old and frustrated uncle as he proceeds with his chastising speech. "And everyone is poor here, everyone because without freedom, money can only get you a few things here and there but cannot buy you happiness, can't buy love or time. In Cuba, only a few are not considered poor, but their day could very well come soon if the government suddenly decides to turn on them and take whatever they do have… Just because. Ouch!" concludes the old man…

Jaime now looks out to the ocean in trying to take a snapshot of the view, and even though it is nighttime, he can make out the foam forming from the sea water hovering over the rocks ashore. He can see the lights afar. He can smell the salt in the air, and he pauses here for a moment as if wanting to put the entire space into a small pocket of his heart. He proceeds to walk slowly along a deserted stretch of the oceanfront as the melancholy sound of the surf and the endless slapping of the rolling waves echo in his own isolated turmoil. Jaime fixes his eyes out at the water and stares at it for a moment, knowing that on the other side, just ninety miles away, lies freedom and the land of opportunity. He makes a 180 degree turn to look at the entire city of Havana behind him. He takes a picture of it in his mind closing his eyes tight and capturing it for one passionate moment, and he exclaims, "Yeah! My city. My lost city! My prison!"

Jaime smiles as an air of melancholy surrounds him, and with his eyes still closed, he grasps his fist as if taking hold of everything inside his heart. His mind races at 300 miles per hour, and he does not want to let go of this moment, he knows there is always something dramatic about leaving home, even if it is just for a few days. This time, though, and for Jaime, it feels quite different from other times in the past. A hunch! Perhaps…

Change Comes to Us All Sooner or Later

THE FOLLOWING MORNING JAIME is sharply dressed and ready for the trip. As they drive to the airport, he holds two carry-on bags on his lap as he waits for the driver to pull over to get out of the cab, a classic '55 Chevy Bel Air in mint condition. Jaime gives the old man driving the car a compliment about the cleanliness of the vehicle and its impeccable condition, "Maestro, su carro es una belleza!" (Sir, your car is a beauty)!"

The driver, a doctor of over thirty years who does this as a side hustle, makes more money driving than he does practicing medicine where he gets paid a miserable salary of about 300 dollars per month, responds, "Thank you! My grandson and I fixed it up nicely, gathering parts here and there. It took us a while but look at it now. We went through hell getting all the parts and looking back now, it was all worth it," proudly replies the man with a smirk, waiting for a response.

Jaime, impressed with the condition of the vehicle, adds, "You did an exceptionally good job! It looks like a new car."

The doctor smiles and immediately replies, "So, you like the car, huh? You just wait until we stop, and I will show you something beautiful!" Jaime agrees by shaking his head as they move on down the almost empty road. Moments later, they arrive at the airport. The doctor, with a smile on his face, opens Jaime's door and says, "Come take a look. You will admire this."

The doctor pops the hood of the car, and underneath it, Jaime can see a Russian car's engine mounted in a '55 Chevy along with homemade spark plugs because it is extremely difficult to find parts for these cars after so many years. Yet, in Cuba, they have ingeniously created unique ways to keep them running. *Incredible*, Jaime thinks. "Oh, and it runs mostly on propane, too! Barely any gas!" Jaime smiles back in admiration. He shakes his hand and pays the doctor for the ride, who gives him a warm hug after noticing the generous tip Jaime has added to the fare. "Thank you, Jaime, you, my friend, are a class act, and you have a safe flight!" continues the doctor.

Jaime nods his head and responds with a huge smile, "Me, a class act? Wrong department for you, my good man, but I will take it. You're the doctor, after all!" concludes Jaime with a smile, he grabs his belongings and walks into the terminal looking back at the beautiful car as the doctor drives off honking the horn.

Jaime is anxious, nervous…as he hears the loud crescendo roar of an airplane taking off. He sighs…with a sigh of relief, reminiscing about the night before when so many thoughts inundated his mind. This was nothing but a prelude to his departure and what appears to be another routine trip out of the island. Even though it is early in the morning, a humidity-stricken soft wind brushes against his freshly shaved face, and as the taxi drives off away from the curb, Jaime looks back at the vehicle, the 1955 Chevy Bel Air in mint condition, which reminds him so much of the great United States.

A confident Jaime walks over to the departure area where he immediately spots a street vendor and buys a Cuban coffee from the man standing beside his homemade vendor cart. Jaime stares at the airport sign, which reads, "Jose Marti International Airport," one named after the great late-nineteenth-century Cuban poet who wrote many of Jaime's favorite books and poems, and for a moment, he is frozen. Jaime then proceeds to walk over to a nearby bench. He sits down and slowly drinks his hot coffee slowly, savoring every drop of the dark, sweet, tiny cup to its fullest, he takes a deep breath…

A plane rises behind him over Havana's contemporary airport, which looked modern six decades ago. Jaime just sits there and stares at the airplane until it disappears between the clouds. A few minutes pass, and Jaime, who takes his time admiring the scenery, watches as international passengers stand in lines at slow-moving ticket windows. In the middle of the floor, Jaime spots a four-man salsa group entertaining everyone passing by. Cuban airport employees are languid and unhurried, and armed soldiers watch the activity within the surroundings meticulously. Outside in a grassy, palm tree-studded departure area, the entire Cuban baseball team is gathered with coaches, managers, trainers, and several of the Black Coats from Cuban national security. A few feet away, another street vendor sells cold drinks from inside a colorful kiosk, and an out-of-place black stray cat runs past it. Jaime spots it and laughs. The Black Coats keep the vendor back as he suddenly notices the baseball players and begins to walk towards them, calling their names to catch their attention. One of the Black Coats picks up the cat and places it over by the bushes behind them, and Jaime puffs on his cigar and smiles. Jaime keeps a close watch on his tight group. He watches the boys proudly, especially the four from the Pinar del Rio team; Chuchi, Papo, Panchi, and Tito. Right away, Jaime realizes the boys are a little edgy, and he becomes curious. There is something rather strange about their behavior, and it feels almost awkward, uncomfortable. A prickly silence hovers, and Jaime knows these boys well, maybe too well, as he just knows either something is bothering them or something is about to happen. Jaime is not quite sure, but they are acting a bit unusual, and he cannot quite put his finger on it. Suddenly, someone calls out, and they all grab their luggage and hustle off. Jaime frowns at the suspicious thoughts going through his head but tries to ignore them all while staying attentive. Outside the terminal, family members and a local entourage of high-spirited patriotic Cuban fans pat the boys on their backs as they walk by in a single file, wishing them all good luck in their trip. Some of the fans bring homemade signs with players' names and numbers on them.

These people are loud and proud, and they treat the boys as a family and not just ordinary baseball players. They do not bombard them with a petition of autographs, but rather with common love and affection. In the middle of the commotion, Jaime yells at Panchi, who amazingly walks off, forgetting one of his bags, "Hey Panch, Panchi... Come on, pay attention! Your bags, son!" The young man is embarrassed, and as he apologizes, he retrieves his duffle bag along with a small suitcase and quickly joins the others. Jaime follows closely, carefully watching every detail of the departure as usual. One of the Black Coats sees this and frowns. One by one, the entire team boards the plane along with managers, trainers, the Black Coats, and Jaime, who is the last one in as the doors close behind him.

Just a few moments later, the entire team, along with all others on board, wait inside the plane on the airfield for departure. Everyone is anxious. Unease covers the ambiance; nervousness invades the players, and mistrust occupies the minds of the Black Coats. Everyone is in their own world as the plane is about to take off. Everyone is on edge! Tropical logos adorn the hull of the small commercial plane, which sits all alone on the runway awaiting departure. Jaime and the boys all wait impatiently for takeoff.

The plane finally begins moving, and the players chatter excitedly, pointing out the windows like boys on a school trip. Some have never been on a plane before, and most of them have never left the island. This is a young team, an exceptionally talented but young team representing Cuba in these games. For most of these guys, this is their first international event, for Jaime, just another trip. Seen one, seen them all! The remaining seats are occupied by coaches, managers, and trainers, and there are also various passengers most likely visiting from Panama who are not part of the Cuban delegation...and, of course, the Black Coats...the guys from Cuban national security, the Gestapo, who seem more like life-size Greek statues as they sit there motionless and expressionless as always, robots. Jaime sits in the back beside Chuchi, and from the closed lavatory door comes the sound of someone vomiting. Jaime becomes a bit uneasy, and just moments later, the door opens, and Tito emerges, wiping his mouth, and his face is pale and sweaty. Tito takes a seat in front of Chuchi and buckles his seatbelt. Jaime looks at Chuchi and asks, "What is going on, Chuchi?"

"What do you mean, he gets airsick," replies the young man with a smile.

Jaime glances at him and comes back with a smart and convincing remark, "Listen, I know you boys better than your own mothers. No BS, what is really going on here?" Jaime suspiciously asks, and Chuchi fires right back:

"We're the number one seed in the tournament. Listen, Papa, we are nervous, okay. I understand you're concerned, but so are we!"

Jaime stares straight ahead, and with barely a whisper, he intones, "Alright…You can trust me, Chuchi, what's up? You got to come clean."

Chuchi, feeling beat, begins laughing and picks up a magazine, playing it all off: "Oh, come on, Jaime. I don't know what you mean, man. Give it a break!"

Chuchi puts his headphones over his ears and tries to ignore Jaime as respectful as possible. Steely-eyed, Jaime looks out the window, distraught. He knows for sure something is up as even the air feels different, and the boys are acting just too weird to ignore. They are not being themselves…

After a few hours in the air…suddenly, the silence is broken as one of the airline attendants speaks over the intercom, "In just a few moments, ladies, and gentlemen, we will be landing at Tocumen International Airport in Panama City. Please do not remove your seatbelts until it is announced." Moments later…the plane has landed, and everyone begins to pour down the aisle. At the open door, the Black Coats attach themselves like glue to the players as they debark. Jaime stands in the back watching, making sure everyone deboards the plane and nothing or no one is left behind. He begins walking up and down the aisle and checking empty seats. A few airplane personnel passes by, and suddenly, someone bumps his shoulder, and he looks up.

"Don't look at me, Chuchi" as he pretends to be making an adjustment overhead, the pilot whispers urgently before Jaime can explain he is not Chuchi. He continues, "Do not draw any attention to yourselves. Speak to no one and take care of the others. You will receive further instructions. Mr. Romero will find you." The pilot briskly walks off and is gone before Jaime can say anything. Jaime remains silent for a short moment, shaking his head, and unloads the plane.

As they slowly descend the flight of steps, the boys look around at their surroundings, admiring the unique circumstances and knowing this once-in-a-lifetime moment is one to cherish. Though still nervous and confused, Jaime accepts the opportunity, he takes hold of the moment simply knowing the time has come, and while preparing for the worst, he chooses to anticipate the best instead. This is it! As he arrives at the baggage pickup area, bags are tossed, and clothes rifled through as the team's luggage is checked by airport security. Full of suspicion, the Panama security men act like secret service agents, talking into earpieces and barking endless questions. Perhaps some suspicion may have been raised, perhaps not, and though this is quite unusual to us here in the US, maybe not so much in other places around the world. A group of men and women from Panamanian media anxious to talk to the Cuban players are roughly turned away by the Cuban Black Coats, who surround the players like a fortress, keeping them lassoed in a tight-knit contained group. Jaime just sits there and watches. He thinks to himself after the interesting episode with the pilot confusing him for Chuchi, *what a careless mistake on behalf of the pilot, this could have ended lives…* But once again, Jaime knows what this is, a defining moment and surely a sign from God. "Have a mind that is open to anything but attached to nothing." A Wayne Dyer quote, which his uncle often reminded Jaime, that he would just know, he would inexplicably know when it is God's thing and a time to act when that intimate light would come up and shine upon his understanding one day. Well, this is it, and Jaime feels it right about now as the players look both fascinated and rebuked. Chuchi seems overly hyper as his eyes roam uncomfortably.

The entire group is now moved by bus. The boys' necks crane as they look out the small windows trying to get a glimpse of a new country. They literally look like prisoners being transported instead of ball players. Jaime's mind continues to race, *But when? How? What is the plan…?* They finally arrive at a hotel, and everyone in the bus is hustled through a modern hotel lobby and straight toward the elevators. Papo pauses to look out the window, but Chuchi pushes him on with a stern look. Jaime and the ball players are all taken straight into their hotel rooms, and they are told to just stay inside until given further instructions. A few hours go by, and it is now the middle of the night. Beds are occupied as well as several sleeping bags on the floor. Someone snores lightly. The team has been divided equally into several different rooms; it is not a comfortable situation for anyone, but Jaime is awake, and he is thinking…his mind in obvious turmoil *and was it cruel fate that I was mistaken for Chuchi…?*

Jaime now lies on one of the beds, staring at the ceiling and thinking, wondering, doubting… *Or was it a miracle?* he asks…as he finally drifts asleep for the night.

The following morning the team is moved by buses to the Panama City stadium, which sits in a somewhat secluded little depression surrounded by small hills. There is a cluster of buses and commercial vehicles outside, but the parking lot is empty. Inside it is a multicultural, Olympic-like circus as athletes, teams, and trainers from all over Latin America practice and train for various events for the upcoming Pan American Games. The stadium seats about 25,000, but the bleachers are all vacant, and this is just the perfect scenario for the perfect plan. Armed security guards are posted at entrances and exits and down on the field. Jaime watches his players with eagle eyes from only a few yards away as they train. Jaime cannot sit still, he cannot concentrate, and he knows he must decide the most important decision of his life. At night, armed security guards pace outside the stadium, and the bright stadium lights are on as if it were the middle of the day. Inside the locker rooms, the players dress and gear up. They are exuberant and rowdy as they innocently get ready to play the game they love. No jitters and no butterflies, just bring it on. Let's play!

"Yeah, baby, our first practice game. About time!" yells one of the young players to one of the managers, full of energy and with much enthusiasm. The ever-present Black Coats chat with the trainers near the exit, keeping tabs on the boys, and a stadium janitor mops the showers while another ball player makes an untimely remark…

"Hey bro, did you see them? The other team… They are not a team; they're more like a herd of cows."

Suddenly, Jaime immediately walks up from behind and half pulls, half drags the young man next to the lockers…and in a low but serious tone scolds him, "I don't remember giving you the mic or the stage to give your all-knowing expertise in cows. Do you even know what a cow looks like? When was the last time you saw a cow, city boy? Let it be the last time. Your job is to play baseball and leave the talking to me! You got that?" The young man, with his head bowed in utter embarrassment, walks away feeling like a fool after being reprimanded by Jaime.

"My bad," he whispers as he walks away. Holding a clipboard, Jaime proceeds as if nothing has happened, and he pretends to concentrate on checking attendance. He knows these boys like sons and is acutely aware that Chuchi, Papo, Panchi, and Tito are unusually quiet.

"Like playing our mothers!" wittily comments another player, looking Jaime right in the eye, and as the banter continues, they all break out in laughter, trying to ease Jaime's solemn demeanor, and finally, he forces a fake smile of peace to them and stops this from getting out of hand. The players continue inside the locker room, and the janitor inconspicuously mops his way over until he is right beside Jaime.

"You must be Chuchi, right?" the janitor whispers, and covering his surprise, Jaime glances at the man, who keeps mopping with his head down.

After a pausing moment, Jaime replies, "Yeah, I must be."

"We need to know how many? How many of you are there?" the old man whispers right back, and without stopping nonchalantly, the janitor keeps mopping toward the other end of the locker room.

Jaime's heart races, and for one grueling instant, he is frozen with utter surprise at the fact that the much-awaited moment is finally here. Then he catches Chuchi's eye and motions him over to the side as the young man already in full uniform approaches.

"What's wrong, Papa? You don't look so good."

Jaime turns away from the others, pretending to be tying his shoe, and confronts Chuchi, "Chuchi, who else?"

"I don't know what you mean, man..." Jaime looks him in the eye.

"Who else? I'm only going to ask you one time, Chuchi." The realization drains life from Chuchi's face. One of the Black Coats is watching, but Jaime winks at him and pats Chuchi on the back like he is giving the boy a pep talk.

"Papa, please...I might never have another chance..."

Jaime frowns...and looking him right in the eye, he whispers: "I said how many?" Jaime, now extremely frustrated, asks the young man, giving him a stern look and clenching a tight fist with anger and sounding harsh and demanding to dig the truth the young man obviously tries to hide. Jaime is once again just doing the job he suddenly hates as the look in the eyes of both men collide with clashing interests. For a moment, Jaime has a flashback and is transported all the way back to Ijaba's days. He sees himself chained amongst other African slaves in the dark containment of a slave ship.

He looks around in horror and then suddenly returns to the present moment...

Jaime remembers his job is making sure the chains are not broken. The chains of slavery, the chains of bondage…and as he is now certain all the suspicion he felt was right on the money, he knows for sure that what once appeared to be only a suspicion is, in fact, a reality and what he did not know now is, and so he presses Chuchi for an answer.

After a few moments, Jaime has pushed Chuchi long enough, and the young man, now exhausted, finally cracks and gives in: "Four! Okay, Jaime. There are four of us!" Chuchi finally answers, defeated and exhausted… Completely beat and feeling like all the air has been taken out of his only chance.

Chuchi looks down, and almost simultaneously, Jaime fakes a cynical laugh, ruffling Chuchi's hair as he walks away. Chuchi looks at Jaime and shakes his head in disbelief, pale and disappointed but at the same time relieved. He then leaves the locker room and stumps out with the others who are already out on the field. Jaime, now aware of the inevitable situation, proceeds to pretend to be checking lockers and uniform inventory on his clipboard as he methodically inspects them one by one. He then casually passes the janitor, and with all the courage in the world and forgetting everything he knows, all he can see in front of him is the possibility of being a free man at last. For an instant, he visualizes his dream… Ijaba's dream! A wish fulfilled! And just like that and with all the courage in the world, Jaime passes the janitor and whispers, "Hey, man, not four, it's five. Five of us… You got that?"

And in the blink of an eye, fate takes form in one simple decision. Now five men who have been prisoners all their lives can be free. Only because of one man's decision to follow his dream, and now he and four others are set to spread their wings and fly. And isn't it remarkable how the very same thing that holds many of us back from fulfilling our lives' dreams, which is decision-making, may deliver others from bondage forever in one single instant simply because they acted? Jaime's decision to take a leap of faith towards something he so strongly believed in, though extremely dangerous, would eventually open the doors to so much more later in our story, but at this moment, it was just a decision made and not even a well-thought-out decision, but a gut instinct, and, as a matter of fact, it was just the single act of one man listening to his heart that can finally deliver them for once and for all from the chains of bondage.

Shortly after, out in the middle of Panama's national stadium and under bright lights, a small crowd of baseball fanatics watches a practice game between Cuba and Puerto Rico. Out on the baseball field...we hear a loud... *Thump!* As Chuchi bunts the ball unexpectedly, drops his bat, and takes off like a bullet to first base. He is safe! The small crowd cheers with the game now in full swing, the bleachers are almost empty still. Armed security guards cover all the exits of the stadium, and Jaime, who puffs on his cigar, watches expressionless from the dugout. He uses a white, neatly folded handkerchief to slowly wipe the sweat dripping from his forehead on this humid evening, a familiar trade his old uncle so often applies. Jaime is extremely nervous and probably the tensest he has ever been in his whole entire life, but the excitement of the game and the humidity help cover the obvious. As the game continues, Chuchi trots over home plate to score in the fifth inning after hitting a double and then stealing third base. He scores on a single by Tito, who flies to first base, makes a turn, and looks, and almost gets caught on a sharp throw by the outfielder. A dumb mental error and something Tito usually is more careful about, but these mental mistakes prove to Jaime the boys are thinking about something else, about their big opportunity, about their break, but when, how, what is the big plan? Is there one? What's next?

Jaime is too nervous and subdued. Papo, who is usually in good spirits, does not even smile after making several great plays in the infield the following inning, and back in the dugout, Jaime makes eye contact with Chuchi...Papo...Panchi...and Tito... We look over to the scoreboard, and the score is, the fifth inning: Cuba 2–Puerto Rico 0.

Panchi, now playing left field, seems to have grown eyes in the back of his head as the Black Coats watch closely. Suddenly, Papo at the third base catches a hard grounder and whips the ball to Tito playing shortstop, who catches it, but this time, steps on the bag, and he simply throws the ball to first base to make the seemingly easy double play. There is no little dance afterwards, just strictly serious baseball. In the eighth inning now, the Cuban team is winning by four runs, and in the dugout, Jaime turns his gaze from the scoreboard and makes significant eye contact with Papo, Panchi, Tito, and Chuchi yet again, who stand just beside him. Tension is palpable. Jaime looks for a sign from the boys…but he gets none. Chuchi moves closer to Jaime. "Papa, I hope you are sure about this. It is not too late, you know." Without making a single comment, Jaime takes the cigar stub from his mouth, he deliberately drops it to the ground and grinds it with his heel.

He looks at Chuchi and smiles…but immediately follows with, "Chuchi, this is it! I'm in. We are all in this together, and there is no going back."

The young baseball player, who could pass for a younger version of Jaime, smiles with a wide beam from ear to ear in complete acknowledgment, and although Chuchi says nothing, Jaime's comment brings music to his ear. He never wanted to leave Jaime behind anyway, as doing so would have been a huge sacrifice, and the young man is extremely happy to hear Jaime's words making his decision that much easier.

Suddenly…the stadium lights go out! In complete darkness on the field, there is massive confusion as managers and trainers rush out to players stranded in the middle of the baseball diamond. The Black Coats and security guards leap to action. Everyone is running, shouting, and panicking. A hundred commands are shouted out at once, there is chaos in this place. And before anyone knows what is happening, five figures are running up through the bleachers in the darkness and growing hysteria. Hearing someone approach, a security guard spins around aiming his automatic rifle, but he is suddenly struck with a thrown baseball. The wounded guard falls onto the ground in pain, and the rifle goes flying in the air.

The five figures run past the man on the floor, holding his face in obvious pain as the man moans at full volume as blood pours down his face. While the guard lies on the floor yelling for help, Jaime and the boys slip out an exit and out of the stadium with their hearts racing one hundred miles per hour. Jaime and the boys run for their lives...

"Nice arm, Papo," Chuchi compliments his teammate, and as they run past a set of dumpsters, there, in one of the gloomy alleys of the stadium, is a white van full of beer logos parked outside the stadium waiting for them. Chuchi then yells, almost out of breath, "There! That is our van."

Without hesitation, the five men beeline toward the white van parked in the shadows of the stadium parking lot with the engine still running and dark smoke coming out of its exhaust pipe. Jaime follows the boys. He is out of place and confused, but he goes along with just mere instincts, not knowing exactly what the plan is. Jaime simply trusts the boys as he is completely oblivious of specifics of the plan to escape, and since he has not been part of any of the instructions previously given to the boys to vanish from the grip of the Cuban watchdogs, Jaime faithfully tags along. In his mind, he tries to believe this prearranged escape has been well-thought-out and meticulously planned by Chuchi and the others with the help of someone on the outside. Jaime hopes it is someone who knows what he or she is doing, but as it is, he just follows his gut feeling and allows the moment to dictate the flow of the circumstances on pure adrenaline, somehow knowing it is the right thing to do; the only thing to do, and the only hope of him ever being free from Castro's rule for once and for all.

As they approach the escape van, the back doors suddenly fly open, and hands come from nowhere and push them all inside.

Instantly, the van takes off over the bumpy terrain. The doors are yanked and closed, and Jaime and the four young men are all inside, breathless and scared as the white van disappears into the dark.

"Home run!" Chuchi exclaims, and suddenly, Jaime and the boys hear gunshots behind them. They all duck in panic.

"Get down! Hold on!" yells the driver of the van as he stirs dangerously, caroming over the rugged land in the darkness with no headlights on. Pitched about, everyone hangs on for dear life as the short drive seems like an eternity, and then, as they are finally about to reach a road, the van nearly overturns as it surges over a ridge and onto the pavement. Everyone screams!

After the driver realizes there are no pursuers in sight, he removes his foot from the accelerator, slowing down a bit and now a little calmer; the van continues to speed unseen down the dark road. The driver finally turns on the headlights and proceeds down the empty road. With the ride now smoother, Jaime and the boys look around the van, and they see several men, all wearing ski masks. One of the men begins to hand out several pieces of old clothing to them. Then the man tells Jaime, with a strong Spanish accent, "Put these on." Jaime and the boys stare at each other, a bit frightened and exhilarated, and begin to change their clothes. They are all puzzled, but no one says anything, stuck in an incredible state of mind where the sun is about to come around the mountain of anticipation. The man continues: "Do exactly as you are told. Today you begin new lives. Free ones. You are about to experience the removing of your shackles forever," the man adds, pointing with his index finger at every one of them, one by one. Jaime looks at the boys, and without words, they each know exactly what he is trying to say. He winks at Chuchi, and they all smile back at Jaime.

Moments later, they arrive somewhere in the middle of Panama City, finding themselves driving through ghetto-like rows of old and dirty project-style housing like the inner-city streets of Old Havana back home. These small apartment buildings, all in ill repair, are crammed along dark streets, and there is garbage everywhere. Homeless people sleep outside, and several stray dogs wander the streets, barking in the quiet of the night. The van proceeds slowly through the empty streets, and it finally stops in a shadowed alley, and the men get out. The driver of the van removes his mask, showing a shaved, clean-cut appearance, not at all what Jaime expected from these types of men and the job they were performing. The man politely guides Jaime and the ball players into a cheap motel room while the other two stay in the van, still wearing their masks. Wearing local clothing, Jaime and the boys stand clustered together in the small room. There is no telephone and only one single mattress on the floor. The Latino man, who finally introduces himself as Julio, stands at the door of the motel room, smiles, and gives them specific instructions, "I'm Julio, you will not leave this room for any reason." He looks at Jaime and continues, "You will open the door, only at the words 'orange juice.' Is that understood?" Jaime nods. The man shakes their hands, one by one, and he tells them, "Welcome to freedom, gentlemen!" Then he leaves, closing the door behind him.

Chuchi looks at Jaime, confused, and Jaime intones with a childish smile, "They think I'm you."

Chuchi agrees, "I got that! It isn't the first time this happens…"

Panchi stands to his feet and whispers, "That was hard…scary, weird! The adrenaline rush was insane!"

The others, sitting on the floor, do not say anything, but they agree with Panchi in silence, and they keep their heads bowed in deep thought, knowing that, in fact, it was because of their hardship that they decided to take a chance in order to gain their much-anticipated freedom, for had they been comfortable, nothing would've ever taken place. Sometimes change is inevitable, the only option!

The young baseball players, still in disbelieve and shock, rock back and forth, waiting for anyone to say the first word…anything, and finally…

"Free at last! I cannot believe we are going to be free at last!" Papo whispers...and then Jaime adds:

"We are not going to be anything, Papo, we are already free! We may be sitting in here apparently doing nothing, but in all reality, a whole lot is happening. We are being strengthened, we are being established, and we are being perfected and refined for what is ahead. So, hang on, boys, I have a feeling the future looks very bright for us all."

The boys keep their heads down, not yet understanding the power of Jaime's words, almost prophetic. Inside the tiny room, they sit, sprawl, stand and pace nervously around in the dark for the next few hours anxiously as there is nothing to do but wait, Panchi bites his nails, and Tito bangs his head against the wall lightly in deep thought. And suddenly, in the middle of the silence, Papo begins to quietly sing a popular Tom Petty song, "...The wait...ing...is the hardest part..." Panchi laughs quietly, and Tito interrupts:

"Wrong song, bro, it should be... I'm free... Free falling (another Petty song)."

"Yeah, I already miss my CDs, bro."

Chuchi steps in, "Be quiet! You do not need any CDs right now, shut up!"

Then Papo throws in his two cents, "Whatever, I just want to play for the Yankees. Seriously!"

Panchi, more relaxed now, adds, "After I'm signed, I'll pull some strings for you...okay?" Papo pushes him, and the youngster snickers quietly. Tito jumps on top of Panchi, covering his mouth to keep him from making any noise.

Jaime just sits there in the corner of the dark room, and he watches the boys as they play around immaturely in almost complete silence to not make any noise as instructed and without any real understanding of what they have just done. In the scheme of things, what these guys have just accomplished is quite a feat while punching Castro and his corrupted government in the face by defecting. By doing this, they are inspiring just about everyone in Cuba with moral encouragement that there is hope and at the same time rewriting the book of their lives. Yet, they do not quite realize what this means, but for the first time in their lives, they are free! Even if it is just sitting in a dark, cramped room in the middle of some Panamanian ghetto.

Minutes later, in hushed tones, Chuchi paces back and forth, trying to exhaust bitter thoughts.

"I don't get it. Castro has been in power longer than anyone in recent history, and he laughs at America and the pressure they put on Cuba sucking everyone dry. The embargo only hurts the people, not him. It has been too long, and it has not accomplished anything other than separation between those over there and the rest of the people who are forced to leave, and his bank account is probably bigger than Bill Gates'. He does not care about the people. Never has and never will, especially now that he is finally dead. The man caused enough pain, so God have mercy on him, but I have a feeling he will not be residing in a very cool place in the afterlife."

Panchi jumps in, and Papo follows, "Meanwhile, we live our whole lives in rooms smaller than this, just dreaming. Hey, did I tell you guys they promised me a telephone line two years ago? But never delivered… Look, all I know is I feel more alive trapped in this little room than I ever did walking along the streets of Havana."

"Yeah, it feels good to know there is no going back!" Panchi agrees with Papo, and his teammate replies:

"All I know is it feels good right now, even in here."

Jaime absorbs all this as Chuchi continues pacing, adding on to his previous statement, "I don't get it. What kind of power does he (Castro) have over the people? He is just one man, and he is only ninety miles away from the greatest power in the world, but after all this time, he is still there, even after his death, it is like his ghost still runs things in Cuba. He outlived a bunch of American presidents too. How much longer? How many more children must die in shark-infested waters trying to escape?"

Tito, who has not said much, now jumps in, "Well, after today, he has no power over us. None!"

Chuchi interferes and finishes Tito's thought, "Listen, man, Castro himself will have to shove me in the trunk of a car and drive me out of here. The only way I go back is dead." Chuchi looks around for consent, and he gets it. The others hold out their fists in solidarity, and they all grasp hands. Chuchi continues looking at Jaime. "What do you think, Papa?"

They turn to look at Jaime, who has been silent, just listening the whole time. He walks over and joins them. "I think we've been given a gift." At this, he reaches out and clasps hands with the boys. "I can't wait. I can't even imagine what it must feel like to just be and do...freely!" Jaime adds, smiling.

A little while later, the talk is now depleted, and everyone is silent, either asleep or simply resting from the long night. Just waiting as there is nothing else to do but wait. Another hour goes by, and the sound of soft snoring can be heard...

Suddenly, there is a soft knock at the door. Jaime leaps to his feet and motions to the others to be quiet. He creeps to the door and puts his ear against it. The man on the other side of the door whispers, "I have your orange juice! Open up..." Jaime unlocks and inches to open the door. He recognizes the man; it is none other than one of the men from the van, who peers in, glancing around the room until he is satisfied, then he speaks, "Gentlemen, I have a message from Mr. Romero. Everything is clear, America is next."

Jaime and the four young ball players look at one another, and they shake their heads in agreement. And just like that, several hours later, Jaime and the boys find themselves at a small airport in Panama waiting to fly to America. They can hardly contain themselves as they all stand next to the dirt runway of a tiny rural airport somewhere in Panama. The airport is nearly empty, and the airfield is unpaved.

Moments later, a small commercial plane comes rolling in, and Jaime and the boys are hustled onto the small plane where they wait for take-off. The boys sit grouped together, barely able to contain their excitement. No luggage, nothing but the borrowed clothes on their backs and in desperate need of showers and shaves, and they could not care less. This is their "new" most exciting day of their lives.

A well-dressed gentleman suddenly takes a seat beside Jaime, who does not yet realize he is Mr. Romero. Mr. Romero quietly intones to Jaime, "Your name is not Chuchi." Jaime glances cautiously at him, and Mr. Romero continues, "The pilot was misinformed. He was told to approach the team's rep, you see. An easy mistake, but it could have ended lives."

Jaime nods and absorbs this. "I assure you; it wasn't intentional. Our hearts were racing…but you can trust me. I am in this 100 percent, sir."

Mr. Romero accepts Jaime's words as a promissory note by simply giving him a sharp look, but no handshake follows. Jaime feels a bit awkward, but sensing he is in no position to prove anything, he only shakes his head several times as if telling Mr. Romero, *I'm your man*. With a rumble, the plane finally moves. Out the small window, Jaime and the boys see the airfield accelerated by, and at last, the plane leaves the ground. The boys all scream with joy, celebrating and lifting their hands up in the air as if riding on a roller coaster. Jaime, watching them, turns back to Mr. Romero, and they continue their conversation. Jaime humbly extends his hand…

"Sir, my name is Jaime Rondeau Colon. It is a pleasure to meet you." Mr. Romero, sizing him up, offers his hand also, and they shake hands for the first time.

"I'm Mr. Romero."

Jaime is excited like a child; he replies, "I know, I know! I know exactly who you are, and what you have done for us is greatly appreciated."

Outside the airplane window, cotton-like clouds now blanket the earth far below. Jaime turns to Mr. Romero and politely asks,

"Why are you doing this, Mr. Romero? If you do not mind me asking. I understand it is not for the money..."

To this, Mr. Romero gladly responds, "Well, see, I am a businessman, Mr. Colon, a wealthy entrepreneur, and perhaps I have friends in high places with a fiscal interest in baseball. Perhaps I am blessed and simply feel a humanitarian responsibility to help others. That, of course, depends on whom you ask. Let us just say I have had a good run of luck, okay, and I am just paying it forward." Jaime nods gratefully. Mr. Romero continues, "I know what you have gone through. I even know what is going through your head right now, but I tell you this if you have the courage to do what you have done, which not everyone has the guts to do, then you can pretty much do anything you set out to do in life. The gate is wide open. The flood gates of opportunity await."

Jaime agrees, accepting the wise words, and then he adds, almost apologetic, "Mr. Romero, we were just desperate. We are not heroes. Something just comes upon a person when he is against the wall, and you simply act."

"I agree with you, but I am not talking about that. I am talking about your dreams!" Jaime, almost giddy, looks back out the window.

"My dreams! What about my dreams?" Mr. Romero just smiles but says nothing...and Jaime continues to look out the window while Mr. Romero now reads through a magazine.

After a few short hours in the air, the private plane lands at the Miami International Airport. It is a gorgeous day, and the airport is huge and crowded, the third busiest airport in America and a major immigration port where people from all different nationalities and different walks of life toddle through here. As the doors open, Papo, Chuchi, Panchi, and Tito descend the private plane's flight of stairs, excited and whooping it up. At the bottom, they join Jaime, and laughing, they drag him along the tarmac like a reluctant leader. Mr. Romero stops and shakes hands with the boys and congratulates them all, giving a special explanation to Chuchi, "You are the leader of this bunch, make me proud."

"Yes, sir, with pleasure," responds the young man who suddenly catches Jaime...

As he stops in his tracks, seeing an American flag waving in the air at the airport (in slow motion)... Jaime fixes his eyes on the beautiful, tricolored flag, knowing what it represents. He stares at the colorful stripes and the white stars, almost as if counting them, then he wipes his eyes with his hand as he is overcome by tears of joy. He then whispers to himself, "I am indeed a blessed man to have this opportunity. I have dreamt about this moment my whole life." Mr. Romero places his hand over Jaime's shoulder...

"Well, how does it feel?" he asks...and Jaime quietly responds:

"Ijaba, a wish fulfilled." Mr. Romero turns to Jaime.

"What did you say, Jaime?" Mr. Romero asks, and Jaime quickly responds, diverting the question:

"Ahh, I feel like a bird out of a cage, Mr. Romero! Allow me a minute to stretch my wings, sir..."

Mr. Romero likes his answer, and then he greets Jaime properly for the first time, "Welcome to America, son!"

But, before they even reach the terminal, Chuchi, Papo, Panchi, and Tito, unshaven in their mismatched clothes, are swarmed by a pack of eager sports agents and representatives. A dozen reporters from different sports affiliates and major league clubs introduce themselves. The four boys look at each other in disbelief, and as Jaime starts to go to their aid as they are suddenly swarmed by all these strangers from the media, Mr. Romero gently holds him back. "Jaime, let them enjoy being The Beatles. Do not worry, you won't be cut out." Jaime pauses...

"How did they know? How did they find out about the boys being here?" Jaime asks, surprised, and Mr. Romero responds:

"Outside the cage, my friend, the world is a global village. Of course, you will learn that very quickly, Mr. Colon." Jaime nods his head in agreement, and the two men shake hands cordially. As they look at the entire picture of the modern airport, hundreds of travelers and immigrants of every race, creed, and color move in and out of the terminals, a sea of people everywhere. The Miami airport, overwhelmingly large, is like a multicultural city. Jaime then turns to Mr. Romero.

"Sir, even the air feels different out here." At this, Mr. Romero looks at Jaime and gives him the biggest grin Jaime has seen in the short time they have known each other. A sign Mr. Romero is pleased with Jaime's sudden understanding of the priceless gift we enjoy here in America... Freedom!

"And that is why people from all over the world take the chances they take to make it here, leaving everything behind and for many, not knowing if they will ever make it or ever return home," Mr. Romero suddenly softly adds to Jaime's childish but true statement. "Jaime, do you want to know why the air feels different? That, my friend, is the smell of liberty!" And the second Mr. Romero replies to Jaime, the two men nod their heads in mutual agreement, and they share a smile at the same time.

Meanwhile, at the terminal entrance, the boys have discovered vending machines. Mr. Romero gives them some cash, and they busily begin to feed them money while talking to agents and media reps. Jaime taps Mr. Romero on his shoulder. "Look at them, drinking their first Coca-Cola in America. I am going to have mine. Mr. Romero, do you realize I am having my very first Coke ever?"

"It'll be the best Coca-Cola will ever have. You will never forget the taste...you will never forget the moment, Jaime," Mr. Romero tells Jaime with a smile, they share a look of mutual respect, and with an opportunistic thought, Jaime reaches in his pocket and takes out a cigar. Standing there, people rushing all around, he lights up his first cigar in America. Mr. Romero stares at him and enjoys the look on Jaime's face, who relishes the moment with his eyes closed.

"Ahh!"

Again, Mr. Romero lets him live the moment for a noticeably short time before he lets him know, "Hey, Jaime, of course, the embargo makes it illegal to have Cuban cigars here in America." Jaime, not listening to Mr. Romero's words, produces another, offers it to the old man, who, grinning, accepts and continues his previous thought, "Jaime, what you asked me back on the plane? Why I do what I do? Well, the answer is the look on your face at this very moment. That is why I do it. I enjoy seeing people opening their eyes to this, America, God's gift to the world, Jaime." Now beaming with excitement, Jaime blows a smoke ring just like his old uncle used to when celebrating anything, and he watches it slowly float into the air as the American flag continues to wave in the background. Jaime takes notice of how beautiful it is, fixing his eyes on it...again! He pauses for a moment and enjoys watching it float in the wind.

"Yes! Freedom!"

Finally, they board a van that waits for them and leaves the airport, and later that evening in a Miami project, the boys, Jaime, and Mr. Romero arrive in the airport van. They get dropped off, and the van leaves. It is an ugly projects-like complex covered with graffiti. Mr. Romero, apologetic, directs his words to Jaime and the boys, "It's not the Miami Hilton."

Jaime shrugs his shoulders and walks next to Mr. Romero, not at all interested in the appearance of the place, and he tells him with a smile and one single word that says it all, "Okay!"

That evening Jaime and the guys squeeze themselves into a cramped one-bedroom apartment somewhere in Miami. It is bland, with a tiny kitchenette and with only the bare essentials. Mr. Romero stands in the doorway, apologetic. "Just until your paperwork goes through. All the immigration stuff... It should not be exceedingly long. Just procedure at this point. As you know, Cuban immigrants only must touch American soil, and they automatically receive political asylum because of the current situation and agreements made between the two countries. It used to be the Coast Guard could rescue Cubans at sea and bring them in, but now they must touch American soil before they can be given proper legal entrance into the United States. Even if they are rescued ten feet from shore, they are sent back, but once they touch, I mean, touch land, that is it, they are granted asylum."

Jaime takes mental notes of the facts and gives Mr. Romero the same answer as before, "Okay!"

As the boys look around the apartment, Jaime brushes a cockroach into the sink and turns the water on. Chuchi approaches. "This is great, huh? It is a castle! We will take it… You have no idea how beautiful this is. We are in America, baby!"

"It's not the Hilton, but give me a few days, I'm working on it!" Mr. Romero presses forward…

"I'm really okay here, just knowing we are not still in Cuba brings a smile to my face. I think I can speak for all of us when I say we would sleep in a sewer as long as we are here in the States," Jaime tells Mr. Romero, and not sure he heard right, he takes out his wallet…

"Jaime, they look like they've already have slept in a sewer. Here! Take this…" He counts out cash into four neat piles on the table. The four young men stare wide-eyed as Mr. Romero counts the money, pile by pile. This is the most money they have ever seen in their life other than in movies. When he finishes counting the money, Mr. Romero gives Jaime some money too, and he leaves for the night.

The very next morning, we find ourselves in the big city of Miami, glamorous and sunny and surrounded by skyscrapers, palm trees, massive billboards, and, of course, the traffic. Ahh! The famous traffic in Miami, which comes with 95 percent humidity, but everyone looks so happy and relaxed as if the whole place is on vacation. Women wear shorts and skirts only Miami can offer, and the shiny sweat beats off anyone's skin as if part of the regular local attire with the high humidity. Now in Downtown Miami, Chuchi, Papo, Panchi, and Tito have taken a taxi, and they stare like awestruck tourists at the sights and sounds of the busy streets, the bustle, and the hustle of endless people… In a clothing store, they emerge from dressing rooms in colorful outfits, gleefully admiring themselves in full-length mirrors. This simple pleasure hereto unknown, even though they were supposed to have been celebrities in Cuba.

...Tito, who carries a dozen outfits, is stopped from entering the dressing room by a clerk who indicates a "limit three items" sign.

...Wearing splashy new clothes, the four Cuban athletes swagger proudly down the Miami street. They are surprised by all the Hispanics they see, especially Cubans, and they are equally surprised when they discover all the street signs and writing, even music in Spanish. Chuchi then approaches Papo. "It almost feels like we're back home... Only with food."

"Yeah, and freedom. No one walking around asking where we got the money to buy this or that..." replies Papo with a sigh of relief.

They stop at a street display and try on new sunglasses crowding each other to peer in the tiny mirror, oblivious to the amused looks they receive from the vendors and all the people walking by.

...Afterwards, they swagger down the street in their new sunglasses. In a tourist shop, they take great care selecting postcards to send to their families back home.

...In the street, passing other Cubans, their eyes meet with camaraderie. It is obvious they have just arrived as there is always a certain something that identifies newcomers, and then something a little more urgent catches their attention when their heads swivel as skimpily dressed suntanned college girls roller-skate by, and Chuchi loves it. "Think I'm going to like it here, bro."

Inside a sports store, Chuchi and the boys are like kids in a candy store. Chuchi browses baseball gear and becomes amazed at the wide selection of bats. He tests each one of them, swinging for the fence each time. He enjoys this. Papo, just like Chuchi with the bats, meticulously examines every single sneaker displayed on a wall, one by one. Panchi tests new infielder gloves, putting them on and slamming his fist inside the leather pockets, and Tito, now sporting a new gold chain, checks himself in a mirror.

Papo is delighted to find a fancy pair of Nike cleats that light up, and a pretty salesgirl laughs at his innocence. Chuchi interrupts the girl, "You don't understand. Where we come from, it is prohibited…"

"What's prohibited?" the salesgirl asks, and Chuchi responds with a smile:

"Everything!"

The salesgirl does not quite get the smart response, but she laughs anyway at Chuchi's seemingly innocent remark, not knowing he is telling the truth as in Cuba "everything" is prohibited indeed, and now the opposite is at hand here in America. Chuchi grabs his shopping bags and waves goodbye to the salesgirl, she smiles and waves back. From the shops, the four young men take a taxi and head towards the beach. Just a few moments later, they arrive. The beach is a nonstop parade of bikini babes. Everywhere they look, women prance around in eye-popping thongs without a care in the world, almost gloriously nude and flaunting it. "Welcome to Miami Beach!" another huge sign proclaims. Everything is big in America, more, bigger, taller, extra, additional, just a true sign of abundance everywhere they look, and the boys are marveled by it all. Right about an hour or so later, now in swimming trunks and his new shades, Chuchi rubs suntan lotion on his new friend, the salesgirl, who has joined them at the beach. The girl, whose name is Brooke, has a knockout body, and she's not alone, she has brought three of her friends with her, and Papo, Panchi, and Tito could not be happier as her bikini-clad girlfriends meanwhile shower the boys with attention. These guys are in heaven, and as they look at this scenario, only imagined in their wildest fantasies, they would be happy to die at this very moment. Chuchi looks at Tito, and he points back to the sign, which reads, "Welcome to Miami Beach." The young men break into happy laughter as they high-five each other with excitement.

New Beginnings

In the late hours of the night, Jaime arrives at his new apartment in Miami in a taxi. The cab pulls over next to a well-lit, middle-class at best apartment building to drop Jaime off, and Jaime, who is returning from a day like he has never had before, shopping like a Beverly-Hills-spoiled rich girl with her daddy's credit card, is happy to be home. The driver, who converses amiably with Jaime in Spanish the whole way home, gets out of the car to open the door for a tired Jaime who isn't used to such service, and he refuses, but the man insists, and feeling like a newly crowned king, he accepts. Jaime pays the old man, and the taxi drives away, leaving him all alone in front of his new home. Jaime stands at the door, looking around and hoping someone will see him entering his new bachelor pad, but no one is there to watch him enter. He proudly takes the keys out of his pocket, and the keys rattle, making the familiar jingling noise keys make...and Jaime enjoys this. His first apartment in the US, and he savors the moment, rattling them again and again, amusing himself, smiling and looking around in utter surprise, happy to be home. As he opens the front door of his apartment, the dark room reveals a small but nice modern apartment; it is brand-new and unfurnished. For a moment, Jaime just stands there, arms full of shopping bags and groceries, and he looks around at the clean, freshly painted empty space, realizing this is his own apartment in America.

"Whoa! If they could only see me now!" Jaime exclaims, dropping the bags at his feet. He then opens his arms and slowly moves around the apartment like a soaring bird in flight. He smiles as he covers every corner of the apartment in disbelief...finally, his own place. Jaime walks in the bedroom and lies on his bed awake. The bed is the only piece of furniture he has bought so far, and he bought it from the neighbor next door who was having a garage sale, and a brand-new bed and mattress at such a good price would be senseless to pass. And so, he did. Jaime now lies in bed, remembering the words of his old uncle back home, "There will come a time when God himself will want you to hear his voice, and you'll know it will be time to turn off all the noise around you and listen. He lives in us, and He is always watching, monitoring like a surveillance camera. We might not know He is there, but He always is. Just look around you, and you will too see Him… He is in everything!" Jaime looks around, hoping to find someone, something, but there is nothing but empty space around him. A bit disappointed, he lies his head back down on his pillow, and he prays quietly to the best of his knowledge as he does not know much about God or about praying, but he just talks as if hoping someone will hear him, "Lord God, thank you for everything you have done in my life. Though I do not know You, I somehow know You know me, I feel it, and if my uncle says I need to know You, then I want that too. I want to know what it is like to be significant enough to have the Maker of everything, according to my uncle, know me. God, if You really are out there, I want to walk with You, and I want to personally thank You for bringing me here and away from hell itself in communist Cuba. My uncle once said I needed to know the height and the depth, and the width, and the breath of God. I want that."

After his first-ever attempt at a conversation with God, Jaime lies there, maybe expecting to see fireworks, but there are none. Then he waits for maybe some type of audible response, but silence follows, and not sure if he should be feeling disappointed or ignored, Jaime drifts asleep, and he begins to snore lightly, finally resting after an awfully long day. Now, had he only waited a tad longer, he could have experienced what most people would consider a sign or response to his shot at connecting with the Almighty as an inexplicable gust of wind entered his bedroom window unexpectedly, knocking down several items on his dresser, but Jaime slept through it. The irony of it was there was not an ounce of wind outside when this mysterious incident took place. Jaime continues to sleep soundly.

The following morning Jaime rolls in his sheets restlessly before finally opening his eyes. Then suddenly, he jumps out of bed and runs into the shower like someone who has somewhere to go. This morning, he skips his daily ritual of two cups of Cuban coffee before anything else, and after getting dressed, he hurries downstairs and waives at the first cab he sees outside the apartment complex. He gets in and directs the driver towards Downtown Miami. The taxi drops Jaime off in the middle of the busy downtown and drives away. Jaime walks off aimlessly for the first time alone in the United States. He enjoys his walk around the city, and then he takes his wandering to Miami Beach and is absolutely stunned at the beautiful skyscrapers and the sunshine. He admires the modern city and all that goes on around him. The sights and sounds astonish him. He is perplexed as he moves slowly through… Suddenly, a loud shouting match erupts, catching his attention and everyone else around. He notices a fruit vendor and a lady at a coffee stand who fight over a customer. He cannot help but laugh as they make a scene, yelling in Spanish in front of everyone who passes by without a care in the world. The bus stop in front of them is full of people going to work and school, but no one bothers to look, and in Jaime's mind, everyone seems so busy in complete contrast to the people back in Cuba, where time seems to stand still, and everyone is constantly in everyone's business and where minutes seem like hours, and hours seem like days. Where people hopelessly follow their daily routines in the hope of a not-so-distant future that may bring change at last. They dream of a day when they can enjoy all the things freedom brings, the things they see on their television sets when their fantasies can become a real living and not dreaming all the time. Suddenly, Jaime dares to interrupt the old lady at the coffee stand who continues arguing with her neighbor by ordering a coffee. She turns to Jaime and helps him politely, forgetting all about the argument with the fruit vendor, and this impresses Jaime. "Hola, mijo… Como te puedo ayudar (Hello, sonny… How can I help you)?"

"Hola! Si, un cafecito por favor (¡Hi! Yes, a coffee please.)." The lady smiles and hands Jaime a single cup of hot Cuban coffee, and he slowly sips on the tiny cup filled with what appears to be a hundred pounds of caffeine and sugar. Suddenly his eyes light up. "Ooooh! Que rico! Gracias! (Tasty! Thank you!)" Jaime pays the lady, and he tips his hat to a couple of elderly gentlemen sitting at the end of the counter of the shop also drinking coffee, and he walks off. As he strolls through this part of the city, he enjoys the festive sidewalks of Downtown Miami, often looking around like a little boy trying not to miss anything. The whole time he is just grateful to be here in the States, and he thinks, *what a wonderful place this is!* Still in complete disbelief, he is indeed walking in the exact place he has been only imagining in his wildest dreams. And what a huge difference in comparison with Cuba, where only tourists have the privilege to go into the hotels and fancy restaurants and where Cubans are foreigners in their own country; always treated like second-class citizens and with no rights whatsoever. After walking a few exciting blocks, Jaime finally finds himself outside of Mr. Romero's office building. He double-checks the address on the business card to make sure he is in the right place, he rings the bell, still confirming the address matches with that on the business card, takes a deep breath, and rings again. After a buzzer authorizes entrance, he pauses for a short moment, then he opens the front door and walks in the modern office building. Mr. Romero, who waits for Jaime in front of his office, greets him by offering his hand. Jaime shakes Mr. Romero's hand, and they walk inside together.

"Wow! This is your office?" he asks, excited and a bit nervous. Mr. Romero nods his head and opens a small office window behind him with a sunny view of Biscayne Bay.

"Ahh, I love the smell of open water..." vents out Mr. Romero as he peers out the window, then continues his chat with Jaime. "So, Jaime, do you like your new apartment?" Mr. Romero then takes a seat behind his desk. An old-fashioned, hand-carved desk, which displays elegance and good taste but flooded with legal documents and all sorts of paperwork.

Jaime, who now wears a fashionable new jacket and open-collared shirt, sits uncomfortably across from Mr. Romero, feeling a bit out of place in the presence of the man who has helped him realize his dream of coming to the great United States of America, and with a sense of appreciation, he wholeheartedly tries to choose his words cautiously, and he finally intones to the old man, "Mr. Romero, I can never thank you enough for what you have done for me and the boys." Now smiling, Mr. Romero stretches in his leather chair and fixes his eyes on Jaime. By the looks of it, this is the office of a man who spends much time away from it, and it is evident by the piles of what seems to be work undone.

He then points upwards as he speaks, "Don't thank me, thank God." At this, Jaime frowns, and Mr. Romero pauses for a moment and then continues, "Do not judge me by the appearance of the office, I simply don't like it when anyone goes through my stuff, including my assistant and my secretary, and I'm always on the go. So there, that's an explanation."

Apologetic, Jaime replies, almost embarrassed in trying to cover his state of shock, "No, I was taken by your God comment, that's all. So, you are a man of God, huh? That explains."

Mr. Romero removes his reading glasses and curiously intones to Jaime, "Why do you say that? Aren't you?"

Jaime becomes awkwardly uncomfortable, and he fires right back, "Well, you know, in Cuba…"

Mr. Romero interrupts, "Yeah, in Cuba, they don't want you to have any faith other than in their communist agenda, right?"

"Yes," responds Jaime, and he continues to look around the office as an uncomfortable silence follows.

"Jaime, do you believe in miracles?" asks Mr. Romero, now a little more interested in Jaime's answer.

"Well, yeah. I'm here, aren't I? That is a miracle alright," responds Jaime in a child-like tone, and Mr. Romero now stands replying to Jaime's timely remark:

"That is indeed a miracle, my friend. It always is when God allows for someone like you and someone like me a chance to have the opportunities many in Cuba never will, and in that regard, any immigrant, anyone climbing from the bottom up. That is a miracle and a grand opportunity. It changes lives." There is a momentary pause, and Jaime finally agrees with Mr. Romero.

"Don't I know that?" Jaime reminds Mr. Romero with a half-smile, and Mr. Romero proceeds to explain, feeling almost responsible for having to show Jaime the ropes in America while digging deep inside his soul:

"Jaime, let me tell you something, and it is particularly important that you understand what I am about to say to you. You have great things coming your way, and since I feel responsible for bringing you and the boys here, I also feel the responsibility to pave the way for you by giving you much-needed advice. Now, it is completely up to you what you do with it." Jaime sits there motionless for a few moments, just trying to absorb the old man's advice.

Then he intones to his new mentor, "Thank you, Mr. Romero. I have had plenty of time to think about this, and I still cannot believe I am here in the US. But enough about me, what about you? You must really enjoy doing this, huh? Why would a man who has everything in the world take the time to help strangers like me and the boys?" Jaime asks.

Mr. Romero checks his throat and continues, almost changing the direction of the conversation, "Jaime, within two weeks, Panchi and Tito will sign with the Atlanta Braves. Chuchi with the Mariners, and Papo, bless his soul, with the Yankees. Jaime, we have you down as the initial contact and the reason the boys are all here. That means you will receive an exceptionally large commission check. You are going to make a lot of money, my friend, because you are the reason these clubs now have a chance at these players. Feel good about yourself and be proud of the work you have done."

Jaime is not sure he has heard right, and he quickly posts the following question to Mr. Romero, "Let me get this straight, Mr. Romero, they get paid just for signing? Don't they have to play for a while? And I get paid simply because…just because?"

Mr. Romero smiles at Jaime's naïve comment and replies in a soft and convincing tone, "This is America, my friend. I told you, you would not be cut out." Suddenly, disbelief becomes joy for Jaime.

Digging into his pocket, he pulls out, what else...? That is right...a cigar, and looking into Mr. Romero's eyes, Jaime excitedly offers him a cigar.

"This calls for a celebration... Whoa! Yeah, baby!" Jaime tries to persuade Mr. Romero, and before he accepts the cigar Jaime is about to hand him, he looks into Jaime's eyes, and the old man speaks softly...but firm, in wisdom and understanding:

"Jaime, remember that with much money comes much responsibility, and son, responsibility defines a man's character. Do you understand this?"

Jaime slowly nods in agreement, and after a short pause, he replies to the old man respectfully, "Yes, sir, I understand clearly. My uncle always said, to lose your honor is a crime against God." Mr. Romero, now pleased with Jaime's apparent full understanding, takes a deep breath while pressing a forced smile as if not very sure Jaime is truly grasping his hard-pressed advice.

But he goes along anyway, "Good, I wanted to make sure you understood this before the money you have never even heard of lands on your lap. Jaime, it is a whole bunch of money, my friend! All these papers here will tell you about it. Let us go over it."

As Jaime holds out the two cigars in his hand, Mr. Romero accepts one but regards it with suspicion while reading the cigar label, and Jaime explains, "Sorry, mine ran out, so I bought these at a newsstand outside your office." Mr. Romero looks at the cheap cigar, and they proceed to light up. Jaime takes a puff from the cigar and immediately gags. "I've smoked better rope. What is this? Don't you know any good cigar shops around here?" Jaime asks innocently after taking a quick puff at the apparent not-so-fine cigar with the fancy label, but after another puff, only a face of deep disgust expresses the nasty taste deriving from it. Mr. Romero smiles at Jaime, acknowledging his dislike for the cigar while they continue talking inside Mr. Romero's office.

"That good, huh?" Mr. Romero sarcastically asks, looking at Jaime as they discuss legal paperwork. As they sit there in each other's company, Mr. Romero begins to tell Jaime about the importance of learning how to budget and protect big bucks. Jaime does not understand much of it now, and he gets lost from time to time in trying to follow Mr. Romero explaining all the money talk, but he likes what he is hearing even if it sounds like a foreign language now, and he genuinely enjoys listening to Mr. Romero's wisdom and his intense ability to clarify all the complicated terms of the business lingo.

Mr. Romero has quickly become Jaime's new mentor, almost playing the role of his old uncle back in Cuba, who was always so accustomed to showering Jaime with good advice and common sense. After a few moments and following many instructions given by Mr. Romero, almost overwhelmed, Jaime has signed a bunch of paperwork related to his professional affiliation with the boys. Jaime then leaves Mr. Romero's office and decides to go out in search of a decent cigar. He takes a taxicab and heads back to Downtown Miami. Moments later, Jaime is spotted walking into several tobacco shops downtown. He walks out of the first shop; he unwraps a cigar and lights up. He takes a couple of expectant puffs and makes a face of disgust remarkably like the face he initially made inside Mr. Romero's office. He throws the cigar into an ashtray outside the fancy shop and walks away. Next, Jaime walks out of a newsstand not far from the first shop, and once again, he unwraps a cigar, lights up, and takes a couple of puffs only to make the same face of disgust. This time he spits into an ashtray, tosses the cigar in it, and walks away frustrated. Again, and again, Jaime walks in and out of several tobacco shops only to have the same disgusting experience, and he finally tosses one of the cigars into a trash can on the sidewalk with anger and walks away, nodding his head, even more frustrated. He continues to walk down the busy sidewalk and towards a taxi line by the curb, he gets into a cab, and they drive off.

That same evening at an Atlanta Braves press conference, Panchi and Tito are beaming in front of numerous cameras as they answer reporters' questions from many different television stations. Flashbulbs go off. Tito amuses reporters with a demonstration of his famous shortstop dance. Everyone laughs, enjoying his little performance. At a Seattle Mariners press conference, Chuchi confidently fields questions from reporters through an interpreter like he has been doing it all his life. Dressed like a shiny brand-new penny, the young man acts maturely as if he has done this his whole life.

Meanwhile, back in Miami, Jaime walks out of yet another tobacco shop; he lights up and makes the familiar face of disgust. At a New York Yankees' press conference, Papo leaps and literally whoops with joy as his dream of becoming a Yankee comes true. Reporters around him laugh at the childish demeanor, and all the flashbulbs catch his antics. A short acceptance speech follows, "Thank you and God bless America…that's all. As my English gets better, I will be making more interviews… Go, Yankees!" The reporters before him laugh and pat his back as he steps off the podium. The young man is truly in heaven. Outside one of the cigar shops, Jaime watches Papo's interview on television, and he laughs along with a few others who observe through the glass display window at the shop. Papo continues his chat with the reporters, "This is a dream come true for me! America is truly the greatest country in the whole world. I mean, where else can a man go from rags to riches in such a short time? Where else in the world do dreams come true in this Cinderella fashion, even for those who have not been allowed to dream their whole lives? This is 'genie in the bottle' stuff, this is amazing, unbelievable." At this, we take a step back as Jaime has a flashback of his family back home in Cuba… His old uncle, surrounded by family, sinks into a cozy chair with a cigar in his mouth and begins to tell one of his stories… One of the young cousins crawls up on the old man and takes a seat on his lap, sucking on his thumb. The old man puts his arm around the young boy and continues telling the now-familiar tale.

And back in the US… It is late at night, and Jaime has gone back to his home in Miami. A taxi pulls over next to the curb and tired Jaime gets out of the vehicle with just a briefcase in hand. He waives the driver off, and the cab drives away. Jaime is glad to be home at last, and as he walks in the door and turns on the lights, he rushes to the kitchen and makes himself a drink. Not interested in checking any messages, he ignores the flashing of his cell phone, letting know he has voicemails. He then walks straight to his bedroom. His apartment is now fully furnished with many pictures of the boys adorning the walls and sports memorabilia. Still fully dressed, he lies down on his bed with his eyes wide open, and he begins to think... He takes a few deep breaths and then places the glass on the nightstand next to the bed. He makes himself comfortable on top of the neatly made bed, and still wearing his shoes, he lies on his back, staring at the ceiling like he so often does. And just moments later, Jaime falls asleep peacefully. Jaime begins to dream... There is complete silence. An impenetrable, dark fog covers the land, and unlike the first dream, Jaime sees himself now as a young man in his teen years. Moving cautiously through the familiar fog...representing the turmoil in his life, he moves forward slowly... His outstretched arms feel blindly for guidance... He is lost. He sees the same dream figure from the previous and now-familiar dream up ahead, elusive in the mist... Hardly clear enough to see, the figure now glows with a soft light... Unmoving as if waiting, inviting in the near distance. "Who is it?" Jaime asks himself as he frowns with doubt and perhaps curiosity...and now closer to it, he looks down and sees his own bare feet walking amid small, green, leafy tobacco plants. He peers at the interesting figure a distance away as it slowly begins to disappear in the fog up ahead... Jaime again tries to try in defining the identity of the mysterious character, but it may be too late as the image is now gone, dissolving into the fog and leaving Jaime standing there all alone, empty and clueless, simply frustrated. "Who was that?" Jaime asks as he continues to lie in bed. Now in a deep sleep, he snores lightly, and the night moves slowly as he sleeps comfortably.

Early in the morning, Jaime jumps out of bed and runs to the shower. He gets dressed, and this time he skips his morning routine of one cup of Cuban coffee before hitting the road. He does not light up a cigar either. Jaime leaves his apartment in a rush and heads towards Mr. Romero's office. He flies out of the apartment building and calls a cab outside. He gets in, gives the driver hurried instructions, and they immediately take off. Upon arrival, the cab pulls over outside Mr. Romero's office, and a doorman approaches in a fancy uniform, Jaime runs out. He runs inside the office building, bypassing the reception desk and straight into the elevator. Inside Mr. Romero's office, Jaime does not stop at the door this time; he walks right in and tosses a half-dozen *cigar magazines* on the old man's desk. Mr. Romero, who is sitting at his desk writing, slowly lifts his head and looks at Jaime over his reading glasses, almost as if telling Jaime, he has lost his mind. Unapologetic, Jaime stands proud with both his arms pointing at the magazines...and almost out of breath and half-smiling, he finally speaks, "Yes, sir! I finally got it! I am ready for big changes in my life, Mr. Romero." Surprised, Mr. Romero glances down at all the magazines thrown on top of his desk and over a pile of important documents. He glances back at Jaime with a look of amazement and shock, and Jaime, feeling he owes Mr. Romero an explanation, proceeds to give his well-rehearsed speech. Unexpectedly, Mr. Romero patiently awaits it. Jaime clears his throat several times before he directs himself to the old man, "Mr. Romero, when you loaned me and the boys' money to get us started, that was an advance, right? When they signed their contracts and got paid, that was an advance, right? You took care of us when we first arrived as an advance. I mean, stop me if I am wrong. Well, I remember you once said to me that if I had the courage to risk my life leaving Cuba behind, my family, my life, and coming here the way we did, to a place where I did not speak the language and where I didn't know anybody, then I could do anything, right? I clearly remember you saying this!" Mr. Romero removes his reading glasses and stands in front of Jaime, a bit confused.

"Good morning to you too, Jaime! Okay, where are you going with this? Are you okay, son?" interestingly replies Mr. Romero, and with a curious frown, Jaime lights a cigar, offers one to Mr. Romero, who declines, and then Jaime, who pauses for a short moment, clears his throat yet again and proceeds:

"Gourmet cigar clubs, Mr. Romero. Nothing but the best cigars money can buy!" Mr. Romero stares at him hard... Jaime continues, "I'll be brief." Jaime begins pacing back and forth as he prepares to pitch his well-rehearsed plea to the old man, who patiently waits. "Mr. Romero, the smoking of a fine cigar is a time of contemplation, relaxation, and appreciation. I have said that a million times before only because I believe it. My uncle said it a million times too because he too believed it. A fine cigar is no different from fine wine or perhaps a great steak. Now, I have given this a lot of thought... You look around, and we live in an increasingly smoke-free environment. Fifteen years ago, secondhand smoke was something firemen worried about, but today the evening news tells us it is invading our restaurants and schools, and we should avoid it like the plague. The EPA blasts it as a 'known human carcinogen.' People do not really know what that means, but it sounds too close to another C-word, right? You enjoy cigars, I enjoy cigars, and there are probably other few out there who also enjoy smoking a fine cigar from time to time. So, where do we go without being a pariah? Mr. Romero, I am convinced there is a true market out there for a comfortable, guilt-free, hassle-free establishment that caters to cigar smokers who cannot smoke in peace anywhere else."

"You want to open a cigar club?" surprisingly asks Mr. Romero, who then scratches his head, looking down and as if expecting Jaime to withdraw his previous comment, but now that Jaime knows he has Mr. Romero's attention, he becomes even more passionate, and he lets it flow...just like in the movie *The King's Speech*.

"Yes! Envision it! A gentlemen's club for the cigar afficionado where for a modest membership fee, they can enjoy the best gourmet cigars, which cannot be found anywhere else... I know I have looked. In a relaxing atmosphere both soothing and private where businessmen and guys who just want to kick back after long office hours or just simply cigar lovers who want to indulge their pleasure. It is an untapped luxury, Mr. Romero! And with your help, we could import fine hand-rolled cigars from, say, Nicaragua, which has some of the finest tobacco outside of Cuba because of its similar soil and climate, and we can hire experts in the art under my supervision to make the best hand-rolled cigars just like my family used to back in Cuba. Mr. Romero, I guarantee you in a year, two at the latest, we could see a nice profit." Jaime quickly catches his breath after pausing for a moment and giving Mr. Romero a moment to react.

"So, you want me to help you import tobacco? replies Mr. Romero, a bit stunned and thinking Jaime has completely lost it.

"Yes! And…well…" As Jaime tries to come back… Mr. Romero interrupts him this time:

"Jaime, slow down for a second," clearing his throat, "and you need some seed money… Are you asking me for a business loan?" At this, Jaime spreads the magazines over the desk without saying a word.

"Not just a business loan, but also your contacts to allow us to be able to do this the way I envision it and going after the crème de la crème, I guess the right way. Nothing ordinary or mundane, nothing common. I have already done my research. There is a huge market, and people pay for the best, and with your help, I am in a unique position to give it to them. I am from Vuelta Abajo, Pinar del Rio, Home of the Cigar! The Colon family, my family, has seen some of the best tabaqueros in Vuelta Abajo for ten generations! Our tobacco produces the best tasting cigars in all of Cuba! Cigar-making is in my blood! I was crawling in tobacco fields before I could walk! And this…this is my dream, Mr. Romero. I know how to make a great cigar; God knows there is a great demand for it, and we owe it to the world to deliver on that promise. What do you say, Mr. Romero? Do you share even a glimpse of my vision?" Jaime has suddenly worked up quite the momentum, and he believes he has finally impressed Mr. Romero after completely exposing his mind and pouring his heart, or has he? And subsequently, after a tight moment of silence, the calm is finally broken by Jaime, who adds, breathless and almost out of words, "Mr. Romero… I have it all worked out. I know I can do this; I know it in my heart. What do you say?" Looking at his watch, Mr. Romero stands, and without saying anything at all, he walks up to Jaime and shakes his hand. The old man then softly pats Jaime on his face with an open hand, and he turns around and says nothing as he fixes several documents in his briefcase. Jaime is stunned. Defeated! Heartbroken and humiliated, Jaime turns around and walks out of Mr. Romero's office. He trudges crestfallen into the empty elevator with rejection written all over his face. He is more embarrassed than anything else, but even worse, he feels crushed as he knocks his head against the doors of the slowly descending elevator.

When the elevator finally stops all the way down at the bottom floor, Jaime exits, and as he passes through the sleek lobby toward the building's front glass doors, one of the receptionists at the desk calls out, handing him the telephone:

"Excuse me, Mr. Colon? It's for you, sir." Jaime stops, making a 360 turn in front of the reception desk, and he looks at the young lady who is holding out the phone in her hand. Jaime is perplexed. He walks over and takes it.

"Hello?" Jaime utters shyly and confused.

"Let me buy you lunch..." Mr. Romero asks at the other end of the telephone, and at this, Jaime, smiling, accepts:

"Yeah, sure... When? Where?"

Jaime and Mr. Romero meet in front of the office building just minutes later, and they walk across the street to a small restaurant with colorful umbrellas covering nicely decorated stainless-steel round tables in the courtyard. They talk over hearty plates of rice and black beans, Cuban steak, and fried bananas at one of the outside tables of the popular Cuban restaurant. The sign outside the restaurant reads, "El Soñador—Cuban Restaurant," which in Spanish means "The Dreamer," and what a fitting name as Jaime continues to glance at the restaurant sign over and over the entire time. The crowded little place, it's an ideally located restaurant in the middle of Downtown Miami, surrounded by office buildings and the usual madness of a busy city.

"So, we grow tobacco in Nicaragua, using the very finest of Cuban tobacco seed, and then we hand-roll cigars at a local factory here in Miami, and then we sell them locally?" Mr. Romero suggests.

"No, we hand-roll the cigars there, and then we bring them here already boxed and ready to sell. There are plenty of tax loopholes for Central American imports, I have done my homework. We use my uncle's traditional methods for the entire cigar operation, and the entire process is kept secret. The Colon family secrets stay alive, and we will give the world of cigars a product never seen before," adds Jaime, excited...

"So, let me get this straight, we import the cigars here already boxed, and we sell them at an exclusive club in Downtown Miami, right?" Mr. Romero inquires as the conversation turns into a war of one-liners.

"Yes, exactly. There is no embargo on Nicaragua, and we can produce a great cigar there. It is all in the way we treat and irrigate the soil, plant the tobacco, in the way we baby them, and, of course, in the way we hand-roll them. We keep it members-only, Mr. Romero, and we will put out a great cigar unmatched by the rest of the competition. We will make the world fall in love with our cigars, Mr. Romero. Cannot stop this train now... It is all in full gear and traveling at a hundred miles per hour. Can't you see it? Close your eyes for a moment, dream with me, Sir...I implore you. I beg you!"

Mr. Romero pauses, he looks away, and suddenly replies to Jaime, "You don't have to beg, Jaime, because your passion alone can move mountains, and you know what? I think your idea is crazy enough it just might work. You are crazy, son!" Jaime smiles...

"I know. I know. Thank you for believing in me." And the rest of their time at the restaurant they spend making plans and drawing out a strategy to begin working on Jaime's dream right away.

Just weeks later, Jaime and Mr. Romero begin preparing to fly to Nicaragua to scout the area where the cigar plantation and the factory will be assembled. And just like that, during a wide-open space, a small plane is spotted in the air flying over Central America. Inside the plane are Jaime, Mr. Romero, and a few business associates. Also on board is Mr. Romero's daughter, Stephanie, who sits across the aisle reading a poetry book. Stephanie looks almost out of place among a bunch of boring businessmen, but she does not seem to mind as she is lost in her reading. Mr. Romero has mentioned her many times before to Jaime, but this is the first time he brings her around and the first time they meet in person. Mr. Romero sits with Jaime next to the window, and the entire time all they talk about is business. Then suddenly, he approaches Jaime in an almost remorseful tone, "I apologize for bringing my daughter, Jaime. I thought I could talk her out of it, but she has never been to Central America, and when Stephanie sets her mind on something, forget it."

"She's not a problem; she seems very smart and prudent. Now the other guys, those guys you should have left back home. They just won't shut up…" Jaime tells Mr. Romero, smiling, but somehow Mr. Romero senses he is telling the truth. Perhaps the investor types may not be the most pleasant people to be around on a long trip, but this is the money behind the dream. These guys are forking out the cash to make Jaime's dream a reality. So, it is all tolerable.

"I know. We will leave them next time, but unless you promise me this is something we can do ourselves without any risk whatsoever, we need these guys' money for now. And by the way, I never invest my own money in any business venture, always use someone else's, OPM, other people's money. Sell the idea like you have the answer for world hunger, and you never have to worry about your own cash being at risk," Mr. Romero tells Jaime, who quickly adds:

"Yeah, I wondered about that, but I was embarrassed to ask."

Mr. Romero continues, "Any time there is risk involved but a promising opportunity on the table, I offer others to participate in making a profit while their seed money goes in first, and that way, we test the waters using their cash before we dive in with our own once it's all clear. I am already violating the first rule in investing, which is to 'never invest in anything you don't know or understand,' but I believe in you, though, and I believe in your dream, so I tell you the truth, I don't know much about cigars, I don't know anything about that business, but your passion and your vision are too strong to ignore. So, I am breaking the rules simply on a weird hunch here, I'm literally taking a chance on you." Jaime agrees by shaking his head, and his eyes grow misty, hearing the old man's words. Mr. Romero continues, "Now, Stephanie was a 4.0 student at the University of Miami, she majored in Economics. A whole different way of thinking from these old geezers, and she seems to love the idea. She is the one who sold them on it."

"Is that so? Wow! 4.0?" Jaime whistles and follows with a genuine innocent question, "What is 4.0?"

"Yeah, exactly..." counters Mr. Romero, thinking Jaime is bluffing and not knowing he really does not know what he is referring to by 4.0 because, in Cuba, they use a completely different method to calculate grade point average in school. Mr. Romero then fixes his tie, and he gives Jaime a strange look as he again pats him on his face. "You are one funny guy, Jaime."

The small private plane lands in an open field in Nicaragua just hours later, in a remote farming region called Jalapa Valley, where Mr. Romero's business associates have confirmed this to be a perfect spot for their endeavor. The lush green fields and rolling mountains are absolute paradise and remarkable like tobacco rival Cuba. The climate, the breeze, the colors are all indicative of a pleasant smile. Stephanie is stunned by the beauty of this place, and the others are completely hypnotized by the surroundings as well. After landing, they are all moved by bus to the tobacco fields through an empty rural road; nothing but God's humble creation all around. Jaime, Mr. Romero, and the others take notice of the beautiful country surrounding them in astonishment as they move closer towards the tobacco fields. Soon after, they begin to spot straw-hatted Nicaraguan workers laboring in a nearby tobacco field. There are hundreds of them. A few minutes later, the bus arrives at their destination and future tobacco plantation. Adjoining the small field, there are two structures there, an old curing barn and another smaller barn, which they intend to use as a cigar-rolling factory. There is nothing else for miles around, and Jaime likes it. He acknowledges the place as if he has picked it out himself. He is amazed, they all are. The bus stops, and they unload and begin to inspect the entire area. Jaime runs out first. As Stephanie gazes up at the blue sky and the sunshine, Mr. Romero and his associates watch Jaime carefully examine the tobacco plants, the soil, and the area. He slowly walks through the rows, chatting amiably with the workers and shaking their hands as he introduces himself. At the end of one of the rows, Jaime kneels and sifts the rich, jet-black soil through his fingers. "Perfect!" Jaime whispers, and

Mr. Romero's associates mutter among each other in recognition of Jaime's knowledge. Mr. Romero looks back at them, and they affirm by nodding their heads with wide smiles on their faces. They all walk through the tobacco field and eventually into the small cigar factory not far ahead. Once inside, Jaime smiles with his arms in the air, and Mr. Romero and his associates make faces of disgust as the rough, gutted barn has no electricity and only the dusty sunlight, which slices through bare windows and seeps through cracks in the wooden slatted walls, provides the ethereal half-light in which a dozen poor Nicaraguan cigar-rollers sit at benches rolling hundreds of cigars in not so good of a condition. Like the Colon family's factory back in Pinar del Rio, this is a small and primitive operation, unchanged for generations, and Jaime seems to love it, but Mr. Romero and his business partners have second thoughts. Mr. Romero watches as his business associates share a dubious glance...probably asking themselves, *this is really a cigar factory?* They look to Jaime, differing with his expertise, and Jaime simply nods enthusiastically... He loves it. He is all smiles, he is satisfied. The men with him, however, think differently as they walk outside, where Stephanie remains transfixed by the gorgeous, secluded landscape, where she continues to take photos with her cell phone. She listens to the birds singing with her eyes now closed, and Mr. Romero approaches. "Is my little girl bored?" asks Mr. Romero, and Stephanie replies with much enthusiasm:

"Are you kidding, Dad? This is beautiful. So peaceful, so untarnished by buildings and traffic, it truly feels like it has been placed right here just for me."

Mr. Romero jumps in and adds his two cents, "Well, it practically is. I always wanted to buy a little place in the middle of nowhere for you because I know how much you like nature, and this whole country is smaller than Florida, you know? They can certainly use our business here, and that was Jaime's idea, Stephanie. I will not take credit for it; the man is a true genius if you ask me. How did he know without ever coming here before?" Stephanie smiles shyly at Jaime and touches her father's leathery cheek...

"I know, Daddy. And Mr. Colon, I think you have a wonderful idea. 'The ancestor to every action is a thought...' you know?"

"Ralph Waldo Emerson… Great writer, great thinker," replies Jaime with a smile, at which Stephanie is completely surprised that he knows the quote, and Jaime adds, grinning, "Yeah, we read books in Cuba too." Stephanie smiles back at him, feeling somewhat stupid, and Jaime returns the smile.

Mr. Romero steps in, "Cuba is actually the only country in the world where there is zero illiteracy, did you know that? The entire country knows how to read and write. Even back in the '40s and '50s, wealthy American families sent their kids to school there, and then the man with the beard took over in '59, and all hell broke loose. Now he trades a good education for freedom…because for some reason he does not think people should have both," explains Mr. Romero…and Stephanie and Jaime listen curiously.

Jaime and Mr. Romero enjoy their time in Nicaragua as they inspect the area to fit their plans for their cigar operation, but that same day Stephanie and the investors fly back to the US. Jaime, however, and his mentor Mr. Romero spend a well-deserved time alone and away from the rest of the world as they continue to draw a map for their cigar plantation's future. After working nonstop and with almost no sleep, Jaime has mapped out a perfect blueprint for the cigar operation. Just a few months later, Mr. Romero's business partners have bought Jaime's idea in its entirety. They have invested even more money than originally discussed for the expansion of the old tobacco field and the factory, suddenly bringing the operation to full motion.

With things now up and running smoothly and business moving in the right direction, Mr. Romero asks his daughter Stephanie and her team to launch an international advertising campaign using the latest marketing tools to begin to make the *Ijaba Cigars* brand recognized worldwide as the cigars they produce are nothing short of an amazing delicacy behind the exquisite elaborate work Jaime demands. The workers at the cigar factory and on the fields fall in line behind Jaime's specific measures, closely following all the original instructions given by his old uncle. The results are just what Jaime expected as Ijaba Cigars turn out to be a top-notch product in a class all by itself in the form of possibly the next best cigar the world has seen. And then suddenly, Mr. Romero and his business associates decide to invite a neutral group of world-renown cigar connoisseurs to come in and inspect their fabulous merchandise. At the end of their visit, they unanimously agree that, and I quote, "Ijaba Cigars are just a raw perfection and a joyous opportunity for the cigar afficionado in its purest form." And unexpectedly, this single review causes a restless curiosity among cigar lovers everywhere, and it instantly begins to make a splash in the world of cigars. When questions about the sudden success of Ijaba Cigars arise, especially "What is the secret to your out-of-this-world creation?" Jaime simply responds by saying, "When those in the cigar business curiously and impatiently ask what the secret to our out-of-this-world-creation is, I simply tell them… Ijaba Cigars is nothing, but the product of an ancient family secret and a tradition once used by our ancestors for generations to come while creating nothing but the best tasting cigar. We kept it alive using traditional earth flavors, unique spices, which produce freshness and a distinctive flavor, which gives our cigars its exceptional taste and a unique aroma that is unmistakable. Plus, its delicate texture, it is to die for. Just nothing but an exceptional display of the best leaf selection and rolling etiquette, also a family pride dating back for centuries. To top it off, even the appearance and presentation of these fine specimen of extraordinary cigars are impressive. Now answer this, how can anyone match such a heavenly and authentic perfection?" To which question silence always follows, creating even more questions…suspense and intrigue!

Just after a few more months have passed, there are now twice as many field workers and twice as many cigar rollers in the factory who crank out more and more cigars. These magnificent cigars are a delightful product of desire and prideful elaborate work, excellence at its best. The competition asks many questions, but no one can explain the unique enchanting taste in these cigars. What is the secret? What is the recipe? What is the formula? But to no avail, and business hits its peak. In only a short period of time, Jaime's cigar business is now named after his family's legacy, "The Colon Cigar

Factory," and they have improved production by more than 50 percent. The workers, always willing to work, keep the operation moving in full gear as Jaime works alongside them as equal, and this inspires them. After another six months have gone by, back in the US, sitting outside their now-favorite Cuban restaurant, Mr. Romero and Jaime have a strategic business meeting with their associates to expand their operation. At the same time, at one of the other outside tables, a man reads a sports magazine, and the cover reads: "Overnight success for Cuban Bullet." The magazine features a full-page color spread of Chuchi looking grand in his Seattle Mariners uniform. "When life moves, it moves fast…" it reads… Consequently, one of the shops next to the restaurant, which has outside display windows, shows on TV two sportscasters give plaudit as game footage of Chuchi bunting and running like crazy to first base… Also, on TV: Panchi and Tito appear together on a late-night talk show. Tito demonstrates his little dance, and the talk show host comically tries to imitate it, almost falling to the ground. The audience breaks into laughter. On another channel: Papo appears alongside hipster Vee-Jay to introduce a new music video. Sneaking a product endorsement, he holds up a sneaker that lights up. As Jaime takes notice of all this, his eyes water with excitement at all the publicity the boys are receiving, and he stands and walks away from the table to recover his composure. Mr. Romeo follows Jaime, and handing him a napkin, he adds, "Jaime, get used to it, son, this is only the beginning for those boys and for you, my friend, so be ready. The sky is the limit."

Living the Dream

JUST A FEW WEEKS later… Arriving at the Miami Airport, crates of cigar boxes are opened and examined by customs officials. Jaime and Mr. Romero observe. Impatient, Jaime jostles up and takes out one of the many fresh cigar boxes contained inside. "Here you go, Mr. Romero, put these inside the humidor in your office. These don't taste like rope. I am going to fill your humidor, and I will make sure it stays full all the time." The brand-new cigar box is lavishly old-fashioned, recalling classic stone lithograph artwork from a century ago. It features the image of a young black African princess who represents Jaime's ancestor, Ijaba. The box reads, "Ijaba Cigars," as Jaime has officially named his cigar brand after his ancestor to keep her memory alive.

A short time goes by, maybe a few more weeks or so, and it is now nighttime. Mr. Romero and his business associates take Jaime to a surprise dinner… Supposedly! As they arrive at the mysterious location, they cannot help but see a huge spotlight waving through the Miami night sky heralding. As they approach the bright sign at the elegant new location, it reads, "Ijaba Cigar Club—Miami." The hoopla of the red carpet opening outside a high-class club catches Jaime by surprise. He tries to look for Mr. Romero, but he is nowhere to be found, letting Jaime enjoy this moment by stepping away from all the action. Jaime is stunned by the surprise celebration, and he can barely contain his emotion. He weeps as Mr. Romero steps aside, keeping low-key and allowing Jaime to have this moment of triumph. Jaime cannot believe his eyes as a Latino-dominated crowd of well-dressed people Jaime does not even know is all in attendance.

Limousines and cameras flash as VIPs appear, a complete nonstop parade of guests have shown up at the grand opening of the club. Truly in shock, as he reads the discreet and tasteful sign, Jaime becomes teary-eyed. "Ijaba Cigar Club—Miami." His eyes grow misty in disbelief, his heart pounds in excitement, and what a glorious moment this is. Inside the club, there is a classy party as Cuban music plays.

The tropical décor of the club is designed with a relaxing, private atmosphere but classy and chic, but tonight is a social celebration. Over a few hundred guests, friends, a few sports stars, and even a few celebrities dance, drink, and smoke cigars. Surprisingly, there are several women with cigars in hand, and Jaime likes it. Just like he envisioned it. Jaime spots Mr. Romero and Stephanie, and he waves. Mr. Romero, who continues to keep his presence low-key in the corner of the room, is regal in a tuxedo. He approaches Jaime and gives him a hug and congratulates him. Stephanie, lovely in a designer gown, mingles shyly with some of the guests. She excuses herself and, like her father, hugs Jaime and congratulates him as well. "You did it, Jaime. You did it!" she tells him with a sincere smile, and as Jaime looks around, all he can do is smile back and admire the moment in disbelief. His dream has now become a reality. Unable to contain his tears, he thanks Mr. Romero as he tries to hide his emotion with his typical man ego by quickly wiping the tears before they become too obvious. Jaime can only hope his ancestor Ijaba, the little African princess who became a slave and who later inspired generations of her descendants, including Jaime, is now looking down at him, and at this very moment, her name has come to life again in the form of a fine hand-rolled cigar brand. Ijaba's name lives again!

Inside the club, there is a fully stacked bar, plush booths, luxurious couches, and chairs. Also, an arcade area with antique pinball machines, billiards, and video games. The place is filled with a jubilant crowd, and Jaime loves it. There are tasteful display cases of exclusive Ijaba products: shirts, cigar boxes, humidors, cigar storage tubes, cigar cutters, and all sorts of accessories. Also, there is an entire wall full of all kinds of different hats with the Ijaba Cigars logo on them, and the food here is just exceptional as Jaime has hired the best chef in all of Miami to perform his finest culinary art skills. Suddenly, Jaime almost leaps with joy when he spots the boys walking towards him; all four of them are here. Jaime screams in one breath, "You guys! Great to have you here! My God, who put this thing together? I did not even know... What the heck are you guys doing here? Don't you have games?" And Jaime, almost out of breath, just stands there with open arms. The boys run to him, and they hug as a group.

"Papa... We got it under control. Just relax and enjoy your night. This is all about you right now," answers Chuchi with a smile while hugging his good friend Jaime, he grabs his drink and walks back with Papo, Tito, and Panchi, and they all stand a few feet away watching the show.

Mr. Romero places his arm over Jaime's shoulder and gives him the answer to his previous question, "Why do you want to know who put this thing together? See, Jaime, you have good friends. You are one of the lucky few in this world who do, cherish it, enjoy it. Friends are priceless, and friends do this kind of things for their friends." He then pauses and softly pats Jaime's face as he now has accustomed to.

Suddenly, Stephanie steps in, "Oh, Dad...You are always trying to preach. Just enjoy the night, Jaime, the moment. We all pitched in a little bit of our time. Between daddy and his friends, they organized this whole thing and put this party together for you. At first, they thought you were crazy, but now they all think you are a genius, go figure."

"Wow, I don't know what to say..." exclaims Jaime, surprised as he looks around. The boys all wave at Jaime, who, like an excited little boy, raises his glass and drinks a toast. They also raise their glasses from their table across the room. The four young men, who have all flown in for this momentous occasion, would not have missed it for the world. Stephanie and Mr. Romero also join them in a toast. Humorously, the boys have all worn matching Hawaiian shirts, and they too have a toast among themselves. They all raise their glasses, Stephanie, Mr. Romero, Jaime, and the boys, and they drink a rowdy toast. Jaime is truly seeing his dream come true as he takes notice of this splendid moment. As the night continues, they drink and eat, and, of course, they smoke several cigars together in the private room of the club, but Jaime keeps busy talking to reporters who have come to experience the opening of the new Ijaba Cigar Club. The grand opening of the club is a complete success, but the boys' time with Jaime is short-lived. They know there will be more time for fun, besides, this is supposed to be Jaime's night, and so they end up only staying for a few hours because they all have games the following day, but the important thing is, they came, and they were part of Jaime's club's grand opening like good friends do even though it was such a short celebration as they have to fly right back and get ready for their games the next day. These are the true small sacrifices and the kind that matter, honest tangible moments that last.

As the party continues, now in full swing, a voluptuous Latino reporter who is part of all the media in attendance corners Jaime with a microphone, and her cameraman follows close behind: "Excuse me, Mr. Colon, Jackie Lopez, with Channel 8 News. Now, Mr. Colon… Why a cigar club, may I ask?" Jaime looks up, and a cameraman is filming.

So, he clears his throat and replies as politically as he can with a cigar in hand and a bit nervous, "And why not a cigar club? Gourmet coffee shops have café lattés, I have the finest cigars. Let me remind you: 'The smoking of a fine cigar is a time for contemplation, relaxation, and appreciation,' my old uncle always said." Looking for approval, Jaime puffs on his cigar, expecting a positive response.

"Looks like you have a huge success on your hands. Now, why do you think no one has had this much success doing something like this before?" the young reporter asks, expecting a serious answer from Jaime.

"Hmm? Good question. Let me think here… Why didn't the Egyptians invent the telephone in 1500 BC? Timing is everything, my dear," Jaime follows in a sarcastic tone, not really having the answer, and the young reporter laughs and continues with the interview:

"You have had an illustrious last couple of years, defecting from Cuba, leaving family behind, a government-sponsored job. Now, Mr. Colon, I understand you come from a family of cigar makers… Is that right? Taba...queros? Is that how you say it?" She tries not to mispronounce it...and he helps her:

"Tabaqueros... Yes, and they taught me how to enjoy life for an hour or two..." Jaime adds, and the reporter tags along with timid curiosity:

"An hour, Mr. Colon?" she asks, and Jaime fires right back:

"Hey, if you can smoke a cigar in less than an hour, it's not the best. Okay? Smoking a fine cigar is not a sprint, but more like a marathon. You look around, enjoy the moment, the company, and you usually have a nice topic of discussion in conversation or a nice drink in hand."

The young reporter, now acting coyly, throws Jaime a curveball, "Maybe you'll have to teach me sometime. This whole cigar thing is kind of interesting, even for us girls." She eyes him with interest, and Jaime proceeds innocently, just talking about cigars, but she has other ideas in mind.

"Definitely. Why not? You do not have to be a man to indulge in the finest tobacco sold anywhere in America. To appreciate good company, have a drink and relax for a little while. There are plenty of beautiful women here, like you. This place is now home to all of you, cigars are no longer a man thing, so welcome!"

"Why, thank you, Mr. Colon. I understand Ijaba means 'a wish fulfilled.' Is that correct?" Jackie replies coquettishly, and Jaime looks at her square in the eye, and if he did not know any better, he could swear she was flirting with him right in front of the camera.

"Very good, you have certainly done your homework."

As the party winds down and most of the people in attendance have now left, a limo driver holds the door for Mr. Romero as he embraces Jaime with sincere, fatherly pride and admiration. "I am immensely proud of you. I'm sorry if I had my doubts at first, but your persistence was such this whole thing had no choice but to happen for you."

"For us," Jaime adds, and Mr. Romero immediately follows:

"This is only the beginning for you, son. Do not allow anything or anybody to put out your fire. This is special, remember that. Use it to your advantage, for your purpose, use it to do well, and do not become careless or greedy. Never fall in love with money, for money is a snake that can bite you while you are sleeping, and always remember where you came from, your roots and the roots of your dreams will guide you." An uncomfortable silence follows.

"Yes, sir. I will remember that". Jaime replies, and Mr. Romero and Jaime shake hands. Stephanie offers her cheek, and Jaime gives her a soft kiss. They get in the limo and drive away. Jaime then returns to the corner of the room, where a few friends are still hanging out, drinking, and having a good time. He finishes his drink, then he tells them it is time to go, bids them all a good night, and he leaves the club. He stops on his way to the taxicab several times and looks back at the sign with the name of his new club in lights. He smiles as he lifts his right hand, holding a cigar as if bidding good night to his dream, now a reality.

Moments later, a taxi pulls up outside a small apartment building, and Jaime gets out. Slightly drunk, he reaches in the car and takes someone's hand. It is none other than our sexy news reporter Jackie, who looks up at the building but remains in the cab. "This is where you live? I expected something…hmmm! Perhaps more promising," she says to Jaime without any prudence, and somewhat disappointed and embarrassed, Jaime notices the cab driver has heard her rude comment, and he quickly tries to counter her smart remark:

"Well,…you know, I put everything into the club for the last eight months. It was just a small sacrifice for a while…" He then bends down and kisses her tenderly, but she glances back at his disappointing apartment building and replies with little interest:

"Nah, probably not a good idea, Jaime. It is late, and I have a long day tomorrow. Maybe another day."

Jaime, caught by surprise, quickly tries to offer a valid reason to justify his current living situation, "Wait a minute, Ms. Jackie, don't just judge the book by its cover so quickly, maybe the inside walls of the apartment are made of gold. Never know! Unless…" He humorously attempts to change her mind, but she quickly interrupts him with haste before he can finish his apologetic comeback:

"Oh no, Mr. Colon, this girl doesn't go for kissing the frog first and hoping it turns into a prince. The outside is always important. The house, the car, the wallet… Don't be fooled by fairy tales." He scoffs and then giggles a bit nervous, but he doesn't have a response for her as she just smiles with hurtful cynicism. "Perhaps our next interview can be at your new condo in Miami Beach, Mr. Colon. You know some Realtors work around the clock, yes, 24/7… It's a thing you know!" Then she smiles and closes the car door… And just like that, the taxi drives off. Jaime stands there all alone, half-drunk, and completely embarrassed at the obvious materialistic remark by the young woman.

What did I do wrong? What happened there? Am I losing touch… Huh, am I losing it? This is a nice place… Isn't it? Jaime asks himself, looking back at the building, which to him and in comparison, with his home in Cuba is a very nice apartment, but unable to cope with reality, his drunkenness has overtaken any realistic chance of understanding what just happened. Besides, whatever the young woman said to him does not hit home quite just yet, and the alcohol consumed is much stronger than his ego at this very moment. Feeling numb, he decides to ignore the insulting episode and walks upstairs, and goes right to bed, putting an end to the eventful evening.

Decisions, Decisions, Decisions...

Several months have now gone by, and all Jaime has done is work on his dream like a dog day and night. He has barely had any sleep as he flies back and forth between Miami and Nicaragua, trying to build a strong enough foundation for his tobacco business so that it will be able to sustain itself even after he is gone, through thick and thin, and for many years to come enduring any possible economic hiccups along the way. It is apparent Jaime has been listening well to Mr. Romero, and he has learned a thing or two about building and running a successful business and about having to work extremely hard to build a dream. Nothing comes easy in this world; nothing is handed to you in life. If you want it, you must go get it. As Jaime walks down the street by himself after shooting a television commercial for Ijaba Cigars, he suddenly spots one of the tobacco shops he visited when he first came to America. To his surprise, the shop now features a massive display of Ijaba retail: there are Ijaba cigars, a cascade of Ijaba T-shirts, humidors, cigar cutters, storage tubes, and more; a complete sign of success. And sure enough, prominently displayed in front of the store is a poster with the largest issue of *Gourmet Cigar* magazine, which features Jaime's face on the cover. "Wow! That was quick!" Jaime exclaims after noticing the magazine cover, and he reflects for a moment and reminisces about everything he has had to go through to arrive at this point of his life.

He thinks about all the decisions he has made in the past leading to this moment, some easy ones and some painful ones too. All the people he has left behind and all the people he may never see ever again. He reminisces about his inability to save everyone along the way, although he wanted to, and he is now beginning to understand for the first time that in life, choices must be made, and sometimes if you save yourself first, then, and only then you can go back and save many. But if you sink with the ship, then everyone else dies too. Sacrifices! This simple lesson Jaime learned the day he boarded his first airplane when the flight attendant gave the preflight instructions as they so commonly do before departure, and it stuck in his head: "If you are traveling with a child, first put on your oxygen mask, then the child's..." Thus, acknowledging that if you are not able to help yourself, how then can you attempt to help anyone else? Pick yourself up and place yourself in a position of power by becoming an asset or by being a contributor instead of being a drain on others by simply being a liability. Be a person of value! Hmm...?

The best way to explain this is not just working like a dog all the time and leaving no time or energy for yourself, which is exactly what Jaime has been doing as he's had no time to enjoy the money his cigar business is making him nor has, he made time to go see the boys play.

And looking back at the not-so-distant fateful evening when at the hands of a young reporter, Jaime felt as if he was not worthy of her company simply because of where he lived; he understands that we do live in a material world. And was it his insecurity? Perhaps his sense of needing someone by his side to share the success he was suddenly having...who knows? However, this lingers inside his head, swirling other ideas that bring about so many questions to an already perturbed man, and he asks, *does wearing expensive name-brand clothes make a man more intelligent? How about driving an expensive car, does it guarantee you are going to reach where you are going? If you buy or build a multimillion-dollar home, does it mean you will enjoy luxury? How about marrying a wealthy person, will it guarantee a happy marriage? And does winning an argument mean that you are right? Hmm?* Jaime remembers his uncle telling him once that "the clothes a man without wisdom wears doesn't make him any smarter, but it can certainly help open doors that otherwise would have remained closed... only to expose his foolish character the minute he opens his mouth!"

The clothes you wear do not make you! Just like the cleats, an athlete wears will never make him any faster on the field. But a man's ego can pitch him the perfect and unrealistic scenario of the many unnecessary needs he is missing in order to find happiness, and that is just nonsense impulses driven only by a voice that does not come from a good place. The possession lie… I am what I drive, where I live, and what I wear. Seriously though, I am not that! What we do to impress people doesn't matter! "Our ego is the right voice to ignore," Mr. Romero tells Jaime, and though he remembers this, he probably should have consulted with Mr. Romero first, but he didn't, and instead of finding happiness, he was only trying to avoid pain remembering how the young reporter had made him feel refusing to come up to his apartment.

In all honesty, Mr. Romero would have advised him to continue working on building his dream and not to worry about the car he drove or the home he lived in, both of which he would have ample time to secure to his complete satisfaction once his dream was accomplished and fulfilled to his total satisfaction. However, based on Jaime's present emotional state, he would not have listened even if Mr. Romero were standing right in front of him. It is incredibly deceptive and purely mockery to see how human beings can be so easily fooled by their ego when cornered by self-doubt and desolation.

Sometime later, Jaime has now bought one of the suites at the pan-up high-rise apartment building in Miami, a million-dollar apartment. He wanted to make sure he would never feel the way he felt that fateful night when Jackie, the young reporter, refused to come up to his humble apartment. Apparently, Jaime forgot for an instant where he came from, like it often happens to many of us, and he will not be the first or the last to forget his roots as he climbs the ladder of success. Many are those who go from rags to riches, suddenly forgetting the rags part of their lives, it is easy to do and perhaps convenient but let's face it, Jaime now has the means to afford such a luxury, after all, money is beginning to flow like milk and honey, and lack thereof is not an issue anymore. So, he treated himself as he called it, feeling he deserved it after all his hard work. Pan-up is a sleek modern apartment building with some of the best views in all Miami, and when Jaime told the Realtor to find him the best, he was not kidding. The bright sun glints off expensive glass and steel architecture here at Jaime's new home. It is truly an impressive private building that declares success and accomplishment. But does it really make Jaime any better a man than he already is? Does it add another hair to his head? Unfortunately, currently, people believe they are judged by where they live and what they drive... Talk about vanity! Reality check! Hello! But in all reality, the opposite is often the case, as described in the book *The Millionaire Next Door* by Thomas J. Stanley and William D. Danko, where the authors compare the behavior of those who are truly wealthy, and to their surprise and mine, real millionaires devote their income to savings and investments rather than luxury goods and status.

For the wealthy and in their wealthy minds, it isn't uncommon to find some who are worth millions driving an older model car that is paid in full and living in modest neighborhoods as they share their idea that in America, we like spending tomorrow's cash today, which is the leading cause of debt and lack of net worth accumulation. See, they think right, and Mr. Romero tried explaining these small details to Jaime once upon a time, and I am sure he probably thought Jaime was listening, or was he?

In the meantime, at the front entrance of the building, a uniform doorman opens the door for Jaime as he leaves his new home. "Good morning, Mr. Colon," the doorman at the luxury condominium greets Jaime, and as he exits his new residence with pleasure, he looks back at the reflection on the sparkling glass wall behind him, and he cannot believe his eyes. He pinches himself over and over in accepting reality.

"I still can't believe I am really here," Jaime whispers as he walks away from his new home, and he heads towards the beach, walking along the sidewalk. He takes notice of all that is going on around him, and he admires his new neighborhood. "Look at this right here in front of my eyes, at my fingertips at last. I am finally starting to live the American dream. This is the dream and the life. Only in America!"

Jaime stops at a corner coffee shop, he buys a newspaper, and a new magazine suddenly catches his eye. He grabs it and begins to read from it. Jaime has a cup of coffee and calls Mr. Romero from the coffee shop, and he agrees to meet with him at his house. A few hours later, they meet. Reading aloud from the magazine with his picture on the cover, Jaime strolls with Mr. Romero outside his house and along a private stretch of beach, both smoking cigars.

"'Due in no small part to Colon's good looks and flair for promotion, Ijaba Cigars have transcended its status as a celebrity den of sports stars, politicos, and movie stars. It now claims the most trendsetting VIPs of all… Rap stars and the beautiful women that accompany them. When interviewed, these elite moguls-to-be say they enjoy the elegant power Jaime Colon's club surrounds them with.'" Jaime chuckles. "How about that? What do you think, Mr. Romero?"

Mr. Romero slows to a stop and intones to Jaime without looking him in the eye, "Did you invite me out here to read about how cool you are now? Please say it is not so, because I have a million things to do inside." Jaime stops beside him catching his attention and grins…

"No, not at all. I have another idea that is crazy enough, it just might work. I came to talk to you about something I only wanted to say in person. Can you please hear me out?" Removing his sunglasses, Mr. Romero turns his gaze to Jaime, who smiles at his mentor, paying close attention as their eyes meet.

America Is Indeed the Land of Opportunity

It is now nighttime, and inside the Ijaba Cigar Club, the usual happening environment is alive. Great business, as usual. A few models take pictures at the front entrance of the club, and inside, a group of young rappers hangs out at the bar, each with a cigar in his mouth as a production crew sets up to begin shooting a music video. Bright lights adorn the front of the club, and even the palm trees outside are lit up and dressed in Miami fashion. The club is relaxing and discreet. Cuban music enhances the tropical atmosphere with a vibrant style where several couples dance almost in rehearsed mode. Other patrons retreat to the plush booths, couches, and chairs, while some congregate in the arcade area talking and having a good time. In one of the private rooms, several elderly couples celebrate their anniversaries where Jaime has graciously comped all their drinks, and several servers and club employees attend to them. In other private rooms, businessmen smoke their favorite style of cigars. Perhaps a celebrity or two are here as well, a few familiar faces that are all treated like family and not like movie stars also hang out at Jaime's cigar club.

The display cases of exclusive Ijaba products are all well stocked and growing, from torpedoes to robustos, panatela, and anything you can think of related to cigars, the club has it all. This place is what all cigar afficionados in the area had been waiting for. Another room is stacked with cigar humidors of all sizes. Seriously, nothing but an exclusive array of the most beautiful hand-carved wooden humidors. The club is a complete smash, a success. In a quiet VIP room, Jaime, his lawyer Hiram Triana, and Chuchi sit over a bottle of Havana Club, Cuba's best rum, and a gift from Hiram to Jaime imported from Canada, where it is legal.

"Hey, Chuchi, do you mind if Hiram hangs around? He is my lawyer and good friend. I introduced you guys, right?" Triana offers his hand, and Chuchi shakes it.

"It is a pleasure to finally meet the Bullet. You are one exceptional ball player."

"Uh-oh. Yes, sir, same here. Pleasure to meet you, and thank you for the compliment," Chuchi staggers his words…and shakes the lawyer's hand.

"Go ahead and shake his hand, he doesn't bite; he doesn't bite my friends anyway. Get it? Sharks…Lawyers…" humorously adds Jaime, and they all laugh, shaking hands. Jaime then turns to Chuchi again. "So, you bought a beach house here in Miami, huh? I hear things…" They click glasses, and Chuchi replies:

"Yeah, good news travels fast. Plus, you know me, I like the sun, but how did you know, really? I figured you would be too busy with all of this to pay attention to gossip," replies Chuchi sarcastically, and Jaime responds:

"'I hear things,' I said, but no, you, my young friend, like the thongs, the bikinis, I know you, Chuchi. Sometimes I feel like I gave birth to you guys instead of your mothers."

"Oh, really? Well, I am closer to you now because someone has got to keep an eye on you, Papa. Your ugly face on magazine covers? The next thing you know: 'Eligible bachelor eaten alive by the rich and famous, the young and beautiful and the miserable and lonely.' Soap opera stuff!" And at this, Jaime stands up to his feet, a bit uncomfortable and almost upset.

"What is it with everybody? Do I look lonely?"

Chuchi quickly tries to calm Jaime down to not ignite an argument between them, "Come on, Papa, chill, I'm just kidding, man… Whoa! Come down. Testy, aren't we?" Jaime instantly downs his rum, and he pours another.

"Chuchi, you're acting like a nagging wife, I don't need a wife, what I need is a new investor. I am going to expand, and that's why I asked you to meet me."

Chuchi looks at Jaime and responds, "Jaime, you've only been open, what, eleven months?"

"Twelve. To be exact," adds Jaime.

"So just enjoy it for a while, like one of your fine cigars. Why expand? Why now?" Chuchi replies with brotherly concern, and Jaime quickly fires right back to make his point:

"Why? You really want to know why I want to expand? Well, first, because this is America and I can, and second, because timing is everything and the time is now. Are you interested or not?" Chuchi looks at Jaime, glass poised halfway to his mouth, suddenly realizing with utter surprise he has been made an offer. The lawyer grins, and putting his glasses on, he places a few pieces of paper in front of Chuchi.

"You didn't think I was here for my charm, did you? Just sign these disclosure forms so that I can approve of what Jaime has in mind for you, and I will get out of your hair. I will prepare the rest of the paperwork, and I will mail it to you this week. My office will follow up." Chuchi is not only surprised, but he is also flattered that out of all the people in the world, Jaime has chosen him to be his new partner.

"Thank you, Papa, this means a lot to me. When I saw the lawyer here, I was not sure what to think. Besides, I need to do something with all that money sitting in the bank collecting less than one percent in interest." Jaime gives Chuchi an uncompromising look and winks his eye. Chuchi winks back, Jaime smiles and then adds:

"Exactly! We are in business then, little brother. I did not want all this success all to myself. The sky is the limit now."

Business Expands and Family Reunites

BACK AT THE JALAPA Valley region in Nicaragua, cigar production of Ijaba Cigars has hit an all-time high at the Colon tobacco factory. The initial limited production of Ijaba Cigars does not meet its early demands, and distributors and sales reps of the new sensation in the cigar world have pushed to expand sales through the roof and not just throughout the entire country, but also South America and Europe now. The supply rooms are being emptied as quickly as they are stocked, and Jaime loves it and agrees that this is certainly a good problem to have. Jaime and his business associates know they must nourish their little golden egg in order to see it reach its full potential, and so they begin to pay more attention to their Nicaraguan operation in order to compete with the giants of the tobacco industry who are now taking notice of Ijaba Cigars and its sudden success.

Rumors of possible attempts to try to buy Jaime out are beginning to circulate, but with Chuchi now on board as Jaime's new business partner and his financial backing, there is much more room to grow, and Jaime's vision expands even more. Jaime and Chuchi make the original business associates Mr. Romero had brought in an offer they cannot refuse, and they end up buying them out completely, making Chuchi and Jaime now the only ones in control of Ijaba Cigars. Seeing his dream is in great shape and heading in the right direction to becoming realized to the fullest, Jaime tells Mr. Romero he wants to spend more time in Nicaragua. He decides to fly there every week to supervise the factory and the fields in person and only returning to Miami on the weekends. Chuchi and Jaime agree to split duties in running the operation during the baseball off-season, but Jaime tells his young protégé he wants him to take control of the cigar club in Miami while Jaime controls everything that goes on in Nicaragua, in other words, Jaime handles all the production end of the business, and Chuchi manages sales, distribution, and marketing.

Now that Jaime has direct control of the way things needed to run in Nicaragua, he immediately takes notice of the poor irrigation system and decides to fix it. He does so by signing agreements with the Nicaraguan government to radically renovate their water and drainage system in the entire area of the country by bringing in American engineers to adequately update it with an effort to provide potable water to this remote area of the country and control all flooding, which for years has devastated many of the farming areas. Jaime also places protective nets over the area where the younger tobacco plants grow in the Colon Tobacco Plantation to protect them from pesticides and bugs that feed off the tobacco plants.

Suddenly, with great results taking place, all the hard work is paying off for Jaime as cigar production continues to grow beyond his wildest dreams. The Nicaraguan government has also acknowledged Jaime's innovative and humanitarian efforts, praising him publicly by having him appear on different nationally recognized television shows to discuss his good deeds and presenting him with many prestigious awards for his company's efforts to improve and help the community.

To this point, everything has been running smoothly with the cigar operation, and everyone is happy, especially Jaime, who works as hard, if not harder than some of the workers at the tobacco fields and the factory. He is always the first one to arrive, often before the sun rises, and he is usually the last one to go home; many times, in the late hours of the night and for many months, Jaime and everyone around him work endlessly to make all the improvements necessary to take their tobacco operation to the next level, hoping the tedious work continues to pay off. The people around Jaime hope their efforts also pay off, but Jaime does not just hope, he knows exactly where all this is going, he feels it.

Several months go by, and Jaime has barely had any time for himself. He has been so busy building his dream he has become completely consumed by it and does nothing but work, except for when Chuchi and his pals pay an occasional visit to the area, and that's the only time Jaime takes off to entertain them and spend time with his good friend.

In the early hours of the morning, Chuchi, Mr. Romero, and a few others have just landed at the nearby airfield. They arrive at the tobacco fields, and only the peaceful sound of birds singing and scattered voices of Nicaraguan field workers are heard as they labor in the now greatly expanded tobacco fields. Mr. Romero, Chuchi, and several others become completely shocked at all the new advancements Jaime and his crew have made at the Colon cigar plantation; this looks like a different place. The visitors watch as Jaime walks through the tobacco rows, examining the plants and chatting with the workers from a short distance away. The entire tobacco operation has now been expanded and renovated greatly, and all the hard work and dedication are paying off vastly.

Back in Miami, more and more crates of Ijaba Cigars continue to arrive. Jaime, who continues to work his normal long hours, does not know Chuchi and the others are here, and he carries on with his daily routine. He is now as sunburned as his old uncle back in Cuba and all his workers on the field, and if they did not know any better, he is just one of them. Jaime has made sure to earn his workers' respect by working among them as equal, and this is his way of showing them he is no better and no smarter but simply a man proud of his work and living his dream. He not only pays their salaries, but he also inspires these people to perform their daily work with pride and honor, knowing their hard labor is being recognized and appreciated. Jaime stops to demonstrate to a younger worker with a spray bottle how to care for the plants, telling him that once the aroma spray soaks into the tobacco leaves and it's absorbed by them, it nourishes the plant, and it also gives it a unique and distinctive flavor when the cigar is rolled. These aromas include earthly tones, rum, different herbs, fruits, and even charcoal, giving Ijaba Cigars a wide variety of unique flavors for the cigar aficionado to indulge in. Other field workers take notice of Jaime's genuine love for his business, and as his employees, they look forward to working hard for Jaime, who treats them well and just like family. These are hardworking people who make almost nothing working elsewhere, and most of them have had little or no hope of ever having a good-paying job, but Jaime is making things different for the workers who now feel appreciated and are paid much better wages for their labor. Many of them do not know how to read and write, they do not have any health insurance, and if they are let go tomorrow, they have nothing left, but Jaime intends on changing all this one day. Some of the people who work in these parts of the country are devoted tabaqueros, but for the purpose of making a true difference, Jaime has found a way to have some of them sent here from all areas of the country to work. Among them are also some who are misfits in society, ex-addicts, alcoholics, men and women who have had criminal issues in the past, and it even includes women of the night and ex-prostitutes. Within the laborers, we can also find glue-sniffing kids from the streets of Managua, the capital of Nicaragua, who are brought here by churches to try to heal them from their addiction and to offer them some form of rehabilitation through work. What Jaime has offered them is clearly an opportunity to help reinstate these people back into society, and this is his way of giving back and showing appreciation to the country and the people of Nicaragua who have made it possible for him to produce his now world-renown cigars. "If only I could have done this back in Cuba, it would have given much joy, but since it could not be there and this is where we ended up, then so be it. It is ideal. It is working well, and I am incredibly grateful for it. So why change a good thing? It has all fallen into place almost perfectly, and by the way, have you had your Ijaba Cigar today?" Jaime points at the camera smiling as he explains during a television interview the sudden success of his business, why he opened it here in Nicaragua out of all places, and the many questions everyone has about some of the people he employs. Jaime continues, "Do you know why these children as young as seven- and eight-years-old sniff glue out there in the streets of these poor areas? It is because the chemicals in it are so strong it gets them so high, and this way, they can forget about hunger, cold, or whatever misfortune they might be feeling after sleeping in dumpsters and in the streets. Sometimes, they bunch up in groups of eight and ten orphan children because it is easier to survive in the streets if they stay together. They can protect each other from molesters, child traffickers, and people who try to take advantage of lonely orphan children in the streets of Managua," explains Jaime, who recently learned this from local social service offices, and he has now made a move to help with this. He keeps on in front of the cameras even more fired up now, "Also, by gathering all the food they collect as a group, of course, there is more variety in their meals, mainly made up of food found in trash cans and leftovers. This sad but fact about the forgotten children in the streets of Nicaragua, whom we have made an oath to protect as part of this project, is a concern, and we are trying to help." Jaime's huge heart and ambition to want to help these great people have not only helped acquire hardworking, grateful individuals who have now become full-time permanent employees, but he is also doing a great deed in saving and reshaping lives. Jaime's redemptive work does not go unnoticed just by those he helps, but also the word now begins to spread outside the tobacco plantation, and many influential channels are hearing of the good news. The Nicaraguan government has taken notice of these great deeds, and more help has begun to arrive in the form of transportation to and from the confines of the cigar plantation, food, and even medical assistance for the workers. All this ignited by Jaime and his dream.

Inside the barn cigar factory, the number of cigar rollers cramped in the rough, gutted barn has tripled since the expansion. The laborers sit elbow-to-elbow hand-rolling cigars at a rapid pace, and Mr. Romero, Chuchi, and the others watch carefully, often in mouth-opening awe at their ability to do their work with such efficiency and dedication. This is an incredible showcase of fantastic cigar-rolling skills, but still, there is no electricity, and no bathrooms, except for the outhouses around the barn factory. It is dim and claustrophobic inside, but the workers look at Jaime and smile, who smiles back but remains undisturbed examining the labor, and he knows the time has come to make it better for them. "We are going to need a bigger boat," Jaime tells Mr. Romero noticing the uncomfortable conditions, which to them is just life as usual in these remote parts, but while seeing these people's desire to work hard for him, Jaime knows it is time.

"I know. It is all happening too fast," the old man replies to Jaime and walks away. Jaime puffs on his cigar stub, thinking, planning.

Just a few days later, an old-fashioned community barn-raising is underway. Hired Nicaraguan locals seem incredibly happy to be employed as they construct a large new cigar factory. Entire families crawl on scaffolding, hoist beams, and hammer away. All this may sound primitive by our standards, but these humble peasants know how to work with their hands. There are just a few lumber trucks in sight, but no bulldozers and no ravaging the land. Suddenly, from behind a pile of dirt pulls up a big electrical truck, and everyone claps and cheers loudly. Nearby, more workers are expanding the tobacco fields by several hundred acres as Jaime watches proudly, talking to himself, "Yeah, we're going to need a bigger boat alright, and someone very qualified to steer it..." Jaime decides to fly back to Miami after a routine hard week of work to meet with his mentor, Mr. Romero. The following day he and Mr. Romero find themselves at their favorite Cuban restaurant having a late lunch; alone. The two men enjoy a delicious lunch along with a couple of cigars and, of course, the usual Cuban coffee as they discuss Jaime's new ideas for their cigar operation. "So, I ask myself, Mr. Romero, where does a guy like me find the most qualified tabaquero in the world to supervise this outfit?" Jaime sarcastically asks in a very diplomatic manner, and slowly, Mr. Romero grins with understanding.

"Okay...Give me a month. I will see what I can do..." And exactly a month later, at a tiny rural airport in Nicaragua, not too far from Jaime's tobacco fields, a small airplane unloads a handful of passengers on a dirt airfield. Mr. Romero watches a short distance away as Jaime runs out with open arms to greet his old uncle, grandmother, his idealistic young cousin, and a dozen other members of the Colon family as they step down off the small airplane. They all look petrified and thrilled at the same time as Jaime finally embraces them in an emotion-charged reunion. They greet each other loudly, and full of excitement as touching tears run down their faces.

"My know-it-all nephew from Havana shows me a day I never dreamed I would live to see," screams the old uncle, making sure Jaime hears him high above all the noise and excitement of the moment, with tears of joy running down his sun-browned face.

"I dreamed it for you, Tio. I did," Jaime answers, also with pleasant tears in his eyes, and after he hugs and kisses the old man, he runs to his old grandmother, who is the last one off the plane. Jaime carefully picks her up, sending her old sandals flying into the air. The old lady weeps silently at the emotional reunion, unable to say one word, and she holds on to Jaime, tightly pressing against his chest and mumbling joyous words in Spanish. She does not want to let go, and neither does Jaime. Their emotional hug seems everlasting, and it is charged with much passion and love.

Following this, Jaime has arranged to have several vans transport the entire Colon family to a nearby hotel where they can clean up, eat and celebrate their arrival to freedom after the long, exciting journey. Even though all the Colon family members who have just arrived did not have to go through the same dramatic process as Jaime and the boys to escape from Cuba, they too had to escape, and this is a definite reason to celebrate. The way Jaime snuck them out of Cuba and to freedom was quite dangerous and, like most Cubans who escape, each unique. He had arranged for a speedboat to take them away from the southern coast of Cuba down to the beaches of Cancun, and from there, Jaime had them delivered to him much like a precious overnight UPS package to Nicaragua. They were all transported in a van from their home in Pinar del Rio to an isolated beach area, and for several hours they all hid inside bushes in a secluded area very close to where the Bay of Pigs invasion took place back in 1961, in the southern part of Cuba. In a remote swampy area located near the coast, the Colon family waited until the boat arrived. Then they were cramped into the speedboat and taken all the way to Cancun, where the Mexican coast guard had been paid off to ignore the speeding boat coming through. From there, they all jumped into the small airplane that finally brought them to Nicaragua. The two men who served as guides in making the whole deal go through also stayed with them, and they are now free men as well. This was Jaime's gift to them for their loyalty, and they sure appreciated his grand gesture. The following morning as the celebration continues, Jaime has a surprise plan. Once again, the entire Colon family is transported by the same vans, but this time Jaime is taking them to the new and beautiful cigar plantation, which still sits among the lush green fields and rolling mountains of the Jalapa Valley but has been completely renovated. The new cigar factory, now filled with scores of new workers and cigar rollers, is large, clean, and well-lit. The workers listen to a local radio station in Spanish as they hand-roll cigars, and a few infants play in playpens while their parents work.

The old factory is now being used as a second curing barn where women string harvested tobacco leaves along fifteen-foot-high rows of horizontal wooden poles, literally sewing them in place with large needles to allow them to dry up while windows and doors are open for air curing. The fresh smell of young tobacco leaf is rich, the ambiance inviting, and everyone seems so happy here, the old uncle certainly is, and suddenly, he directs himself to Jaime with much exhilaration, "Jaime, please tell me I have a job here?" Jaime smiles and replies gracefully to the old man who stares at him with the eyes of someone who happens to be expecting exceptionally good news.

"No jodas (Are you kidding me)? Tio, this whole place is yours to run. Who can do a better job? Who is more qualified?" At this, the old uncle begins to giggle in disbelief, just like a five-year-old opening gifts on his first Christmas. Jaime enjoys this moment, and the old man begins to dance comically in celebration.

Just days later, in the early hours of the morning and while still dark outside, it is the old man's first day at work, and he and Jaime take a walk around the cigar plantation. The old uncle, excited and confident, wearing a sharply pressed guayabera shirt, licks his finger to test the wind and then calmly sighs with his eyes closed as a sign of approval. He smiles again with a face that expresses wisdom but mostly gratitude. It's beautiful out here, and even though it is still dark outside, a thin layer of new daylight hovers over the mountains as the first rays of sunlight slowly begin to appear in the pitch-dark sky. As the horizon begins to slowly brighten with the coming of the sun, Jaime and his uncle each puff on a cigar; proud and in high spirits, the two men prepare the way for the new workday by setting up the work schedule before any of the laborers set foot on the field. The weekend comes fast, and Jaime flies to Miami as usual. He and Mr. Romero get together to go over routine paperwork and business prospectus inside his office. Mr. Romero gazes at Biscayne Bay out his open window. "I love the smell of open water…" Jaime strolls around the office, smoking a cigar in his designer label clothes, and he is all passion and confidence.

"I know this may sound crazy, but, Mr. Romero, if you can recall…"

"Let me guess? Crazy enough, it just might work? I remember," the old man implies finishing Jaime's sentence, and Jaime fires right back at him with much enthusiasm:

"No, wait. Just listen, I know we can do this. I already have three churches willing to sponsor." Mr. Romero turns to face Jaime and begins reading from the documents Jaime has handed him.

"Oh, no! Now you have really lost it. You want to hire ex-cons and former drug addicts?" Mr. Romero asks, surprised.

"I've already been doing that, Mr. Romero…just didn't want to tell just yet until it was all in place. It works," replies Jaime, a bit uncomfortable, and Mr. Romero smiles at him and points with his index finger.

"Be careful, Jaime…" Jaime glances at Mr. Romero with the innocence of a child but with the sudden wisdom, he has quickly acquired from his old uncle in running the cigar operation in

Nicaragua. Working alongside the old uncle, Jaime has quickly learned how to run his cigar operation from the man who taught him everything about life, and running the business is not much different if one applies quite simple but critical rules.

"Such as 'if you say you are going to do something, you do it, and if you do it, you do it right. The same goes for anything you write down in the form of a business plan. You design it in your mind first, then you transfer the ideas to paper by writing them down, and then you put it all into action. No sense in wasting time, no procrastination, all basic stuff, and nothing new. The same way it was done a hundred years ago, that is the way we do it today. Why reinvent the wheel?' This is the old uncle's simple way of running the show, running the business. Plus, half a century of experience behind rolling cigars to perfection, picking the best leaves, treating and irrigating the soil, selecting the seed that will produce the best harvest, and a few other important facts about running a successful tobacco business. Nothing too complicated if you have been doing this for many, many years, right? Oh, and the most important part behind a successful business, any business, is making sure the employees are treated fairly. Treating the workforce behind any business in the same manner one would like to be treated almost guarantees instant success. It creates a state of comfort, knowing that if the workers perform their duties with enthusiasm, then the rest is easy, just guiding along and supervising the result," Jaime finishes his long speech and is just amazed at how easy the old uncle makes it all look, but it is indeed an extremely complicated process that not just anyone can do. After all, the goal is making the finest cigar in the world, no big deal, right? No pressure.

Right about a month later, back in Nicaragua, at the Jalapa Valley region, like an orating prophet in the sun, wearing a straw hat and holding a spray bottle, the old uncle gives his colorful spiel to dozens of ex-cons and former addicts, young and old. Some are scarred, some or most tattooed, and they carry years of struggle in their eyes, but they all listen to the old man like little children at story time and in appreciation of the new opportunity given to them.

Jaime turns to Mr. Romero, who watches, surprised. "Who needs compassion more than those who've been chained their whole lives, huh?" asks Jaime, and Mr. Romero nods in agreement as they leave and go back to the factory where a line of new and old workers stand outside to begin their day, and Mr. Romero asks:

"How in the world did you get this to fly, Jaime?"

"Well, I don't know. I just had a hunch, a feeling. See, I offered to teach them a trade when no one else will give them a chance. I demanded excellence and respect in return, and I allow them to find self-worth and value in their lives by being part of something making them feel worthy. I doubt many of them will blow this second chance but if they do, if any of these men and women here decide to throw away this grand opportunity, then shame on them. 'Losing your dignity is a crime against God, and no man can escape from the wrath that comes with it,' my uncle always said," Jaime explains and looks away, following his emotional words. He then spots his old uncle, who sits at a table peering down through new spectacles to make sure each worker signs a confidentiality agreement. The old man shakes his head as some of these people mark an "X" instead of their names or a signature because they do not know how to read and write as many who live in these remote areas have never been inside a school before. Honestly, some have never even held a pencil in their hand.

Not too far from where Jaime's uncle is with the workers, a couple of ministers oversee this charitable operation they have now sponsored in Nicaragua. This is truly a good thing they are doing here, and the ministers know that without Jaime's help, some of these people do not stand a chance in life. Meanwhile in Miami, Jaime and Mr. Romero sit in his office, and they go over a new business plan Jaime has presented to him. This time the material is much thicker, Jaime much more passionate about his intentions, he sits there serious as Mr. Romero rifles through the pages almost in disbelief. Mr. Romero lights a cigar, and he continues, fixed in the documents before him. "Okay, Jaime, let me get this straight, you need my help because I'm a humanitarian with inscrutable contacts in the, shall we say, import/export business?"

"Mr. Romero, you know everyone, and a lot of people owe you favors. You are in a great position to help me out with this."

"I see…Anything else?" Mr. Romero anticipates something coming, and before he can say another word, Jaime speaks again:

"I want to give them pensions, yes, a monetary reserve they can tap into later in life when they need it. Think about it, that is unheard of around here," Jaime adds proudly. "Can you imagine pensions in this neck of the woods? In this corrupted corner of the world where only a handful own everything, and the rest just handle the workforce? Mr. Romero, if we are going to make a difference, let it be something that leaves a mark. If we are going to do this, we will do it right and with an everlasting impact, don't you think?" Jaime continues proudly, and Mr. Romero has heard it all, believing Jaime has completely gone mad.

"Come on, Jaime, what are my ears hearing? And exactly how are you going to do this? These people are not ready for all that; they are content to just have a job. You are doing plenty already."

"I don't know, but we'll figure it out," Jaime tells Mr. Romero confidently while patting him on the back, but he walks away a bit concerned about how exactly he is to put this huge endeavor together. As Mr. Romero kicks around all possibilities, he sees a tornado of ideas flying before his very eyes, but he becomes troubled thinking that Jaime may want to do too much for people who may not appreciate all that he is trying to do, and maybe they're just not ready, and as they battle with these new ideas, questions to continue to arise… Can they pull this one out? Can Jaime really accomplish an idea that may only work in theory but never in practice? Can these people be trusted to straighten their lives after such a short time? Can an addict really recover from their addiction for good? All these questions with only speculations of a positive result make matters complicated for Jaime and those who try to help because, on top of it all, it is a huge gamble for sure. Jaime tries to act as if everything is under control. He sees a lot further out than anyone else around him, and his vision allows him to walk confidently towards that ultimate goal, and towards an unclear finish line only he sees, leading only to a positive conclusion to prove the presumption he felt all along. They say all geniuses have one thing in common, they seem crazy to everyone else, but also only genius understands what no one else does. They see a triangle when everyone sees a circle, and they can stay calm in the middle of a storm, knowing that not one hair on their head will be harmed when everyone else panics. Call it faith; call it confidence, I like to call it simply knowing. When you know that you know, nothing can stop you. Nothing needs to make any sense to anyone else but you, and no one must believe you either. Only you need to know, and so long as you believe in your idea, that is all the power you will need to conquer it.

Meanwhile, everyone else seems content to just watch because remember that we live in a world of watchers, spectators, and only a handful of participators. Jaime is one of those individuals willing to take a chance, regardless of what everyone else thinks.

In Nicaragua, out in the tobacco fields, the young fervent cousin supervises new workers who treat the now-irrigated soil to protect it from insects and bugs. The old uncle does what he does best as he instructs new cigar rollers the proper way to select the best leaves. Jaime, however, continues to work on his plan. This once incredulous plan, which involves paying the laborers well above what they have ever been paid before and treating them with respect and not as cheap labor, is slowly proving to be an effective masterpiece as not one of these so-called misfits has failed to meet Jaime's expectations. These people who were all dread to society not too long ago have now become an intricate part of what is possibly shaping to be the next up-and-coming giant of the cigar world. Jaime believes deep in his heart in return, they will continue to perform their jobs with pride and integrity, having found self-worth and purpose in life.

Jaime wants to show the world that people can change if given the opportunity. Suddenly, the risky venture, which Jaime knew all too well would take some time and hard work to develop, is paying the high dividend, and who would have known? Believe it or not, in a very short period, Jaime's tobacco operation begins to show much improvement with the help of many folks the world has long gone given up on, and in Jaime's mind, if it could only have worked sooner, how many more lives could he have saved?

At the tobacco fields, workers erect elaborate protective nets over the fields of young tobacco plants while the church ministers watch. They are all caught in a state of disbelief and extremely impressed at the vast improvements made in such a short time, and not just the improvements made to the cigar operation and the factory, but the incredible turnaround by the people, the workers, who just a few months prior were begging on the streets to support their addiction. Now, these men work for Jaime, and they have literally transformed their lives. One of the ministers scratches his head and mutters to the others taking notice of all the changes in the people. Jaime smiles…and with an amusing tone, he adds, "People can change, Pastor, people can change." The following day Jaime stands on a grassy field with some of the ex-cons and ex-addict workers throwing a baseball back and forth and goofing around together as equals. Jaime tosses the ball to one of the ministers, who surprisingly catches it with a comical acrobatic move, and everyone laughs. The old uncle approaches, and pointing at his watch, he tells everyone, "Break is over! Back to work, guys!" Jaime keeps in mind his main objective, working like a dog to make his cigars known to the world, but at the same time, he knows the importance of trying to enjoy himself in the process, and this includes mingling with his workers from time to time. He has been working endless hours since they began their project, and it is beginning to show. Jaime looks tired and worn down, but it does not seem to face him… He has a dream to fulfill. Days and months slowly go by, and as the cigar production continues to grow, so does Jaime's desire to see his dream through. Many times, he stands there and stares at nothing, just envisioning a not-so-distant future for the Colon Cigar business when the name Ijaba Cigars has a complete global expansion.

It is a beautiful Monday morning, and Jaime wakes up earlier than all the others, and he goes for a walk as the sun comes up. The lush fields and purple rolling mountains glow with the amber rising sun, the new expanded cigar plantation is well-ordered and impressive. Birds chirp… Jaime goes back to the house and brings his old grandma with him. They now stand at a hilltop overlooking the valley. The two of them, though generations apart, hold hands together, but neither one says a word as they survey the breathtakingly beautiful view, Jaime is proud of his achievement. Grandma kisses him and begins to hum an old song. Jaime recognizes the sad song, and he directs himself to the old grandma with concern. "What are you thinking, Abuela?"

"What do I think? I'm eighty-seven years old, and I've left my home and all I've ever known, if anyone cares what an old woman thinks…" Approaching, lighting a cigar, the old uncle overhears.

"Viejita (my dear old lady), that home you left, Abuela, has been gone since 1959. We did not leave it either; it left us a long time ago."

Jaime places his arm over his old grandmother's shoulder, and as he turns to her, he whispers softly, "This is your new home, Abuela." The old lady grabs both Jaime's hands, and a lonesome tear rolls down her face.

She then replies, "And I am incredibly happy to be here with you, Jaime. Thank you for everything, son. I love you so very much!"

"Then why the tears, Abuela?" Jaime asks, and she replies:

"My sadness comes from having to say goodbye to my home, Jaime. In all honesty, I cannot say I miss the misery. I do not miss the desolation, the…" Suddenly, she breaks into emotional tears, remembering her surroundings back home, her circumstances, and the painful life she lived as a proud woman who always tried to be strong for her family through it all. She places her arms around Jaime's waist, and she kisses him with much adoration. She smiles, and then she adds, "I love it here, I really do, Jaime, but Cuba will always be home."

Jaime Hits the Big Time!

"Hollywood," reads the famous sign, which can be seen from miles away, and it glows as the Californian sun reflects on the hard-to-miss gigantic letters. Beautiful palm trees that only grow here in the farthest southwest end of the country let us know we are in the land of the sun. The people of California alone accent the Golden State as multi-cultures collide in a colorful melting pot of immigrants and locals coincide just like in Miami. Los Angeles is an iconic place where natives and new arrivals from all over the world exist side by side, from surfers to corporate suits, bikini babes in roller skates, Hispanics, Asians, people from all over the Middle East, Central Americans, South Americans, Hawaiians, and all islanders and descendants from every race and corner of the world we can think of, crowd the busy ambiance of this magical place. California is not only beautiful but also an incredible display of a perfect mixture of colorful human art and perfect weather. Not just ethnic differences, but social and economic diversity as well. In Beverly Hills, where a homeless man rolls his cart with his personal belongings past a multimillion-dollar mansion and at Venice Beach, a tanned, blonde-hair beach bum carefully places his surfboard on the back of his convertible Volkswagen and calmly heads back to USC to teach a political science class; where a rich, runaway girl from the Midwest plays her guitar with a collection hat next to her to help pay for an almost unaffordable one-bedroom apartment by the beach, and she sits on the sidewalk wearing only flip-flops, ripped jeans and a tie-dyed T-shirt.

From the looks of it, it is obvious she may very well be a new arrival at the Golden State and a transplant, now a Californian. The girl looks up and notices a tall, thin man in Rollerblades who skates past wearing a turban on his head and an unusual outfit like that of a Persian sultan, playing his guitar. This man has been there forever, and he has become a fixture here at Venice Beach, with his picture appearing on many paintings and even billboards of the area.

As the girl picks up a postcard and continues to write on it to send back home, she smiles as the man's picture is on the postcard as the well-known trademark of Venice Beach he is, expressing the freedom this place has to offer where from beach bums to hippies to suit-wearing corporate types, Venice has it all.

California is the second-largest state in the country and home to a fascinating display of different cultures, making it a delight for both visitors and residents. The hot sun, the Pacific Ocean, and the mountains rising from every angle and in no specific direction clash together, harmoniously and welcoming anyone who dares to dream. A billboard on the side of the massive freeway where about a dozen different routes connect displays a most fitting sign, "Welcome to Hollywood." Land of the sun! The freeway looks like a massive connection of spaghetti strings and what fine engineering and design where the traffic is horrendous, but it always gets you where you are going. Jaime loves it, his first time here, and he now has his sight on "Ijaba Cigars Los Angeles" to expand out west and to a whole new entrepreneurial level of success. And just like that, Jaime's once crazy idea has now invaded Los Angeles as well. "We are in California, baby!" exclaims Jaime as he is interviewed by a journalist from one of many Spanish television networks here in LA, Telemundo. The man interviewing Jaime, who is completely amazed at how quickly Ijaba Cigars have spread from one corner of the country all the way out west, insists on wanting to know how Jaime has been able to accomplish such a difficult undertaking in such a short time but Jaime dodges all questions with an indirect answer, and he gives his now trademark answer, "Hey, I believe God knocks on all doors...

and whoever answers! Bingo!" Jaime's dream has rapidly reached a point even he never expected, and after surprisingly wrapping the entire South Florida tobacco world under his thumb, Jaime, Mr. Romero, and their business associates have now taken their business to Hollywood, where it is also a smash.

The glamor of Southern California combined with the sudden success of Ijaba Cigars; it is a match made in heaven. The new location has elevated the short-lived success of Ijaba Cigars to a point where no one had ever imagined, certainly not Jaime. The much-anticipated opening night of Ijaba Hollywood turns into such a monstrous event one could swear it was the hottest movie to come out in years and written by the best screenplay writer in the business.

As they prepare for the grand opening ceremony of Jaime's newest location, cameras flash, and the usual multitude of paparazzi here in LA stand along the curb as a carousel of limousines begins to pull in front of the building and along the sidewalk. A line of uniformed policemen keeps a large group of fans away from the slow-moving vehicles as the guests begin to arrive. Celebrities, movie stars, and all sorts of famous people parade the red-carpet spectacle as only Tinsel Town can host it. An extremely large, shiny, elegant limousine approaches the front of the club, and Jaime slowly rolls down the dark tinted window and sticks his head out. He takes notice of the huge glowing sign in front of the new building, which reads, "Ijaba Hollywood," in bright colors. Jaime smiles proudly.

Like stars in tuxedos, Jaime and Chuchi emerge from their limo to an assault of flashbulbs, shouts, and cheers. Reporters try to interview them as they walk through the multitude, but bodyguards avoid the mob, and they finally make their way inside, where a toast awaits them. Jaime and Chuchi join the ribbon-cutting ceremony, and following this, once again, the celebration goes into the late hours of the night. The grand opening of Ijaba Hollywood is a complete success as the new location could not be more ideal… Fine cigars in a world of beautiful and famous people, I repeat… A match made in heaven, but before they can say much and before allowing the opening of the grandest cigar club around to sink in, Jaime and Chuchi have expanded again. This time… Las Vegas! And then suddenly… Welcome to *Las Vegas*! The City of Lights. In the blink of an eye, the Las Vegas strip is now being invaded by Ijaba Cigars as the blinding neon extravagance of all the bright casinos is an adult circus and a sore eye for Jaime, who has never been here before, and he is just shocked and not shy about it as he twists and turns to try not to miss anything. It is apparent Mr. Romero and his business associates have been working nonstop promoting their cigars through a huge marketing campaign in trying to establish Ijaba in the most centralized markets, and Las Vegas could not have been left out. We spot Jaime, who emerges excited from yet another limo with a cigar in mouth and under high-watt lights for another red-carpet opening, this time of the brand-new Ijaba Las Vegas. And once again, they cut a ribbon, and the celebration goes into the late hours of the night. Jaime, surrounded by both friends and strangers as the lively crowd of partiers fills the new hot spot in town, shines like a brand-new penny. Ijaba Las Vegas is such a huge splash, instead of celebrating in one of the many world-renowned nightclubs here in the City of Lights, everyone comes to Jaime's club, and I mean everyone. A den of celebrities gathers at the opening of Jaime's new club to celebrate with him, and ironically there are no overly expensive bottles of liquor to toast with, but fine Ijaba Cigars are handed out in celebration of the new spot in town. Everyone in attendance holds a cigar in hand. The women, too, all wearing designer gowns, look almost funny, each with a cigar in hand. A smooth cloud of smoke hovers over the large gathering of friends and strangers, but before they can take much time to absorb the new expansion, the once small business has now become a global sensation, and, of course, New York City must be next. At a distance, the famous New York City skyline is lit up as always, and a new sign has now been added to it… What else? Ijaba, New York. Jaime steps down from yet another limo with a cigar in the mouth and amid more flashing bulbs and glitterati for a New York red-carpet treatment. He is all smiles, and he points at Chuchi with the thrill of this historic occasion. Jaime shakes his good friend's hand and whispers in his ear, "We did it, little brother, we did it. New York City? Are you kidding me? This is the Mecca of all Mecca..." Chuchi, along with everyone else in attendance, is proud of his good friend. Jaime, like the rookie that he is, continues to amaze every person here with his naïve comments and childish demeanor as he knows he is blessed to have this opportunity; he is thankful and grateful and not haughty and deserving. His pleasant personality welcomes the media bumblebees, making them all feel right at home, and all they write about Jaime and his cigars is nothing but spectacular. Even in a city like New York, which is home to the most critically acclaimed and brutally honest journalists in the world who are well known for being cruelly honest, and "cruel" being the essential part of this comment. Everyone knows at times these exceptional journalists and writers can beat anyone down to a pulp, and some newcomers to the city of New York find it difficult adapting to such sincere and brutal honesty. Many are those who end up leaving or completely going into hiding in NY because they cannot take the harsh forward approach. These writers and journalists are the best at what they do to get their stories, but so far, Jaime's experience has been nothing but positive, and he likes the idea of waking up next to a reporter sitting on his bedside at any given time or simply camping out outside his front door. I am exaggerating, of course, when I say, "...waking up next to a reporter," but Jaime likes the attention, and he does not mind their direct and to-the-point, brutally honest style, and even their dry humor. He says their sincerity shows their passion for their work, and that is the only way he would want it. "I hate hypocrisy, I despise fraud and lies, and as long as you guys don't make up anything about me that isn't true, I will always give you the time to publish my truth. I am a wide-open book if you guys continue to be a sharp writing machine. Deal?" Jaime tells them while in front of the cameras and offering several cigars to the reporters. The small crowd of New York media reporters laughs, and he pats them all on the back one by one as he leaves, and so far, they seem to love Jaime.

Perhaps Jaime makes a clear comparison between New York reporters and himself back in Cuba when he played a role a bit similar, only Jaime could not be as straightforward and passionate about his job because he was doing exactly what he was told. So, he can completely relate to what some may call annoying reporters as simply passionate professionals simply doing the job they love.

In the morning, Jaime takes off from his hotel, and he has a taxi take him down to Columbus Circle, where he takes a shopping stroll in Manhattan; his first time all alone in the Big Apple. Jaime immediately falls in love with New York City. It reminds him of Old Havana in so many ways, the old buildings, the crowds, the traditions, and the history. After a few hours walking around the city, he now carries expensive designer shopping bags as he strolls around enjoying the culture and the sights. Suddenly, he stops for a hot dog and a cold Coca-Cola reminding him of his first Coke in America. He slowly drinks from the refreshing soda pop, and everything around him moves in slow motion. For those who have always had Coca-Cola at your fingertips, you will never know what it must feel like to have your first ever as an adult, which was the case for Jaime, and it is truly an experience you never forget. Jaime cherishes it, remembering his first when he arrived in Miami just a short time ago, and he has a conversation with himself. "Having your first Coca-Cola is like seeing the sun for the first time. I still remember mine. I remember seeing the old Coca-Cola billboards only on pictures and in movies back home, and I always wondered if I would see the day when I would be able to have my very own. Crazy, huh? Something so lightly taken by just about everyone in the US and around the world," Jaime thinks out loud, and looking like a million dollars, he now strolls through crowded Columbus Circle in Manhattan. Jaime is amused by all the pigeons he sees and suddenly coming upon a four-man salsa group playing for a crowd, Jaime pauses for a moment, and they seem familiar... He suddenly has a flashback... Jose Marti International Airport—Havana, Cuba... The same four-man salsa group entertains passengers waiting in ticket lines in the Cuban airport departure terminal. Armed soldiers watch the activity. Jaime recognizes them, and without hesitating, he pulls out his wallet, and with a magnanimous smile, he drops several hundred-dollar bills in their collection hat. The group stops playing for a moment...astonished. Then they continue at a joyful double rhythm as they notice the money in the hat but do not recognize Jaime. How could they? He looks like a new man; he glows with prominence. People around them become inspired by the happy sound and begin to dance; more money now begins to be dropped into the hat. Jaime smiles and walks away without saying anything to the musicians to try not to interrupt their flow.

With the cigar clubs now in full swing and the tobacco production in Nicaragua under the supervision of Jaime's uncle running flawless, business is at its highest. The cigar production in Nicaragua has hit an all-time high, and the number of laborers is in the hundreds. Jaime's uncle runs a smooth operation over there, and crates full of Ijaba products continue to crowd the Miami seaport daily. Business is good! Jaime continues to fly back and forth between Miami, New York, Las Vegas, and LA, reassuring the cigar clubs are running as they should, and with Chuchi's marketing group handling all the publicity, things could not be any better. Between Jaime, the old uncle, and Chuchi, they work hard in a perfect triangle to obtain maximum results, and what an incredible accomplishment when just a few years prior this was only an idea and now, fully implemented, is a dream come true for a man who was categorized as a just dreamer by so many who probably laughed behind his back any time, he would utter words expressing his ambition. Now that Jaime's dream has become a full-blown reality and as some would call it, some kind of Cinderella story or Starbucks-type success, only faster and maybe not with the same magnitude as the coffee giant, Ijaba Cigars are quickly climbing the ropes of achievement and becoming the talk of the cigar business. And not just related to cigars, but the entire business world is as astonished as Jaime is at the sudden widespread explosion of his popular cigars. Even the name is catchy, and everyone keeps asking what the name means, at which Jaime always pauses to proudly explain. The logo is too attention-grabbing, and the passion behind all the work is almost inevitable to feel. Jaime, who continues to be in constant awe and disbelief at the magical and rapid prosperity of Ijaba Cigars, tries carrying on with the daily activities, never taking for granted the awesome and once-in-a-lifetime opportunity he has been given as Ijaba Cigars have quickly transcended as a new trend and an enormous novelty amongst just about everyone and not just cigar lovers.

A few weeks later… It is a beautiful morning in South Florida, and the sun shines over an affluent neighborhood in the center of Biscayne Bay. Elegant, tall coconut trees and beautiful palms adorning the streets alongside trendy shops surrounded by lush tropical landscaping edge a subdivision of modern wealthy and secluded homes. This is where Jaime's new house is. He has rented his apartment to one of his new business associates, who is an investor and part of the great business expansion because Jaime does not dare to sell now. He knows the market continues to skyrocket, and therefore he rents it instead like many wealthy people do to capture the wave of the real estate market, and this shows he's been listening to all the advice Mr. Romero has been giving him. This and other types of new business endeavors, though all new concepts to Jaime, he has been slowly learning and implementing, thanks to Mr. Romero, his accountants, and all his new business-savvy friends who think Jaime's story is impressive while he absorbs all he can from them. Everyone flocks around Jaime and everyone loves him, and why wouldn't they? Not only because of his charming personality but knowing how a guy who was making around thirty dollars a month just a few years ago is now the founder and CEO of one of the fastest-growing and trendiest chains of cigar clubs in America? That is just beyond inspiring, and this is what makes America great. Everyone has an opportunity! Even a guy like Jaime gets a break to make his dream a reality. Only in America!

Jaime's new home, a small mansion in a secluded neighborhood, is elegant and classy, a replica of the old-fashioned mansions of the great Hollywood movie stars. He had always dreamt of owning one of these, only he probably never really thought it would happen in his lifetime, but he dreamt it, he visualized it, and now he has it. "They say, if you can dream it, you can have it, and if you see it in your dreams, then it is always in reach. It's all a matter of taking advantage of the opportunities thrown your way," explains Jaime during another interview for one of the local magazines. Somehow, Jaime's charming personality has allowed him to fit right in with the publicity and attention he faces daily, and as exhausting as it is at times, he likes it. He enjoys it, and he fits right in with the paparazzi lifestyle. Meanwhile, back inside Jaime's new mansion, a limousine pulls up from a security gate and stops in the richly decorated landscaped circular drive. A fresh-faced young chauffeur, Jordan, gets out and opens the back door. Jaime, who is finishing a drink, emerges exhausted. He is glad to be home at last, and as he thanks Jordan, he mumbles, "Home sweet home. Thank you, Jordan."

From inside the spacious garage, Jaime's butler Enrico rushes out and welcomes Jaime back home, "Welcome home, Mr. Colon."

"Enrico, I'm glad to see you again. Get me a rum, would you?" Jaime asks…

"Better make it four, your guests arrived about an hour ago, Mr. Colon," the butler tells Jaime, and he walks inside the house. After removing his coat, Jaime rushes out to the arms of Chuchi, Mr. Romero, and his daughter Stephanie, who have been waiting for Jaime in the back patio where nestled amid a beautiful tropical garden is a swimming pool with a built-in waterfall.

Jaime's backyard is nothing but acres of private, secluded land beyond, and he saunters onto the patio with rum in hand as he joins his guests and good friends. "So, what do you guys think of all this? Not bad for a frustrated and washed-up baseball player, huh? I know what this place is missing, a miniature golf course. Right over there…" Jaime points with the same hand holding his drink. Chuchi, Mr. Romero, and Stephanie rise from the poolside table where they have been sipping drinks, and they all embrace Jaime in warm greeting. Jaime apologizes for his flight being delayed, and they disregard the waiting.

"Papa, you are going to be late to your own funeral, but I've waited in worst places. Old Fidel himself would be jealous of all this.

I am proud of you. It's genuinely nice," adds Chuchi as he points around at the mansion.

"Stephanie, you look lovely," Jaime tells her as he places his arm over Mr. Romero's shoulder and embraces the old man, intoning, "Thanks to you, Mr. Romero, you made it all possible."

"No, I will not take any credit. It was all, you kid." He pauses.

"So, cigars bought all this?" she replies, looking around the magnificent house.

"Cigars? No, my dear friend, not just cigars, these are the finest cigars in the world, but it was cigars and a dream."

At this, Chuchi interrupts, "Yeah, and he is humble too." Stephanie laughs, and Jaime pulls out a gold cigar case from his pocket, and Chuchi and Mr. Romero accept cigars.

Stephanie declines, and Jaime continues, "This is my own little piece of Cuba right here, my own paradise. I had the best landscapers flown in from Britain. See those flowers right there? Those are more exotic than the ones I saw in the hotels in Vegas, even Steve Wynn would appreciate this…"

"Okay, now…the old man has had too much to drink," Chuchi adds, and Mr. Romero begins to laugh. Jaime laughs at himself and acknowledges his childish remarks, but it is all good fun, and they are all friends. So, no harm intended, and none taken on Jaime's behalf.

"So, you live in this kingdom all by yourself?" Stephanie innocently asks.

Jaime puts his drink down, and he slightly snaps, looking at Chuchi, "What's wrong with that?" Chuchi smiles, and Stephanie looks stung…

"It was just an innocent question, don't get all butthurt about it…" Mr. Romero exclaims as he takes a puff of his cigar.

"No, she's right… What the heck am I doing in this ridiculous thing? It is always empty. I mean, I am never home anyway." Jaime looks around, and he takes notice of all the luxury surrounding him. He puts his drink down. "I'm sorry I snapped. I'm only tired…but really, I'm not alone, though, I have a cook, a maid, Enrico, and Jordan. Come on, let me show you guys around." Mr. Romero and Chuchi look at each other and laugh, sensing Jaime must be tired from his trip. Jaime ignores them with a scoff, he grabs Stephanie's hand and leads the way.

Jaime proudly shows his friends his new house and all his new toys, much like a newly arrived hillbilly in the big city. He almost looks like a poor kid who has never had any toys before on his first Christmas ever. As they walk around the modern home, Stephanie and Mr. Romero compliment Jaime prudently as he shows them around, but Chuchi, on the other hand, threatens Jaime by saying he is going to buy one better of everything he shows them as they walk through the beautifully decorated mansion. Jaime shows them all his new possessions, obviously reflecting a man who is new money, and though he is humble about it, it is extremely comical to watch him give his friends the tour of his home. His friends go along and enjoy the personal tour, often giggling at Jaime's naïve remarks and comments.

Stephanie thinks Jaime's actions are "cute," as she calls it, but her father, on the other hand, thinks Jaime sounds like a country boy who has never seen the city before because that is exactly what it looks like. Jaime's good friend Chuchi thinks the old man has lost it, and he lets him know it in such a goofy manner they have no choice but to just laugh the entire time like children, like childhood buddies.

But all jokes aside, the three friends are truly proud of Jaime's accomplishment, and their admiration is sincere. After all, Jaime has indeed worked extremely hard, not wasting one single day since he arrived from Cuba, taking advantage of his grand opportunity. When he is done showing them around, they sit and talk for several hours, enjoying each other's company. As they finish their last drink, Stephanie and her father leave to get ready for a party Jaime is having later that evening right here in his house in celebration of Chuchi's accomplishments in baseball. The young man, meanwhile, sticks around and spends time with his good friend. They sit out on the patio; both light up cigars and catch up on lost time. Jaime goes on telling Chuchi about all his recent business endeavors, and he tells him about how challenging it has been learning the ins and outs of business outside of Cuba. He also mentions how big of a deal it has been having Mr. Romero around to show him the right way of doing things. "But enough about me… Tell me more about you and the guys. I find it more interesting learning about your success in the majors, and again, I apologize for not being more involved in your careers. I promise things will be different from now on."

Chuchi looks Jaime dead in the eye, and with a nice smile on his face, he puffs on his cigar and tells Jaime, "The past is the past. We are all busy, Papa, let us make it count tonight, and from now on, no more gaps, deal?"

"Deal!" Jaime agrees by raising his glass as Chuchi raises his in a promissory toast. They continue chatting, and Chuchi tells Jaime all about his short stay in the minor leagues and about his dealings with the many sponsors and his million-dollar endorsements. Jaime is just amazed, again and again, at how good not just Chuchi but all the boys have done, but mostly at how easy it is for these endorsement companies to fork out millions of dollars in advertising money, knowing well how little people make back home, but Chuchi reminds him that not everyone can hit a ninety-five-mile-per-hour fastball either, and they laugh, reminiscing about the past. Never forgetting the painful memories and the struggle. Jaime brings out a box of his best and finest cigars, and Chuchi quickly puts it away to take back home with him, but Jaime lets him know there is more, much more, and the young man explains:

"Papa, sometimes I forget I'm here in this world of great abundance. I forget what I am doing, and it blows my mind to think we are making this kind of money playing the same game we played as kids. It almost feels like a Cinderella story…" Chuchi takes a deep breath.

"I know, me too, but it is a Cinderella story and not a day goes by I don't relive the whole thing in my mind, Chuchi. We can never forget and never take for granted the great gift we have been given," Jaime replies with sincere affirmation, then he goes on to add in a more convincing manner…while trying to make sense of it all,

"I have to pinch myself from time to time, but it isn't a bad thing, you know. America has given us an opportunity, and we have taken advantage of it. That is all, son. No guilt, no harm, no foul. You have done it one way, and I have done it another, but in the end, we waited for a good pitch, and we swung hard… Gone! Out of the park… Do you know how many of our guys back home have thought about it, talked about it, but have done absolutely nothing about it? I know a few…who have nothing to do but wait to die, wondering what it could have been. What if?" Jaime pauses for a moment, and he and Chuchi exchange looks.

The young man now speaks with the wisdom of someone much older, "Yeah, it's called 'analysis paralysis,' a term used to describe when a person thinks and thinks but never takes action. We are blessed indeed, Jaime. I see the films, and I read about the European immigrants at the turn of the century when they first arrived in Ellis Island, and the Cubans in the boats back in 1980 and later the rafts in '94, and the many stories of those who have made it here from all corners of the world in search of the dream. It is all incredible, huh? Jaime, I wonder what the boys back home think of us for leaving?" Chuchi frowns as he asks.

Jaime thinks for a split second and replies, "Honestly, Chuchi, I bet you all this right here, they all wish they were in our shoes right now. I will bet they would have traded places with us when we were inside the van trying to get away, horrified and scared to death. It is no secret they all know the reality of things.

"The Cuban government honestly believes they are smarter than the average bear, but they are not. I've seen guys come and go through the years, leaving family and country behind, knowing freedom is truly a cause worth dying for, and there are those who do die and never make it, but I think they would do it all over again if they had a chance to; it's the ultimate goal for all those guys back home, even the ones who don't say it." Chuchi frowns again… Jaime keeps on, even more inspired, "Do you really think for a moment the people in Cuba don't know that ninety-mile stretch of water between Cuba and Key West is infested with hungry sharks? They know, and they know about the huge waves and how deep the water is, but this is a risk they are willing to take. When the opportunity arises, you must take it. Just like we did, little brother. No different than not swinging at a fastball straight down the middle of the plate, you just may not see another pitch like that again. You got to strike when the iron is hot!" Chuchi takes a puff from his cigar and acknowledges Jaime's comment by shaking his head.

"Yeah, I know. I know, believe me." And placing his arm around Jaime's neck, he hugs his good friend. Jaime and Chuchi go on to enjoy their time together for several hours, just talking and making up for lost time as their new lives have completely taken them apart from one another the last couple of years. The business of everyday life in America has gotten in the way like it so often happens to us all oftentimes, allowing us to drift apart. They have become too busy and, in doing so, have allowed the burden of everyday life to dictate when, if ever, there will be time for those they love. In the end, family and friends are what really matter. Relationships and the moments we share with those we love last forever, things and possessions, they do not. We embark on a mystical race to accumulate "things" our entire lives, and when we run into the many speed bumps that are guaranteed to come just as is death, the end result is leaving it all for someone else to enjoy. But this is one of the many blindfolds we wear as we walk through life, always wanting more and collecting possessions half the time we do not even need. In America today, we live in a material world, and our brains are being programmed to accumulate more, newer, bigger, better, and now with technology, faster, while forgetting what really matters.

Jaime and his young protégé go on talking about everything that has happened to them in such a short time, and they agree on one thing without ado, that adjusting to life in America hasn't been easy, especially after coming from a place like Cuba. "Look, most people think that upon arriving in the US, any immigrant who has been deprived of the American way of life is desperate to become Americanized right away. Not quite. Immigrants are proud of their heritage, and as much as they desire the freedom America offers, this way of life can be cold and materialistic, a system, which forgets about their elderly and their veterans, yes, the very people who built it and protected it are often forgotten and buried aside, left without proper healthcare and even homeless. Of course, it is not a perfect system, but I would not trade it for anything else. Where else in the world would we have had the chance to do what we have done, Jaime?" Chuchi explains in a serious tone. Jaime agrees. As time slowly creeps in, they begin to allow the moment to dictate the conversation, often laughing and reminiscing about the past and the present. They go on about how everyone has a different experience, referring to those restarting their lives in a new land and about the choices they make; from learning a new language, making new friends, and learning new costumes, for centuries now, millions have made their way to this great country just like Jaime, Chuchi, and the boys have, and they have all left a trail and footprints. It is a known fact that this is the land of opportunity, and if people work hard and simply follow the blueprint other successful immigrants have left behind throughout time, they too can be successful in their own way. The footprints are all there, engraved in history and in time. It isn't very difficult to follow a path already laid by others. It isn't reinventing the wheel, and it is a real shame how many are those who come from all corners of the world to make it in America, and yet there are those who are born in this country and who have all the same opportunities, they have an advantage having lived here their whole lives and knowing the language but still fail to take advantage of it. Sometimes I think having it all can be a curse and perhaps exactly what they take for granted. When was the last time you saw a homeless man begging on a street corner that was not American? As a matter of fact, you will rarely see an immigrant doing so. Ever seen an oriental street beggar? Never! The same thing with most Hispanics, they will offer to clean your windshield and sell fruit at the side of the road, but very seldom do we find these people begging or holding a homemade sign involving God…after all, even in the Bible, it is written that "…those who work, will eat." Many are those who come to the US from other parts of the world to work hard doing whatever it takes, from picking tomatoes to sweeping the sidewalks, to going to school to excel in whatever their profession, often being treated unfairly because of the language barrier or for their lack of contacts enabling them to find good jobs, in the end, many overcome and make the grade as this great nation was built on the backs of immigrants, and sure enough, as it so often happens, many who initially had the apparent advantage by having been born in this country, they are the ones who end up working for these same immigrants later on. This is a fact, and look around… Who are the hotel owners and the owners of many large companies and CEOs of large corporations? Many are immigrants, that is, immigrants and sons and daughters of immigrants who end up receiving an education many Americans neglected, and plenty of times, they end up speaking better and more proper English than our own people here in the United States. This is not an insult to anyone, just the shameful truth that haunts this great nation daily, and if not corrected, it will become the demise and possibly the fall of this young empire we know today as "The Greatest Country in the World." Yes, we are barely 250 years old, which makes us one of the youngest world powers compared to some of the European, African, and Asian countries that have been around for thousands of years. I have always said this country is so divided amongst itself and its own people. Maybe rather than calling us the United States of America, we ought to be "the Separated States of America" instead. We are indeed a nation of "watchers" as we love to watch others succeed, we watch others make it, and we become spectators instead of participators in the arena of life, and shame on us! I believe we should be making and selling everything to the world instead of the other way around. The "Made in America" sticker has disappeared from many of the items we purchase, and it needs to come back, contrary to what some college professors teach about economics, preaching that a strong economy is built on buying instead of selling, which I disagree with, but that's just my take on this matter. Also, our farmers must be made a priority, allowing our land to yield its best products and only purchasing from abroad what we absolutely must. We must become the leaders of the world in alternative energy, allowing Mother Earth to breathe and cutting out the billions of dollars spent buying oil from the Middle East. I say if we invest more into alternative energy, then we will need less oil, which we can surely supply ourselves within the United States' resources in Texas, North Dakota, and Alaska. Just a long unrehearsed thought to air out and perhaps express a bit of my frustration. But in our story, Jaime takes advantage of his situation, and he makes the best of it. So do Chuchi and the other boys, and let's be fair, though, and let's say that Chuchi and the guys are gifted athletes, and he and the other three ball players have an obvious advantage over the average person out there because of their incredible talent as baseball players, and I'll give you that, but what about Jaime? He did receive some seed money when the boys signed their contracts to play professional baseball, but a lot of people have won the lotto or inherited lots of money, and two years later, they are simply broke again. In America, we tend to take for granted many of the opportunities and freedoms we have. We have lost the hunger and the ambition to reach our highest potential by not taking advantage of what is in front of our noses. Education in America has become a joke, our teachers make almost nothing compared to a drug dealer or even a valet parker at a good hotel who's probably never set a foot inside a college classroom, and a Realtor, who is not required to have any formal education other than passing a real estate written exam, can make a six-figure income by selling two homes per month...and I ask, where is the logic? The government laughs at the thought of a better health system, and they allow every black neighborhood in America to become the ghetto. Yeah, why is that? Why is it that almost every Black and Hispanic neighborhood is considered the bad side of town? Is this plot or conspiracy to allow people to live in poverty and on welfare and food stamps for several generations at a time? Or is it the people? The government can't make anyone go to school and receive an education, but neither should they be responsible for those who decide not to in order to make a better future for themselves. Whatever the case, there should be limits on how long people use the welfare system, force them to go get regular jobs, spend the money educating them, training them, so they have no excuse. Instead of giving free assisted living to people who are healthy enough to work, and walk and talk, make them responsible for their actions and put them in control of their lives. The government should not be responsible for people's laziness and lack of ambition either. In this country, lower-income whites are often categorized as people who live in trailer parks instead of striving for more, for better, and ultimately, for the dream, when in all reality, there are those who may choose to want to pay a lower rent by living in a trailer park instead of being enslaved by a thirty-year mortgage they can barely afford and thus being seen as what some call "trailer trash…" Stupid if you ask me, but the deal is everyone is often categorized in America by prototypical classes based on outer appearances, race, and ignorance. It has been encrypted in their heads from generation to generation to keep them ignorant, and this way, not allowing them to see straight, and in my eyes, it is deteriorating the core of this nation and fragmenting us as its people. Yet, many of our doctors are from other countries, our college professors too, and all we can do is complain and hate when what we really should be doing is striving to excel and become that person we dreamt of as kids because if we remember when we were kids, we never said we wanted to be unemployed and be collecting food stamps. Neither did we say we wanted to spend our lives working for someone else, and don't get me wrong, no job is shameful, and anything we do to make an honest living is a justifiable means of being a contributor to society because we need all kinds of people doing all kinds of different jobs, otherwise everyone would want to be a doctor, and no one would want to be the other guy. So, with that being said, I rest my case, love what you do, and do what you love. It is all at reaching distance for everyone to grab; our own dreams are right there, just waiting to be snatched by all of us who really want it and for anyone who dares to dream. It has been proven that if we want it bad enough, we can have it all. There are no excuses, only lack of desire, lack of planning, and lack of action. They say good luck is when opportunity meets preparation…so, I say, always be prepared by continuing to grow and by learning something new every day. Never neglect a moment of learning. If we are not growing, we are dying. Look around, who are the ones in charge, who has all the money? Look at our politicians. Who are these people? Some do not even know how to speak properly but still receive our votes to put them in office…or should I say our lack of votes? We need to take advantage of our ability to have our voices heard as we live in a democracy. People die to have this gift and to live in a place where we have the freedom to choose who runs our government and who makes our laws, but a handful of Americans do not take advantage of this. Only a percentage of people pay attention to who these political candidates really are, barely ever taking the time to research their backgrounds or their intentions. So, a bunch of crooked and corrupted lifetime politicians end up being the ones running the show while the bottom part of the pyramid is kept busy trying to make ends meet while complaining about their senators who have no business being in office because at their old age they can't even tie their own shoes, and just about every decision they make is irrelevant and bias. Governors who have no clue about politics but are popular enough to be put in office and even presidents who steal and cheat and get away with it right in front of our noses. This is a great country, the greatest nation in the world, but at times we have allowed it to be run by immoral individuals driving it to the ground. Let us take America back, let us start dreaming again, and let us make a difference by being the difference!

A few hours later…at around nine o'clock at night, there is a party going on inside Jaime's house. The richly decorated rooms are filled with a hundred guests, mostly a Miami party crowd of good-looking, fun people. There are buckets of champagne and all sorts of booze everywhere. Cigar humidors are on each table with Jaime's best cigars, and the music is loud as Enrico the butler is kept busy at the front door meeting and greeting everyone who arrives. Outside at the pool, there are several people splashing and having a good time. Beautiful women in bikinis all over the place filled with festive lamps strung from the trees outside provide the half-light the ambiance calls for. Caterers bring out hors d'oeuvres and all kinds of mouth-watering food to the bar area, where two bartenders prepare drinks for the guests. The place looks like a sultan's palace in one of the stories from Aladdin's days, only short of a magic lamp and a genie. Among all the people in attendance is Jaime's lawyer Mr. Triana, who quietly enjoys himself along with other guests downning rum and feeling no pain, Hiram is drinking Black Label and water, his trademark drink.

Inside the house, Jaime meets and greets guests in the main hall. He is the life of the party as he shows off his new giant humidor covering an entire wall, his furniture, and all his new toys to his friends and half the people there, half of them whom he does not know. "Look, Sony, a ninety-five-inch HDTV flat screen with 3-D. Has the visual quality of thirty-five-millimeter photography even though I don't know what that means...but I saw the commercial," Jaime jokes and as he plays host, one of the guests, Ramon Saucedo, is impressed.

"Very nice, Mr. Colon, you could buy a Third World country with the money you must have paid for that, huh!" And as he says this, Ramon notices some of the women are drinking Matervas, a popular soda in Cuba, and he comments, "Matervas, huh! Only tourists can drink those in Cuba anymore."

"You've been there? Cuba?" Jaime asks.

"I'm from Pinar del Rio, just like you, Mr. Colon. The most beautiful land on God's green earth," Ramon explains and offers his hand. Jaime shakes it. "Ramon Saucedo, it's a pleasure to finally meet you, Mr. Colon. I have heard so much about you, I feel like I practically know you. Heck, I know about everything there is to know about you; very impressive, to say the least."

"No, the pleasure is all mine," Jaime responds, quite ecstatic at Ramon's charming details, and they talk for a little while before Jaime ushers Ramon into the spacious kitchen. The kitchen is littered with numerous empty bottles and half-eaten plates of food. Ramon tries hard to impress Jaime, telling him all he knows about him and his sudden success, but Jaime replies almost apologetically as Ramon continues to shower him with all sorts of compliments, "Look, Ramon, I'm new at all this, but I've become pretty wealthy in a short period of time simply by helping other people. No magic there, so why do I get all this credit? I intended on creating a good cigar, and in the process, a great cigar turned out. Oh, and hundreds of people now have found heaven working for us on our tobacco fields and in our cigar factories, but all the credit goes to them, they do a great job. If you call that 'greatness,' I will take it, but I certainly wasn't looking for it."

"You are certainly a humanitarian, Mr. Colon," Ramon adds...

"That, my friend, depends on whom you ask. Can I offer you another drink?" Jaime pours a few ounces of rum into a small crystal glass containing several pieces of ice and offers it to his new acquaintance, but Ramon politely declines. Instead, he offers Jaime his business card. Jaime reads it, "Financial advisor, huh? Third one tonight, you guys certainly have my number."

"Actually, Mr. Colon, I'm more than just an advisor. I am an expert in the field, and all those other guys either know me or know of me. I have been around the block and made a name for myself by making people money," Ramon replies, but disinterested, Jaime puts the all-black business card in his pocket and continues:

"Sure, everybody is an expert. An expert in finances from Cuba, and that is why you've been on me like glue."

"Well, yes, sir, I am Cuban, but I went to school here at the 'U,' and my offices are here in Miami, of course, and like you, my business too involves helping people, Mr. Colon. We have much in common," Ramon adds, grinning, and Jaime slaps him on the shoulder, and they laugh together.

"I was just giving you a hard time. Maybe I will see you around. Nice to meet you, Raul..." Obviously, Jaime has had one drink too many as he mistakes Ramon's name for Raul.

He turns his back to the man who now stands there, staggering his own words, and walks in the main hall where other guests await him. The party is now in full swing, with people laughing, dancing, and drinking. In the corner of the room, several guests are secretly sniffing cocaine, and looking up, they see a commotion at the front door. A group of women flocks around Chuchi, who has just arrived. Chuchi, now a full-fledged sports celebrity, is offered lavish attention by everyone at the party. Waving a cigar, Jaime navigates through the crowd to meet his friend. "Chuchi, my little brother... Come on, leave the muchachas alone, I need to talk to you. Come on!"

Suddenly, Jaime pauses, and seeing the hurdled cocaine group, he jostles his head into their private circle, and they are all smiles. One of the guys offers Jaime a tiny silver spoon heaped with white powder, "Mr. Colon, it is an honor."

Jaime looks at the man as if he wants to kill him, and trying to control his anger, he replies, "You've got two minutes before I call the cops. So, get your wasted behinds out of here right now before I do something you will regret." The partiers think he is joking and break out laughing. Jaime gives them a deadly look that kills it and then whispers to the man, "Thirty seconds…twenty-nine…twenty-eight…" But before Jaime can say another word, two huge men, looking like linebackers for the Miami Dolphins and wearing all black, escort the entire group outside and out of the house.

Moments later… Inside Jaime's spacious car garage with the feeling of a miniature showroom of expensive cars all sparkling like new, it is quiet and private out here. Jaime and Chuchi take a break from the party, both with drinks and cigars in hands as Chuchi checks out a Limited Collector's Edition Hummer, the military-bred massive jeep-like truck with television sets everywhere and shiny 28" rims, and he adds, "Desert Storm was good for something, huh? Too bad these monsters did not become the wave of the future everyone anticipated…maybe it was gas prices, huh!" Jaime ignores him, feeling a bit drunk, and Chuchi quickly moves to a classic Harley motorcycle from the 1940s and looks for Jaime's approval as he straddles it like an excited kid. Jaime approves by giving him a thumbs up. "Same as James Dean had in the old black and white movies, remember?" Chuchi pauses, then he continues, a bit somber now, "Jaime, I wish the guys were here with us. We could all go riding, I miss those fools. Isn't it funny how in Cuba, we did not have any of this, but we always had time for each other? Now, we have it all, and it collects dust…with no time to enjoy it!"

Jaime agrees with his young friend, "Yeah, something like that, but we should make a real effort to have a reunion soon, just the five of us. It would be nice. Cannot get all caught up in the cobweb of life". At this, Chuchi is hit by a pang of guilt as he sits on the bike.

"You know, one of these bikes could feed an entire town in Cuba for a year. Ever think about that?"

"First, a Third World country and now a town in Cuba. What is this, a guilt conspiracy?" Jaime adds, feeling a little…awkward and a little drunk.

Chuchi then replies, "I'm just saying, we now have so much. I mean, I never thought in my wildest dreams… How a snot-nosed kid like me…"

Jaime quickly interrupts, "Listen, I've known you since you were twelve years old, Chuchi, you were a skinny, unwashed kid playing ball outside the stadium, just waiting for that door to open to go fetch baseballs. You came from nothing, my man, just like me, so feel good about yourself, about the principles and the possibilities that you have within you. God knocks on every door, you answered, that is all, and there is no room for regrets! If you could trade places with someone else right now, would you?" Chuchi nods his head, accepting Jaime's explanation, almost breathing a sigh of relief.

Then he shoots right back, "So, what'd you want to talk about, Pops? I got a babe sandwich waiting inside…"

Looking at Chuchi, Jaime quickly responds, "Sandwich? I saw a buffet in there waiting for you. Just give me five minutes because I have been walking around with this crazy idea for a week." Jaime begins pacing back and forth. "Stop me if you heard this one before… I want you to go into business with me. I need you in order to expand, and I need a *yes* from you, because being negative does not help us grow." Jaime then proceeds to lay down an entire business plan before Chuchi with the intention of bringing him in as his new business partner, and Chuchi likes what he hears but the young man has one legitimate question for Jaime before they launch into their business adventure together:

"Hey, Pops, I have one question for you. What do you really think of this guy Ramon? Is he as good as you say as a financial advisor? Have you met with other advisors and compared? Did you check him out?"

After a short pause, Jaime fires back at Chuchi, "Chuchi, the guy is solid. He knows his stuff. I saw all his credentials, and I looked up all the people he currently works with, his clients are all high-end. We begin to feed him a little here and there to test him out, and we will take it slow at first. He says we need to diversify our interest, and I believe that is true. It only makes sense; we should not have all our eggs in one basket. He says he knows how to make me passive income versus active income or something like that… Passive income is where my money works for me instead of me having to work for my money. Something along those lines… You know that is not my thing."

Chuchi takes a deep breath and replies, "Jaime, I know what you are saying, but this table you are talking about holding all those baskets has to be a solid table because it doesn't matter how many different baskets, we put all our eggs into, if the table only has three legs, then what happens, huh?"

Jaime thinks for a moment, then he answers, "I know, I know. I will be careful. Just sounded good to have someone who knows how money works manage it for us. An expert, and it sounded even better to be able to double and triple my money by investing in the market, I mean, it seems like all successful people put their money in the market, right?" Jaime tells Chuchi, unsure and somewhat worried.

The young man stops him and gives Jaime a piece of his mind, "Jaime, do you know who Warren Buffett is? He is one of the wealthiest men in the world, anyway, he says most of the people investing in the market should not be doing so because they have no idea of what they are doing." Silence follows… At this, Jaime puts his head down and says nothing to his friend. They finish their drinks and go back inside to join the others.

The next day Mr. Romero, Jaime, and Chuchi gaze through a wire mesh fence at an abandoned, rubble-filled lot outside Downtown Miami. "Now, I've really heard it all," Mr. Romero whispers to himself as he is flanked by Jaime and Chuchi, who are looking at an inner-city empty lot, which runs the length of graffiti brick walls for almost an entire block. A razor-topped fence encloses this eyesore of hazardous fallen debris, piles of dirt, strewn garbage, and maybe even rats. This is an abandoned lot with nothing but garbage in it. "Jaime, you want to turn an entire city block into a kids' park?" asks Mr. Romero as Jaime turns to the old man, puffing on his cigar.

He adds, "You know how some inner-city families struggle. These kids need a place to go, a place to run and be free; otherwise, they will get into all kinds of trouble. They…uhm! Tell him, Chuchi."

Chuchi checks his throat…and proceeds, "Great, thanks a lot, Jaime…put it on me. Well, I don't know about you, Mr. Romero, but when I was a kid, this would have been a dream come true for me and for all my friends back in the old neighborhood." Mr. Romero frowns…

"And you need my pull at City Council to make this dream of yours come true, right?"

Jaime responds, "A lot of people owe you favors, Mr. Romero. You know everyone," Jaime quietly replies, and Mr. Romero fires right back:

"Do you have any idea what it takes?"

Jaime gathers his thoughts and quickly intones to his mentor, "Look, I have a church sponsorship right here in Miami, just like in Nicaragua. Church youth groups that will double as a clean-up crew. These kids will work their tails off, they will earn it, and it will keep them off the streets. Don't you see? It will be a miracle for this neighborhood if you can help me turn this mess into a park for the kids."

"Yeah, it'll be a miracle alright. Jaime, this is a noble thing you want to do, but in case you have not noticed, there are powerful men lining their pockets with things just the way they are. Not everybody wants to see a clean-up crew in here. This is a drug heaven in the day and at night, a battlefield for the local gangs. The last thing they want to allow in here is a remodeling crew."

"That is why I need your pull at City Council, let us clean this place up and give these kids a future, we will give them hope. What do you say, sir?"

"Jaime, don't 'sir' me… I know how you operate by now. You are one persistent and pushy dude, and when you get an idea in that big head of yours…forget it!" Mr. Romero responds as he sighs, running his arm through his forehead in wiping the sweat off. "You are crazy! You know that, Jaime?" Jaime smiles, and Chuchi, not too sure Mr. Romero has agreed, raises his arm at Jaime to give him a high five. Jaime hugs Mr. Romero as if knowing the old man has already agreed to help. "Alright, alright… Put me down. I will see what I can do."

Jaime smiles, and he turns to Chuchi as he tells him, "It is a done deal."

The following morning at Biscayne Bay, picturesque sailboats float in the sun on a beautiful sea of calm and crystal-clear water. Among all the lustrous sailboats, one gleaming forty-foot yacht stands out. The back of the boat reads, "Ijaba." When Jaime was a little boy, he had promised his old grandma one day he would buy a big boat, and he would name it "Ijaba" in honor of his beloved ancestor. First, Jaime named his world-famous cigars after his African ancestor and now the beautiful *boat*. This is quite a promise after all these years, huh? Well, now a kept promise. And just like that, the day has finally arrived, and now Jaime, cigar, and drink in hand, entertains a few friends, and among them is Ramon. The financial advisor he met at the party and the same man who has not left Jaime's side for weeks, giving him all sorts of priceless Wall Street advice. All these people hang out on his newly acquired forty-foot *multi*million-dollar yacht.

The yacht is occupied with friends, anonymous guests, and bikini-clad women all partying on deck. Even young Jordan is there, chauffeur's uniform unbuttoned and flirting with the girls aboard. Jaime and Ramon sit alone as they overlook the action from the top deck, both holding cigars. "I will be honest with you, Ramon. What I know about the stock market would get lost on the head of a pin, and *The Wall Street Journal* looks like Latin to me. So, when you talk about all this stuff, I am as lost as a little boy inside a funeral home. I can barely turn on a computer, but I do know cigars…"

Jaime giggles clumsily, and Ramon, looking Jaime in the eye, fires right back, "And I know how to make your money work for you, Mr. Colon; I have done it with hundreds of my clients. I can show you how to save a bunch of money in taxes, how to secure a future, and even leave a nice legacy behind. I have brought you all these recommendation letters I have gotten from some of my clients. I deal with bigwigs only, and I know my business."

"Alright, alright... You had me at hello. Let us start small, and we will take it from there, deal? I will go along, but it better be for real. No games," Jaime tells Ramon firmly after the man's persistence becomes almost overwhelming.

"Mr. Colon, my clients love me because I make them money. Listen, Jaime, last year you hit it out of the park with your cigar clubs and your tobacco production, and that means you are ripe. Time is not money, money is timing. It is all about being in the right place at the right time and not always by design. Does that make sense? Listen, Jaime, if I started today, I could triple your net worth in six to twelve months. Timing is everything, and the time is now. Wall Street is where the American dream is made. If your money is not making you more money, it is losing you money." At this, Jaime begins to reply to Ramon but is interrupted by a soft hand on his shoulder.

"Senor Colon... Hello!" In an instant, Jaime turns to find himself staring into the eyes of the most seductively sexy woman he has ever seen, Rosie Padon. He is speechless. "Mr. Colon, I saw you on a magazine cover. I am Rosie. I have wanted to meet you ever since I read the article. *What an incredible man*, I told myself. *What an accomplishment*."

At this, Ramon jumps up and explains, "I apologize. Mr. Colon, Rosie is a friend of my sister. I should have introduced you when we first boarded, but you were so busy talking with everyone. Anyway, allow me to properly introduce you two. Mr. Colon, this is Roselyn Padon. Rosie, this is Mr. Colon," Ramon introduces Rosie to Jaime, and shaking her hand, Jaime just melts.

She smiles and replies, "I didn't mean to intrude. You see, I was born in Havana, and that is why I had to stop and say hi and shake the hand of the man we are all so proud of. I have read all about where you come from, and believe me, how you got to where you are today...is simply amazing. You inspire me, you inspire all of us! What you have accomplished is incredible!"

Jaime is mesmerized by her beauty, and looking right into her eyes, he adds, "Well, I really believe God knocks on all doors and whoever answers…boom!"

Rosie looks warmly and seductively into his eyes; Jaime cannot look away. He is glued, paralyzed, and after a prolonged gap, he is returned to reality by another one of her comments: "You make it sound so easy, but it has been a long, hard road for you, and still you have endured, and you have crossed the desert in much less than forty years." Jaime, a little lost with her analogy, agrees by nodding his head but has no idea what she just said as she was referring to a story in the Bible when the Israelites spent forty years in the desert after leaving Egypt in a journey that should've taken only a few months at the most, but instead, it took them forty years. "But there was a good reason why, and that is because they were stubborn and disobedient," she continues, and so Jaime only agrees to try not to disagree with the beautiful woman. Jaime, who is still hypnotized by Rosie, does not see she has Satan written all over, and as the celebration continues inside the club, he is grabbed by two gracious members of the media who have been waiting to talk to him. He says goodbye to his new friends, and he takes off to entertain the rest of the people in attendance.

A few hours later, Jaime's limousine pulls away from the marina, and young Jordan glances at Jaime in the rearview mirror as he drives. "I have to say, Mr. Colon; it is a real pleasure working for you. That was the first time I have ever been on a yacht. Honestly, my father did not treat me this good, God rest his soul… I mean, he is not dead, but he just had never really been around. You know what they say, any old fool can make a baby, but it does not make him a father."

"Uh-hmm…" Jaime mutters, looking out the window…

"I heard you never knew your old man either…" The young chauffeur glances back in the mirror, trying to ignite a conversation with Jaime riding in the back of the limo; Jaime has a glowing, daydreaming smile on his face and has not heard a word Jordan has said. His mind is somewhere else, he is thinking about Rosie… The limo pulls up outside Mr. Romero's office, and Jaime gets out with his briefcase in hand and walks right in the building. The limo drives off.

Inside the office, Mr. Romero and Jaime's attorney Mr. Triana listen to Jaime, who has been talking up a storm about his new plans to put his money in the stock market. He raves about how he is going to triple it in no time, and Triana stands quietly off to the side as Mr. Romero is not impressed with what he is hearing. "Jaime, you don't even know this man. Didn't you just meet him?" At this, Jaime tosses a bunch of papers on the desk, a resume, and financial brochures to go with it, and the old attorney, Mr. Triana, just stands there without expression.

"Look at his credentials. Ramon is an expert in the stock market. He knows how to invest, and he promises he will be able to deliver by tripling my money in a few months, and I want to believe him because I really don't have time to be learning how to invest in the stock market... Ramon does that for a living; let him handle it for us. I don't want to spend my time trying to learn what he is already an expert at." Mr. Romero gives him a strange look.

"Do not be greedy, Jaime, put your money into real estate; buy expensive art, gold, diamonds. Jaime, you do not know the first thing about the stock market. The stock market is unpredictable and difficult to understand. Jaime, the first rule in investing is 'never invest in anything you don't know or understand.' Most people in the market simply should not be in it. Even I know that, and I am not a financial guru like this Ramon guy," calmly replies Mr. Romero as he sips on a glass of water, and Jaime jumps right back at him.

"I am not greedy, Mr. Romero. I only see an opportunity to put my money to work for me, just like all the rich people in America do. Besides, every other wealthy person in America invests in the stock market, so why wouldn't I? That is where the money is made, are they all wrong too? And they all go through a stockbroker or financial advisor, right?"

Mr. Romero tries to continue to convince Jaime, "Buy land. God is not making any more of that. Jaime do not put your money in the hands of someone you just met. What makes you think rich people put all their money in the stock market, huh? What do you know about that? Just because Ramon told you. Have you ever heard of the rule of 100? Answer me, Jaime? Don't you realize real wealthy people only gamble with the kind of money they would bring to Vegas for a wild weekend with the fellas?" There is a moment of silence…

"Jaime, Mr. Romero is right. Ramon may be a charming and persuasive fellow Cuban, and he is smart, he knows his business, and he has many high-end clients, but we do not know much about him. Just give it a little time before you go dumping a bunch of money into the hands of someone you just met. By the way, Mr. Romero, what is the rule of 100?" Triana advises Jaime and curiously asks the unique question…

Mr. Romero answers, "Well, the rule of 100 is a diversification strategy where one can determine how much of our investment portfolio should be allocated into the market or into a risky game plan based on our age. You simply subtract your age from one hundred, and that is how much of your money could be invested in the stock market or any market-driven investment. The remaining, equaling your age, is always to be placed in a more promising or safer strategy. Perhaps a fixed rate of return deal."

"Oh yeah, that makes sense. It makes a whole lot of sense. I get it!" replies Triana, knowing that the older a person is, the more difficult it is to recover in the event the market takes a dive and one loses a bunch of money, sometimes overnight, because of the market's unpredictability, always looking like a heart rate monitor, zigzagging up and down without any steadiness.

"Listen, son, money is called bread for a reason. It can go bad very quickly if it does not sit in the right place. We are talking about millions, Jaime, is that clear? You have worked extremely hard for this money, now protect it. You ever seen all those so-called money experts on MSNBC, CNN, and Fox News sit there and discuss finances and investments? All they do is argue but never come to any kind of agreement on what exactly makes our money grow, and that is because they don't even know, it is impossible to tell, all speculation, they don't have a crystal ball. If they knew, they would be geniuses," Mr. Romero continues to try to convince Jaime of how volatile the market really is, but he is not all there…and after a short pause, Jaime replies a bit angry and on the defensive:

"Look, I know what we are talking about here. Now I cannot even play around with the money I have worked so hard for without your opinions or permission, right?" Mr. Romero coughs and takes a gulp of bottled water.

"Excuse me, the doctor tells me I have to drink more of this. No, Jaime, that is not it at all. You have always asked me for my advice and support, and most of the time, I have given you my blessing on almost every decision, but right now, I am just saying, be careful, that is all. You have not signed anything with this guy yet, right? I am a man who prides himself in finding baseball talent in unusual places, and I am a rather good judge of character… I find trouble in your eyes right now, Jaime. What is it, son?" Jaime turns away, and Triana's expression says it all. Mr. Romero looks at Jaime, concerned. "Jaime… Tell me you have not signed anything." Silence follows. "Jaime?" Mr. Romero pauses for a moment. "Your calm says it all, son. I cannot believe what I am hearing. Haven't you learned anything? Haven't you heard a word I have said?"

Jaime, feeling cornered, finally responds angrily, "Look what I've accomplished! Look where I came from! Some people find it amazing! Why can't you guys give me any credit?" Mr. Romero holds his temper, just barely, and takes a deep breath.

Then proceeds to talk to Jaime calmly, "No one is saying anything different. Jaime, you are flying high, and I am raining on your parade. Listen, why don't we consider this calmly. Let us sleep on it. Okay?"

Jaime turns away beat and now completely defeated, he whispers softly, "My friends don't call me greedy." Mr. Romero and the attorney exchange looks, Mr. Romero is not happy, but he also realizes Jaime is an adult and the type of mistake he has made luckily is only a monetary blunder, yes, it could have been worse, and everyone hopes he has learned from this foolish mistake. Just moments later, Jaime then gets up, and he walks out, slamming the door. Mr. Romero stares angrily at Triana, and the lawyer, who is embarrassed beyond words, excuses himself, and he follows Jaime out the door.

Mr. Romero sits alone in the office chair and runs his hand through his gray hair as a sign of disbelief and frustration, but also trying to piece together their next move.

Later that day, behind Jaime's mansion is a melancholy Floridian sunset exposing a display of multiple colors covering the horizon. Jaime's limo pulls in the driveway. In the drive, Jordan opens the door of the limo to loud music, and Jaime steps out with a drink in his hand. There is a party going on inside his house as usual... Salsa music plays as dozens of guests are drinking and dancing. Enrico opens the front door for Jaime, who looks sarcastically at the festive crowd. "Anybody I know this time? I did not even get an invite...and I am not really in the mood for parties." Not interested, Jaime walks straight into his bedroom and closes the door behind him, ignoring the festive ambiance and feeling like a stranger in his own home. A familiar occurrence by now.

A few months have now passed, and much of Jaime and his team's effort has been placed in trying to recover the money that was lost, but a rebound in the market sometimes can take years, and frustration continues to build. Jaime is learning for the first time about the struggles of the rich, struggles that may seem all too distant from the battles of the poor, but at the end of the day, struggles, nevertheless. These trying times can consume a person emotionally and physically, Jaime deals with it to the best of his ability, but he often feels incapable of producing good enough results. His battle is real and one only he can face in an effort to overcome the deplorable situation; however, his demons are many, his strength is lacking. Jaime falls into a deep state of depression, he feels like he is losing control, and his disappointment points to only one person, him. So, he hides from the world the best he can in shame and disgrace, but unable to disappear completely, he continues to sing his song.

Several months later, in front of a huge crowd, a gigantic pair of scissors is poised to cut a massive red ribbon... We find ourselves at the opening of the brand-new Colon Playground on the site of the formerly abandoned lot and Jaime's dream project, which had been put in place a short time back, has come to fruition. After much work and dedication by those Jaime had put in charge, the day is finally here. A lively crowd spills out onto the street to celebrate the opening of the kids' park. The transformation to this once crime-infested area is nothing short of remarkable, as the entire place has gone from a war zone to an exclusive compound surrounded by lush green shade trees and lights everywhere in sharp contrast with the dark alleys it once conveyed. Inside, nearly an entire block of new swings, slides, water spray fountains, wading pools, a huge jungle gym obstacle course, and basketball courts…all enclosed within fifteen-foot fences and multiple tall light poles to keep the park well-lit at night. There are several lifeguards around the pool areas, and a large group of people surrounds a podium as the mayor of the city of Miami speaks over a microphone, "On behalf of the city of Miami…and especially our children… I present to you the new Colon Playground." At this, dozens of inner-city kids dutifully erupt in cheers as Miami's handsome Cuban-born mayor gestures broadly toward Jaime, who, with a cigar in mouth, holds the oversized scissors ready. Chuchi is also here, and he stands next to Jaime as they continue to listen to the mayor speak, "I want to extend my profound gratitude to Miami's honorary citizen, and fellow Cuban American, the illustrious Mr. Jaime Colon," applause follows, "…and to another fellow Cuban, the Seattle Mariners, the Bullet—Chuchi Aguilar…" More cheers follow. "…Kids, the playground is now open!" Amidst all the cheers and applause, Jaime cuts the ribbon with a half-smile on his face, and the kids rush in, happy as water bursting through a dam. Chuchi and Jaime raise their hands like prizefighters. Jaime beams like a man on top of the world and at the height of complete success in an effort to try to hide everything else that clouds his mind. He does a good job at it, and Chuchi is not buying it, but they both play along, and it works.

The highly anticipated opening of the playground is a huge success as kids play, frolic, and romp in the new playground, and Jaime, Chuchi, the mayor, and assorted local politicians glad-hand

and work the crowd. Jaime bathes gracefully in all the attention. Stephanie walks up to congratulate Jaime. Her father is conspicuously absent. Jaime kisses Stephanie on the cheek; she hesitates and then embraces him tightly. Proud of his accomplishment, she stares at his eyes and lets him know how she feels, "Jaime, just like you said. You did it! I am proud of you… This is quite an incredible thing you have done. Be proud of your accomplishment." As Jaime hugs Stephanie, he notices among all the people in attendance, Ramon is also there, and his eyes light up when he sees Rosie with him. He excuses himself from Stephanie and the others and walks up to greet Ramon and Rosie. She is looking amazing in a fitted low-cut dress, and as she gives Jaime a demure smile, she looks down. Jaime and Ramon shake hands.

Then Jaime gives Rosie a gentle kiss on her cheek as it is customary for most Cubans to greet each other in this manner and goes on to compliment her appearance, "Rosie, you look stunning."

"Thank you, Jaime," she thanks him and then quickly comments back on the kids' playground and what a great idea it was to have something like this built in this part of town.

Jaime puffs on his cigar, and with a smile, he replies, "Isn't this great? It all happened so fast." She eyes him firmly before replying…

"You have a lot of courage, Mr. Colon. Walking in here and building all this…" replies Rosie.

Jaime takes it in and then responds calmly, "It's all about vision. For some people—seeing is believing, but for others—believing is just enough… I just knew it would work. A hunch!" Jaime exhales…

"I like that. Confidence," she replies, somewhat surprised. Perhaps she didn't expect for someone who had only lived in the United States just a short time to be this wise about the way of things in the business world, and as they continue to talk, she studies Jaime methodically and carefully while mingling in a group of friends and new acquaintances.

Rosie tries to be extremely careful in not revealing her inner plan; she does not want him to know she may be interested, but at the same time, she is obvious about her intentions… But men, we are so dumb in understanding women, he does not get it! And at this, Jaime invites them all back to the cigar club for drinks. Rosie quickly accepts along with all the others there. On the other hand, Ramon apologizes for not being able to join them, and he promises to be there the next time. He explains he has a particularly important client to meet, and it is impossible for him to get out of it on such short notice. With a frown, Jaime takes a particular liking to this, and he makes Ramon promise to join him another day for drinks and a cigar, and he is not at all insulted by Ramon's refusal, on the contrary, he assumes Ramon is an extremely professional individual who puts his clients' needs ahead of having a good time and is glad to be doing business with him. They say goodbye to Ramon, and Jaime and Rosie jump in a cab.

Later that night, inside one of the VIP rooms at the club, Jaime and Rosie eat together in quiet private luxury. The room is plush and relaxing, the lights low. "When you said… Let us get some Cuban coffee… I thought you meant the corner deli," she says Rosie to Jaime, and he grins, still hypnotized by her beauty. Rosie simply looks glum. He frowns. "I'm sorry, Mr. Colon…" she adds and looks away.

"Not in the mood for bad jokes?" he asks, and she immediately takes the napkin and gently wipes a tear from her eye…

"I don't know if Ramon told you, but…" She pauses. Jaime shakes his head, concerned, and Rosie continues, "I'm getting a divorce. It has been overwhelming lately. Ramon thought it would be a good idea for me to get out before things worse between him and I." She pauses, and Jaime listens. "He is in Boston. We cashed in our chips over a year ago. I do not see him. It is just…the lawyers, all the expenses…it is overwhelming, and like I said. It's too much…" She looks up at Jaime, her big brown eyes brimming with tears, and she continues, "I'm about to lose my home. My ex drained all the equity from home, and I am so upside down now I just cannot make the new payments anymore. It was an adjustable loan, I did not know, but I do not need to overwhelm you with all this, I just wanted to air out. Oof! I apologize, this is none of your concern, but I wanted you to know where my mind is in case I'm acting a little off." Suddenly she uses her napkin again to dry her eyes from the tears, and her soft perfume and revealing dress arouse more than Jaime's sympathy. Slowly, he reaches for her hand on the table. She does not wear a ring...

"Would you like a drink, Rosie?"

It is now in the late hours of the night, and Jaime's mansion is unusually quiet and empty tonight. The pool looks like a picture of a romantic island somewhere in the Caribbean. No one is in it. The waterfall is the only noise, and the low lights cast the appropriate mood. Inside, Jaime's lavish rooms are silent and empty. All the lights except for a single lamp are out, and two empty wine glasses sit on the dinner table. Upstairs in the master bedroom, soft romantic music plays, we see Jaime and Rosie there. Their minds spin as the clock slowly moves, and the soft music continues to play. Neither one notices time slowly passing into almost the early hours of the morning, and Jaime wishes this blessed moment would never come to an end.

The following morning Jaime wakes up bright and early, and he carefully jumps out of bed to try not to wake up Rosie, who is sound asleep. He leaves the house and drives to his office, feeling like a million bucks. As he enters, he tells his secretary to bring him a Cuban coffee, and he sits at his private bar, returning a few phone calls and looking at his day planner. Jaime's office is large, expansive, and overly rich. It features a full-size flat-screen TV, which plays on SportsCenter, the volume has been muted. Opulent potted palm trees, black leather couches, and a massive desk adorn the modern office space. All his furniture has been imported from Italy, and his office is decorated by the best interior designers in all of Miami. On top of his desk, there is a new desktop computer monitor and a huge ashtray next to a new box of Ijaba Cigars...and nothing else. There is no telephone, no paper tray, and no printer. Jaime's office is as modern as *The Matrix*, and he likes it, but still he often complaints about how much it cost to have the place decorated in a way he can't do anything without his secretary, who does everything for Jaime, from printing a piece of paper to making a phone call, to making a cup of coffee. "What happened to personal attention? The poor girl does everything for me…and she talks to my clients more than I do. What is the point; she might as well be the boss, right? I bet you no one even knows I run this place…" Jaime talks to himself as he stands there just admiring the panoramic view of the ocean from his office window. "Wow, look at that view! I need to do this more often… What is the sense of having all this if I never have any time to enjoy it?" Jaime calls on his phone, and suddenly, someone answers on the other line. "Hello, it's Jaime! Yeah, it is a mortgage. I just want to help her out with a small loan…" Jaime pauses for a second, listening to the other end of the conversation. Jaime listens. "No problem. I will call you back with the information." He hangs up, and as he turns around, Triana walks into his office. He looks far from happy. Jaime offers him a seat, the lawyer declines.

"Jaime, I'm your friend, but this is insanity. Have you lost your mind?" Jaime's face darkens with anger…

"What are you talking about? Wait a minute, Triana, my friend. Who built this mini empire? Me or you?"

"You did, Jaime, and all I'm trying to do is help. Just please slow down. This meeting is happening way too soon, and we need to talk about it," responds the old attorney, serious and concerned about Jaime's untimely decisions. All Jaime can do is just stare at him with anger.

"Listen, if it bothers you so much… I tell you what, go home! You are off the hook… I can handle this myself!" With a burst of fury, Jaime storms out, and Triana just stands there with his arms crossed, and he is whispering to himself:

"Idiot!"

The next morning, inside a fancy conference hall in a hotel in Miami Beach, an assemblage of corporate types in 3000 dollars suits sits around a large conference table. These men observe as Jaime, with Ramon at his side, signs papers. Triana, Jaime's lawyer, is absent. Jaime has now authorized Ramon to move some of his money around and into several extremely prominent investment opportunities. The future looks very bright for Jaime, according to Ramon, and his money should be doubling in almost no time. Good call on Jaime's behalf to have listened to Ramon's advice, and no wonder so many people have financial advisors to guide them in the complicated process of investing in the stock market and feeling like a billion dollars, Jaime smiles with a sense of certainty.

Several weeks have now passed, and Rosie and Jaime have become a couple. They have been almost inseparable during this time, and Jaime has been nowhere to be seen. He is not even returning any of his calls while neglecting many of his obligations, both here in Miami and in Nicaragua. He has been to many of the ball games to see the boys play; however, always bringing Rosie with him. Jaime's personal life is beginning to enjoy what it lacked. He seems to have found what was absent, and it shows. Meanwhile, business is beginning to suffer at the hands of his absence as the control he usually applies to his business is now in the hands of other people who do not perform the job with the same level of diligence and respect as he.

Jaime and Rosie return from a recent trip to the Bahamas, and they sit inside the VIP bar at the club in Miami like royalty, both dressed spectacularly. Chuchi, who is there with a Brazilian model hanging on his arm, joins them. He has flown in a few days before his team plays the Florida Marlins in interleague play. Rosie sits closer to the young model while Jaime and Chuchi sit together at the edge of the bar. Rosie decides to establish a conversation with the young lady to break the uncomfortable silence, "Jaime used to play ball too, you know." Rosie stands and frowns over Jaime, kissing him. The model also stands and places both her arms over Chuchi, sort of claiming her territory…and softly whispers in his ear:

"Was he as great as you?" Chuchi looks her in the eye…

"Taught me everything I know. Jaime was an incredible baseball player too," explains Chuchi, and the model giggles.

"I doubt that…"

Chuchi quickly replies, "No, seriously, he did. He has always been my biggest fan, but also my mentor and teacher."

"That's nice. Well, excuse me. I have to go to the ladies' room," the model pleads as she struggles to her feet in the skin-squeezing miniskirt, and Jaime and Chuchi laugh. Rosie also excuses herself and joins the young model, and the two women walk off, garnering admiring looks from everyone at the bar. Jaime and Chuchi watch them depart, and so does everyone else in the bar area.

"I am so lucky. I think she was God-sent. I really do," Jaime tells his younger friend, and he kindly waves to the bartender for another round. Chuchi regards him with concern, as Jaime is now slightly drunk. Jaime continues, "Did you hear what I said? I'm so lucky, I think I'm in love, bro." Jaime eyes Chuchi, and he responds sarcastically:

"Well, something like that… I saw how much money you blew to bail her out of her little problem and then asked her to move in almost immediately. Papa, you are either in love or insane."

Jaime, not liking the tone Chuchi uses, fires right back, "I didn't blow anything. Besides, who is the teacher, and who is the student here? Why can't you be happy for me?" Jaime replies, annoyed and almost raising his voice, he slams his drink on the table. He then gives Chuchi a look that says everything, and Chuchi defends himself:

"Chill, I'm kidding with you, Jaime. I tell you; you are letting the bottle take the best of you," Chuchi responds and waives to the bartender. "Just water for me, thanks." Jaime dives into his drink, and Chuchi hesitates, "Hey, Papa, why don't you call it a night after that drink?"

Jaime gives Chuchi a stern look, and without wavering, he utters his fatherly response, "Junior, respect your elders. I can handle my rum," Jaime replies defensively, and Chuchi fires right back:

"Yeah, I know, Papa, you're drinking scotch, though…" Jaime then looks at his drink. So he is. Not feeling any shame, he takes the glass to his mouth and slowly downs it. Chuchi immediately turns to Jaime, and in a low tone of voice, he explains, "Listen…Papa, you know I love you like a father, don't take this the wrong way, but coming from a place like Cuba where we didn't see a liquor store for miles and landing here to the land where booze flows like tap water is quite a stretch. Jaime, you are letting the alcohol take you over." Chuchi keeps his eyes on Jaime, hoping he does not freak out on him, but Jaime instead changes his tone to a calmer mood, and looking right back into Chuchi's eyes, he asks his good friend:

"Are you lecturing me?"

Chuchi eyes him carefully…and responds, "It clouds your judgment, your responsibility. That is all I'm saying."

Jaime, much calmer, leans back, and placing his hands on both sides of Chuchi's face, replies, "Oh, and you're saying I've lost my sense of responsibility now? Now you are an expert on responsibility? Come on, kid… I've got it all under control, trust me." Jaime, beginning to feel interviewed and harassed, lets Chuchi know he does not like the awkward turn the conversation has taken, and he tries to change the subject, "So, what do you think of Rosie?" Chuchi gives Jaime a strange look as if telling him he is not a kid anymore…

"Don't change the subject. I'm serious, Jaime."

Jaime answers, "Well, well. Listen to the ball player calling out his mentor. Do you have what it takes to correct me? Mr. Experienced, all of a sudden?"

Chuchi thinks for a moment, gathering his thoughts before responding to Jaime, "Well, I had a good teacher. You could even say he was my hero." And at this, Chuchi stands and walks off, knocking on the door to the ladies' bathroom as he walks by. "Honey, let's go!" The young model immediately comes out of the ladies' room and latches onto Chuchi's arm, and they leave. Jaime turns his back as Chuchi walks away with his girlfriend, and he instantly takes a seat in one of the couches at the bar, and he lies back…

"Well, yeah. Everybody is an expert!"

Moments later, Jaime begins having one of his flashbacks, and he finds himself back in West Africa during the 1600s, where he is suddenly transported to idyllic scenes of nature. A sparkling waterfall, a mountain range carpeted by green jungle, and a paradise where antelope and gazelle graze grassy fields… Hundreds of colorful birds accent the sky… In the African village, it is now nighttime, and suddenly the calm is shattered by a group of pirate-like white European men who storm in with muskets. Knives and torches… In a slave ship, at night, he finds himself in a claustrophobic, dark, stinking cargo hold crushed amidst African men, women, and children chained together like wild animals, starving, bleeding, vomiting… Through the sweaty tangle of bodies, Jaime makes eye contact with half-naked, dirty, and frightened young Ijaba, Jaime's ancestor. She looks back at Jaime, who has been standing right in front of her this whole time, just watching, weeping. Suddenly, Jaime sees himself as one of the slaves below deck, gazing back at innocent young Ijaba, who is chained and bleeding. His eyes are screaming with shame as he pleads for forgiveness for his inability to help. His mouth wrenches open, and he expounds with every ounce of mustered strength at the top of his lungs, but only forceful silence trickles out… Jaime desperately cries in frustration.

It is the middle of the night, and inside the master bedroom of his mansion, Jaime jolts awake. Sweating and heart-pounding, he takes a moment to catch his breath from the horrible nightmare, and he turns to Rosie sleeping beside him. "Rosie…" He touches her gently…and calls out again, "Rosie…"

"What is it, baby?" she mumbles, and as he sits right up on the bed, she turns to him and places her head on his chest. "Jaime, you're sweating… Go back to sleep."

Jaime, now wide awake, feels he must explain: "Rosie, my life was nothing but a lie. I was a slave, and now that I have gained my freedom, it feels like I am slowly creeping back into the same chains I had once removed." Rosie snuggles closer with her eyes shut, nearly asleep. Jaime stares in the dark and continues, "I knew it. I knew it was a lie. That is what made it unforgivable…a man who lives a lie is only half a man. That is why I left, Rosie. That is why I escaped from Cuba and came here, but my past haunts me still. They say the only thing that is the same anywhere you go is you. So, if we have demons to deal with, there will never be inner peace regardless of where we escape to. We can run, but we cannot hide." Rosie just mutters and kisses his cheek as Jaime confesses his pain, "It's about much more than just making my dreams come true. I want to live my life true, Rosie… I believe a pure conscience gives you the keys to heaven. A true heart allows you to walk with God. Yet, I do not know God… I do not have a pure conscience, which is why the memory of Ijaba, my ancestor, just will not let me be." He pauses for a moment…then he continues, "Do you believe that, Rosie? Do you believe in God?"

"Yeah…I believe," Rosie mumbles just vaguely as she drifts back to sleep. Jaime wraps his arms around her, kissing her face. He presses his chest against hers with his eyes wide open.

"Rosie? Did you hear me? I have been alone since I was ten; I'm tired of being alone." At this, he pulls her closer and holds her tightly, and the long silk curtains hanging from the window blow softly as the midnight sea breeze enters the room. A few minutes later, Jaime and Rosie are both sound asleep, lying there motionless in each other's arms, a lonely tear rests upon Jaime's face.

Jaime begins to dream… He hears a soft voice in his dream whispering, "How do I approach trouble times? What do I do in times of crisis? I choose God and His ways… I wait for an intersection or a God moment, and that's when I act…" Jaime is now completely asleep, and so is Rosie. The night slowly moves…

The following morning Jaime is up and running early. He stops for his usual morning coffee and reading the paper, he sits at an outside table in the sun in one of the many coffee shops lining the street. Surrounded by birds feeding off the crumbs from his muffin he has thrown on the ground, Jaime watches the birds devour the tiny crumbs, and he thinks about his dreams. He thinks about how everything is finally happening for him, and he then leans back, allowing the sun to bathe him from head to toe. His own words begin to echo inside his head…and he continues to reflect on the realization of all he had ever dreamt and how it has finally starting to come to fruition. But confusion suddenly startles him. *Wow! After so much work and dedication, it is all finally here, I am truly living my dream*, he adds selfishly, slowly standing to his feet, and after shaking a few muffin crumbs from his shirt, he begins walking away from the coffee shop.

Just a few blocks away, inside a men's clothing store, Stephanie helps her father shop for ties. She is dressed as elegant as always, and her father is as grumpy as usual. "Daddy, I know you're hurt, but try to get over it. You cannot control what other people do or say."

"Hurt? No, I am not hurt, I am pissed. He would not have even had a chance without me," Mr. Romero adds, and Stephanie responds, engaging in their sudden back-and-forth chat:

"Okay, but…" Stephanie tries to interrupt, but her upset father does not hear her…

"How soon we forget. I made everything possible for him. Everything. All I ever asked him was to be responsible and to never act without my council." Holding up a tie and looking for Stephanie's approval, he continues, "How about this one?" Stephanie picks another…

"Orange is much cooler for you. He is not trying to hurt you, Daddy. He just needs to learn for himself. Maybe you need to let him find out on his own, you know, do not baby him so much."

"Oh, sure, so now he's hit his rebellious teenage years," Mr. Romero says sort of under his breath.

Stephanie thoughtfully finds another tie for her father and continues, "We all make our own mistakes, but eventually, we're usually stronger for it. I think you saw the man inside, and he will always be that man, Daddy."

Mr. Romero pauses for a second and then proceeds, "Did you know he hasn't been back to check on the cigar operation in Nicaragua in months?"

Stephanie jumps in, "Well, things are running smoothly now, and he has you to look over it, plus his uncle and Chuchi." Mr. Romero looks at his daughter carefully and nods his head…

"You too…huh?" She smiles.

Several hours later… Inside Jaime's office, Jaime sits facing the panoramic view from his office window, and as he gazes pensively out at the ocean, he is suddenly startled by the intercom buzzer. Rolling his chair back to his desk, he hits the intercom, and the secretary answers, "Mr. Colon, you have Ms. Stephanie Romero on line one."

And just about an hour later, Jaime and Stephanie agree to meet at a restaurant across the street from his office. It is the same restaurant Jaime and her father used to frequent, making it their favorite meeting place when it all started. This little place has now become a meeting landmark for anything related to Jaime and his cigar business. It carries sentimental value, perhaps a little bit of superstition, a bit of empathy? "How about this?" Chuchi, realizing Jaime frequented the place so much, went ahead and bought it without Jaime ever knowing, and now making complete sense why the waiters and the restaurant manager would always tell Jaime his money wasn't good there and never allow him to pay. The maître d' escorts Jaime to his favorite outside table, and immediately spotting Stephanie, he begins to smile, then he pauses…pointing at her in amazement at how wonderful she looks. "Aww, look at you!" She has brought her father with her, and Jaime is now even more surprised. Jaime tries to cover his shock as he approaches the table as they both stand, and he and Mr. Romero shake hands out of respect, and Jaime kisses Stephanie on the cheek. "Stephanie, you look wonderful." He then turns stiffly to Mr. Romero. "Mr. Romero, hello!"

"Don't bother with your hypocritical comments, Jaime, I know I look nothing spectacular, but the tie is genuinely nice, isn't it? Stephanie picked it." Jaime looks at the tie…

"Yes, genuinely nice tie indeed, it really saves you! Stephanie must have picked it out for you alright because I have seen the ones you select." Jaime looks at Mr. Romero and gives him a smirk.

"Ahh, sit down, Jaime, and stop pretending you're still pissed at me." Jaime looks at him cautiously, and Mr. Romero continues, "What? I did not get where I am today in business by holding grudges. Holding a grudge is like dieting on poison. I love you, kid." He then warmly slaps Jaime's shoulder…and gives him a warm hug. Jaime kisses the old man on the cheek with much respect and warm reverence. "Look, Jaime, let us try to have a nice lunch! And let us put all our differences aside, okay? It's a beautiful day."

At this, Jaime grins and fires back sarcastically, "Do I have a choice? No? Then, no objection, Your Honor!" Mr. Romero smiles, and the three of them break into laughter.

They have a nice lunch, reminiscing over Cuban Palomilla steak, white rice, and black beans and a huge avocado salad bathed in olive oil and sprinkled with balsamic vinegar. Also, a nice bottle of red wine sits on the table as they chat amiably. This is a pleasant moment, a nice touch of a friendly reunion. "Just look at you, Jaime, and to think it all started in my old ugly office with a couple of cigar magazines."

"Daddy, no one ever said your office was ugly. Undecorated maybe…a little abandoned…" Stephanie adds…and they laugh.

Jaime follows, "I remember the paintings on the wall. It looked like Picasso painted them while falling asleep." They laugh some more…and Jaime follows, "I beg your pardon, sir, but it all started way before your ugly office. It started with a dream a long time ago inside this big watermelon." Jaime grins, pointing at his head, and Stephanie proceeds:

"'The ancestor to every action is a thought…' remember? Ralph Waldo Emerson…" Stephanie reminds Jaime, smiling and remembering this very conversation, which had taken place some time ago. She then looks at her father, who is busy cutting his steak, but he puts the knife down and turns to Jaime at once.

"Let us get to the point sometime before dessert, shall we? I did not invite you here to critique my office or impress my daughter with literary quotes. Jaime, I want you to know I am prepping an associate to take over my business. I am getting old, and I want to relax a bit at the end of my days." Jaime stares at him carefully. Mr. Romero continues, "No, I'm not retiring. No such luck. You know me, I work, therefore I am, but a few years down the road…who knows. What I have built is too precious to allow an outsider to get his hands on it. It must be run by the right person." Jaime looks at him, surprised…

"Who?" Jaime asks.

"Well, you are looking at her," Mr. Romero replies, and Jaime surprisingly looks at Stephanie to try to catch the expression on her face as the old man says this. He then looks back at her father and back at Stephanie again with utter surprise. A waiter glides over.

"Another Dewar's and soda, Mr. Colon?" Jaime barely nods. He is distracted and somewhat surprised at the news of Stephanie taking over a business typically run by men.

The business Mr. Romero built from nothing and which now handles the lives of many Latin American baseball players and prospects coming to the major leagues. A lucrative business combined with a non-profit, a life-changing company, and a serious noble idea where one man's money and power lifts the human spirit to a whole new level, and which will now be run by none other than a woman with an even bigger heart. "It was her idea. Listen, I am old-fashioned and proud of it. We live in a man's world, for better or worse. Usually for worse, but nevertheless, I told her it was ridiculous, and it is… Of course, I am wrong. She is the most qualified person I know, and I practically know everyone. Do we agree?" Stephanie tries to hide her emotions as she takes her father's hand. Jaime is at a loss with surprising conviction but extremely glad to hear the news, and then suddenly, Mr. Romero clutches his chest and begins to shake uncontrollably. His eyes roll back, and he begins to struggle for breath, Stephanie screams:

"Daddy?" Still gasping for air, he topples to the ground, sending his chair sprawling, and Stephanie leaps to her feet and yells, "Call an ambulance!" Jaime leaps over the table to Mr. Romero's aide.

A few hours later, inside a hospital corridor, Jaime and Stephanie wait outside the emergency room. She is frantic, and Jaime softly touches her shoulder to keep her calm. He gently squeezes her hand without saying one word, and she gives him a tiny smile, wiping a tear from her face. The two of them just sit there, and all they can do is wait in the uncomfortable silence of the hospital hallway. After several more minutes of waiting, one of the doctors from the emergency room approaches, and they rush over to him to try to find out about Mr. Romero's condition. At his reassuring words, Stephanie nearly faints with gratefulness. She then wraps her arms around Jaime's neck, filled with joy and overwhelming relief. Mr. Romero is going to be okay!

Inside Jaime's mansion at night, Enrico opens the front door, and Jaime trudges in. He is drained after a long day…and after taking Jaime's coat and briefcase, Enrico asks with sincere concern about Mr. Romero's condition, "How is he, Mr. Colon?"

"He's okay, Enrico. Thank you for asking. Where's Rosie?"

Enrico hesitates awkwardly and then replies, "She hasn't come home yet, sir." Looking at his watch, Jaime does not say anything, but he frowns, and after running his hand through his forehead and through his hair, he bids Enrico a good night.

"I'll see you in the morning, Enrico."

And just moments later, in the main hall outside his bedroom with a drink in hand, Jaime has passed out in his clothes. He is sprawled on his luxurious Italian designer sofa, with his head back and his eyes closed. An empty bottle sits on the coffee table next to the sofa. A moment later, at the sound of keys in the door, he stirs, and Rosie walks in. Jaime is groggy with a drink. "Where have you been?" Jaime asks Rosie.

"I went shopping. Then I saw a movie. Were you sleeping on the sofa?" Jaime reaches for his glass and sees it is empty.

"Rosie, it's midnight, and you don't have any shopping bags…" She comes closer to him…

"Are you interrogating me? I didn't buy anything. What is the problem? Did you need me for anything?" Jaime surprisingly frowns at her tone, and immediately he tries to ignore it…

He sits up and explains, "Mr. Romero had a heart attack." Rosie stares at him with clear compassion, and Jaime continues, "He's okay…he'll be fine, the doctor says." Suddenly, Rosie is hit with a ton of guilt, and she drops her guard.

"Oh, baby, I'm sorry… I didn't know. We have been spending so much time together, when you are not around, I just feel…lost! Lonely!" She goes to him, and Jaime grabs her, he pulls her down and kisses her, crushing his mouth against hers. He kisses her hard, with an emptiness to fill. She lies down next to him on the sofa and comforts him. Jaime rests in her arms… Finding the sympathy he needs.

In the middle of the night, Jaime tosses and turns on the bed in a complete state of restlessness… And finally, he awakes, startled, he turns to Rosie. She isn't there. Her side of the bed empty. In his silk pajamas, Jaime walks in the dark, looking for Rosie, and he finally finds her sleeping in the guests' room. He gently sits on the edge of the bed, still in the dark. Rosie stirs, half asleep. "Think I'm getting a cold. Didn't want to keep you up." Jaime looks at her blankly.

"Rosie, what happened to the girl I met a few months ago?" There is an empty awkward silence, followed by a long and uncomfortable pause…

"Oh… Don't be silly, Jaime," she whispers in a convincible manner, and as Jaime stands up dully, he turns to leave, but Rosie continues, "Wait!" Her eyes gleam at him in the dark, a bit emotional. "Jaime, you are a good man. You're an honest man. No one can take that away. Okay!"

"What does that mean?" he asks… She then quickly rolls over.

"Jaime, go back to sleep. We will talk in the morning. Okay, honey?" Jaime just stands there in the dark, staring at Rosie as if wanting to continue their conversation, but she covers herself with the sheets, letting him know the conversation is over.

In the morning, Jaime leaves the house early and drives to his office. He is late for an appointment. The appointment is with none other than Stephanie, who has been waiting for him for over half an hour now. She finds herself in Jaime's office, waiting and staring at the young receptionist who spends most of her time inside her computer screen… Finally, Stephanie politely asks, "Excuse me, Miss, is he going to be much longer? I have things to do. I can come back later." But before the receptionist can answer, Jaime walks in, agitated. He was running.

Almost out of breath, he greets Stephanie, "I'm sorry! I lost track of time. Good morning! And thank you for waiting." Jaime kisses Stephanie on her cheek, and he asks her to follow him to his office. She takes a seat in one of the designer chairs inside Jaime's office, and while he perches on the edge of his desk, he watches Stephanie look around his office for the first time. It is impressive, everything money can buy. She then turns to Jaime…and he asks, "How is your dad?" Stephanie clears her throat.

"He's resting now. Sort of, I hired a nurse to watch over him. Poor woman, she has her work cut out for her." She smiles at Jaime and gazes at the magnificent and panoramic ocean view through the office window.

Jaime replies, "I know I don't need to say this, but if there is anything I can do…please let me know. I know everyone says that, but I do not really know what else to say in a situation like this. He is going to be okay, and you should know my offer is genuine." Stephanie agrees by motioning with her head.

"Thank you. I know, but how are you? How's Rosie?" Jaime does not answer. Stephanie continues, "Dad says it must be odd for you, living with someone after being a roving bachelor all your life." Embarrassed, she quickly adds, "Pardon me, you don't have to answer. That was not very prudent."

"Relax, Steph. We are practically family now; I can take words… Is the roving bachelorette worried about me? I'm a big boy, I can take care of myself, you know?" Stephanie smiles coyly.

"Me? Roving bachelorette?"

"Yes. What about you?" he presses, and as she gets ready to answer, again, she clears her throat.

"I suppose I haven't been asked by the right man yet, Mr. Colon. There have been a few guys here and there, but school was always more important, and time just flies. And now between work and daddy, forget it."

Jaime smiles and proceeds, "That's better. Except don't you think it's about time we drop the Mr.?" Stephanie glances at him, and Jaime continues, "You know, my grandmother always said my not taking a wife is either a sin or a miracle."

Stephanie curiously replies, "Well, what do you say, Jaime? Which is it?"

Jaime carefully responds, "I told her I just never found the right woman either. Me and you are in the same boat. It is a jungle out there. Now psychologists say these days it can take up to a year to really see the real person inside someone you just meet. Scary, huh?"

Stephanie gently touches one of his palm trees…and fires right back, "A whole year? I dated a guy for about five years, and in the end…going hunting with his friends and racecars were more important. He was a nice guy but a bit immature for me, maybe I spend too much time with my dad, and maturity matters to me. What about you… Isn't Rosie the right woman, though, Jaime? She is certainly beautiful."

Jaime stops to think, and suddenly, he is saved by the bell as the intercom buzzes, and his receptionist calls out, "Mr. Colon?" There is a pause. "Sir, are you available?"

"Yes?" Jaime answers to the young lady over the intercom…she then proceeds:

"Sir, it's Bank of America."

"Take a message, please… I'm in a meeting," responds Jaime, but she insists:

"It's Mr. Roth, sir, the bank president. He says it is urgent." Jaime excuses himself, and he promises Stephanie they will finish their conversation. Immediately, he picks up the phone while he has Jordan take Stephanie back.

A few moments later we see Jaime heading to the bank to meet with Mr. Roth. At the bank, Jaime sits across from the bank president in his plush office. Jaime is flanked by several dark-suited bank officials as they look over legal documents; he is stunned at the news. Suddenly, there is a knock on the door, and Jaime's lawyer Hiram Triana enters with his briefcase in hand. "I'm sorry, gentlemen; I got here as soon as I could. I am Mr. Colon's lawyer, Hiram Triana. What is it?" Jaime stares, dazed.

He finally speaks, "There must be some kind of mistake here, Hiram." Triana is also in shock, looking down at all the paperwork before him.

He curiously follows, "What is this?"

"He says, Ramon… Well, my financial adviser has forged a power of attorney, and…" Jaime explains to his lawyer, who replies impatiently:

"What about Ramon? What about a power of attorney?" Mr. Roth stands and begins pacing…

"Mr. Triana, you are aware that Mr. Colon's financial adviser, one Ramon Gonzalez, had access authority to Mr. Colon's accounts, is that true?"

"Yes! But he is only authorized to move funds directly approved by Jaime and with a second signature of approval from me. It is all right here in these disclosure forms," Mr. Triana answers, paling, as Mr. Roth carries on explaining:

"Well, I'll cut to the bone. As of eight this morning, this Ramon character has virtually drained every account he was previously managing on behalf of Mr. Colon. For several days we received alerts on unusual activity related to Mr. Colon's accounts, but it was all suddenly explained by these three new corporations to which all the funds were being transferred. Here is all the paper trail backing up these transactions, and until this morning, it all clicked exactly right. However, this morning around 10 a.m., there was a flaw detected in the signature, and that is when we discovered the signature was being forged, and illicit activity was being performed. We immediately placed a red alert to our fraud department, and the agents now tell us he has disappeared. Ramon is gone along with all the money that was directed to these accounts. Gentlemen, I regret to inform that the amount exceeds the eighty-four million dollars' mark." Triana stands there speechless, and Mr. Roth continues to explain, "Mr. Colon, we are doing everything we can. We have already contacted the police and any department that may have anything to do with this. We are trying to locate him, but for now, we need you to press charges. This is far graver than you think, this is federal." For Jaime, everything begins to spin. His lawyer riffles through the paperwork, and the words coming out of Mr. Roth's mouth are now all silent as Jaime is so furious; he is suddenly unable to hear. The man's lips move, but Jaime hears nothing. A chill runs down his spine with the news registering in the mind of a simple man who, just a few years before, had only heard of this kind of money in movies. Certainly not exactly the type of thing he had ever imagined would happen to him. Jaime's awe continues for a lasting moment as reality dawns upon him. He is frozen, paralyzed.

Outside Jaime's favorite restaurant, it is raining, and no one sits at the colorful outside tables as the rain pours down. Inside, only Jaime sits alone in one of the booths, drinking coffee. He is unusually quiet, still in a state of shock, and the waitresses try to avoid him, sensing by his silence he does not want to be bothered. A few moments later, Triana joins him. The old lawyer walks in with his briefcase in hand and an umbrella. He takes a seat next to Jaime, and the two of them have a solemn lunch while Jaime listens, very much stunned, as his lawyer goes over important paperwork, explaining his options. Reaching for his drink, Jaime carelessly spills it, and Triana curses at him. Then the lawyer apologizes while suddenly remembering who he works for. "I just can't believe this, Jaime! How could you have been so naïve?" Jaime quickly lifts his head, giving Triana a look, which needs no words, and Triana quickly responds to smooth things out, "We will try to fix this. You did not know any better, I know. Let me make some more phone calls. Okay? I will contact the custodian of all the accounts, and we will begin an investigation." A waiter brings a fresh drink and cleans up the mess on the table as Jaime keeps his head down well in doubt.

Moments later, Triana has left, and Jaime sits there all alone, feeling like a zombie. He tries to recollect his thoughts and laments his ignorance for a few painful moments, probably thinking of all he could have done differently and how he neglected the basic rules in life his old uncle taught him. "But they tell us to trust our advisors. They swear to God that they know all about the market and where to place our money in the safest form. Their credentials are extremely convincing, their schooling and licenses impressive, to say the least, but in all reality, market-based investment is always risky and unpredictable, and some of these conniving, heartless individuals make a great living misleading many innocent people who see the principal of their investment diminished to almost nothing just a short time after falling in the hands of these ruthless monsters.

In the end, all we get is a statement. There is never any real tangible asset attached, and no one really explains how to read all that mumbo jumbo inside the one-hundred-page prospectus and what all those funny symbols represent. We never really know where our money is really being invested, and we have no control. We are led to believe these value-based investments are our only options, and we trust them blindly. 'Value' meaning when the market is up, we make money, but when it is down, the answer is obvious, right?"

Jaime finally stumbles out into the rain, holding his drink, and the waiter comes after him and politely takes the glass from his hand. Jaime feels lost and confused, and the drinking does not help the situation either, only amplifying his dark turmoil as he curses everyone and everything as he walks away… Jaime tries to recollect his thoughts and laments his ignorance for a few painful moments, probably thinking of all he could have done differently. He mumbles, "I detest dishonest people…a herd of cowards, snakes!"

A few hours later, Jaime makes his way back to his house, staggering through the door like a dead man, Enrico sees him come in and offers to help. Jaime refuses. The butler looks at him, and, disturbed, he shakes his head in pity. Jaime looks awful. He is drenched from head to toe and completely drunk. As Jaime walks in the master bedroom, he realizes Rosie's closet is empty as a tomb. He walks downstairs zombie-like, and as he finishes his drink, he pours another. Dropping several pieces of ice onto the floor, he picks up the phone, and this is when a terrible truth dawns on him, he does not have anyone to call. Minutes later, at a loss, he dials, and after several rings, someone answers at the other end. "Stephanie?"

A short time later… Different is the gloomy expression in Jaime's eyes as a throbbing tear rolls down his cheekbone in repentance and regret. Still drunk, he is lost, and deep inside his burning soul, he knows things are falling apart, and there is absolutely nothing he can do to prevent it.

Jaime Becomes Financially Rich but Spiritually Dead

PRIOR TO THIS WHOLE mess, Ramon had taken complete control of Jaime's investment accounts, basically becoming the handler of all of Jaime's finances, except for a few credit cards and Jaime's personal checking accounts. The initial idea had come about Ramon performing quite impressively with the money Jaime had entrusted him with. He quickly made an impression on Jaime by doing such an amazing job in doubling Jaime's net worth while allowing him to have extraordinary cash flow in truly little time. This was just about the only part of Jaime's life making any sense as everything else just dangled in the wind with him chasing Rosie around and not spending much time overseeing things related to his tobacco business both in Nicaragua and here in the States. At first, Jaime felt quite blessed to have trusted someone with such incredible talent in the field of finances, an area he was not at all familiar with. On top of it, to have doubled and almost tripled his net worth in such little time was a good reason to feel comfortable as well, and every time Jaime checked his account balances and his investment portfolio balance sheet, it was another reason to celebrate as it had literally gone through the roof. "Investment portfolio," who would have ever thought Jaime would be using words like these as part of his vocabulary? When not too long ago, these two words were French to him, but Ramon had diversified Jaime's financial interests into so many different avenues only he really knew what was happening, but it worked, especially for Jaime. However, this is never a good thing as we all know any good investor or, for that matter, anybody in handling money should always know exactly where every single penny is always. Balancing a simple checkbook is one of the most basic things in personal finances, yet many are those who cannot even do this. "Know where every dollar is spent at all times," and always make sure your money balances correctly. Four minus two equals two, it is all basic stuff, but like Jaime, many of us do not bother with these small details, and it is sure to backfire sooner or later. Thinking things were marching in the right direction regarding his money, Jaime's life appeared to be heading towards an incredible bright future, but with Rosie still gone and the many legal issues going on, he would rather not look. The drinking also increased immensely as a way of hiding from responsibility. Jaime was losing control. Quite true, Jaime's financial growth is an impressive display of "placement awareness" regarding his money on Ramon's behalf, but with him not knowing a thing about his own money, it was certainly dangerous, and an inevitable collapse was surely soon to follow. With Ramon spreading Jaime's money in so many different avenues, it was almost impossible to track, and from real estate to oil, gold, and silver, to stocks and bonds, CDs, and all sorts of annuities constantly building up Jaime's portfolio to a point he had never imagined, it made Jaime believe Ramon was the answer, and if it was making Jaime money, he never cared that he didn't know what was happening or how.

Ignorance can be ecstasy to someone like Jaime; to someone who does not know it has a price in the end to not be educated in the things that matter, and every now and then, Jaime's old uncle's wisdom comes to mind as he shamefully remembers the old man's words, "Jaime, there may come a day when you'll have to choose between being a man enough to face the facts or being a man who prefers to live under false illusions." These words of the wise old man would eventually echo inside his mind as Jaime obviously had no idea where the money was going, but all he knew was that it suddenly returned with a large sum attached to it, so who cares, right? Just keep it flowing, baby! Ignorance at its highest, again…but since he had been so busy, coming and going, running the cigar operation at first, and now looking for Rosie, he had absolutely no clue of how

Ramon was doing what he was doing, but the numbers do not lie. Yes, Jaime's net worth has almost tripled in extraordinarily little time, just like Ramon had told him it would when he initially talked Jaime into allowing him to handle his finances, making this about the only pure joy Jaime experienced now as all else collapsed before him. But not for long, trouble was here, and Jaime could no longer hide from the facts.

Apparently, Ramon's expertise in the stock market had secured Jaime a rather interesting spot among some of the bigwigs in the money game, and his name was beginning to sound with that of the big boys in the money circle. Without knowing it, Jaime was starting to become a sort of Mr. Gekko (a character played by Michael Douglas in the movie *Wall Street*) thanks to Ramon, and he was beginning to be viewed as an icon by many in the financial district. His story and sudden success were perhaps viewed as an amazing tale and even an incredible feat, some would say.

Several months later… It is a beautiful morning in South Florida, and inside Jaime's house, soft music plays. The wooden shutters are wide open, allowing the sun to penetrate, brightening the entire house. Out of the blue, the front door flies open, and Jaime enters with a suitcase in hand. He is returning from a short business trip, and to his surprise, he finds several pieces of important documents lying on his desk inside his home office as he walks into the dusty room. In a voice suppressed with deep concern and emotion, he whispers, reading from the document, "What the heck is this? Who put these here?" A single note sits on top of the pile of legal papers, and it reads, "Jaime, take two minutes to look through these documents. Please do not disregard. I will call you later. Chuchi." Concerned, Jaime now begins to open a series of envelopes, which contain specific documentation about Ramon's involvement in illicit business with various members in the drug world on top of everything else. There are also several pictures inside the envelopes, confirming Ramon's association with certain well-known criminals; pictures that show Ramon shaking hands and having drinks with these notorious characters. Jaime becomes angry, and with his face in a state of shock, he picks up the telephone and dials…the phone rings. "Chuchi, what is this, little brother? I need to see you right away. What is going on?" Jaime decides to make his way to see his friend Chuchi who has agreed to meet with him immediately. He does not even change his clothes; all he does is ask Enrico to make him a shot of Cuban coffee, and he leaves. The two had agreed to meet to go over all the new information in the envelopes at a nearby coffee shop, but as Jaime walks out to his house, he realizes he cannot find his keys. He is shaking with anger. He then calls Chuchi and tells him to come to his house instead. He is in no position to drive.

Finally, moments later, Chuchi walks in, and Jaime's mind races with confusion as the young man, wide-eyed and lost in turmoil, finally speaks, "Illegal drugs? Come on, man!"

This is something Jaime never suspected and something he has never wanted to be a part of. Inside the house, Jaime and his young friend go over and discuss the present situation to try to resolve this serious mess. "So much for the land of milk and honey… Huh, Chuchi? This is not what I want," mourns Jaime, and after a long pause, Chuchi replies, looking him right in the eye:

"Jaime, everyone wants to go to heaven, but no one wants to die, they say, from the *Mayflower* to the banana boats leaving Vietnam and the Mariel Harbor in 1980, it is all written in history. This is a country built by immigrants, built by the calloused hands of hard workers, by fruit vendors who make sure their children will have a better life, and small business owners who build it all from the ground up. There are no shortcuts in life, no easy way out and no magic behind building a dream. Yet, spoiled billion-dollar corporations beg the government like breastfed babies to bail them out in times of economic trouble, and they do. Tell me, who bails the little guys out? Illegal drugs are not the answer. Not my thing. No easy fix for success without hard work." Jaime absorbs this in deep thought and approves by shaking his head. Chuchi then abruptly opens up, "Jaime, we are all very different, but somehow, this country makes it work. Except when there is so much greed, it overshadows the greatness of this great land. Look at the banking system, Wall Street; just take a good look at our very own government."

"Very well said, son," Jaime directs his friend in agreement, and they share a look that says they are both on the same page. Soon after Chuchi leaves with a promise that he will help him clear his name of all these allegations hovering over. But sure enough, almost immediately, rumors begin to circulate the financial district about Jaime's possible involvement in funny business, and as they say, when it rains, it pours, and just like that, Jaime goes from Gordon Gekko in his prime to Gekko when he was first released from prison after losing everything and back to being a nobody.

Consequently, Jaime does the obvious, and he stays away from Wall Street, and just like that, a once-prominent hangout for Jaime now becomes a place to stay away from, leaving him with only one choice, to concentrate on his cigar business; all he has left...or does he?

Several months have now passed... Jaime has become so busy and fixated on the global success of his cigars, knowing this is the only thing that helps him keep his sanity. Even though Jaime's personal finances have taken a dive, Ijaba Cigars are now rapidly expanding to Europe as well, and the demand continues to grow. He works on the field day and night alongside his old uncle. Today he sits for a moment to catch his breath and suddenly realizes he has barely had any time to catch any of the boys' baseball games as he works constantly to try to bury all the other stuff that is going on and the little time he has for himself he spends trying to find Rosie still. Jaime realizes that by paying attention to his cigar business, it helps him stay away from the depressing and turmoiled part of his life and his drinking, of course, which has begun to take a serious hold of him as a way of burying his sorrows. Jaime had become somewhat of a jealous freak around Rosie, and paranoia had taken over. Many times, he questioned her rationale for the many lies he received of her whereabouts after spending months together and being almost inseparable, but he could feel her sudden sense of distancing along with a strange cold spirit she had all of the sudden developed. He then went as far as tracking her credit card statements to see where she was having her coffee, lunches, and even where she was doing her shopping. Jaime went on to hiring a private investigator to follow her. It was obvious he was obsessed with Rosie, and he was turning into a complete mess as his personal life, just like his finances, suffered, but his cigar business thrived. Ijaba Cigars thrived only because of the high demand for the wonderful product Jaime and his people had put out there, but not at all because of his undivided attention to the dream that once moved him, and what a shame that at one point he had completely forgotten how it all started, and why? "Remember, work well done does much good to the man who does it, and it makes him a better man at the end." Also, "I like to work, and I like to do good work, for work is the best friend I've ever known." Jaime remembers reading this in a book he very much cherished… *The Richest Man in Babylon*, but his recent struggles had apparently made him draw away from all he learned in the successful and inspiring book as it shows. He had forgotten about his own motto, "Live and dream life!" One he lived by since his youth but now a vague distant memory. However, without his constant supervision and based upon his recent chaotic behavior, his cigar business was starting to suffer, though on the outside looking in, it appeared to continue to thrive. The operation in Nicaragua only survived because of his uncle, but in due time Jaime's neglect was apparent. This was only the beginning of everything slowly crashing, and had they been able to see it clearly, adjustments would have been made. But it crept up under their own noses, going unnoticed until it was just too late.

Jaime had apparently forgotten what hard work was and the same hard work and tenacity, which had catapulted him to the top of the mountain, placing him on a unique spot at the vortex of the cigar world, and this is exactly what was now absent. He probably began to think that it pays better to be smart and to get by without working, for "work was made for slaves," as some people often think once they begin to make the kind of money they never made before.

Well wrong! There is no shame in working hard to build a dream and to leave a legacy or even to pay the bills, but much shame there is in easy money, as easy come, easy go! The low-hanging fruit many times is nothing but a trap, so be careful! To top it all off, Jaime's accountants are beginning to question if the foundation of his cigar business was ever solid enough to support such a large operation in such a short period of time. As a matter of fact, to some, Jaime's success was something only seen in fairy tales, and, of course, his competitors' envy and their desire to take Jaime down was always an issue to keep his lawyers busy as well.

On several occasions, both the IRS and the FBI opened investigations over Jaime's incredibly successful cigar operation only to drop their cases shortly after because there has never been any evidence of any monkey business behind it. Jaime always ran a clean and legit operation thanks to Mr. Romero detailed advice, and not once has the FBI been able to find any reason to shut him down or even slow the growth of the company. As a matter of fact, with every false allegation and every single public accusation, Ijaba Cigars becomes even stronger. With every televised accusation or newspaper article linking Jaime and Ijaba Cigars to illegal activity, it only intensifies sales and serves as great promotion. In the end, nothing illegal can ever be brought against Jaime or his famous cigars, making every negative attempt to try to destroy the now global brand, once again, a tool to intensify its fame and, of course, Jaime's fortune. Being in the news constantly serves as a great way to promote the already popular product, making it even more desirable and cranking its value through the roof every single time. But with all the recent financial issues, there is big trouble in the horizon for Jaime, and the scary thing is that after Ramon's disappearance, all of Jaime's personal assets continue to be frozen while the investigation takes place, being that Ramon controlled Jaime's investments to a point where Jaime was barely involved. In addition, since money continued to pour in like a broken fountain up to this point, Jaime had always trusted Ramon so much he basically allowed him X amount of money to be invested freely and without even running it by him first, and why? Because it was working, everything this man touched would just simply turn to gold, so in Jaime's mind, if it isn't broken, why fix it? And aside from the many warnings Jaime received from Mr. Romero, Triana, and Chuchi, he continued forward with Ramon as his financial advisor almost as if the world were against him, and he wanted to prove everyone wrong. To Jaime, Ramon simply appeared to be a genius of some sort, until now, of course, where Jaime finally had every reason in the world to cut ties with this man, realizing he has been played, but Ramon has completely vanished.

The business structure Jaime built with the help of Mr. Romero, and his business associates had led him right up the threshold of unimaginable fame and success; however, he had failed to remember his first enemy, which was fear. He had become fearless, leading him to act extremely irresponsible and to not listen to counsel. Jaime declined advice from his mentor, Mr. Romero, and from those who genuinely cared about him over a man who made plenty of false promises and empty prophecies, Ramon. This is where everything first began to fall apart for Jaime.

"Quick cash in the hands of a fool is never good, in the end, it comes back to bite him like a rabid dog," yet another Mr. Romero's advice, which still lingers in the air for Jaime who had become careless and had simply forgotten how hard he worked to make his dream into a reality. He had certainly gone past beyond some of Mr. Romero's early tips in life, and one that comes to mind is, "Fear is good, it keeps you grounded and on your guard."

Mr. Romero often said that fear always strikes when you are most vulnerable but only to make you stronger and much wiser once you finally face your adversary. However, Jaime did the opposite. He ran. He ran from responsibility by putting his finances in the hands of a stranger because it had all become overwhelming to him. Learning something new such as managing large amounts of money seemed complicated to Jaime, and it felt uncomfortable, so he found it easier to delegate this task to someone else instead, a so-called expert. After all, isn't that what all wealthy people do? It is no different than the day we finally open the closet door as a little child, turn on the lights and then realize there is no monster in the closet, and afterwards we feel like conquerors. It's funny how many years later that very memory comes back only to teach us a lesson and to remind us that unless we face our trials and tribulations, we can never overcome them. But Jaime never wanted to deal with learning how to manage his own money, so instead of taking the time to learn this seemingly complicated issue, he placed everything in the hands of a professional; a mistake many of us so often commit, thinking it is much more productive to hire someone who is more qualified than us. Ahh, wrong again! A good banker knows everything there is to know about banking, he knows the rules, guidelines, and his training and extensive experience allow him to perform his job well. The same can be said about any type of business or occupation. How can anyone operate a vehicle legally without first obtaining a driver's license and before passing all required testing by the state to confirm knowledge of the rules and laws of operating a vehicle? You cannot, and if you get caught, you will receive a hefty fine, if not jail time. It is common sense; it is called the law for a good reason. During all the current chaos in his life, Jaime decides to pay a surprise visit to Chuchi and the boys who are participating in spring baseball games in Las Vegas. This is a rare opportunity Jaime cannot pass as life has become so hectic for everyone these days, since all their lives have become such a circus between baseball, traveling, living in different cities, different circle of friends, and different love lives, and not to mention Jaime's chaotic life, which is a complete mess at the moment and almost out of control. Although Jaime has mentioned the possibility, Chuchi never bothers inviting him to come out and does not even mention it to the other three. In all reality, a visit from Jaime, though never really expected, would have been a great rare reunion of Jaime, Chuchi, and the boys, and without anyone knowing, Jaime suddenly decides to show up anyway. Upon Jaime's arrival at the new baseball stadium in Downtown Summerlin in Las Vegas and home of the Oakland A's triple a minor league team, the Las Vegas Aviators, one of the trainers rushes out to meet him. Before Jaime can get out of his vehicle, a loud and sweaty old man, almost out of breath, motions to Jaime to roll down his window. "Hey, Jaime, how are you? You will not believe who just arrived yesterday!" asks the overweight trainer, breathing heavy and exhausted from the short run to Jaime's car.

Jaime removes his sunglasses and replies to the old man, "Who? Are you okay, Lou? You look like you are going to have a heart attack."

The trainer catches his breath, and more relaxed now, he responds to Jaime, "I'm okay. I'm okay now, much better. Doctor says I need to lose a few pounds… Anyway, Jaime, do you remember Roly Loredo, the young hot prospect from the Industriales team in Havana, the pitcher with a cannon for an arm?"

Surprised, Jaime responds to the old trainer, "Yeah, of course, I remember Roly. The young outfielder…right?"

The old trainer agrees by bobbing his head and continues, "Yeah, him. He was only about seventeen years old when you and the boys left and one of the hottest prospects in all of Cuba at the time. Well, guess what? The kid became one of their best pitchers, and just a few days ago, he jumped in a homemade raft with a couple of other people and landed in Miami. He is here in the States. Can you believe it?" Jaime smiles…

"Well, yeah, I believe it. I like it too. Where is he? I want to see him. Is he still in Miami?" Jaime beams as he says this, and to his surprise, the trainer adds:

"No, Jaime, he is here, inside the stadium. Right here in Las Vegas. All he needs to do is get himself an agent, pass all the physicals, and then he is money. Teams are already lining up," an excited Lou replies, and Jaime gives the old trainer a huge hug with much delight.

"Boy, good news sure travels fast," Jaime mutters, and right away, he and the trainer walk inside the stadium to talk to the young prospect who is already surrounded by a group of media guys…

"Alright, guys, let the kid breathe, would you? Besides, he is here to talk to me, not you," Jaime jokes, and upon hearing his voice, young Roly jolts out of his seat, and he runs to Jaime. Roly gives Jaime a huge bear hug.

"Alright, Jaime, mi hermano (my brother)! So nice to see you, old man. Wow, look at you. You look great. America has been good to you. Did you have a face-lift?" jokingly adds Roly, and Jaime replies:

"Nice to see you, Roly. Welcome to America, kiddo. You got to tell me all about your odyssey," Jaime tells the 6'3", 220-pound young man with sincere admiration, almost sounding like Mr. Romero, but before he can say another word, he is grabbed by Roly's big paws and lifted in the air.

"Jaime, I'm really here, man. I am here, in the United States of America, brother."

A short distance away, Papo, Chuchi, Panchi, and Tito witness the pleasant reunion, and they can't help but laugh as Jaime is tossed around like a rag doll by the young player who is extremely happy to see him. At this, Jaime receives a glimpse of exactly how Mr. Romero felt when he and the boys first arrived in America just a short time ago. Jaime suddenly understands the real reason why a successful businessman like Mr. Romero would take his time to do such a rigorous job as to find and bring Latin American baseball players to the majors while giving these stellar athletes the opportunity of a lifetime.

And just like that, for the next few hours, Jaime spends quality time chatting with the newly arrived kid while the other guys continue their practice out on the field. And as soon as practice ends, Jaime goes over to the rest of the guys and showers them all with hugs and all kind of fatherly affection. Afterwards, they all go to a nearby restaurant and enjoy a nice time together. Inside the restaurant, Jaime and the boys converse like old neighborhood buddies, catching up on lost time. "So, Pops, enough about us, where is the Rolls-Royce? Where is the chauffeur? We know you are living the life," asks Tito comically in an effort to have Jaime say something about himself since it has all been about them since he arrived.

"No, Tito, none of that. I did not even tell anyone about this trip. This is all about you guys right here, about you, the boys, and Roly. I just wanted to come see the little guy before he got snatched by the vultures, just like you guys were not too long ago. I wanted to enjoy a few moments of nobility with Roly before he becomes a big shot, know-it-all, like you." At this, the boys all laugh, Tito bows, accepts Jaime's remark, and replies sarcastically:

"Ahh, listen to the old 'fool-osopher' speak." Chuchi, however, exchanges a look with Jaime, knowing that everything is not as peachy as the rest of the boys think, but he says nothing in front of them to not ruin the momentous occasion, and Jaime appreciates this. Jaime and the now five young men continue chatting cordially, and before long, this unplanned late lunch turns into a five-hour ordeal as time flies before their eyes, sharing each other's stories of the past few years, and time dissolves here…

At the end of the night, Jaime leaves with Roly to begin working on finding the young ball player a new team. The others, Chuchi, Panchi, Tito, and Papo, join their teams before the curfew bell sounds. Chuchi and Jaime hug, but no words are exchanged at this time. Jaime pats him on his face just like Mr. Romero would him, and they both smile.

The next day Jaime and Roly arrive in Miami early in the morning and immediately head to Jaime's office to begin marketing the new young arrival to major league teams. As Jaime hastily prepares several phone interviews and a few live appearances before the local media, Roly maintains glued to the wall, reading all the articles posted in picture frames about Jaime and the boys of the past few years. Then Roly turns to Jaime. "Wow! What a fool I was to not jump ship earlier."

"What? When you were three years old? Roly, the time is now. What matters is that you are here now, and you haven't even hit your prime yet," replies Jaime without lifting his head as he continues to type in his laptop, and Roly suddenly asks:

"What are you doing over there, Jaime?"

Jaime looks at the kid over his reading glasses and responds, "I'm putting together a profile of you to send out along with this killer game film we have here. These highlights are just awesome, champ. You are an incredibly talented ball player, and these major league clubs are going to be salivating over you, maybe even swallow you whole, so be ready!"

"Oh...cool. Nice. I am ready. I was born ready!" humbly answers the young man and turns back to the wall with all the articles and continues reading. Jaime picks up the telephone and begins contacting several teams he knows are in desperate need of a player the caliber of Roly, and before he can hang up the phone, all the phone lines are flooded with major league agents and managers inquiring about Roly. Jaime's email is full as well, and Roly is jolting with excitement. "Jaime, are you serious? How do they know?" asks the young man, and with a sense of responsibility, Jaime answers:

"Roly, sharks can always smell fresh blood in the water, little brother. This is how it works, that is their jobs. It is all they do all day long. Sometimes they know before you even know!" Jaime smiles, and the young man is most impressed with how quickly the information moves out there, and he proceeds to rehearse a few lines Jaime has given him on how to respond to the media when being interviewed. By the end of the day, Jaime has already scheduled several trips to meet with major league clubs, and half a dozen teams have already sent their reps to meet with Jaime and the kid.

It is now the following Monday, and departing from the Miami airport on their way to Philadelphia to meet with the front office of the Phillies, Jaime and Roly field questions from reporters as they await their flight. Jaime, feeling more like a watchdog, keeps a dozen or so reporters from local television stations from trampling the kid. Roly does not seem to mind, but the eager group of reporters does not give much ground to the competition as they elbow one another to keep close to the young ball player who fields all their questions with grace. At the end of the day, Roly and Jaime arrive at their hotel in Philly, and they both look as exhausted as road groupies following a rock band on tour. "Were you expecting all this?" Jaime asks the young man, who replies enthusiastically:

"Not really. How do they know all that stuff about me? I thought they didn't watch any Cuban baseball here in the States."

"Roly, these guys are the best. They know their stuff and especially a high-profile prospect like you," replies Jaime, and Roly continues with his array of naïve questions:

"What, did I have the word 'defector' written all over my face when I was playing in Cuba?" asks the young man, feeling a bit on the defensive...

Jaime laughs and responds sarcastically, "Son, every player on the Cuban national team has the word 'defector' written on his face. It is almost expected for everyone to try to jump ship. Even the most loyal guy... I mean, who would have thought I'd escape. My hypocrisy can only go so far, and there comes a time when it is impossible to show impartiality towards that government, no matter how much you try to hide it, it finally pushes you to do stuff never imagined possible." Roly just sits there and thinks for a moment.

"I guess so, huh? The guys said that I was only one of the many young men on the team who were expected to flee, but if they were to keep us all home to avoid that risk, then they simply just wouldn't have a team at all to go out and compete," Roly adds with a half-smile on his face and looking for Jaime's approval.

"Yeah, that is true, but what about your family? Are they going to be okay?" Jaime curiously adds...and Roly answers:

"Jaime, this is my family now. You, and the guys and whoever my teammates end up being from now on wherever I land. There is no time for sentimentalism when we only live once, this is my life, and I can do more for them playing here for one season than playing over there my whole career," surprisingly responds the young man with a sudden wave of wisdom, and Jaime clearly understands what he is referring to, having been there not too long ago.

For the next few months, Jaime becomes Roly's own Mr. Romero, simply teaching him the ropes and showing him the way around the complicated business of baseball as he tries to protect him from malicious schemes by those who constantly feed off these new millionaires and from being lowballed by the teams going after him. Jaime, who now officially acts as Roly's agent, finally comes to agreement with the Philadelphia Phillies, and Roly signs a five-year contract even King Tut would be jealous of. Roly is in heaven, and now, all Jaime has to do is protect Roly from doing anything stupid with all his money, but for now, he helps the kid, of course, to develop a consistent routine to prepare for the upcoming season physically and mentally. He sets him up with a personal trainer and a pitching coach, and they immediately begin working together. The major league is no joke, it is a profession and a business, not just a game, and it is the ultimate goal for all aspiring baseball players, but not a permanent home to anyone because of injuries, free agency, and the overall game inside the game. Many are those who pass through the professional baseball circuit, but with thirty-two clubs trading players around constantly while looking for those few gems, it leaves only a selected few out of all the ones who try out and get drafted to become superstars and this is Roly's dream.

Initially, Roly does all the right things as he brings Jaime along before making any important decision, and he fills Jaime in before he makes any crucial arrangements. From the girls he dates to the car he buys, and especially before signing any sponsorship agreements with the different advertising agencies that bombard him daily, Roly does not do anything without Jaime's blessing. Before long, Nike, Under Armour, Chevy, and a few others have lined up to put the young player's face on their product endorsements. Without a doubt, his anticipated baseball debut piques everyone's interest, but one thing for sure is, Roly is expected to be a well-known name in the game very soon, barring any unexpected injury.

For several months, everything seems to move according to the plan, but right before the season begins and after an extremely successful spring training, Roly suddenly disappears. No one knows his whereabouts, including Jaime and the boys, for several days, and the top guys from the Phillies organization are extremely upset about the whole thing, and sure enough, Jaime receives a call from the manager of the club in the middle of the night, asking for Roly, "What is going on, Jaime? Where is the kid?"

Half asleep, Jaime responds in the sincerest way he can, and calm as can be for a two o'clock in the morning surprise telephone call, "I don't know where he is. Last time I saw him was in your office, exactly a week ago," responds Jaime…

"Don't give me that, Jaime. You guys all sound the same…" At the loud sound of the manager screaming over the telephone, Jaime sits up on his bed and turns on the light behind him.

"What does that mean? 'You guys' as in us agents? I am not like those guys out there, and you know it. Have you ever had any problems with me in the past? I don't party with my clients, and I certainly don't condone them doing anything stupid. You know what happens under my watch, so do not even answer that because I know the answer is no. Never before have you ever had any problems with me or any of the players I have brought to you. I am actually concerned; it just is not like Roly to just disappear for days at a time," Jaime assures the manager, and he now responds in a higher tone of voice:

"Well, my job is clearly on the line on this one because I talked these guys into giving him all that guaranteed money, and now I look like a clown." He coughs and continues a bit calmer. "I am sorry for snapping at you, Jaime," more relaxed now, answers the manager, maybe feeling a bit stupid for the unnecessary tone of voice he uses, and Jaime accepts his apology and gives the old manager what initially appears to be well-deserved advice, but he is too just hoping, praying, speculating.

"Well, Greenie, let us not panic, if I know this kid well enough… wait, actually, I don't know him all that well, so I hope everything is okay."

"Me too," replies the manager and hangs up the phone, leaving Jaime with a few things to say. Unexpectedly, Jaime hears a loud banging on the door of his house, and the doorbell begins to ring endlessly. Chuchi has driven up to Jaime's house to see him, and he continues to bang on the door in horror and desperation.

"Jaime, open up. Jaime, it's me…" Jaime opens the door, and Chuchi walks in. "Jaime, something is wrong."

"What are you talking about? What's wrong?" Jaime asks Chuchi, and he notices the young man shakes hysterically.

"Jaime, something is wrong with Roly. His girlfriend found a note in his hotel room."

Jaime is frozen by what he hears and unable to contain his curiosity, he finally snaps, "What in the world is going on here? What happened? What note?" Chuchi hands Jaime a note Roly had left his girlfriend, and Jaime reads it. "Oh no! This is bad. Where is the girlfriend? Who is she?" Jaime grabs Chuchi, interrogating him, and Chuchi explains:

"She is a sports anchor for a local affiliate, she is a good girl, but she says Roly's new friend was very weird the last time she saw them together." Frightened and concerned, Jaime jumps in…

"What friend?" asks Jaime, and Chuchi quickly replies:

"She says his name was Ramon, a savvy financial advisor from here in Miami. Well, actually, she says the guy is from all over… Sounds familiar?"

Jaime takes a second to proceed, and then in the most astonishing way, he asks, "Do you think?" Jaime somberly asks Chuchi, knowing what his response will be…but hoping he is wrong.

"Yeah, I'm almost positive it is him. I am afraid so, Jaime. Her description of Ramon fits him perfectly."

Jaime is paralyzed for a moment, and then he shouts at Chuchi, grabbing his coat on the way, "Have the authorities been notified? We got to move, let's go." Jaime and Chuchi fly out the door, and immediately jump into Chuchi's car and drive off.

At a Miami-Dade Police Station, Jaime and Chuchi file a report with an officer, and inside a closed glass door, Roly's girlfriend sits with several detectives as they take a statement from her. She cries hysterically as the detectives take notes and overwhelm her with a hundred questions. Jaime finally stands; he walks over to the office and knocks on the glass door.

"Excuse me, detective, I'm family. Can I be of any assistance?" One of the detectives wearing a dark suit and holding a clipboard stands, offering Jaime his hand with a demanding look on his face.

"Mr. Colon, nice to meet you, sir. I am Detective Prendes; of course, you can come in. I am a big fan of yours and your cigars."

"Thank you," Jaime adds, and offering Roly's girlfriend his hand, he introduces himself to her, "I don't believe we have met, I'm Jaime." The young lady shakes Jaime's hand, wiping her tears with a tissue. Her makeup runs all over her face, and Jaime offers another tissue as one of the detectives holds the box up to him.

"Finally, nice to meet you. Roly talks the world of you… He… umm…" At this, she breaks down, sobbing frantically. "He is a good guy. He is so good to me."

The lead detective, Detective Prendes, comforts the young lady by placing his hand under her chin and raising her eyes up to him, he assures both the young lady and Jaime they will do everything they can to find Roly, "Miss, we are experts in this field. I promise we will do our best to find him as soon and as safely as possible." Jaime agrees by shaking his head. The girl smiles at the detective, and with her eyes full of tears, she hugs Jaime, and he hugs her back with compassion.

Several days later, at a nearby abandoned parking lot, Detective Prendes opens the trunk of a car only to find Roly's body in it. The detective covers his nose with a white handkerchief to avoid the obvious rotten smell of the body, which has been here for a few days now. The abandoned vehicle had been reported to the police by the security guard of the car lot next door after one of his dogs continued to bark endlessly and refused to leave the site of the suspicious vehicle, apparently letting the officer know there was something in it. This vacant parking lot where the vehicle was found happens to be just minutes away from Ramon's apartment; a large bloodstain on the door and a broken windshield indicate there might have been a struggle. Also, Roly's coat is found lying in the backseat of the car, with Ramon's business card in it and several legal documents in its inside pocket. The documents prove to be the final nail in the coffin of the investigation, though as it is now apparent, Ramon had smoothly conned the young man into a legally binding agreement behind Jaime's back in which Roly would agree to facilitate the names of Cuban baseball prospects who may also be interested in fleeing the country to come to play in the major leagues. In the document, it clearly states Ramon had agreed to smuggle other players out of the island in an effort to bring them to the United States in exchange for a huge monetary sum upon them signing baseball contracts in the majors, which is exactly what part of Jaime's job entails in some ways, therefore, Ramon would be undercutting Jaime and obviously becoming Jaime's competition and rival. There in writing is an accord between Ramon and Roly where he offered to manage the young man's finances at no charge to him once he signs with a team in exchange for future contacts with players currently in Cuba. It is apparent Ramon has impersonated Jaime's work in his dealing with Roly while breaking all the rules and doing it all against the way Jaime and Mr. Romero conducted their business, but there is more… All of a sudden, there is also possible evidence of Ramon's affiliation with a known Mexican drug cartel as a large see-through plastic bag containing white powder sits inside the car as well. The cocaine bag with red writing imprinted across it reads… MMC, meaning this cocaine belongs to the Montego-Medellin Cartel, a dangerous crime group notorious for their sickening and unusual torture practices applied on their rivals and often used to send a message to the local police, DEA, and the authorities in general. The MMC would move their drugs all the way through Central America and the Mexican drug cartels, then handle getting it to the United States and beyond. These guys and the entire organization are no joke and certainly no one to mess with, and this is why it was so alarming to hear of the possibility of Jaime's involvement with the crime group. It was Ramon, however, who had crossed that line, but not true in Jaime's case. After a thorough investigation, the Miami Police Department have found phone records and even bank documents attaching Ramon to the drug cartel, and the department is on the hunt for him, but he is on the move. His apartment empty, his cars abandoned, and the office he used for business also empty from wall to wall. Sadly so, the blood on the car door matches that of Roly's, proving there was indeed a struggle between him and Ramon before the young man was finally stabbed to death and dropped in the trunk of the car. Medical reports also show the kid had been drugged before the scuffle occurred, allowing Ramon an obvious advantage, even though Roly was much stronger and bigger than he. The detectives believe the two men met at Ramon's apartment, and after several drinks, where Ramon must have drugged the kid, he then tried to convince Roly into signing more legal documents, making him the lonesome beneficiary to all his accounts in case something ever happened to him. Upon Roly refusing to sign on the dotted line, a scuffle must have begun, resulting in the stabbing of Roly. The legal documents had been left on the table ripped in half and unsigned. It is obvious now that once Roly refused to sign the documents, this made Ramon angry, and as he became infuriated at Roly's refusal, it all got ugly, ending Roly's life. But before that, Roly had left his girlfriend a note stating he was on his way to see this Ramon guy and to try to end all business ties with him. In the note, he also stated that if he was not back before dinner, something was wrong, to call the police. That was three days ago. Roly was just twenty-one years old. A phenomenal athlete with an extremely promising baseball career, and just like that, he is now gone forever, and the criminal is on the run.

Living a Lie and a Life of Complete Denial

Hours and minutes pile up, turning the clock into a torturous constant drip for Jaime, and time slowly dissolves here. It is now dusk. The bright orange sun sets over the city of Miami, and neither life nor time has been kind to Jaime as of recent. It is apparent he has found comfort behind the bottle, and his guilty conscience pushes him nearly to the brink of disaster, with many uninvited thoughts crowding his already agitated mind. His inability to cope with the reality of what things have become pushes him into hiding from the world, and inside his cloudy and turbulent head, confusion is bliss as he tries to find rest in his self-isolation, but instead, he gets a visit from the kind of voices no one wants to ever hear, and to try to ignore them, he tells himself the drinking will make everything go away by numbing him to the point where he feels nothing, but it's all in vain. During this dark time, Jaime decides to avoid everyone, especially those he feels he owes answers to. Even though vague and unacceptable by his own standards, the unusual heavy drinking has given him much-needed comfort as he remains secluded from the world in an empty apartment, in shame and self-destruct mode. Jaime has not been home in weeks and after renting the temporary apartment, hoping to sort everything out without having to explain to Enrico or Jordan his current situation whenever he bumps into them at the house. He also stays away from Chuchi and avoids Mr. Romero like the plague to not have to discuss the embarrassing dilemma taking place. Jaime hopes to have a resolution soon and to be able to come back to those in his life with good news; more like he wishes it would all just magically disappear.

Inside Mr. Romero's office, Stephanie sits at her father's desk. Another man, Emir Ruivo, is there. Disheveled and drunk, Jaime enters with Triana after receiving a message the night before about the meeting taking place, and honestly, had it not been for Triana picking him up, he probably would not have shown. Jaime's drinking has become so excessive the last few weeks it is pitiful, but this is the only way he knows how to deal with all that is happening. Stephanie stands and introduces the men to one another, "Hello, Jaime, Mr. Triana. This is Emir Ruivo, my father's private investigator." Jaime is hoarse and disoriented. He checks his throat and tries to straighten himself by adjusting his composure, but his efforts are in vain, he is obviously drunk, and it shows.

Jaime then asks curiously, almost as if standing before a jury, "Tell me. I am all ears…what is really happening here? Just hit me with it…" But no one responds to Jaime as they shuffle through legal documents in an effort to try to organize the files on the table before beginning. As the four of them sit at the small conference table, Ruivo has folders, documents, faxes, and photocopies spread before him.

The investigator then begins explaining, "His real name is Sanchez. He used at least three aliases in the past and probably more. In 1998, he served two years in a California state prison for check fraud. A year after his release, he was involved in a three-million-dollar credit card scam in Las Vegas. A good mafia lawyer got him off. And…let us see…three years ago he was indicted in France for embezzlement, and then he quickly disappeared until now…"

Triana leans over to Jaime and whispers, "I tried to warn you."

And at this, Jaime peers at him and then snaps, "I could care less for you and your advice. I…I was…" Stephanie lays a hand on Jaime's arm and calms him.

Triana replies, "Jaime, I'm just saying you acted against counsel and not just mine."

"Look, Hiram, the only reason this man got to me was because I let him get inside. It will not happen again."

Triana looks Jaime right in the eye and leaning over to his ear, he tells him, "It's too late! You're broke!"

Hearing this, Jaime freaks out, "I can't be broke! You are crazy… Do you even know what you are saying?"

Stephanie now places both hands on Jaime's face to get his attention, and she tells him softly, "Oh, Jaime, you weren't protected. You didn't know what this guy…" Jaime suddenly stands, unsteady, and begins pacing across the office.

"Chuchi's flying in tonight, we'll figure it out. I'll talk to your father when he feels better, and it'll all be okay." He just stands there, lost and confused.

"Jaime, I'll tell Chuchi the same thing. When this sort of thing happens, the bank isn't liable…you are," Triana tells Jaime straight forward and without holding back. Jaime doesn't like what he is hearing, but it is the truth. Triana is not done, "Jaime, I don't want to try to sugarcoat this any more than I have to, I have to be direct and upfront with you. All your cash is gone, the bank accounts have been drained. Unless you begin selling your properties right now, you are going to lose the operation in Nicaragua. Everything!"

"No!" screams Jaime angrily as he stares stubbornly out the open window, and all there is left to see of the sun is the last trace of the now orange-red sunset streaks across Biscayne Bay. He turns around and walks back to the table where the others are still sitting and tells them firmly, "I will not lose my dream."

The investigator Ruivo shares an uneasy glance with Stephanie and then speaks again, "Jaime, there is more." Even Triana now looks surprised, feeling uneasy looking at them sharply and not being aware there was more, and Ruivo continues, "Did you sign over some of your properties to the woman?"

"What?" asks Jaime, and the blood drains from Triana's face. Jaime answers without lifting his head, which he has had down this whole time because he is embarrassed and ashamed, "I wanted Rosie to be part of my life. I guess I was just lonely, and I wanted to have someone to share my life with. Honestly, I did not want her to leave."

At this, Triana explodes, "Are you insane?"

"How in the world could I have known?" Jaime asks, defeated.

"It doesn't matter! You only knew the woman for a few months! It is common sense, Jaime... You're a grown man..."

Suddenly, Stephanie interrupts, "Come on, Triana, haven't you ever messed up? This could happen to anyone."

But before the old lawyer can respond, Jaime answers, defeated and flat: "I loved her. I fell in love. That is the truth, and honestly, as hard as this is to say, I always knew she never felt the same about me, and maybe I just wanted to hold on to her."

"My God, Jaime, how desperate are you? You would have given up everything for the first pretty face that comes around? Has all the booze turned your brain to mush?" Jaime loses his cool and starts at him, ready to tear him apart, but Ruivo leaps up and grabs him, gently holding him back. Stephanie watches in alarm as Jaime, fist-clenched, fights helpless tears, and he places both his arms around his head and lays face down on the hardwood desk. Both Stephanie and Ruivo crowd him in, providing a little comfort.

That night, at the cigar club, inside the VIP room, Jaime sits over a bottle with Chuchi in the smoky room. It is late, and they are all alone. Jaime is bleary-eyed. "Her real name is Maria Solano. She has been his wife for two years." Jaime slams his fist on the table and continues, "She was sleeping with him the whole time she was with me too. She studied me, they played me, and she figured out how to get to me right in front of own my nose. So did he. They worked me well. So much for a big bad street guy, huh? Stupid and naïve, I know." Trying to show a little compassion, Chuchi places his hand over Jaime's back and pats him softly several times.

"It'll be alright, Pops. You know how it works, bro. You make yourself out of sugar, and you are food to the world. Especially to those with a sweet tooth, isn't that right?"

Jaime looks at Chuchi, and nodding his head, he replies, "Chuchi...screw your wisdom."

"No, Jaime, I'm just saying, baseball in America...isn't riding your bike to practice feeling the sea breeze in your face and the sun on your shoulders like back home. In America, it is business. You learn these things; agents, managers, contracts, and all that…" Chuchi notices Jaime has tears in his eyes as the painful sorrow of betrayal dawns upon him, and he has no choice but to pity his good friend.

Jaime exhales out of his mouth, tired and defeated, "Chuchi, we made love. How could she do this to me? We made love…" With a surge of anger, Chuchi snatches Jaime's glass from his hand and hurls it smashing to the floor.

"No, you made love, Jaime. Stop feeling sorry for yourself. It is my money too! '…We made love, we made love…'" the young man mocks Jaime deliberately to let him know he isn't happy with his careless and irresponsible handling of his money and his dumb way of handling this, but perhaps this isn't the time or the way to say this. Jaime is hurt, heartbroken, and in letting Chuchi know this, he just stares at him with a stern look as if wanting to kill him but also sensing his friend is right. He knows he acted irresponsibly and naïve, and now he pays the price. Chuchi gives Jaime an astonishing look, he takes a deep, calming breath, and then he follows apologetically by adding, "No, I mean… I just wasn't looking for anything serious because between all the traveling, training, plus I just knew I'd be jumping ship one day and didn't want any unnecessary attachments."

"Yeah, I hear you. Well, I feel the same, but it seems like this sort of thing tends to happen when you least expect it. Trust me. No one is ever ready to have their heart broken, and no one is exempt. To me, it always felt like committing suicide to open my heart and to allow someone in. Only when it happens to you, that is when you really understand the true meaning of heartbreak. It is literally the worst feeling in the world. Giving your heart to someone to only see everything thrown away in the end and to have every ounce of trust washed down the drain, it is just disheartening, to say the least. A broken heart cannot be mended with apologies or regrets…it is useless, it is worthless, I'd say."

Jaime grew up a poor boy in Cuba, and today he feels like the same poor boy from years ago, vulnerable and helpless, returning to his not-so-distant past as he is humbled by life. However, there is a good lesson to be learned from a disloyal heart, it strengthens us, it builds us up by tearing us down at first but thankfully, so, in the end, we all become stronger by it. We cannot mend a healthy heart since there is nothing to heal, but when the heart is broken in two, that is when the healing process begins.

To think that losing sometimes can be viewed as winning is not only irrational but absurd. At first, it is never to be seen this way as in a crisis all we tend to see is the crisis, of course, but it is quite the site to have enough wisdom to see past beyond the pain. The death of someone's innocence by means of betrayal can become the birth of great capacity and overwhelming comprehension of things to come, and in fact, we all would like to avoid it at all costs, but most of us eventually are glad to be bitten by this bug. It simply happens, and as they say, what does not kill you makes you stronger, and sooner or later, Jaime will too get over this painful deception. There is always a light at the end of the tunnel, and this is the great hope we await as we navigate through inevitable times of tribulation. Oftentimes, someone else comes along unexpectedly and patches up the broken heart by mending together all the shattered pieces, and in some instances, only time can restore the wounds making the healing process almost as stagnant and as excruciating as the tear itself...but eventually the heart heals. And at this, I ask... If a heart can heal with time, why is it that after all these years, time has been so unkind to my homeland? In Cuba, where the high humidity covers the air overtaking the entire ambiance and where thousands of tourists take pictures of the mess it has become like it is a grand village, and while they focus on the old buildings and the beautiful structures, I was able to see the story inside the walls. I was exposed to the tales written all over the faces of those who filled the space within the walls, those who painfully endure their decaying existence. I was heartbroken by their struggle, and I immediately became one of them for a short while, feeling their pain, their suffering, and the ugliness of being trapped in a world of agony; no different than what Jaime's ancestor Princess Ijaba must have felt when chained up with rusty shackles on her way to America. In deep thought, I looked out at the blue waters of the

Havana harbor, and suddenly they were not so blue anymore, just as the sparkle in a tear is never so sparkly when the tear is caused by pain. Awe…a tear… How can something so beautiful usually exhibit moments of affliction? And yet the same tear can roll down your face during a time of contentment and joy? In analyzing this, the reasons why do not really matter, and only the resolution becomes the most intricate part of this unsolvable mystery. So, whether we laugh or cry in shedding a tear, the answer is always the same, either we scream in silence, "Get me out of this mess," or we scream, "I don't want this bliss moment to end…" but ultimately, a tear is nothing but a silent scream, in the end becoming the only voice unheard. Jaime is left there probably wondering what did he ever do to deserve this? Trying to justify such heart-throbbing and wrenching pain at the hands of an almost total stranger just a few months prior seemed senseless, but why does it have to hurt so much? Now, knowing there is no easy resolution for a broken heart, Jaime is suddenly more concerned with his personal issues than he is with his money being gone, and Chuchi senses this. Chuchi stands up; he grabs the bottle on the table and smashes it against the wall with all his might. A second later, with all the anger in the world, he screams, "Ahh!" And then leaves.

Several hours later, Jordan picks up Jaime at the club and takes him home. At Jaime's mansion, Enrico rushes out to the aid of Jordan as the young chauffeur tries to pull Jaime from the limo. Jaime is rambling incoherently, blindly drunk. Inside the house, the two men half drag, half carry Jaime as he continues to ramble, "It's all a joke…let us laugh it up, come on, everybody… Heh! Yee-haw!" Jaime stumbles forward and lands headfirst on his luxurious designer sofa. He does not move as he lays there motionless. He begins snoring loudly right away. Enrico and Jordan look at each other with pity towards Jaime and then walk away.

Meanwhile, back at Mr. Romero's house, it is a large and beautiful old home nestled among exotic trees on a shady, secluded lot off the road. The house is quiet, and only the sound of soft music plays as Mr. Romero continues to recover.

Mr. Romero looks weak and fragile. A nurse gathers up his uneaten breakfast, and Stephanie stands at the doorway, watching. He sits on the bed, sipping on a cup of tea. "Look what I've become... You are my life, Steph; all I have left. You are my little princess...but he too felt like a son to me. A wild and exciting son that..."

"Shhhhh...Come on, Daddy, you have to rest now. We will figure it all out..."

Mr. Romero impatiently waves off the nurse who tries to fix his robe and proceeds, "He wasn't ready. He was too naïve. Too green, and he needed to ripen. You have to build a dream, and it usually takes a lifetime. You must cultivate it, and it has to have a solid foundation... It all happened too fast for Jaime. He just wanted it too bad." Stephanie approaches and takes his hand. She kisses his cheek.

"I'll take care of everything. I promise," she tells her dad, and he lets her know:

"I know you will...but let me tell you, our wise actions accompany us through life to please us and to also help us. Just as surely as unwise acts follow us to torment us all day long. The latter cannot and should not be forgotten as the memories of the things we should have done and the many opportunities that came our way, and we did not take advantage of. Now, let me tell you something else..." Stephanie leans close, and Mr. Romero continues, "He was just lonely. That is why he wanted to believe in her. He was looking for attention, sympathy. It is almost a trademark for people who are raised without a mom and a dad. I think...do not quote me on that one, what do I know?" Looking up into his daughter's face, he cradles her hand in both of his and whispers, "Loneliness is like that. We try to deny it, but everyone knows you cannot, and it grows under the surface. I know, after your mother passed away, I went through it, and it took years of hiding behind my business and pretending to be strong. Until one day, it gets so desperate, it grabs the first body it sees." He peers into his daughter's eyes and continues his speech. She listens attentively. "But you know, Steph...it does not have to be denied, loneliness does not have to come from weakness, it comes from being too strong, from being proud, and pride is one of the seven deadly sins. Heck, it knocked Lucifer from heaven forever...and he was the angel of light." Stephanie meets his gaze, and she becomes overwhelmed by the understanding and empathy that flow between them. "Steph...He likes you; you know," Mr. Romero tells Stephanie with strong conviction, and she hesitates and tries to dodge her father's remark by replying with a fair-minded comeback:

"I promise I will take care of everything," she adds, and Mr. Romero smiles, satisfied.

"I have always said I can't think of no one more qualified to take over my business than you, kiddo. I am proud of you, and I'm proud of the woman you have become."

The following week, Stephanie sits at the dining room table of her father's house, conferring with Triana and Chuchi, who looks like he has not slept in days. "So, let me get this straight, everything's frozen? All the properties, even every one of the cars from his collection?" Triana asks, now angrier than ever before and almost losing his cool as he takes notes. His briefcase is wide open with apparent important documents all over the table. He stops writing, removes his reading glasses, and nods his head in frustration. Stephanie looks at them both, concerned, knowing they are right but trying to play referee and serve as the only neutral party involved in the discussion. Both Triana and Chuchi have every reason in the world to be disturbed and even upset at Jaime and at the present situation, which seems to be an unsolvable puzzle, and it literally gives an air of defeat to an unbeatable champion who is about to be knocked out. Suddenly, there is a heavy crash from the bedroom.

Stephanie leaps to her feet in alarm and screams, "Daddy?" Immediately they all run to Mr. Romero's aid.

Hours later, inside Jaime's mansion, he has passed out in his clothes on the sofa. His phone rings. Jaime does not stir. The phone rings again and again, and then it stops. Again, Jaime's cell phone begins to ring. Moaning, he rolls over and feels blindly for it, he finally answers his cell, "Hello?"

Jaime receives the bad news about Mr. Romero and is unable to absorb what he hears; he has Jordan rush him to the hospital right away. Unwashed, unshaven, and wearing the same clothes from the night before, moments later, Jaime makes it to the hospital. Outside the emergency room, a badly hungover Jaime gathers Stephanie in his arms. Her face is pale, tear-stained, and swollen from crying. She looks at Jaime. "I'm glad you're here, Jaime."

"How is he?" Jaime asks, almost disoriented, and Stephanie responds:

"He is unconscious but stable." There is an awkward moment of silence. Then she proceeds, "I read somewhere that hearing is the last sense to…you know. I hope he heard me say I love him." She sobs into Jaime's shoulder.

He holds her tight and replies, "He just did." Following this, they share a long warm embrace in pain and loss. Then Jaime looks into her eyes, and without thinking, he leans in and kisses her on the mouth. Initially, it is a soft and gentle kiss, but as it continues, it turns into a long passionate one, and Stephanie, needing the compassion, pulls Jaime even closer to her, and the two become one for a moment. Then Jaime suddenly stops, realizing what he is doing. "I…I'm sorry!" Stephanie shakes her head, and then she places her index finger over Jaime's mouth in an effort to shut him up…

"No, thank you. I really needed that; you did nothing wrong." She then clutches onto Jaime's chest, hugs him tightly, and softly begins to cry. Jaime holds her.

The next morning as Stephanie, Jaime, and a few close friends chat, the doctor informs Stephanie that her father peacefully passed away while he slept. The doctor also assures her Mr. Romero suffered no pain; his heart just gave in the middle of the night, and he went to be with the Lord. Stephanie takes it well. She turns to Jaime, who had slept at the foot of her bed, and lets him know, "It makes me feel good to know he didn't suffer any pain, and I know he knows I'll be okay." Jaime does not take it as calmly as Stephanie, and he silently finds a corner of the room and weeps solemnly without anyone noticing.

A few painful days have now passed, and Jaime has remained on Stephanie's side, helping with the preparations for the funeral, and the two have become almost inseparable. On a beautiful April morning, a private burial service takes place to put Mr. Romero to rest and to send him onto the next life. Somber mourners, family, and friends, all dressed in black, stand in a loose circle around a casket over the open grave in a private cemetery. Mr. Romero's pastor, also dressed in black, directs himself to the small crowd, "Ladies and gentlemen, this life is a place in which we spend little time in comparison with eternity. The majority of our existence will be spent in an everlasting place God has designed and prepared for us, heaven. Mr. Romero knew where he would go when his days here on Earth came to an end. He was a good man, a man of God, and one who made a living helping others, and he enjoyed doing so. He was a true follower of Christ's greatest commandment, 'Love one another…'as mentioned in John 13:34, as he showed it with his actions, not just words. He was a doer, not a talker. I think we all can agree with that. Mr. Romero will be missed. May our Lord have him in His glory. Amen."

Many of the people in attendance weep, especially Jaime, who perhaps had a thing or two to say to Mr. Romero but never did. Sometimes, many times, we allow pride to get in the way of our words and our actions, leaving us with unfinished business and often thinking we have plenty of time to do so. Wrong! Jaime weeps quietly as the pastor continues to speak. He knows that he and Mr. Romero were so alike in so many ways one could say they were related. They were both stubborn and proud, and Jaime now feels like a part of him has died along with his mentor. Mr. Romero was Jaime's good friend and teacher, but pride stood in the way of many things that were never said. Among other things, Jaime never told Mr. Romero how grateful he was for all the help he offered to lift his dream off the ground, and he never really spent quality alone time with the old man as they were both constantly busy. It was always business talk, and most of the time, others were around, but he was never able to truly spend quality time to get to know his mentor from a personal stance, and that hurts Jaime. There was plenty more he could have learned from Mr. Romero as he was a brilliant man, much like a treasure box full of untapped information, which Jaime sees deep inside as a terribly missed opportunity mainly due to all the great knowledge he could've learned from this great mind, and now that he is gone, Jaime sees it as a missed occasion. Mainly because he was so green when he and the boys first arrived in the US, and he felt like he had nothing to offer to an established businessman like Mr. Romero. Also, feeling like he was only robbing him of his time when it came to sharing ideas and information back and forth and not knowing this was exactly what Mr. Romero would have enjoyed most. Second, Jaime also felt intimidated by Mr. Romero's vast experience and understanding, and he would rather just listen to the man as he gave him one piece of advice after the other. This was Jaime's way of paying tribute to the man who taught him everything about life in America. In all reality, Jaime never really got to know Mr. Romero, the man, and now that he is gone forever, Jaime acknowledges this with a heavy burden, weeping in silence and buried in the shadow of an oak tree across from where the burial takes place as he reminisces, and laments Mr. Romero now gone. After several minutes, Jaime composes himself, and he climbs in the limo, and they slowly roll down the drive and closer to the burial location.

We as humans have to value those people that mean the world to us while they are here because death comes to us all, and it usually comes unexpected. There is nothing more painful than having unsaid words for our loved ones and then having them suddenly taken away from us. To the people we love, we owe our time, our respect, and our undivided attention. The people who absolutely love us do not need to be showered with material gifts in order to make them feel loved, but they do appreciate the time we spend with them. No material thing can take the place of time well spent with a loved one. Our loved ones do not need expensive reminders of our love and affection, but they do need to know we value them, and sometimes just a simple hello…a phone call, an "I love you," an email or even a short visit every now and then can make them feel important and appreciated, and that isn't too much to ask from anyone. But we claim we are always too busy and too involved, doing unimportant things until it is too late. Jaime is feeling this pain now. Stephanie, who wears a black veil covering her face and is dressed in a stunning Armani dress, keeps quiet as everyone gives their condolences. Chuchi is there as well with the boys, and a line of limousines wait on the cemetery drive just about a hundred feet away. Jordan stands patiently outside his limo with his arms behind his back, Jaime is inside. Jordan opens the door. "I'm sorry, Mr. Colon. I know he was like a father to you. Would you like to come out now?" Jaime does not hear a word Jordan says, and inside the womb-like comfort of the limo, Jaime brings a pint bottle to his lips; he drinks and then tosses the bottle under the seat. When he finally crawls out, his eyes are filled with tears, and after taking a deep breath, he nods, clears his throat, and his intention is to walk off to join the others at the cemetery. After taking several steps in the direction of the cemetery, Jaime turns around and gets back in the limo. Jordan does not have time to open the door for him, and Jaime tells him it is okay and that he just needs some time alone. At this, Jordan shrugs his shoulders and obeys.

The man Jaime is today, who he has suddenly become, is so much different from the man he was back home in Cuba and even who he was when he first arrived in the US. He has a hard time looking in the mirror and recognizing the image before him, and in the midst of all the recent struggles, he has learned humility, heartbreak, and disappointment. He hopes he has become a wiser and much more compassionate man. He is certainly a much humbler man learning to accept life just as it comes, first the storm and then the calm. Life has a way of doing this to us, and if we learn to roll with the punches, we are usually okay in the end; many times, even becoming exactly who we were always supposed to be just by design, organically. It is those who expect things to go smoothly all the time who have the hardest time dealing with the speed bumps in life, those who become weak in front of the storm, folding and hiding their heads in the sand. Those who do not have the strength to face the giant, like in the story of David and Goliath, when a young boy was able to kill a giant, even the most courageous warriors feared using just a slingshot and a stone. But some people fail to seize the opportunity before them by becoming the victims when they were supposed to have been victorious all along. For Jaime, there are still many troubles ahead, but thus far, he is learning how to gargle bad experiences along with the many dreadful curveballs life throws at him. He now knows these are necessary obstacles in life, and now he knows that by handling these tough moments with the best of his abilities, it helps strengthen his foundation as a man, and the better he becomes at dealing with it, the better it will go for him. One situation at the time, one problem at the time, and so it becomes apparent the solution to all his problems magically develops right in front of these very adversities. It is no different than building a muscle, the more one flexes it and the more resistance it faces, the bigger and stronger it gets. Jaime admits that in this road called "life," there are many injustices in the form of unexpected circumstances, but there is always a way out. God always provides an eject button, a parachute, or exit door to each and every one of the situations we encounter along the way. As long as there is work to be done, there will always be thorns in the way and giants and enemies to fight, but ultimately, a victory lies ahead for those who see these obstacles as an opportunity to persevere and not as a time to run from it. It is not always easy, but it is not always difficult either. Life is full of ups and downs. So, buckle up on the way up and simply enjoy the ride as the breeze hits you in the face on the way down; lift your arms high up in the air and just let go! We cannot control it all, most of it anyway…so why fight it? Just learn to deal with whatever comes our way and roll with it.

A few weeks later, Jaime's drinking has increased drastically. His problems continue to pile up, but the biggest enemy he faces is his guilt. Jaime is having an extremely difficult time dealing with remorse, and he sees it building up in the corner of his mind, feeling responsible for everything that has happened so far, including Mr. Romero's death; Jaime continues to struggle. Maybe *I should've done more to stay on top of things… Maybe I should have kept better track of where all my money was being spent and invested... Maybe I should have listened to Mr. Romero more... I know, I know...that was my biggest mistake of them all, not listening to the man God put in my life to show me the ropes*, he keeps reminding himself... And as Jaime continues to kick himself for not being on top of things, the situation continues to get worse. All his assets have now been frozen, and so has been any income from other previously reliable sources. All the money from the operation in Nicaragua has been intercepted and placed into an account to prevent anyone from getting their hands on it as the investigation against Ramon continues. The real estate that had been signed over to Ramon has also been placed under court protection, unable to be sold or transferred during the investigation. The clubs are losing money every single day, all advertising is canceled, and the bills are not being paid. Neither is the mortgage on his mansion, the furniture, his cars, and more...

Outside Jaime's mansion, we now see two large cargo moving trucks are parked in the drive, and a moving crew carries the Italian designer sofa out the door along with other furniture, paintings, and many items inside the house. Many Realtors weave in and out of the mansion, taking pictures of the beautiful property, which has not yet been listed for sale, but in case it becomes part of foreclosure proceedings for upcoming auctions, prospective buyers are already lining up. Coming around the corner is a large diesel towing cab with an auto transport attachment for hauling expensive classic cars, and it backs up to the garage. Inside, Jordan and Enrico, who are stunned at the unexpected scene, watch silently, and finally, Enrico speaks, "How could this happen? He had everything a man could want." As all this domino effect takes place, Jaime sits alone under a shade tree in the backyard. He wears a small straw hat, and without a cigar in his mouth, he sits on a bench with his back to the house in deep thought, completely out of it, lost. To the average guy, this would be the end of the world, but let us remember that not too long ago, Jaime had nothing to his name, and to him, though it cost him much hard work and dedication to build everything he now has, it all happened so fast he may still be in a state of denial. The whole Cinderella story may still feel more like a cruel fantasy than anything else, and after all, Jaime is still so thankful to be in the United States and maybe feeling like if he is going to fall on his face, what better place to do it? The US is the ultimate destination for those who dream and especially for those who come from a place like Cuba, a communist country where freedom is prohibited, and Jaime knows this. He knows that at least in a place like America, one can fall from its high horse, and there are many opportunities to get right back up. But it still hurts, and he is feeling the pain even as he tries to numb his sorrow behind the alcohol while he is only slowly dying. The deliberate process is probably the most painful part of it all, and just watching everything gradually crumble in front of his eyes is too humiliating and just simply not fast enough. So, he would rather not look, and this is why he turns his back on the house as they take away all that is inside in the huge moving trucks. In a state of disbelief, Jaime would like to think this entire recent nightmare is something temporary. He probably assumes he will just be able to pick up where he left off and rebuild everything right back up, as it happens with most of us who have seen this sort of thing take place in the past. Losing material things is never a pretty sight, especially when we are made to feel worthless and defeated by the modern society we live in that these items such as home, a car, or financial comfort all serve as a sign of stability and what we think is the norm. Just ask anyone who has ever had a car taken away for nonpayment because they lost their job, or someone who had their home foreclosed on and their family thrown on the streets because they fell behind on their payments as we saw happen during the mortgage crisis of 2008. That mortgage meltdown wounded many Americans, and not just the poor or the financially unprepared, but many were those crushed by this event as the unprecedented crisis hit everyone like an unavoidable avalanche. Now, do not discount the possibility of this repeating itself in the near future because even though it was one of the most devastating social-economical catastrophes of our time, dragging along some of the largest companies and giants of the finance world, it is apparent that like Jaime, we haven't learned anything. Many experts believe it is looking obvious for history to repeat itself, and this next time around, it may be even worse than it was in 2008, calling it "the Mother of all Bubbles." Being financially unprepared is no different than going into a fight not ready, or a better term may be going to war untrained. As it typically happens, when things begin to fall apart in our lives, many times we tend to not want to admit the reality of things, and in most cases, we lean towards blocking it out thinking, or maybe "hoping" is a better word, that it will all go back to normal in the morning. We tend to look the other way as we wait for rescue, we go into denial mode, and some of us run away while others hide in shame and disgrace. Through this whole dilemma, Jaime often reminisces about his ancestor Ijaba, the African princess who was lucky enough to have survived her life-changing nightmare when she was ripped away from her home and brought to Cuba as a slave. Though she suffered much after being taken captive and surviving the horrific trip across the Atlantic, upon her arrival in Cuba, she was blessed to have been bought by a slave owner who took her in like family, and she was never sent to the sugar fields like most of her fellow slaves to die. See, Ijaba still suffered the dramatic trauma of being ripped from her home and more, but her circumstances were much different than that of most of her fellow African men and women brought to the New World against their will. After all, the average lifespan for slaves, once they arrived in Cuba from Africa, was only nine years, and regardless of age or physical strength, only in nine short years after leaving their beloved home, many of these men, women, and children would be buried in a strange land and forgotten forever. Like Ijaba, Jaime is also blessed to have survived an unforgettable experience, and after all, experiencing Castro's regime his whole life and living under communist Cuban rule was no cakewalk. Jaime lived a life terribly similar to that of a slave in Cuba, always being told what to do, being told how to think and what to be, very much like that of his ancestor Ijaba and her fellow slaved countrymen. Jaime feels he was given a fair chance for redemption and a true opportunity of a lifetime for a fresh start in America; however, after his devastating financial meltdown, he feels as if he has squandered his moment, throwing it all away. He senses that before the eyes of his family back in Cuba and even his ancestor Ijaba, he let them all down. Jaime acknowledges this every time he looks in the mirror, and it is difficult for him not to feel shame and dishonor while constantly reminding himself, "Many of my countrymen and women are not as lucky, at least I made it here alive, and I was able to accomplish much, maybe too much and more than I ever imagined or expected. Too much for me to handle for sure, but what do I have to complain about? In any case, I was able to experience even if only a brief time of the greatness of America, a brief flash of it. For the average American waking up to a bowl of cereal and the morning news is a normal day in everyday life; nonetheless, that very lifestyle we find so normal here in the States is more like luxury to most people in Cuba and around many parts of the world. This explains the reason why people from all over the world risk their lives attempting to make it here in search of that bowl of cereal, and why they take the risks they take for a sniff at the dream. I keep saying that America is indeed the greatest country in the world, even if some may not totally approve, and believe me, I do agree it isn't perfect, and I know there is much work to be done, but to me, it is worth of risking it all. If you don't believe me, just go ahead and ask a missionary returning from a poor part of Africa or ask someone returning from one of those remote corners of the world where there is no running water, and just listen closely to their answer… Or simply go travel the world and compare. Now, imagine this for a moment, you wake up in the morning, the kids are asleep, a husband or wife is asleep, the fridge, if you are lucky to have one, is empty, and there is nowhere to go buy anything to eat. There are no twenty-four-hour grocery stores in Cuba stocked with everything imaginable and without any limits of how much you can buy. There is always someone watching over your shoulder and asking where you got the money to buy, and you are having to whisper constantly because saying the wrong thing can land you in jail. Yes, we are indeed blessed to live in the US, so let us celebrate our freedom and pray for those who do not have it every single time we have the opportunity because it can always be worse."

In Cuba, housewives are more like "magicians" because they have to figure out what to make for breakfast, lunch, and dinner on a daily basis and out of thin air. How do they do it? I do not really know, but they do, and yet no one starves to death there. The entire country of Cuba, except for a few lucky ones, suffer from lack of everything but have learned to live off the land where everything is organic and not infected with pesticide, and they've learned to buy and sell in the black market as their only means of survival. Now, a father and husband, who is supposed to be the breadwinner and provider, gets up in the morning, and his wife tells him there is nothing to eat. Now, this man has to go out and find provision, and somehow, they do. "How?" you may ask. In a place where there are no 7-Elevens, no supermarkets, and no gas stations filled with convenient food stands and other goodies. One thing they do have is the most efficient system to make a pound of rice, beans, and a few ounces of chicken last an entire month. It is called "creative willpower." All discovered by the people themselves because over in Cuba, there are no seminars to attend or motivational speakers to teach people how to survive their crisis, only generations of experts in a course known as Survivorship 101, and this is why so many people who come to the US as immigrants make the very best of it, knowing they have been given the opportunity of a lifetime and a rare chance at a new start with endless potential to succeed. In this country, we tend to measure our level of success by the material things we accumulate and how much money we have in the bank, but the freedom we enjoy itself already makes us rich, yet not everyone appreciates this as it is a priceless commodity, we so often take for granted. I only pray we never lose that gift because it would be a devastating experience and one many of us may not survive if exposed to it. See, most immigrants may arrive in America by air, by sea, or land, but one thing connects a number of them, which is a hunger and a desire so strong it is difficult to deny. Their purpose is that much more vigorous than any obstacle they may encounter. For immigrants making their way to the US, the word "no" means nothing in comparison with the number of difficulties they may face along the way, and all they need is just a glimpse of hope to ignite their thirst for a shot at the dream. A thirst so strong it helps them get through the hardships they may brush up on along the way by focusing on the dream itself. Jaime, for example, after many rookie mistakes, sees the world is quickly collapsing around him, and unfortunately, he has found refuge behind the bottle. He has lost his sense of responsibility and dignity, and the shame alone is killing him knowing he has betrayed the chance of a lifetime by trusting the wrong people and by not being careful with his money, and now he is allowing alcohol to cloud his judgment with only one objective, to hide from the world and forget about his troubles.

Outside one of the docks in Biscayne Bay, two workers scrape "Ijaba" off the hull of Jaime's forty-foot yacht, and all he can do is watch from a distance. A million guilty thoughts run through his mind, and there is not a thing he can do. They say guilt is not only a horrible thing, but it can kill a man. Watching from the dock, Jaime slowly looks up at the sky…as if talking to God, perhaps Ijaba. *I'm sorry. I have let everyone down.*

Within days, inside the Ijaba Cigar Club in Miami, employees tear down Ijaba display items. On the floor is a discarded framed enlargement of Jaime's face on a magazine cover. One of the employees clumsily steps on it, cracking the glass. At night, people begin looting the former exotic establishment, leaving it practically in ruins. The alarm suddenly goes off, but no one seems to care, and the looting continues until the cigar club is empty. Some of the employees watch in disbelief, and there is nothing they can do to stop the barbaric display. The following day the club is empty and dark. The bar, the plush booths, and couches are all lost in the shadows. The arcade is shut down; pinball machines are smashed in, and the private room is vacant. All the display cases are bare. There is garbage everywhere, all the windows have been smashed, and the once lavish club is now in ruins. The Ijaba Hollywood club is now closed as well. Ijaba Las Vegas is closed. The sign outside is dark and cold, and the windows are boarded as if preparing for a hurricane to hit. Ijaba New York is the last one to close as some of the patrons try to recruit other regulars to host political parties inside the Ijaba Cigar Club right before the elections to spark up a sudden boost to help keep it open, but it is all in vain, and before long, the fancy New Your City hangout is now too closed. Unable to control the avalanche, Chuchi is devastated, all of his efforts have fallen short of his intentions to try to save the clubs. He takes time away from his off-season workouts to attempt to revive Jaime's dream, but it is too late. Chuchi cannot believe this is happening, and he has not been able to reach Jaime for quite some time, making the situation even more difficult for him to hold things together. And just like that, everything is gone. The dream is over!

Back in Nicaragua, the cigar plantation is deserted, and all the production has come to a halt. The once large and overpopulated tobacco fields are now empty, and the adjoining factory and curing barns vacant. Not a single worker is seen in the confines of the hundred-acre plantation where hundreds of workers once performed their daily duties. On top of a hilltop and overlooking the entire area, Jaime's old uncle and his gray-haired grandmother stand in a state of shock as they look down from up high, and a view of the lush fields and beautiful rolling mountains seems melancholy in the serene calm of the amber sunset glow. Wordlessly and sadly disenchanted, the grandmother turns her back on the fields and walks away. The old uncle holds back tears as he begins to puff on his chewed-up cigar stub. He tries to think of what Jaime could possibly be doing at this very moment as if he had some kind of telepathic powers, but all he can see is Jaime bursting into quiet choking tears as he realizes his dream has now vanished. The dream is gone! After a few somber moments alone, the old uncle turns around and follows the old grandma back to the house. The sun slowly continues to hide behind the dense mountaintop until it completely disappears from sight… and just like Jaime's dream, the sun suddenly becomes vapor in the air. Gone!

Jaime's Inevitable Downfall Arrives

Back in the States, Jaime has completely vanished from the public eye. Even those close to him do not know his whereabouts, and suddenly, the new boy in town and a sudden splash of the cigar world quickly become dust in the wind and forgotten as out of sight, out of mind. It has been months now; everyone is beginning to think the worse, and Jaime not showing up at Roly's funeral was a clear message that he was in trouble, and everyone is worried sick about him, sensing the unthinkable. Jaime had attended the funeral with the intention of paying his respects to Roly but never stepped inside the cemetery where the service was being held because he was not ready to be seen in the condition he was, and everyone assumed he just did not show.

Several months go by, and at a small motel somewhere outside of Miami, Jaime finds himself all alone in a tiny room in the murky half-light. The thick, drawn curtains hide his defeated and worn-out body as he lies tangled in the sheets of a single bed. He stirs and turns, trying to sleep off whatever amount of alcohol he had consumed the night before. If one did not know any better, Jaime has the appearance of someone trying to drink himself to death. The many empty bottles of liquor on the shelf appear to say so. Jaime rolls over, waking in the middle of the day and looking in the mirror, he is shocked by his wasted appearance. Disheveled, distraught, an empty shell of a man, Jaime has lost an alarming amount of weight, and his eyes are dead. He opens the door to the small refrigerator in the tiny motel room, and he has nothing to eat. Two empty bottles of cheap beer lie inside the dirty fridge. Jaime grabs one of them, walks over to the sink and fills it with tap water, and begins to drink. He coughs as he attempts to drink the unfiltered water straight from the sink, all dehydrated from the long night sucking from the bottle, plus he is run out of booze. The cough continues for a minute.

Moments later, Jaime gets up to use the bathroom, and when he comes out, he decides to make his way to a nearby bar only a short distance away.

He walks there, staggering his steps and groggy enough to have to hold on to whatever he can as he makes his way to the bar. Once he arrives, he fixes his shirt like he is walking into a job interview, he looks himself in the mirror hanging from the wall by the bar entrance and proceeds inside. The place is dark, secluded, and an anonymous refuge for a few regulars. A black and white movie plays on the TV above the bar, and the sound is muted. Loud rock music plays. Jaime slides onto a barstool, and the bartender nods.

"What will it be?" Jaime shrugs blankly, bleary. This will be his first drink of the day and one he desperately needs. His body calls for it, demands it, and he feels no choice but to obey.

He then turns to the bartender and asks, "What would you be drinking if your world was upside down, my man?"

The bartender walks over to Jaime and responds, "If I had a dollar every time I was asked that question, I'd be rich… Now order a drink or take your self-pity somewhere else, I'm busy."

Jaime takes a second, organizing his thoughts, and responds calmly and perhaps curiously, "You'd be rich, huh? What is rich? Do you even know?" Jaime asks without looking at the bartender, and the young bartender places both his hands on the bar and faces Jaime as he explains:

"Yeah, I know. I know exactly what rich is. I get to work my tail off getting guys like you drunk every day, then I go home to my beautiful wife, I wait for the kids to come home from school, and once a year, we go to Disneyworld. If you ask me, that is a slice of heaven, and one day, I will have enough money to open my own place, and I will be working for myself. I will be my own boss, and to me...that is rich! Having a plan and a dream makes you the king of the world." After this, Jaime raises his eyes to the young man behind the bar and smiles.

"A dream, huh? I heard of that," Jaime scoffs...then suddenly, a drunk at the end of the bar begins to clap his hands clumsily, with his hands almost missing every time.

"Yeah, baby! And I am the king of the world number two. Dreams don't make you happy, dreams die. The only true comfort in life is in this tiny glass right here. Yeap!" The drunk man mumbles, immediately diving in his drink, and Jaime looks at the bartender, who shrugs his shoulders and smiles. "Who knew there are two kings of the world," he adds. "And after that speech, just give me another double. I'm ready..." The drunk slurs his words as he downs his drink and walks away.

Jaime, looking blank and depressed, replies to the bartender in a serious tone of voice. A tone so serious the young bartender has no choice but to pay close attention. "Same for me, a double...apparently the drink of choice tonight." Jaime checks his hoarse throat and continues, "Hey, kid, don't ever let anyone or anything take that dream of yours away. If you can do that if you can hold on to it and see it through, I tell you the truth...a dream realized...there is nothing else like it in the world." The bartender absorbs this. Jaime finishes his thought, "Then you will indeed feel like the Richest Man in Babylon."

After a much-needed drink, plus a few more...and a few more... Jaime leaves the bar and feeling drunk not just from the alcohol he has consumed but mainly beaten to a pulp by his conscious, which has decided to torment him, waging war on his intellect and bringing him to the brink of self-destruction. Perhaps Jaime feels more nauseated from the reminder that his dream is now gone forever than the actual drinking. Later that night, Jaime walks through the motel's dark parking lot on his way from the bar, and he staggers, drunk, running into everything he can find. As he approaches his motel room door, he fumbles his keys in his hands and drops them in the dark. He does not notice someone getting out of a car behind him.

He is drunk. He continues to look for his keys: "Hmm! Come on!" By the time Jaime finally finds the keys, Chuchi is standing right beside him. Jaime's eyes take some time to focus on the old friend, and as he recognizes Chuchi, he is surprised to see him. He turns to him, and almost whispering, he intones to him, "Chuchi, I don't remember leaving a forwarding address."

The young man responds, "Papa…Ahh, remember Stephanie's private detective?"

Jaime looks like he would rather not and changes the subject, "So, how's baseball these days, kiddo?" Chuchi does not respond, he helps him up, and they go inside the room. Jaime removes his coat and drops it on the floor. "Welcome to my new home. My most humble temporary home, which, of course, is yours too."

"Thank you, Papa, I'll have to remember that," Chuchi answers sarcastically, and he helps Jaime onto his bed as he is falling off his own feet. Sprawled on his dirty, unmade bed, Jaime drunkenly attempts to light up a cigar. He finally does after several attempts, and he tries to blow a smoke ring, but it dissolves half-formed. He laughs without mirth. Chuchi doesn't.

"Drugstore stogie…they make lousy smoke rings." Sitting by the edge of the bed now, Chuchi hides his shock and pity as he looks around the dirty apartment. The cheap room is a disaster, and Jaime does not look good.

"Papa, this is a joke. What are you doing to yourself?"

"Don't call me that, I don't deserve it. I deserve this. This right here is what a man like me deserves. I deserve everything that's happening right now…" Chuchi stands, and he comes closer to Jaime.

"That ain't cool, and you know it." Jaime regards his cigar with distaste. He looks into Chuchi's eyes…

"I let everybody down, son. I got lost in a dream, and I allowed you to go down with me. Chuchi, I am so sorry, son." He looks away in shame as he almost drops the chewed-up cigar onto the floor. Chuchi attempts to grab it and put it out, but Jaime pulls it away.

"I came to take you out of here. You do not deserve this; you have people who love you. You do not go from prince to pauper overnight. This is impossible."

Jaime then jumps up and responds to his good friend in anger, "No, wrong... It is possible. Chuchi, this is America, anything is possible, my friend! The good and the bad. Look at me, this is real." Chuchi shakes his head.

"No, you could've saved it. There was still money coming in, and I have known you since I was a skinny, dirty little kid, and you have always been my hero, Jaime. I will tell you what I saw, Papa... I saw a guy deprive himself of love his whole life, then go crazy for it at the first woman he lets in his life. It is not too late. We can fix it."

Jaime drops the half-smoked cigar inside an empty beer bottle, and with his eyes half-closed, he responds, "Ramon and his woman got it all, and who even cares." Jaime closes his eyes and swallows this. "She played me, brother, he played me, and they played me. They played us. Yeah, they played us both!"

"Listen, Papa, we'll take care of them later. For now, Stephanie says she needs to see you. I told her I knew where to find you; everyone is worried sick about you. You have been gone a long time. You just vanished out of thin air, and we were all thinking the worse after what happened to Rolly," Chuchi, with tears in his eyes, half yells, have whispers...and Jaime, with his eyes still closed, asks:

"No, not like this. Why? Why would she want to see me?"

"Look, she didn't say...but she wants to see you."

"She doesn't need to see this. I'm a disgrace..." replies Jaime, and then he rolls over and turns his back on Chuchi. Who takes a deep breath, and...he utters:

"Papa? Papa?" But there is no response. Jaime has passed out.

The following morning, Jaime stirs amid tangled, dirty sheets. Still in his clothes, he stumbles out of bed and slowly staggers toward the bathroom when something catches his eye, skillfully placed on the nightstand are two objects that weren't there when he fell asleep, there is an envelope with the word "Papa" written on it and a box of Ijaba Cigars. Bleary-eyed, Jaime picks up the thick envelope and opens it. It is stuffed with cash. Jaime looks away, spiritless.

Around mid-afternoon, a figure knocks on Jaime's motel room door. It is none other than Stephanie, and she knocks again and calls out, "Jaime? It's me, Stephanie…" She tries the door, and it is unlocked, she then peers inside the tiny dark motel room. "Jaime?" Stephanie walks inside the room, and Jaime is gone. The bedsheets have been removed, and the dull motel room is vacated. Stephanie immediately notices the box of Ijaba Cigars on the bureau. Untouched! She storms out, gets in her car, and calls someone from her cell phone as she drives away.

Inside a nearby bar, loud music plays. It is dark and crowded, and there are a handful of dancers on a stage, topless. Jaime sits at the bar, sipping his drink. He is numb and in a world of his own. He does not notice two men pointing at him. After a moment, they approach Jaime, shouting over the loud music, "Hey, you're that cigar guy, right?" Jaime looks up from his drunken stupor, wasted and lost. Hoping to recognize the men, but he does not.

"Do I know you?" Jaime asks…and the men come even closer.

The one guy loudly and rambunctiously screams, "With the clubs? Came from Cuba? Yeah, it has to be you. Maybe a little thinner, dirtier, and sporting a beard, but it is you. My man!" Then the other man with him finally realizes who Jaime is…

"Oh my God… I know who this is. I know who you are talking about, we should party!"

About an hour later, in a dark alley behind the bar building, Jaime finds himself leaning unsteadily against the wall, barely tasting the cheap cigar in his mouth, and starring into the two strangers' eyes. "You probably think I'm playing, man, but it is really an honor partying with you, my name is Miles, and this here is Rico," Miles, full of tattoos from head to toe, including the top of his bald head, shouts at Jaime as he removes a bag from his pocket and then glances around to make sure they are alone. Then Miles takes out the baggie of white powder. "You should open another one of your cigar clubs right here in the neighborhood. There were lines of people outside your clubs, waiting to get in all the time, I remember. I was one of them. I remember when you first opened too. You were hot..." Miles scoops a tiny spoon and sniffs it up.

Jaime, who is slow to react, responds, "No, I don't do coke... No, no..."

"Neither do we. This is better, much better...you will see heaven open up right in front of your eyes. It is just a little taste of heroin. We like to snort it." Miles takes a hit, and elated, he offers the baggie and spoon to Jaime, who just looks at it. A moment passes like an eternity...

"Well, I guess it doesn't matter anymore." And without hesitation, Jaime too takes a hit of the unknown powder. His eyes roll back, and all you can see is white in them. His head rolls back too, and as odd as it may sound, Jaime just stays up that way. As if someone was holding him steady in the awkward position. Miles and Rico look at each other, and they laugh.

"Bro, have you ever seen this happen before?" Miles mocks at the way Jaime's body stays up in the oddest of all positions as if being held up by someone because otherwise, it would be a physical improbability for him to sustain his body the way he stands, head leaning back as his body is erected, but there is no one holding him. Miles thinks it is creepy, but he is too high to make any sense of it. Rico is too out of it to comment. Eventually, they walk away, and Jaime finally falls onto the ground and just lies there. A few hours later, at a dark and empty park, Jaime is rustling through secluded trees, and by now, he is out of his head, dizzyingly high still from whatever Miles gave him. He mutters to himself, slurring and rambling. He trips and falls. He cannot get up, and he just lies there laughing... He laughs at his clumsy gestures and movements, looking at his hands, apparently hallucinating. Jaime moves his hands in front of his face to try to make something of it. After a while, Jaime is finally able to get up, and he manages to slowly walk away into a dark alley until he disappears behind two large trash cans filled with garbage to the top.

As the sun rises, he is awakened by the noise of a garbage truck emptying the waste from the large containers behind the liquor store.

Jaime looks horrible. He is unshaven, and his clothes are filthy. He has mud all over his knees like he had been crawling on them. His hands bleed. He walks into the liquor store and stands at the counter, buying a bottle. He offers to pay with cash from the envelope Chuchi left him in his room. The liquor store owner looks at him funnily as he glances at his appearance and back at the envelope, which is completely stuffed with cash. "Hey, do I recognize you?" Jaime opens the bottle and takes a drink.

"I don't know, do you? No, I don't think so, but my friends call me… Christopher Columbus, does the name sound familiar to you? Ha, ha, ha!" He begins to laugh as he places the bottle back into a brown paper bag and walks away. The store owner watches Jaime as he leaves and nods his head in pity, thinking he recognizes Jaime from somewhere, but he cannot quite place him. It is now raining hard, and Jaime is standing outside the motel office window, roaring drunk. He is drenched, waving the envelope containing the cash at the motel manager, pleading for a room. But the aggravated manager pushes him outside as Jaime tries to walk in and slams the door in his face.

"Get out! Stay out! Take your money somewhere else… You bum! Loser!" Jaime just stands there, motionless and stunned after the man in the motel kicks him out, and he takes a seat against a midsized tree, which is planted right next to the motel. He slowly leans back, and almost instantaneously, he falls asleep in the rain and with his face against the mud. The rain splashes back onto his face, bouncing off the hard ground, but Jaime feels nothing.

At night, Jaime, now awake, makes his way into a dance bar close by. Music and dancing are oblivion inside. Suddenly, Rico and Miles, who sit at the bar, see Jaime come in, and they look at each other surprised. They watch Jaime shuffle in, completely out of it. They wink at each other and get up as if expecting him. They finish their drink; they place the empty glasses back on the bar and walk over to Jaime, who does not even notice them. They grab Jaime's arm and guide him back outside and into the back alley where Rico takes something out of his pocket as Jaime mumbles nonsense words,

"Yeah…told her, meaning of life, Rosie, pure conscience, gives you keys to heaven…live your life true, true heart, lets you walk with God…"

Rico and Miles laugh.

"Yeah, man, we're walking with God alright…" Rico holds a syringe in his hand as Miles, wearing a secondhand store suit that looks two sizes too big, places Jaime on the ground and holds him as his partner shoots Jaime up. Jaime falls back and lies on the ground motionless, his eyes roll back, breathing hard, and finally, he relaxes after a few moments of struggle when the drug finally kicks in. The other two laugh and take turns drinking from a small bottle of hard liquor they find in Jaime's pocket. Jaime has passed out. After a moment, Jaime is hallucinating. He talks to himself and laughs awkwardly. His body shakes loosely, and he begins to take sudden turns from side to side. He is paranoid and skeptical.

I suppose a man should be capable of controlling his own destiny, right? That is what most people say… And that upon his decisions, he should be man enough to carry his own weight…something like that, but in many instances, it does not even seem fair. One can lose so much in so little time it can be scary. One careless mistake can take a man from the heights of success down to the pits of hell in a noticeably short time, and Jaime is not alone, how many people do we know that are sitting pretty one day and the next, they have no idea of which way to go. It is really that easy, so much for a man being able to control his own destiny then…

In the early hours of the morning, a commercial plane flies through the sunny sky. Inside first class, walking down the aisle, is a flight attendant who hesitates as she leans indiscreetly to one of the passengers on board. "Pardon me, Mr. Aguilar. I am not supposed to do this…" Chuchi looks up at the pretty lady flight attendant with the overdone makeup, maybe in her early 40s, and who looks like she has been doing this for too long as she holds a small notebook and a pen. "Mr. Aguilar, it's my son's birthday. An autograph from his hero would mean the world to him. Would you please?" Chuchi reacts to the word "hero," and forcing a smile, he signs.

"Yeah, no, no problem. What is his name?" Chuchi autographs the notepad and returns it to the flight attendant, who gladly checks the autographed signature and thanks him again:

"Thank you, Mr. Aguilar, he is going to be incredibly happy."

"No problem at all. It is a pleasure knowing I have a fan." She smiles warmly, and after returning the notebook to the flight attendant, Chuchi continues reading through a pile of scattered legal papers sitting on his lap. All of which have to do with the clubs and the cigar operation in Nicaragua.

At the same time, outside a liquor store, the streets are deserted, and the business district closed. Looking like a homeless man, Jaime tries to go inside a liquor store, but the doors are locked. He kicks the door in disappointment and slams an empty trash can against the wall with anger and frustration. He then notices a bright fluorescent sign across the street and slowly moves toward the twenty-four-hour minimarket with the huge blinking sign that reads, "Open." As he walks across the street to the dirty and unkempt eighty-year-old store, just being there brings music to Jaime's ears. Jaime goes inside. He then joyfully carries three bottles of cheap wine to the register, and the clerk frowns as he approaches and automatically assumes Jaime is another one of the junkies in the neighborhood. The clerk's face lights up at the sight of Jaime approaching the register, holding the bottles of cheap liquor. His look is that of someone who has not bathed in days, and the smell is intolerable, but the clerk proceeds to help him anyway. "Hey, you new around here?" Jaime is groggy and so busy counting the money to pay the clerk he does not hear the question, which the clerk takes as rude, and it frustrates him even more. Jaime proceeds to try to set the bottles down on the counter to pay the man, but he accidentally drops one of the bottles, and it smashes onto the floor. The night manager angrily jumps over the counter and ushers Jaime out the door, leaving not just the broken bottle on the floor but also the other two he so desperately needed on the counter. Jaime panics…

"Wait! It was an accident. I have money, I've got money!" And just moments later, in the dark shadows of the back alley, moving deeper in the wet, dirty, garbage-strewn alley, Jaime has passed out behind a dumpster. His face filled with tears and dirt. He does not even lie on top of the newspapers, which are now drenched from the rain. The many pieces of hard cardboard he has gathered to lay on top of are drenched too, and he is lying on the wet, bare concrete floor. His mouth is dry, and his lips are cracking. He has grown a nasty beard, making him almost unrecognizable, and his clothes bring shame upon the dirtiest man around. Jaime is missing a shoe, but he could care less. He sleeps soundly even as it begins to rain a little harder, and nothing seems to bother him. As Jaime now snores lightly, someone suddenly kicks him to rouse him. He barely stirs. The man then kicks him harder, and Jaime just opens his bleary eyes, only to see Miles and Rico standing before him. They lean over to check Jaime's pockets and immediately make a face of disgust as Jaime's body odor hits their nostrils. The two delinquents find the envelope containing most of the money Chuchi had left Jaime and begin to count the cash. Suddenly amazed at all the cash they see, Rico mumbles something to Miles, and he immediately begins to prepare a syringe. Miles shoots Jaime in his arm with the poison, sticking the rusty needle right through the vein of the almost motionless man. Jaime stirs just enough to let the men know he is alive, but he has once again passed out and left there alone on the wet and dirty pavement as the two men walk away with his envelope full of cash, counting it and high fiving one another. And into the shadows of the night, they disappear.

Inside Mr. Romero's house, Stephanie sits all alone in her bedroom. She tries to find comfort leaning against the bed board, pretending to read a book. She twists and turns without any luck, and finally, she fixes her eyes on the unopened box of Ijaba Cigars she had found in the motel room, now sitting on her dresser. Stephanie, in her nightgown, looks at it, and her eyes water instantly, wondering about Jaime's well-being and his whereabouts. Her eyes burst like a broken dam with painful tears as she slides off the bed and kneels down on the floor and begins to pray out loud…for Jaime: "Lord, please…! Hear my prayer… I don't want anything for me but for Jaime. Please be with him wherever he might be. Watch over him, and return him back home safe and sound…"

She continues to pray on the ground, almost as if reciting endless poetry, and she nearly falls to sleep on her knees.

A few more months go by, and outside on the street is raining. It is early morning, and pedestrians with umbrellas swerve in and out to try to avoid someone passing through. It is none other than Jaime, who is wandering aimlessly down the street. Now a full-blown junkie, he looks sick, he is dirty and tattered. As he comes to a halt, he slumps against the wall of a restaurant, holding out his hands like a beggar. He does not hold up any catchy sign to attract attention, nor does he have a collection can, he only holds out both his hands as if pleading for mercy and forgiveness, and not for just money or food, but for mercy most of all. Jaime is shaking, needing a fix as he is now hooked on whatever Miles and Rico injected into him… Jaime drops down to his knees on the sidewalk and waits with his arms up in the air as the rain runs down his sallow bearded face. He truly looks pathetic, sick, and everyone who comes either in or out of the restaurant steps around him in repulsion as they walk by. Many of the people walking by make criticizing comments as it is easy to judge such an appearance, but Jaime hears none of it. Soon after, several security men emerge from the restaurant along with a few local politicians escorting a VIP. They open their umbrellas, and it is none other than the mayor, who glances sympathetically at the sad homeless man, and he mutters to one of his men and then walks on. The security man comes back to Jaime and hands him a five-dollar bill as instructed, and he takes it. Jaime looks at the neatly folded paper bill and puts it in his coat pocket without lifting his eyes as he keeps his face buried down in shame and pity. Suddenly the mayor pauses, he looks back at the homeless man, and without saying anything, there is a silent moment of recognition, which is hard to miss, but before he can say a word, Jaime slinks away into the back alley.

Jaime continues to walk aimlessly around Downtown Miami, often stopping to try to recollect who he is or who he was not too long ago but without any luck, as he cannot remember who he was just a short time ago. With his vision bleary and his mind lost in sorrow and despair, Jaime feels like a lost sailor at sea. The not-too-distant past has been temporarily erased from his memory, and all he can think of is his next fix, his next drink, and nothing else. With so many crack houses in the area, junkie hangouts, aloof back alleys, and rat holes to find refuge in these parts of town, it is easy for these people to stay attuned to their miserable lifestyle. The spooky nightmare may sound like nonsense and like a miserable joke of some sort to us who are sober, but it is heaven to those living in the dark hell of such a horrific drug addiction, making this world all they know and want. Besides, no one who has never been in this position should dare open their mouth and criticize because unless they have been there, they will never know. Just like someone who has never been incarcerated telling a person doing time that they know how it feels. There is no way they do! Now, for a man like Jaime, who had never tried any kind of illegal drugs before, and for someone who only had the occasional drink here and there prior to this ugly episode of his life, it all happened so fast his addiction was even more severe than that of any regular addict. The drinking quickly began to creep up as soon as things started melting in front of Jaime's eyes, and in the end, he could not do without some type of alcohol in his system to help him deal with reality. Then he quickly became absorbed by the cheap heroin as soon as he arrived on the streets. This was a much stronger kick, chemically induced and straight to the bloodstream, and also new to him, and making it even more addictive. There is no way to really explain to a person who is not addicted to a substance how someone can fall victim to an addiction so quickly. Something that can so easily happen to just about anybody who becomes unguarded and unprotected while looking for an escape. How do we explain such quick dependence on drugs? But maybe that in Jaime's case, only a desperate man, a man ashamed of his actions and someone so disgusted with the results of a few bad mistakes, would be so inclined to do such a thing. And perhaps a man who knows nothing about faith in a God who can fix it all in the blink of an eye…would do such a thing, thinking there is no other way. Only a man who feels condemned for his actions, not realizing all of his debt was already paid back at the cross, according to Jaime's old uncle, who preached this constantly to Jaime's deaf ears throughout his entire life. Only a man who does not know God's true character of redemption and only a man who does not know of Jesus' love and compassion feels the way Jaime is feeling right at this very moment. So, he hides, just like Adam and Eve hid from God back in the garden when he asked them…what had they done? And soon after they ate from the forbidden fruit in the Garden of Eden, they shamelessly hid from God. Jaime runs and hides as well. He hides from his pain, from his shame, and he takes refuge behind his self-pity and destruction, which is inevitable at this point. We could say it is natural for all human beings to not know how to deal with responsibility after we have messed up. Jaime is there right now; hiding is a normal, natural reaction commonly done by many of us who are ashamed of our actions. We have all done it, we are all guilty of such a thing. None of us are exempt, so before we go pointing the finger, let us take a good look inside and truly analyze our very own lives. Just saying…

As night falls over the City of Miami, so does Jaime's desire to live another day, now finding comfort on the ground and over several pieces of cardboard he has gathered to use for his bed this night. Jaime rests, and as he begins to drift into a deep sleep, two men charge him, and all he can do is lie on the ground, unable to defend himself. He makes a vague attempt to defend himself, but he is too weak, and all his efforts are to no avail. One of the men holds Jaime steady as the other shoots him up. Jaime closes his eyes in oblivion, realizing it is Rico who injects him… Jaime does not move. The two men laugh hysterically, and they too shoot each other with the poison, taking turns, sharing the needle. Moments later, nodding off, Jaime slowly tries to pull himself up, but Rico helps him down. Jaime sinks into the garbage-littered ground for a second time and again tries to stand, but he loses his balance and nearly falls. Miles and Rico steady him. Jaime mumbles, "Gracias, hombre." Something falls from his pocket all of a sudden, Rico bends and picks up a crumpled, torn, and taped-up envelope with "Papa" written on it. Seeing it, Rico is amazed that it still contains a small amount of cash. This was the last of the money Chuchi had left for Jaime back at the motel. Feebly, Jaime snatches it away. He holds it preciously to his breast, but it is now too late as Rico and Miles have seen it. Miles takes Jaime's arm and pulls on it to straighten him up.

"Come on, brother, you are only making this harder on yourself. Let it go, we are going for a walk in the park," tells Miles with Jaime almost completely out of it. The two men, Miles and Rico, half drag Jaime through the empty park's secluded trees, Jaime is in oblivion drug-hazed and has no clue of what is happening.

He then asks, "Are we going to your place?"

"No, Jaime, we're just taking a little shortcut. Just a little bit further..." They pass in the darkness behind bushes and shrubs, looking in all directions and making sure no one is following.

Jaime continues to mumble, "...It doesn't have to be fancy... We would sleep in a sewer for this chance...that is what we said, remember? When we first arrived in America... Yeah, me and the boys... Remember?" Not listening to a word, he says, the men continue dragging him away when suddenly Jaime is tackled to the ground. His face is pushed hard into the wet grass as Rico and Miles hold him down and grab for his pockets. Fiercely, Jaime rolls around, punching and kicking, as instinct takes over. He starts to cry out for help, but no words come out of his mouth. He feels as if he is suffocating. Then a fist pounds his face and then another, and another, snapping his head back. He can hear his clothing rip as his body is ransacked for the envelope with the little money left in it. Swinging wildly, Jaime fights back and manages to get to his feet. He tries to run...but he trips and falls. "Somebody help me..." Hands grab him. Jaime whirls, and Rico immediately hits him again in the face, and Miles punches him brutally in the stomach. Jaime crumbles to his knees, his face is bleeding and badly cut open. The two men grab him, and he continues to struggle violently. "Please...Stop..." Infuriated by his dogged struggles, their fists continue to assault him violently without mercy. They pummel him relentlessly and nonstop, beating him senseless. Jaime's fingers claw the earth as he literally tries to drag himself away, and suddenly, a shoe slams into his back, and something cracks. Jaime screams… Rico and Miles freeze for a moment. As Rico pulls Jaime's arm to turn him off his side, he pulls too far on his arm and dislocates it. Jaime screams. With his face bloody and swollen, he loses consciousness, and in a flash, they rifle through his clothes, find the envelope with what little money is left, and run off. The total amount of money left in the envelope was twenty-two dollars. A vicious and cruel beating over twenty-two dollars…that could have cost a man his life. Go figure!

Jaime's bloody body lies twisted and silent in the dark…as if left for dead. The following day…the bright sun creeps up over the park, and there are birds singing and squirrels scurrying about. A young woman jogs on the running trail with her headset over her ears, listening to music, and another young woman rides a bike. There are a few elderly people enjoying the morning air, and another couple sitting on a bench talking, a man in a suit reads a newspaper, and there is a mother who glances up at the sound of her little girls' laughter. She calls out, "Girls, over here, where mommy can see you."

The three little girls do not respond to their mom calling them and continue to race around the bushes, playing tag and giggling with one another. Suddenly, the girls stop dead in their track as they discover someone lying in the bushes. There in the grass, lying in his own vomit, is a man unconscious and with dried blood all over his face. He looks dead… The oldest of the three little girls tries to cover her younger sister's mouth to keep her from screaming, but without much delay, a loud and terrifying sound comes out of the little girl's mouth as she takes notice of what looks like a dead man…that is none other than Jaime: "Ahh! Mommy! Look! Mommy!"

The Road Back

INSIDE A NEARBY HOSPITAL, Jaime recovers. It has been several days since he was brought in. He had been picked up by an ambulance shortly after people at the park, where he was lying almost dead, called 911. The call was described as "attention, all units, there is a [dead man] at a park..." of course, using the right codes the rescue units use over the radio in following protocol. Upon their arrival, the ambulance crew does not give Jaime much of a chance of survival, and after intense effort on behalf of the rescue team, Jaime finally begins to slowly recover his consciousness. He was immediately taken to the nearest hospital, where doctors continued their efforts of reviving him, yet still not giving him much of a chance after finding him in such ill condition. With his vital signs low enough to have pronounced him dead upon arrival, the doctors give extraordinarily little chance of him fully recovering, but these health professionals are absolutely amazing everyday superheroes who fly under the radar, saving lives every single day. Thank God for our doctors and hospital staff, true everyday supermen and superwomen who are often underappreciated and, in many instances, underpaid, but these anonymous heroes continue to save lives, and it happens that Jaime is their latest achievement as one more life is saved...his heartbeat miraculously begins to pick up.

After several hours of trying to figure out his identity in an effort to locate any relatives, the hospital human resources department finally contacts Stephanie to come and try to identify Jaime. No, he is not dead, but he had been very much close to it. Stephanie, who had just returned from a trip to Nicaragua where she continues to deal with all sorts of legal issues related to the cigar operation, enters her house and immediately hears the telephone ringing. She drops her bags to the floor and answers her cell phone buried deep in her purse, and after listening for a split second, she falls to her knees and begins to praise God upon hearing the news that there is a possibility they have just found Jaime.

It had been almost a year since Jaime had gone missing, and perhaps she had already lost hope of ever finding him, but this is good news, and Stephanie is perplexed for a moment, paralyzed. Soon after hanging up, without any hesitation, she jumps in her car and drives to the hospital at the drop of a hat. She leaves the bags unpacked and even the front door wide open, and she drives hysterically to the hospital. She prays the whole way there, and when she finally arrives, she leaves the car in front of the fire lane and runs inside. Once inside the hospital, in one of the recovery rooms, Stephanie finds herself peering over Jaime as he lies unconscious in a hospital bed. She gazes at him, and tears of joy sway down her face at the sight of someone who looks nothing like Jaime. His face blotched with now fading bruises, seventeen stitches on his cheekbone, and bandages wrapped around his torso. An IV feeds his arm. Jaime is a complete mess, but nevertheless alive…just barely. One of the doctors assures Stephanie he will have a slow and painful recovery, but if he is as strong as they need him to be, he will be fine. The doctor continues, "Ms. Romero, it's going to take a long and painful recovery, but he'll be fine."

"Thank you, Doctor. How long has he been here?" The middle-aged doctor with a long name too difficult to pronounce and with several different eyeglasses on his white hospital robe pocket closes the door behind him before he responds to Stephanie. Then he proceeds to cautiously answer the concerned young woman who stands before him with her face swollen from crying and makeup running all over:

"Listen, he has been here in this department for about a week now, but I've only worked on him these past few days. He was unconscious for a while, and now he is in and out. He is incredibly lucky to be such a strong man because usually many of our patients in his condition do not make it. He was in pretty bad shape. It is really a miracle to see him alive."

"You mean to tell me he was worse than this?" Stephanie asks, and the doctor simply agrees by nodding his head. She then breaks into emotional tears. As the doctor leaves, Stephanie takes a seat beside Jaime's bed, and with much sadness and aching heart, she feels compassion for his condition and stays with him the remainder of the day. Although tired and hungry, she often bobs her head to try to stay awake, but she does not leave him.

The next morning, Stephanie softly feels Jaime's bandaging, and suddenly, Jaime slowly wakes up. He gradually opens his eyes to see her face and gives her a half-smile. Stephanie is surprised to see him awake, and she greets him softly, "Good morning there!"

Jaime looks around and responds hoarsely, "Heyyyyy…there she is… How long have I been here?"

"Almost five weeks, they tell me. You've been in and out, but I doubt you'll remember any of it."

Jaime slowly reacts with disbelief, "Wow! How long have you been here?"

"Shhhh…you need to rest. Can I get you something to drink?" As Jaime prepares to reply, he notices her eyes are flooded with tears.

"Hey now… I have done enough crying for both of us. There is no need for that; I am going to be simply fine…"

Stephanie cradles his bandaged hands with hers, and wiping a tear, she agrees with Jaime, "Yeah, I know. I know…" Then Jaime suddenly drifts back to sleep, and Stephanie allows him to rest.

He is in and out for the entire day, and the following morning, he wakes up, and Stephanie is already there, by his side. "Good morning," she greets him.

Jaime, more alert than the day before, replies, "Stephanie? Why am I so sore? My body hurts all over. I am jittery and shaky…but mostly sore."

She moves closer and replies to him, "They operated on your back. You also had a concussion, and you were in a coma for several days when they first brought you in. You have been on morphine to control the pain the whole time, and the doctors tell me you are going to have to be strong in order to fully recover. It is going to take time and much work, but right now, what you need is to rest." Jaime tries to adjust his eyes to have a better look at her, but he is too groggy. So, he just mumbles:

"And you've been here the whole time?" Stephanie smiles gently.

"Nahhh…Jaime, you would have done the same for me." She checks her throat. "You have had some pretty entertaining hallucinations there, Mr. Funny Guy," she tells him, trying to cheer him a bit, but Jaime averts his gaze and stares off at nothing.

"I messed up. I was given the opportunity of a lifetime, and I blew it. My uncle always said losing your honor is a crime against God. I lost more than that, Steph."

"Jaime, look at me. You are going to be okay. God isn't through with you yet," she tells him, looking right in his eyes in conceiving the seriousness of her statement.

"Stephanie? Why did this happen to me?"

Stephanie gives his question some thought, and she replies the best she can for such a complex question, "I don't know, Jaime; bad things happen to good people all the time. Sometimes God engineers chaotic moments in order to reveal Himself to us, I do not know. He also gives us a chance at exercising our responsibility by putting us in front of tough challenges. As we learn to trust in God's sovereign intervention, we learn to wait and watch God's (Christ's) redemptive work… I guess. I ask myself the same thing all the time, though. You are not alone." Jaime is perplexed at her response.

"Wow! That is deep…how did you learn to talk like that?" She says nothing and again smiles… He then adds, "So, now you think I'm a good person?" She smiles…

"I've been watching you… Spying on you, Jaime… Nahhh! Just kidding…" she jokes. "Just messing with you… Jaime, I wouldn't be here if I didn't think you were a good person." He smiles.

"Stephanie, then why do I feel so… Like I'm the worst person in the world?" She gathers her thoughts…

"I don't know...but guilt is one of the many weapons the devil uses to mess with us, and it's working on you right now. Get some rest, would you? Are you hungry?"

Jaime thinks for a split second, and he tells her, "No, I'm not hungry. Thank you. I am not sleepy, not tired... Just feel...sore physically and drained mentally." Jaime looks away, and he stares at a blank as if wanting to just vanish out of thin air.

He is confused, and he feels empty and lost, but glad to be alive and certainly happy Stephanie is by his side. Stephanie breaks the awkward silence and adds on a positive note, "Well, you need to rehab from all that heavy drinking, and you're going to have to detox your body from the other stuff too.

Jaime then asks, "What's that? Detox?" Stephanie frowns...

"Shh! Try to get some rest... I'll be back in a few, okay?" Stephanie turns off the light and closes the door behind her as she walks out of the room and into the hallway, where she begins to cry hysterically after holding it all in before Jaime. The sight of him is a pitiful one, he simply looks unrecognizable. He is bruised, tarnished, and skinny, and Stephanie cannot help but feel for the man.

After several more weeks in the hospital recovery room, the doctor gives Jaime the green light to go home. Stephanie insists he goes to her father's house so that she can keep an eye on him, and finally, Jaime agrees. At Mr. Romero's house, in the Miami suburb, which is now Stephanie's home, a group of medical staff arranges Jaime's hospital bed and other equipment inside the guest room. This will be Jaime's new home during the rest of his recovery and detox period. The front of the house has the appearance of a modest home in an affluent and secluded area and, from the looks of it, just the average fifty-year-old house in one of the many exclusive neighborhoods in Miami, but there is a reason why this particular neighborhood is such a desirable spot. It is not so much the front of the homes here that attracts people to this area, but the distinctively decorated backyards. This part of town is known for having extremely lavishly decorated yards and patios, some with lagoons, extravagant swimming pools with waterfalls and cascades along with exotic birds and wildlife, which may include tigers and other colorful animals. Inside the confines of Mr. Romero's backyard, there are rare ducks, geese, and many other birds that roam freely, including some unusual ones such as peacocks and flamingos. Stephanie feels this will be great therapy for him and a far much better environment than the old motel anyway, and she laughs when she mentions this to Jaime. There are also horses and llamas wandering inside the ten-acre property and around a dozen or so full-time employees constantly performing their daily duties either gardening, handling the maintenance of the estate, or attending to the stables and the animals, and with ample space to still feel much privacy, Jaime and Stephanie are never alone.

Days later, Jaime begins his physical therapy sessions. With time he begins to make progress even though he battles the pain and discomfort that comes with it. Days later, he begins to slowly walk around the living room with the help of a nurse who has been assigned to watch over him and assist him in anything he needs twenty-four hours a day. Jaime, who is gripping a cane, now sits on the couch in the spacious sun-filled room and watches Stephanie, who stands there a little awkward, telling him the plan of moving forward, "Jaime, I prepared the guest room for you, but you can stay in my room if you want. It is bigger, much more spacious than the guest room, and closer to the kitchen. I can move my stuff to one of the other rooms, I do not need that big of a room anyway. There are plenty of rooms to choose from so, please make yourself at home. I want you to feel comfortable here. It is the way daddy would have wanted it. All your stuff is gone, but I will get you more clothes and things. Just let me know what you need, okay? I will be working from home, but I will keep out of your way. I can take one of the smaller rooms in the back, better view for me anyway," she repeats in an effort to show him she is really trying to make him feel as comfortable as possible.

Jaime is awestruck…asking himself what in the world has he ever done to deserve such royal treatment, and he finally asks, "Why are you doing this?" Stephanie does not answer, but she looks at him, and her face speaks the deepest empathy Jaime has ever seen. Jaime honestly has nothing left but this, the compassion of a genuinely good person, which is exactly what he needs at the moment, and in clear understanding, he smiles and accepts it. Stephanie gives him a smirk but keeps her silence.

As the days continue to go by, the situation becomes even more difficult every day rather than getting better. Jaime, let's face it, had become a full-blown junkie, and his body demands the drug it was so used to feeding on, and sadly so, before Jaime lies a long, difficult road ahead and one even he is not sure he can cross. As doubt and guilt clutter his already tumultuous mind, Jaime senses these feelings are too attacking his intellect and his security.

It is now almost dark, and the shadows of the night approach rapidly as the loud sound of vomiting comes from the bathroom. Immediately, Stephanie runs to Jaime's assistance, he uses his cane to try to stand over the toilet, and she helps him by placing her hand on his forehead in support while her other hand pats his back softly. Jaime misses his target almost every single time, making a smelly mess and wishing he could just disappear, and his embarrassment is such he cannot stop apologizing to Stephanie, who continues to labor by his side in an effort to control the situation.

When he is all done puking his guts, she gently helps him back into the bed. He is pale, sweating, trembling, and weak. Stephanie then asks in a soft tone of voice, "Jaime, if you think this is too hard…too much…please let me know, and we will…" Jaime then quickly interrupts her.

"No, I can do this! I have got to do this," he answers with a lost look and rolling his eyes in doubt and confusion, and not yet completely out of the woods with his health issues and his recent addiction.

Stephanie tries to talk some sense into him, and she uses an extremely soft tone to get her point across, "Listen, Jaime, I'll come with you to the detox center at the hospital if you want. I will stay there with you…they have professionals there. People who will help make it easier. There is no shame in it." At this, Jaime takes a deep breath, realizing he is beginning to lose his cool and knowing his current health condition does not warrant any emotional outbursts, and he calms down.

A little more relaxed now, he keeps going, "Steph, I have to do this…do you understand? Nothing is easy in life, my dear, nothing. I got myself into this mess, and I will have to deal with it in getting myself out. Freedom is a disappearing act where we make the ego disappear. 'EGO stands for Edging God Out…' my uncle used to say. Me, me, me… I always think I can figure it out, but maybe it is time I ask for help. Would you please help me? I need your help; I just cannot do this alone. It is way too hard but let's try it here at home first." Stephanie nods in a painful accord, knowing fully this difficult process is something only Jaime can surpass, and with much emotion, she accepts to allow him to proceed with his detox plan at home instead of the hospital now that he has agreed to accept her help.

She also knows he is being stubborn in wanting to do this on his own, but in a worst-case scenario, if it doesn't work out after a few days, then she can take him to the detox center, but for now, she will just see how much Jaime can take of this self-inflicted inferno. She knows this trial and tribulation is the result of careless abandonment on Jaime's behalf but also a true test of character. Can Jaime do this? Will he be able to finish the race?

That same night, inside the bedroom, Jaime lies on his bed wide awake. Feverish and shaking, and all of a sudden and without any notice whatsoever, he goes into unbearable withdrawal, shaking harshly and making loud, painful noises. Suddenly, he flings off the sheets…landing on the ground. He screams loudly, "I can't! Oh, God! I can't! Stephanie! This is harder than I thought. Help me. I need to… I need some. Give me some…" Stephanie rushes in, hearing him. She sees Jaime on the floor, convulsing like a fish out of water, foam sputtering out of his lips, shaking. "Stephanie… I need some. Get me some, please, I am going to die. Please! Give me some, just a little… Make it stop! Make it go away!"

With an alarmed look on her face, Stephanie leans over him, feeling his forehead. He is boiling up with a high fever, and he is shaking like a demon-possessed person. Stephanie is in a state of shock, and she does not know what to do. Does she call someone? Does she throw him in the car and take him to the hospital? What does she do? Instead… She prays, and she prays…placing her hands over Jaime with her eyes closed tightly and frantically scared. Jaime continues, "I'm dying… Please, don't leave me."

At this, she finally drags him out of bed and leads him in the tub with pajamas and all, she turns the shower on cold water in an effort to bring down the fever, and as the water begins to splash on his convulsing body, he suddenly begins to cool off.

Jaime's shattering carries on almost the entire night, and Stephanie finally leaves his side after he has fallen asleep. Right around three in the morning, she is dead tired from the recent events and in much need of a shower and sleep. Stephanie checks on him once more before he retires for the night. She looks at Jaime with pity, shaking her head, and then glances at the clock on the wall acknowledging the time. It is late, and she is dead tired. His lips are dry, and he is drenched in sweat, his face pale, but he finally rests peacefully after a harsh episode of withdrawals.

This is quite common for people who become addicted to anything; really, even cigarette smokers go through withdrawals after attempting to quit. When it comes to heavy drugs like heroin and such, the aftermath is much worse, and, in many instances, the addicts never get over the cleansing period and return to the addiction almost instantly to avoid the painful recovery process. It isn't easy, and it isn't normal for a human being to tolerate pain. Pain is the opposite of pleasure; pleasure is the opposite of pain. As Jaime lies in bed comfortably, it is the calm after the storm, and he begins to dream. His dream is nothing but a continuance of a familiar dream now…the same dream he has had his whole life.

Jaime comfortably walks in the now-recognizable cloud-like mist. No longer afraid, he sees his own bare feet walking in the midst of a green tobacco field. Jaime, at his present age, slowly comes to a stop and realizes he now stands in the center of the familiar bright cloud-like mist from the previous dreams. He gazes straight ahead… at the same elusive figure from before who is coming down with the clouds of heaven. Still not clearly seen at a distance and in the foggy mist, the bizarre but no longer unfamiliar figure in a robe white as snow waits patiently before him with open arms… Jaime smiles with ease, he reaches out his hands, and then the robed figure, like a son of man, gently takes Jaime's hands in His own and leads him to His presence.

Suddenly, a warm pure light bathes Jaime. He stares right into the eyes of the man, who suddenly looks like a remarkably familiar face. Then suddenly, for the first time, the man with the robe, who wears a beard, finally speaks…

"I am the way, the truth and the life. No one comes to the Father except through me (John 14:6)," says the man in the glowing light as Jaime looks closer at the elusive figure who has now taken the clear form of a man in trying to make out his appearance. Jaime looks into the hands of the man before Him, and something catches his attention, but the man wearing the bright white robe and whose radiant appearance is as pure as the midday sun smiles at Jaime, and Jaime, no longer afraid, smiles back. The dazzling light upon the man shines almost endlessly and, unlike any light, Jaime has ever seen before. Jaime finally notices His hands, and fixing his eyes on them, he can clearly see the hands of the man have deep scars on them as if His hands had been pierced with thick rusty nails, and at this, Jaime falls onto the floor in agony, acknowledging he is in the presence of *Jesus,* Jesus Christ, and the same Jesus his old uncle so often talked about from the time Jaime was just a child in the many stories his uncle told about Jesus where he described Him exactly as He appears now. And almost instantly, Jaime begins glowing with peace, the bliss of sudden understanding. He immediately drops down to his knees and begins to cry with emotion.

Initially, it is a soft weeping cry, but it suddenly turns into a desperate mourning shedding of emotional and cleansing tears. With his head bent all the way down to his knees, Jaime stays there for a few moments as he mumbles, "Oh my God… My God… It is… You, Jesus, Jesus. Lord, it is You!"

Jaime just stays there bowed down to the ground; he places his head almost at the feet of Jesus, who stands right before him. Jaime's arms are extended, wanting to touch Him with his fingers moving towards Him as if inching closer and closer on the dirt in the direction of Jesus, who smiles as He looks Jaime square in the eye by placing His index finger under Jaime's chin and lifting his face towards His. Jaime weeps uncontrollably without words, fixing his eyes sharply on the radiant face before him. After a moment, Jaime notices the feet of Jesus are too scarred from the same rusty nails, and at this, Jaime almost collapses with compassion and emotion. It takes him a little while to compose himself as the bitter reminder of a cruel death from a long time ago comes to mind; *the cross*, over two thousand years ago. Jesus looks at Jaime, and as the two share a bountiful look, He finally speaks, and His words echo in the air, "Jaime, stand up and walk, you are almost there. Just finish what you started; you are not done. I will give you the strength you will need, and I will be with you along the way. You are not alone; you have never been alone."

Following the miraculous encounter, Jaime is left there speechless and unable to find the words to address Jesus, so he just sits there and reminisces about the magical moment taking place as a million thoughts run through Jaime's mind. *What should I say? What do I ask? Should I ask for forgiveness? Should I ask about heaven?* And as thoughts continue to murmur inside his head, no words can be uttered as he moves his lips, but nothing comes out, and all Jaime can do is immerse in the moment as if not wanting this magical moment to end. He stands there for a split moment and after sharing a look with Jesus that says everything as if his life flashes before his eyes where He discloses every act and deed of his past without the use of words. Suddenly, the glowing reflection slowly begins to dissolve before Jaime as the image of the profound and gentle smile of Jesus with His wide-open arms continue to linger before Jaime…and still overwhelmed with passion, Jaime is taken by the inexplicable warmth provided by the miraculous encounter. After a few moments, the light begins to fade along with the image of Jesus until it comes to complete darkness, and it becomes pitch-dark again. Jaime now sleeps calmly as the night continues…

In the early morning light, Jaime stirs from sleep, the calm after the storm, and Stephanie sits by his side, sipping on a cup of coffee. "Good morning!" she says, and Jaime looks around a bit lost as if looking for someone else, but it is just him and Stephanie inside the room. He directs himself to Stephanie in a bizarre manner and somewhat surprised…

"You didn't call anyone last night!"

"Nope, almost, but you finally slept. I prayed. I prayed for you like I had never prayed before because I had never seen anything like it. Yes, I prayed much of the night. It was pretty scary there for a while, but then, out of the blue, you looked so relaxed I felt much at ease, and finally, I too slept," Stephanie tells Jaime, quite convinced and looking right into his eyes, sensing he understands her.

"You must be an angel, Stephanie," he tells her, and she responds with a half-smile:

"I don't know about that." She nods her head…and Jaime continues:

"Hey, speaking of 'angel,' I had the craziest and most real dream I have ever had. Perhaps a hallucination."

Almost ignoring his words and maybe thinking he might have been hallucinating indeed from the high fever and with all the withdrawals from the previous night, she then adds, "Come on, Jaime, I'm not an angel, but I can pray for you. That is precisely what I did. Prayer can move mountains. I know you may think it sounds stupid, but it really does work." Jaime keeps silent, thinking she did not hear him, and Stephanie quickly asks, "What did you dream about last night, Jaime?" Silence follows… She keeps on, "I am very curious because you had the most unusual expression upon your face when you finally slept. It was like there were two different people there last night, before and after…" Jaime pauses, choosing his words…

"Stephanie, last night, I had a revelation…one too crazy to explain." Then he continues as a tear rolls straight down his face, "I saw Him… Steph, His hands were pierced! His feet…the light… The glow upon His face and His soft and gentle voice…" Jaime begins to cry. Stephanie closes in on Jaime, and she puts her arms around him.

"I hear you. I have heard people say that when recovering from many forms of addictions, they tend to hallucinate a bit and see things that perhaps only their subconscious mind can assimilate. It is normal; it is all part of the process."

Jaime looks her right in the eye, and he tries to defend his story, "No, I was not hallucinating. This was different, it felt so real. Too real to explain with just words." Stephanie smiles, looking into Jaime's eyes, and she lets him have this moment as he goes on telling her about his mysterious dream. She listens attentively as he passionately tells her about his experience and about his unusual once-in-a-lifetime encounter. Stephanie is quite fascinated by the extraordinary dream as he becomes rather enthusiastic when he tells her, and Jaime can swear it was much more than just a dream.

She finally speaks after there is a moment of silence, "Jaime, my father used to say that we communicate with God through prayer and that God…"

Jaime interrupts her, "Wait, I know this one… And God communicates with us through meditation…time alone with God. See, he always said, after we are done praying, to just listen in silence, and God responds. He thought I was not paying attention, but I was. I always did pay attention when he talked; I only wish I had listened better. He was a great teacher, a great man." Stephanie takes his hand, and Jaime continues, "He and my uncle also mentioned something about Jesus knocking on my door one day, Revelation something, a chapter in the Bible…it was a specific chapter and verse in there he always talked about, but, of course, I wasn't listening." He chuckles, and she smiles back. "Steph, I think that was last night. I really do… How did your dad and my uncle know about that? This dream, this encounter, was just too real to ignore but as I lay in bed shaking, scared, the only words I could utter were 'Jesus, Jesus, Jesus…'" Stephanie smiles as she continues to look right at Jaime, who now looks much more refreshed and a bit overjoyed after the dismal experience the night before.

"Jaime, the Bible quote you are referring to is Revelation 3:20, I know the verse well, but I tell you this; your recovery period isn't over, and it isn't going to be easy. It may take many nights like last night, but I can promise you, this too shall pass. You have to be strong, and you have to have faith. You are not alone, though, and last night was evidence of that."

"I know that now. I know, well, I do not know exactly how to explain what I do know, but I know." He perplexes as he tries to explain…

"Good," Stephanie replies with a gentle smile, and she hands Jaime a tall glass of orange juice. "Drink some of this. It'll do you well." She continues on, "Jaime, my father had a similar experience a long time ago. You knew my father was Jewish, right?" Jaime frowns but says nothing. "His family migrated to Cuba in the 1930s like many who ran away from the war in Europe, and they established themselves in Havana as businesspeople. Grandpa Jacobi changed his name to Romero because he was afraid of any persecution like many Jews did, and later, many years later, he became one of the most successful jewelers in all of Cuba. True story."

"Wait, I didn't know that!" exclaims Jaime, still frowning…and she replies:

"Only a few do… And do you know how he got the name Romero?" Jaime shrugs his shoulders…

"No. That was my next question."

Stephanie sighs, smiling…and she keeps going, "Ironically, it was a box of Cuban cigars. Yeah, the first time he saw a box of the famous Romeo y Julieta cigars, he thought it read, 'Romero y Julieta,' instead, and people there at the shop mocked him, and from that moment on, everyone began to call him Mr. Romero, and it stuck. So, it was easy changing his name afterwards." Jaime smiles, and he adds:

"I see. Now it makes complete sense that your father would think my cigars idea was such a glorious one," Jaime explains, and Stephanie keeps on, more motivated now:

"Maybe. Dad was a great entrepreneur and a man with great vision. So, he must have seen something in you right away, I did."

"You saw something in me? Jaime asks, rather surprised, and Stephanie fires right back:

"Yes, me. I loved listening to you talk about your dream and your ideas, which you told in such a convincing way as if already accomplished. Dad believed in you too. He was crazy about you. Jaime, you have a way of talking, and people listen when you speak. You wrap people with your passion, you have a contagious personality, and it draws people to you."

"Wow! Thank you, Steph, I only wish he would have told me himself; I would have liked to have heard this from him." Jaime surprisingly adds, and Stephanie carries on:

"You are hearing it from me now. Jaime, my father, was a proud man, a man of God, but he was righteous and bitter because the people of Cuba reminded him of his own people, the Jews of the Old Testament. He always said that in Cuba, they live their entire lives, always idolizing made-up gods and all sorts of man-made statues that have to be tied to something so that the wind does not blow them away. They are dead, no life in them, and all made of rocks and sticks. He said he knew God, the creator of the universe, was angry about all the disobedience, and he claimed Castro was put there as a curse for their defiance just like the Babylonians, the Persians, the Romans, and the Egyptians were put there to torment the Israelites back in the day for their disobedience. Whether that is true or not, it is what he believed, and you knew my dad, once his mind was set on something, forget it."

Jaime sits there for a second and tries to make sense of it all, then he puts in his two cents, "Ahh! That explains... I do not know the history; I have not read the Bible, but it makes sense. There has to be a reasonable explanation for Castro being there all that time; torturing, tormenting, killing passions and dreams, breaking families up, and separating lives. Some kind of legitimate excuse or reason."

Stephanie agrees with Jaime, bobbing her head, and then adds, "Anyway, that's what he believed. My father…"

Jaime keeps quiet for a few seconds, absorbing everything Stephanie has told him, and without any more delay, he intones, "But I thought Jewish people didn't believe in Jesus?" She smiles…

"Well, my father did. He was a messianic Jew, meaning a Jew who also believed in Jesus. He had accepted Jesus as his personal Lord, as Savior when he was just a boy, then he later brought his entire family to believe in Him as well. Many Jews are believers in Christ, though, and it took years for my father to come around, but he said it was the only thing that really made any sense being that Jesus was a man who never sinned, who didn't even retaliate when being unreasonably accused and beaten and who died nailed onto a sinner's cross for the sin of the world even though He was sinless. It is all written in the Holy Scriptures… In the book of Isaiah in the Old Testament even, the part of the Bible Jews read. It says, 'By His wounds we are healed…' (Isaiah 53:5), and that was foretold 700 years before Jesus was even born, prophesying that by Him being nailed to the cross, all the sin of the world would be washed by the blood shed on the cross, His blood. It's been actually proven that all the prophecies in the Old Testament about Jesus came to pass exactly as they were foretold, to a T. Jaime, my dad was an educated man, and he said there was way too much evidence, too many miracles in front of too many people all recorded in history to not believe that *Jesus* was the Messiah and God Himself in the body of a man. Even the Pharisees in the days of Jesus came to realize He was indeed the son of God and the one the Holy Scriptures talked about, only realizing they had made a huge mistake after He finally died on the cross. Three days later, His tomb was empty, and He was taken up to heaven. The way the huge stone guarding His tomb was removed, there were soldiers guarding it, and it would not have been that difficult to find His body or who took it in those days if it were so. I guess you are going to have to read on it.

It is just too much to tell. Okay, I am surprised all that came out in one breath. Wow! I apologize, I got excited."

Jaime is perplexed and simply stunned at all her knowledge. He is left standing there hoping he had a pen in hand and a notepad to take notes of all these new things Stephanie had just told him. Things he senses she could not have repeated if she wanted to, or even better if he only had a tape recorder to keep word by word what Stephanie had just said. Jaime is literally in awe and silenced by the spur of her sudden wisdom and reminding him that "the fruit never falls far from the tree" as she strikes a chord, reminding him of Mr. Romero, his mentor and a good friend, her father.

"Huh! Wow! We learn something new every day but wait…do not stop now. Wasn't Jesus Jewish too?"

"Yes, He was, and even when He was a child, He taught at the temple, but the Pharisees, the religious leaders of that time in Israel, refused to believe He was the Messiah the Old Testament talked about and the prophesied king of the Jews. Regardless of how many miracles He performed in front of them and how many wonderful teachings they learned from Him in the short time He walked among them. See, they were expecting a king in the eyes of the world, not a simple and humble man and son of a carpenter who performed these amazing miracles out in the open; but they wanted a Messiah dressed in elegant garments, who rode on a gold chariot and who upon his arrival brought fire down from heaven, freeing them from the Romans who controlled Israel during that time," Stephanie continues her chat with Jaime, and he seems to have a million questions. She keeps going, "But many did believe, and they accepted Jesus as their Lord and became saved instantly. He healed the sick, made the lame walk, and even returned the sight to the blind among many other wonderful miracles out in the open. He even brought back to life several people who had already died in front of many." Jaime, more confused now, frowns as Stephanie tries to explain, noticing his perplexity, and she tries to clarify, "I know, you are confused, but the more you learn, and the more you study the Word of God, it will all begin to make sense. The Bible also says that faith comes by hearing the Word of God. So, the more you hear it and read it, the more you will understand."

Jaime absorbs this, and he immediately fires right back after hearing her words, "But there are so many religions out there, and everyone claims to have the answer. They all claim they are right, and the next one is wrong. There's Christianity, Buddhism, Islam, and so many other religions, and so much blood has been shed in the name of God throughout time, and why?…when there is supposed to be just one creator, one God." She listens attentively, and understanding his desire to have his question answered, Stephanie tries to satisfy his hunger for a response to the best of her ability:

"Jaime, man created religion. God has always been and will always be. You are right, *He* was the creator, the beginning and the end, the alpha and the omega, but if you want answers, simply pray and ask God Himself to give you revelation. This is the best way I can explain it. I certainly may not have all the answers, but He does. I can only give you my version, my take, based on what I have learned along the way." Jaime is completely taken by Stephanie's clever words as he tries to absorb all he has heard while sending his head for a wild spin, and this raises even more questions with so little understanding, but a deep desire to learn moves him…

Several weeks go by, and Jaime continues his painful and slow recovery. Some days are better than others, but it is all a work in progress as his situation is a slow and painful process one would never wish upon anyone else, but Jaime has agreed to endure it, and he deals with the ups and downs of it all. As the draining affair continues and the poison from the drugs finally begins to slowly leave his body, Jaime suffers greatly both physically and emotionally. The pursuing withdrawals are quite an alarming sight, which portrays Jaime's true mental and physical strength, both of which continue to be tested. Stephanie, on the other hand, continues to work from home as nurses carry on weaving in and out of the house, attending to Jaime's every need.

One evening, as Stephanie and Jaime sit over a quiet meal, he tries to explain he has been humbled by the agonizing events of the past few months. He compares his position to someone going through chemotherapy to have a malignant tumor removed, only chemo is something the body rejects, often times causing the person receiving it to suffer a great physical demise, including vomiting, morning sickness, and constant discomfort and pain, while on the other hand going through detox is similar, but instead of something external being injected into the body, the body calls for what is being deprived of and the very poison that had been inserted into it. It is frightening how the body screams for precisely more of what is killing it because that is our makeup as humans, to desire the very sinful nature, which caused us to fall even at the beginning of creation. We always gravitate toward what is bad, just as sin tends to taste sweet at first only to confirm the opposite later. Why is it that healthy foods never taste as good as chocolate and other not-so-healthy things we eat? And diets, well, the first three letters in the word say it all… (die)…as life itself is full of contradiction. Why is life so complicated? Sometimes I feel life is death's vengeance for the sins we commit, but life can also be beautiful and fulfilling, all depending on how we view it and so long as we concentrate on the critical moments that push us to live with the tenacious desire of trying to enjoy every minute as if it were our last. After sitting there in deep thought, Jaime finally explains, "All the times I had wished to die when I was out there in hell, I take it all back. I regret it all. I would do it all over again, and I honestly continue to say this over and over because I know now, well, I am learning that life is indeed beautiful even as I go through these uncomfortable and unfortunate episodes. Good and bad, it is still life, the only life we get here on earth. Look how many people we get to touch and how many are those who impact us as we walk through this crazy…but beautiful world," he says sarcastically as he picks at his food without any appetite as he tosses the fork back in his plate.

Then Stephanie asks, "Hey…Are you okay?"

"Yes, this is all great. Thank you so much for everything. I do not feel I deserve it, Steph."

She grins sympathetically and continues, "You are very welcome. Listen, Jaime, you do not have to eat if you don't want to, but can you stop thanking me, please? It makes me feel like a stranger." Apologetic, he looks at her…

"No, I lost my appetite," he replies, feeling a bit puzzled and wishing he were in a better position, in a different place, a different state of mind. The pain and aches a recovering addict goes through during his or her cleansing period are such they can literally make the person feel like they are dying. It goes against everything their bodies can absorb. It feels unnatural, and that is just the physical aspect of it.

Stephanie leans in and keeps the conversation alive, "Jaime, how about everything else?"

"Well, it's going to take a long time for me to recover completely, but I have to say, I feel much better if that is even acceptable for me to say under the circumstances. Just wish I were hungrier, that is all. I don't really taste food." He coughs after giving her his best answer to her question, and Stephanie quickly hands him a glass of water.

"It's going to take a while, remember? You didn't arrive here overnight, and it won't be an overnight recovery either."

"I know. Hey, Steph, I feel like today is the first time we have really talked. Well, actually, these last few weeks it has been great. Wait, did I really say that? You cannot call this 'great'?" She scuffs with a fake smile and referring to his physical condition, and he proceeds, "Well, you know. I am not talking about me; you have done more than enough. Steph, you are truly an amazing woman, and I appreciate you." An awkward moment of silence follows, and unable to contain his emotions, Jaime looks down at his plate, and in a more somber tone, he continues, "I don't know what to do. I have lost everything. I have nothing to offer anybody, nothing left."

Stephanie regards him gently, "Jaime, sometimes, we have to lose it all to gain everything. You are here. Life is what you have, not what you lack. Do you know how many people out there never get out of the hole you were in? You did it, you are here, alive. Feel good about what you have done in so little time. It is quite impressive. Really!" Jaime stares at a blank… Stephanie continues, "Have you tried reading the Bible I got you?" Jaime shakes his head. Stephanie grins and continues, "Thought you read books in Cuba?" This brings a small smile to Jaime's face, remembering this question from a previous conversation he had with her.

"We do, again, but you don't read the Bible...the Bible? It is a bunch of little kids' stories. I tried reading it, but I just don't get it. It feels like it is written in a different language. I feel either you have to be highly intellectual or as naïve as a child to grasp it," he mocks Stephanie, and she replies back in the most convincing way she knows:

"That is exactly it, you have to see it as a child would. Of course, that is what I thought too, until one day my dad told me a little story. He asked me to open my Bible and then told me to go to the book of Genesis at the very beginning. He then said to read from the very first chapter, Genesis 1:1...that's the book of Genesis, chapter 1, verse 1, and it was kind of cool there for a moment because I had never read it like that before, and in between rolling my eyes with doubt and a certain piquing curiosity, I got to the part about 'and God said, "Let there be light," and there was light' (Genesis 1:3). Then my dad asked me something I will never forget. He asked, 'Okay, Steph, you're a smart girl, where does the light come from?' And I quickly answered, 'The sun, of course...everyone knows that.' Now thinking I had outsmarted my old man with my quick and obvious reply, I felt very stupid when he said, 'Good answer if you don't know God, but if you keep reading a little further down, you'll realize it wasn't until the fourth day of creation that God actually created the sun, the moon, and the stars. So, where does the light really come from, Steph, if it was there from the beginning?' he asked again. I sat there for a trivial moment, trying to outwit my old man, and I suddenly drew a blank. He continued, 'The answer is *Jesus* if you believe He is the light of the world and who was with God from the beginning. In the Bible, it says:

> In the beginning was the Word, and the Word was with God, and the Word was God. He was with God in the beginning. Through Him all things

> were made; without Him nothing was made that has been made. In Him was life, and that life was the light of men. The light shines in the darkness, but the darkness has not yet understood it.
>
> John 1:1-4

'That last one there is speaking of the world not recognizing Jesus as the son of God, which is exactly what they did,'" Stephanie continues...

Jaime just sits there and listens. She keeps on, "Yes, I was blown out of the water then as he calmly explained like a kindergarten teacher, and I had heard this so many times before, but I like to believe that on that particular day, I was finally ready to hear these words. I was ready to understand, and I got it. I had no choice but to begin reading the Word of God because I just knew I would find priceless information in there, and because my dad made me...it is all a choice, though. No one forces you to open up. I believe you just have to be willing, and God does the rest." Jaime chuckles, but he continues listening to Stephanie...even more curious now. "There is another passage: 'Look at the birds of the air; they do not sow or reap or store away in barns, and yet your heavenly Father feeds them' (Matthew 6:26). Jaime, it is all about faith taking care of your needs. If you have faith...things always have a way of coming to you, and God makes sure of that." Jaime is mesmerized, and she clears her throat, trying to get him to say something.

He suddenly snaps, "Sensational! That...that was very impressive! The way you explained it was so much easier. Now I am the one who feels like a kindergarten kid." He then thinks for a moment, gathering his thoughts, and she laughs at his childish reply. Then he adds, sort of pensive and looking away as if not sure of his words, "You know, sometimes I wish I could just fly away like one of those birds in the Bible."

Stephanie grabs his hand, and looking right into Jaime's eyes, she murmurs, "You will, some day we all will, but for now, let me help you while we are here. Okay?"

Tears fill his eyes as an emotional wave hits his intellect. Jaime holds out his arms, and Stephanie rises; she crosses to him and gently sinks against his body. Her head is on his chest as Jaime embraces her like not wanting to ever let go. "I'm ashamed, Stephanie. I have done the unthinkable by not handling things properly and throwing it all away. I did not know any better. I was stupid and naïve," Jaime says, and at the same time, he releases a heavy burden along with his words. A burden of regret and sorrow for not managing the things he was entrusted with and for wasting irresponsibly a golden opportunity, and within all this, Jaime finds himself wrapped in shame and dishonor, while Stephanie believes they are finally making progress…

See, not knowing the consequences of any action is one thing, but once we know exactly what will happen as a result of any specific wrongdoing and we still proceed with it, then that is precisely what causes the heavy load upon our shoulders. That is where guilt and shame come from, and that's Satan whispering in our ear, reminding us there it is always a high price to pay and a heavy load to carry upon one's consciousness. Stephanie then tenderly takes his face, cradles it between her palms. "Jaime, you've always said life was like a cigar… correct? Well, I think it is more like a song, a song you can sing any which way you like. It is the song of your life! You have to live it true; no one else can do it for you while every day is another musical note, another bar, another magical lyric."

At this, he drinks in her eyes…and he quickly replies with much fervor, "I like that…my very own song, huh! I like it."

"Yes! Listen to me, Jaime…you are not the first, and neither will you be the last person something like this happens to, it can happen to just about anyone. Do not kick yourself, you simply did not know. You were not ready!" Jaime continues to pay close attention to Stephanie as he writes on a piece of paper on the table…

"My song…my very own song."

Stephanie keeps on, even more inspired and determined, "We live our lives from within. Everything that matters comes from here…" She clutches her chest, her heart, and then continues, "Nothing else matters, because if we don't have love, then neither does the world. But if we do, then the world has no choice but to love back, and it becomes a beautiful golden opportunity because there is nothing that can stop a pure heart." She sees a tear spill down Jaime's cheek as he listens to Stephanie's words...and obviously, it touches a sensitive spot. "Jaime, you're an educated man, have you ever heard of a Professor Vyskocil?" Jaime stops for a second, and he gives Stephanie a surprised look...

"Of course, I have, I know who he is, the world-renowned chemist, right? We studied him in Cuba, and I even did a paper on him. He was a big-time atheist, am I not, correct?"

Stephanie is really beaming now with Jaime's surprising grip on this, and she dives in more detail, "Yes, he was until he found God. Or should I say until God found him. He said he believed that the theory of evolution explained life's diversity, but later on, he had his doubts about evolution when he began his studies on synapses. He said he was amazed at the complexity of these supposedly simple connections between nerve cells. Then he wondered how could synapses and the genetic programs underlining them be products of mere blind chance? It really made no sense to him, so he researched it further. He then attended a lecture by a Russian scientist and professor, and during the lecture, the professor stated that living organisms cannot be a result of random mutations and natural selection. Then someone in the audience asked where the answer lied. The professor took a small Bible from his jacket, held it up, and said, 'Read the Bible—the creation story of Genesis in particular.' Later in the lobby, Professor Vyskocil asked the other brilliant professor if he was serious about the Bible. And he answered, 'Simple bacteria can divide about every twenty minutes and have many hundreds of different proteins, each containing twenty types of amino acids arranged in chains that might be several hundred long chains, and for bacteria to evolve by beneficial mutations one at a time would take much, much longer than three or four billion years, the time that many scientists believe life has existed on earth.' The Bible book of Genesis, he felt, made much more sense," Stephanie concludes, and Jaime is just mesmerized.

"Steph, what in the world? Why aren't we writing a book about this? This is good stuff! The world needs to know," Jaime asks, almost as excited as a jack-in-the-box, and Stephanie replies right back in a soft and reassuring tone:

"Good stuff, don't you think? And then after this, when he was asked if his personal belief hindered his scientific research, he answered, 'Not at all. Every good scientist, regardless of their beliefs, must be as objective as possible.' But his faith changed him. For one thing, instead of being overly self-confident, extremely competitive, and overly proud of his scientific skills, he became grateful to God for any and all of his abilities. Also, instead of unfairly attributing the amazing designs manifested in creation to blind chance, he says he and other scientists now ask themselves, *how did God design this?*" Jaime is left there with his jaw dropped and scratching his head.

"Wow! Steph, you sound like your dad… I'm speechless." She giggles clumsily.

"Not my thing, I read all this."

Jaime keeps on, "Steph, that is exactly how I feel. I just don't have the beautiful words to express my feelings like you do, but I, for one… I don't want to be alone anymore."

Jaime comes to a slow pause, and Stephanie senses he is trying to make a point. She looks him in the eye as he continues, "I think… I need…you! Is that wrong? I think I have fallen in love with you, Stephanie. I have fallen in love with you and all that you are. You are truly a beautiful person, and not just physically; an amazing woman I have grown to know and now love in these difficult times by getting to know you better. The real you."

Stephanie blushes, and without holding back, she replies right back to Jaime, a bit nervous and even a tad confused as if the roles have suddenly been reversed, she is the one who is a tad nervous, "I feel the same, Jaime, but I didn't just fall in love with you. I have loved you from the moment we met. I first fell in love with your dream, your passion, and your desire to excel even though you didn't have much back then, not even a clue, but you always talked as if you were predestined for great things in life. Then, as I got to know

Jaime, the man, I could not help but accept the fact that I am too in love with you. I see a little boy inside a man, I see my father inside of you, and I think you are an incredible person too. You are honest and pleasant…" Jaime sighs as he can't believe the words his ears are hearing, and to top it off, Stephanie adds, whispering in his ear, "And very attractive too!" At those words, nothing can hold them apart. Jaime slides the side of his face, which is already touching hers, and without any delay, their lips suddenly find each other. They kiss… there is a long, enduring kiss, and time dissolves here. There is only this moment, the most pure, passionate moment of Jaime's life, and as excited as Jaime is, Stephanie is the one who sighs with pleasure this time. Suddenly, Stephanie takes Jaime's hand, and she stands up before him with the most peculiar look in her eyes. "Jaime, I hate to put a damper on this beautiful moment, but I believe you are ready for this, but if you're not, you tell me, and we'll do this another time…when you're good and ready." Jaime pauses…

"You have got to be kidding. This better be particularly important. What? Ready? Me?"

"Jaime, are you ready to accept Jesus as your personal Lord and Savior? You already know the power behind this; you have lived it in your own flesh. This is going to change your life forever, though; it is going to renew you from the inside out and in total and complete harmony with some of what you already feel." Jaime moves his head in agreement…and Stephanie continues, "The Bible says that in order to become a new person, a new you, in order to leave it all behind and start fresh you must accept Jesus with your mouth, verbally…and be born again spiritually by acknowledging He now lives in you. Not becoming a born-again hypocrite like so many out there, but a new person with a new clean slate. Jesus promised a new beginning in accepting Him as Lord and Savior, He said those who are thirsty come and drink from the fountain of life where you will never thirst again… And He was referring to accepting Him as Lord and Savior." Jaime, like a little boy, is perplexed.

"Huh? Yeah! I did not know there was a process, though… What do I do? Do I have to sign a contract? Or know the Bible inside and out? If so, I am nowhere near ready." Stephanie smiles at

Jaime, who could not be more vulnerable and inexperienced at this very moment, and he listens carefully as Stephanie explains:

"It's a simple prayer of acceptance that connects you with our Lord Jesus Christ forever, leaving the past behind and being born again with a new heart, with a new mind. A Pharisee called Nicodemus once asked Jesus if he had to enter his mother's womb in order to be born again after listening to Jesus preach, and Jesus explained to him exactly what I am telling you now. Are you ready to do this, Jaime?" Jaime nods, agreeing with Stephanie.

"I can certainly use a fresh start. It cannot be that difficult, okay, let us do this… I'm ready!" Stephanie looks at him and smiles.

"Jaime, your life is about to change forever, and I don't mean becoming a born-again Christian like many who give a bad name to the power of a personal relationship with Christ. This is much simpler, and it has absolutely nothing to do with religion. Open your heart and repeat after me." Jaime closes his eyes, and leaning back, he clears his mind of all external noise by solely repeating the words he hears coming out of Stephanie's mouth. He concentrates on her words and takes them into heart with the fervor of an inspired poet. She begins to speak, and he repeats after her:

"Dear Jesus! On this day, I ask that you come into my life. I give my heart to You, and I ask that You take control of every step I take and every word I say from this day on. I ask Lord that You cleanse me of my past and of all my sins, forgive me, Father, for I know I am a sinner. I make You my Lord and Savior, for I know You are the son of God and that You died on the cross for my sin and the sin of the world. Thank You for giving me a new life, thank You for making me a new man. Amen!"

"…and amen!" Jaime finishes, and he is frozen for a moment after finishing this simple but powerful prayer.

Jaime holds Stephanie's hands tight, and unable to say a word, he slowly lifts his head and smiles at her. He then takes a deep breath and begins to slowly weep…and right there and then, pure and wholesome freshness runs through his entire body as if being purified by invisible magic as if his body, mind, and soul had been daubed into a delightful stream of fresh water. And though nothing is apparently happening on the outside, no fireworks, no sounding of noisy bells and whistles…nothing but the inside of a man being immediately transformed.

Jaime stands there paralyzed for a brief moment and had a thunderbolt fallen in the midst of Jaime and Stephanie at this very moment, it would not have amazed them more than it has Jaime's outer appearance. He glows, he has been touched by grace and forgiveness; he has been touched by the hand of God himself. As joyful tears of sudden understanding continue to run down Jaime's face, Stephanie holds him as he cries nonstop in her arms, unable to explain his emotion. He trembles, not with fear, but he trembles with excitement and anxiously awaits all that Stephanie mentioned in the little prayer he repeated after her in his acceptance agreement with his new Lord and Savior, *Jesus Christ*. As he remains unmoved, paralyzed, he is shedding off years of burden and loads of guilt as he continues to weep in silence.

Jaime is experiencing a rebirth of some form as we know it, a miraculous transformation. He is now a new man spiritually as he has agreed to have Jesus Christ take away the heavy burden of his past sins and erase them for good. The Bible says God does not hold any grudge, nor does he bring back any of the erased sins once they are removed and forgotten. Like a sealed record, these sins are forgiven, and they are all forgotten as well, forever… After a few moments, Jaime turns to Stephanie and asks, "Hey, Steph, what's today's date?"

She looks at him and replies, "It's the twenty-second, November the twenty-second… Why?" she asks…and Jaime quickly adds:

"I just wanted to remember, that's all. I wanted to mark this as an unforgettable moment for me. I feel liberated! I feel light! Free!" She then eyes him kindly and agrees with him, feeling his relief and knowing he has been bathed in the spirit of God as the Holy Spirit has come upon him:

"I know, Jaime, I know!"

Months go by, and Jaime continues his recovery process with Stephanie by his side. His whole new spiritual rebirth makes everything much easier, but Jaime still has to fight through the brutally painful undergoing of recovering from his addiction. As the midday sun hovers over Jaime, who now sits on the front porch of the house just rocking back and forth on a wooden rocking chair, he is thinking, and a light breeze soothes him, easing the high humidity covering the air. As the swirling ceiling fans fight to keep the area cool, Jaime now understands why God was always mentioned in the literature used in the AA (Alcoholics Anonymous) meetings and also in the meetings for those recovering from drug addiction.

This was something he always questioned when he first began attending, and many times he meant to inquire about what the idea was to have a seemingly out-of-place subject such as God in the midst of such time of calamity, but now he understands clearly that the power of God surpasses all understanding. It is an undeniable and incredible power, which can withstand any situation, circumstance, or condition and heal all sickness and disease. Jaime thinks, *If only reciting a short prayer in which one gives his heart to God wholly, sincerely, and without holding anything back, no reserves, nothing…can change a man's heart this fast, then imagine what kind of power having a personal relationship with Jesus will have in my life?*

Jaime is thrilled at the opportunity, and he looks forward to his new life, which has already begun, but he also knows this is his take on life, and he is not here to change anybody's belief system or to inflict his newly found peace upon anyone else as this is a personal relationship that only arrives once one is ready to receive it. After all, people will believe what they want to believe, and they will walk in darkness until the day when they decide to open their eyes just like it happened to Jaime. Remember, it has nothing to do with religion, it is all about a personal relationship with the almighty who can make all things new. At the same time, Stephanie's business also continues to expand greatly now, with Jaime involved even as a part-time consultant as he continues to get better. Her partners begin to collaborate with Jaime as well in making many needed contacts with trainers and managers from different Latin American baseball clubs, all of whom have worked with Jaime in the past or at least have heard of him.

After a few short months, Jaime's addition to the team has now been elevated to full-time, and it proves to be a great asset as they now realize he was the missing piece of the puzzle and the bridge to catapult their young company into a globally recognized name in the sports industry.

The once small business Mr. Romero started many moons ago in an effort to simply help expose young Latin American baseball players to the majors is now becoming one of the largest and most recognized marketing agencies in all of baseball. The house is never empty as Stephanie continues to work from home with Jaime now heavily involved as well. Their agency uses Jaime as a silent consultant in discovering new and young talent in the baseball world and bringing Latin baseball players to the majors from places like Cuba, the Dominican Republic, Venezuela, and growing, with the latest addition being Japan and South Korea. Jaime begins bringing in translators in different languages to facilitate a more comfortable environment for those players they bring in, yet pushing the importance of learning English as soon as possible so they can fit in with the rest of their teammates and not have a disadvantage because of the language barrier.

Through it all, Jaime does everything from home while he continues his dreadful recovery, which seems never-ending at times, but he realizes it is going to take time to reach complete recovery.

He endures painful daily physical therapy as well as cold-turkey detox to cleanse his body of all the junk he had injected into it. The process is long and challenging, even after weeks and weeks. And so, Jaime continues his daily activities in growing their agency using the telephone, fax machines, the internet, and even Zoom calls as he works day and night alongside Stephanie and her business partners in taking their company to a new dimension just as he did with his cigars. Now let us remember using the internet was something completely new to Jaime, but he is becoming extremely familiar with it in a rather short time as he learns to generate leads and receive referrals of talented young hopefuls with a dream of one day being professional baseball players, saving him the long trips across the world.

By now, Jaime has learned to use computers so effectively his laptop is always on. Latin American scouts along with major league talent explorers use Jaime as a bridge between them and young prospects trying to make it because of his vast experience in dealing with Cuban baseball, but unlike the modern way of doing business, Jaime still prefers the face-to-face interaction, and that is what makes their company what it has become, one of the best in the business. Thanks in large part to Jaime and that contagious personality of his, which has the phrase "personal care" written all over, oftentimes the missing ingredient in modern-day sports and business in general, as the kind of money paid to professional athletes continues to soar. Jaime examines character much deeper than just physical ability and talent; he conducts background checks on these athletes in finding truly worthy men of this once-in-a-lifetime opportunity and not just hoodlums who can swing a bat or run like lightning. And like his old uncle used to say, "A first impression is of utmost importance. A person says much about themselves with their first impression, and it shall not be taken lightly…" On that note, Jaime adds proudly, "Our company demands personal attention, human touch, and a lively energy that is unmatched, we don't just use handshakes and such, we are a promise met behind the talent we provide. We are the middleman between a bunch of talented guys and what the world sees on TV, and we do not want to be responsible for sending a whole bunch of spoiled and talented millionaires out there, the likes of Ramirez. Those baggy pants, the attitude, and that hair? That is not part of baseball! No offense to you, Manny, but you have to admit, when you first showed up with that look, you certainly caught our attention." He laughs… but by using the clumsy remark, he hopes to get his point across.

As he jokes, and the guys and gals from the media laugh during a live television interview, Jaime makes it a point to explain that personal attention is the main ingredient to successful relationships and even in any type of successful business venture, no matter how advanced technology becomes, personal attention is something people still need and want. A robot or computer can never provide that! "We are still human. We are not robots, not yet anyway," Jaime adds during the live interview in proving his point.

The sudden and inexplicable success of their marketing firm is due mostly to Jaime's charisma and experience with the recruiting of talented baseball players, but mainly, I repeat, because of his ability to relate to these young hopefuls with his now own personal experience behind it. Some people would even say Jaime's story is quite remarkable and an unprecedented accomplishment in this day and age. Jaime, who still struggles with unexpected issues caused by his not-so-distant drug addiction days, continues to battle his demons daily but maintains his serenity and stays busy as a way to living a clean life free of drugs the rest of his days.

Baseball once again becomes the main focus in his life now that his cigar operation has come to a halt, it keeps Jaime busy, and it makes him feel like a contributor and not like a parasite anymore. Jaime has regained his status as an important man, but most importantly, he has slowly recovered his health and his desire to live once again. He has asked Stephanie to find Enrico, his old butler, and to bring him to work with them at Stephanie's father's house, now her house. It would be great to have a few familiar faces around instead of always being surrounded by strangers and recent acquaintances. Enrico, who had spent much time at Jaime's side before and whose loyalty demanded the recognition it deserved, finally joins them. Also, to help with Jaime when Stephanie is not around or is too overwhelmed with work, he has asked that they also bring Jordan back, his old chauffeur.

And just like that, only a short time later and seemingly in the blink of an eye, all that Jaime had requested has been granted, and he now recovers at least part of what he lost in the recent past in Enrico and Jordan reuniting with Jaime, who are there with him once again, and it brings Jaime much comfort to know that both these guys are back, and they too enjoy being back with Jaime.

These days, Stephanie and Jaime are almost inseparable, and they seem extremely happy together as it reflects on everything around them, and with business taking off the way it has, the future looks extremely bright. Jaime explains during a live radio show that he can now grow old through years rather than sorrow as things are beginning to fall back into place. He can once again be comfortable rather than worried by having Stephanie and these guys who mean so much to him by his side. Jaime's life makes sense once again, and he is glad to have Enrico and Jordan back, especially while he goes through his rehabilitation. The process is intensely difficult, as already mentioned, and it seems infinite for someone who was relatively new to these kinds of drugs but who quickly became heavily addicted and dependent on the poison. It literally requires intensive willpower and determination on Jaime's behalf, but mostly many sleepless nights on his knees, praying… Yes, praying! Those around him also have to be strong for him as it is not easy watching a loved one go through something like this; it almost feels as if it is happening in your own skin. Yes, it feels like you are the one living their experience in your own flesh, and it is draining, tiring, and exhausting for those around an addicted person going through recuperation. Outside of all the therapy, Jaime attends weekly meetings to help overcome his addiction, and Stephanie has now offered her house to the group to have their functions there for recovering addicts. Most of these recovering alcoholics and drug addicts do not even know Jaime was the face of the cigar world not too long ago or what he does in baseball, and they just see him as another one of them. Jaime is just one of their own, a part of a lifelong fraternity of recovering addicts, and it makes Jaime feel good to belong once again. Unexpectedly, Jaime has become a person of value once again and one who is now liked for who he is and not for what possessions he has. He often remembers when he was just a puppet for the Cuban government as he watched over the ball players back home and how he felt on a daily basis like a worthless snake. In addition, Jaime lingers on the past and dwells over the time when he had the multimillion-dollar business, the luxurious home, the fancy cars, and all the toys, but none of that matters now. In these recovering groups, he has found good friends and people who share much in common with him, an addiction. Genuine friendships at last! All linked by one common thread, the fact that they all have had a rebirth and a second chance at life. "These are people who like me for who I am and how I treat them, not for what I have to offer and what I can give them. We do not talk about money in these groups or stupid temporary fixes and material things; stuff that can vanish in a moment's time with natural disasters, fire, or simple mismanaging of finances. We spend quality time with one another, knowing that for most of us, it is a miracle we are still here," Jaime comments…

For Jaime, the painful withdrawals continue night after night, and some are worse than others. Many times, he feels like giving up, and in some rare instances, it almost feels convincing enough that he may die from these convulsions, but he prays for strength as instructed by Stephanie, and he magically gets it. Stephanie is always there with him, and she has not left his side since her father died. Who would have thought? Jaime certainly did not, and for a man who honestly believes in loyalty, this is big to him. It spells good character all over, but, of course, he already knew this about Stephanie. Her father made sure she inherited that part of him.

Mr. Romero was truly a good man, and Jaime is glad to have known him. Jaime misses him greatly, and not a day goes by where he does not regret paying more attention to his advice, his mentoring, and his teaching. His daughter Stephanie has filled a great void left by his death in many ways, and Jaime has found a new close friend in her. In more ways than one, she has replaced Mr. Romero in Jaime's eyes.

Jaime tries to hold it together when it gets tough, but sometimes it is almost intolerable. He feels like quitting, like giving up. It is an extremely difficult process, but with God on his side, somehow it feels comforting, easier. He is not alone anymore, and as he walks through the valley of the shadow of death, he just knows this.

It has been many lingering months now, and after an excruciatingly long period of detox and rehab, Jaime is beginning to feel as close to normal as possible. The many extensive sessions of rehabilitation to remove all the toxic waste from his system have completely drained him, and the constant battle against his body's demands, which kept asking for the drug day in and day out, can drive anyone insane, but Jaime has endured. He keeps strong, and he continues to thank God constantly as he pushes through. One evening, while Stephanie goes over work files in her home office, Jaime walks in with a bunch of flowers in his hand. He clears his throat to get her attention…and as she turns around a bit surprised, Jaime suddenly intones, almost apologetic, "Hey, you! Still working?"

"I thought you were sleeping. You said you were going to go take a nap," she adds, much surprised, and he replies clumsily:

"No, I couldn't, so I asked Jordan to take me for a drive, and I got you these…"

"Wow! Those are beautiful. I love lilies. Thank you, Jaime. How do you feel today?" Jaime looks around and stretches his arms…

"You know what? I guess I can say this is the best I have felt in a long time. I haven't had the shakes in a while, and I'm hungry again." She smiles…

"Well, that's a good sign. I'm glad to hear." She pauses for a brief moment…and then adds, "Come sit with me. I'm done working for now. You know, we have more boys coming in for tryouts this weekend. There are a few coming from Panama, Colombia, and from other places too. Things are looking really good. MLB scouts will not stop calling either. That is a great sign."

He smiles, and pointing at her, he replies, "That's what we do best! Right? We make it happen for them, just like your daddy made it happen for us. We pay it forward! It feels good, alright. Doesn't it?"

Jaime slowly walks towards Stephanie and takes a seat next to her. He grabs her hands and then begins to speak softly while staring right into her eyes, "Hey, Steph... Have I ever told you how grateful I am to have had you next to me this whole time? I could not have done it without you."

Stephanie accepts his words, and after a moment of silence, she adds, "Oh, stop it. You are the strongest man I know, plus you would have done the same for me. Jaime, we're family now." He pauses, then he stands up and walks over to the window. He then turns around and slowly walks back to her, who is still sitting...

"What? No, no! Steph, you deserve whatever you may ask of me for what you have done, and I thank you for it. I wish I were in a better position to give you everything you deserve. I am forever in debt to you!" At this, she stands up and faces him.

"Jaime, I've got everything I need right here."

"And what's that?" he asks...and leaning closer to him, she now locks eyes with Jaime and politely tells him:

"You!" He frowns, maybe not expecting her response, and immediately she inquires, "Jaime, do you realize you have never kissed me again since that day? It has been exactly six months and four days..." Jaime is baffled at her ability to remember this with such exact preciseness, and he stands there feeling a little awkward at first in total silence, then suddenly, their bodies begin to quiver like teenagers in love, with desire, curiosity, and anticipation. Jaime pulls closer to Stephanie, he places his arm around her lower back, pulling her even closer to him, and they kiss. Time dissolves here...

It is now nighttime, and inside the master bedroom of the beautiful house, low-volume instrumental music plays, and in an aura of soft candlelight, Jaime and Stephanie lie in bed. Under the silky sheets, they lie in each other's arms. Jaime is in heaven. Stephanie touches his face; her fingertips, soft like a whisper, make Jaime feel alive. Jaime kisses her soft lips ever so sweetly. Jaime looks deep into her eyes, and he does not want this unforgettable moment to end. When Jaime looks at Stephanie, he sees himself growing old with her, and at the same time and without any words, she is expressing the same feeling about him. They both react to one another with respect and admiration as this magical moment seems to last forever, neither one is in a hurry, neither one wanting it to end.

Moments later, Stephanie's eyes are closed, and Jaime has both his arms wrapped around her as if not wanting to ever let go. The silky see-through drapes hanging from a balance beam over one of the many windows in the bedroom blow softly in the pleasant evening wind. The patio doors are wide open, and Jaime can see the full moon outside, with only scattered clouds floating in the clear night sky. He then whispers to himself, "That is exactly how I feel right now, full, complete, just like that moon. I would go through it all over again if I knew this would be the end result. Yes, sir! I feel I have finally made my peace with God, and I think I've found true love at last." He closes his eyes, and they both sleep as one.

As the easy morning light creeps in the room, Jaime dozes peacefully. Stephanie's lips touch his, waking him. He looks up, surprised, and she is leaning over him, already dressed and holding a cup of steaming hot coffee in her hand. "Come on, sleepyhead, I made you breakfast..."

"Is that bad? What does sleepyhead mean?" he asks innocently and pleasantly awestruck as her beautiful appearance is the first thing he sees this morning. She smiles, and he continues, "Am I really here with you?"

"I don't know, maybe we are both dreaming, hallucinating," she adds...and he fires right back with reassuring words in trying to convince her that this whole experience is indeed real:

"Or maybe you being here with me is just proof that God really keeps knocking until we finally answer. This is what I prayed for, Steph. I prayed for God to send me someone who would love me unconditionally and for who I am, and to send me a woman who was real, grounded, and sincere."

She kisses him again and says, "Come on, Mr. Smooth, I bought you new clothes this morning. They are in the closet. Come on, get up!"

Jaime, surprised, suddenly adds, "But…you didn't have to. What time is it?" She looks at her watch.

"Oh, it's late. I let you sleep in. It is almost noon." Jaime gets up, wincing. He shuffles on his cane to the closet, and he looks at the clothes she has bought him, almost in shock.

"These weren't cheap, Stephanie."

"Jaime, you are not in Cuba anymore, and daddy's business didn't leave me poor. Besides, you can pay me back if you want if it makes you feel better!"

"Oh yeah? And how am I going to do that? You got to give me a little time." She smiles…and he proceeds, "Can I tell you something? You know, even when I was rolling in big bucks, I was still afraid to be poor again. I always overspent to let people know I was not poor anymore, and I overpaid, overtipped… I guess in the back of my mind, I was still poor; like I was dreaming or something. Like a poor lotto winner. Anyway, I enjoyed the dream while it lasted, and now I am back to square one, but I am okay with it. I went from rags to riches and again back to rags, funny! Who does that? Me, that is who! I tell you something, though, it was all worth it. I learned a lot about myself, about life, and right now, I feel I have more than I could have ever had when I was flying high with money and possessions. I have nothing, but I have everything because I have God with me, and I have you. Does that make any sense? I have nothing, but I feel like I have more, go figure! However, I feel truly complete somehow." She stares at him with a gentle grin on her face as she walks towards him.

"Oh yeah?" She takes a document from her briefcase, and she hands it over to him. "Well, why don't you read this here? Go to page three, paragraph 2E. It is all there." Jaime looks at the paperwork, and his jaw drops as he reads through it. Stephanie smiles at him and guides him to the dining room table after he almost collapses reading from the document in his hand. They now sit at the dining room table, and Jaime stares at the document, stunned.

"When did you learn about this? When did he add me to his will? I did not know, he never…" Jaime staggers his words and sort of chokes up.

"I...actually, he named me executor of your trust. The same trust he set up for you at the very beginning, just simply fearing this would have happened. He left it up to me, and I needed you to be ready before I told you about this money. Had I not, you would have squandered it." Jaime, close to tears now as Stephanie discloses the news, finds himself in some kind of awe and disbelief. "You know, he thought of you as a son, Jaime. He once told me, people with new money are just like five-year-old kids inside a candy store with a hundred-dollar bill in their hand. They will not think about tomorrow, and shortly after they are broke, their mouth is full of cavities, a true dentist's dream!"

Jaime, wide-eyed, takes a deep breath, and he continues, "That was me, Steph. I was hungry for things I never had and most of it, things I did not even need anyway. Pure vanity! Just a poor man's mentality. Like a newly arrived emigrant, ignorant and foolish!"

"I think 'naïve' is a more fitting word. Jaime..." She pauses and looks down shyly as she continues, "My father...you and I are what he wanted. Or what he hoped for. He was always worried I would never find a man who truly deserved me. That is a father speaking... of course!" Stunned, he gazes at her.

"Does that mean you want me to stick around? I have his blessing then?"

"You silly man," she replies, smiling, and Jaime continues his defensive struggle, still in disbelief:

"Steph, I'm twenty years older than you...and I'm a mess. How will this work, honey?" She takes a second to respond, and when she does, she does it with a huge grin on her face:

"We'll fix you up; besides, do you know what guys my age are doing right now? The nightclub scene and trips to Vegas is not my idea of heaven." He smiles, happy to hear her words. She takes his face, and they kiss...

Later that night... Inside the bedroom, Stephanie sleeps with a smile. Stirring, she rolls over and sees Jaime is still awake beside her, staring at a sports magazine in the dark. "What's wrong, Jaime? Aren't you tired? What are you doing?" She then sits up and turns on the light of the lamp on the nightstand beside her. Jaime sighs. Stephanie leans over and peers at the article he pretended to read in the dark. It is an article about Chuchi and the boys, and it has an old photo of the four of them with Jaime at the airport arriving in America. "Jaime, you have to call them, it's been too long already, and they know nothing about you. Why don't you let me call them for you?"

"Steph, I'm ashamed."

"Oh. Honey…" She wraps her arms around him.

"I ran like a coward. I hid from the world. I lost my greatest power, responsibility for my own life." She frowns, feeling bad for him.

"Jaime, sometimes you have to lose it to find it, remember?"

"I know, but there's no excuse for what I did. They…" Stephanie is filled with compassion and understanding… She steps in:

"Okay, I will fix it."

Moments later, as the soft moonlight penetrates through the bedroom window, they both sleep peacefully in each other's arms. The next morning inside her father's attorney's office, Stephanie and the elderly lawyer are all smiles. Jaime and Stephanie sit across from him, holding hands. "Are you two going to let me in on your little thing here? What is it with the smiles?" Jaime asks, and the attorney removes his reading glasses and intones to Jaime:

"I knew her father since I had hair on my head. He was a great man, a rare breed nowadays. Mr. Romero was a generous man, and I can say that because I am a pretty darn fine lawyer, and I know a good man when I see one. I see you two holding hands like teenagers riding to prom. She is a good person, Mr. Colon." Stephanie blushes. Jaime waits impatiently… Mr. Jacobs continues, "But I digress, okay. The answer is…yes. I am not an accountant, but I took a glance at the will, and I think we can manage what you want." Jaime frowns.

"What is he talking about, Steph?" Jaime asks Stephanie, and she responds:

"Jaime, daddy left some money to make another one of your dreams come true." Overjoyed, Jaime stands…

"Haa! Thank you, thank you. So, I am not broke after all?"

"No, but don't thank me, you better thank Mr. Romero," responds the old lawyer with a grin on his face, and Jaime jumps up and kisses the old man on the cheek. Stephanie laughs.

After they leave the lawyer's office, Stephanie and Jaime take a drive to a nearby supermarket, and they go inside to grab a few things. As they exit the local supermarket, Jaime, with a cane, and Stephanie pushing the cart of groceries. He looks at her and smiles. "This feels so strange, you know."

"Why? Haven't you ever gone grocery shopping before, Mr. Big Shot?" Stephanie responds, squinting her eyes and expecting a good answer from him, and a good answer it is:

"Well, no, not with such a gorgeous woman anyway."

"Oh, you are so smooth," she replies, and he shyly looks away.

Suddenly, an eccentric man comes running through the parking lot towards them. Stephanie knows him; it is one of the neighbors, Rolando, who wears a loud-colored outfit and flashy disco shoes in bright daylight. "Oh God, Jaime, brace yourself…" she warns him as Rolando approaches like a fast-talking zealot.

"Hola, hola! You are Jaime Colon! Hello, Stephanie, you know this man? This man is famous! Ijaba Cigars? The best…I, I remember! What happened?" nervously yells the man. Stephanie turns to Jaime…

"Jaime, this is our neighbor, Rolando." The man keeps on talking, "Señor Colon, may I call you Jaime? I know your whole story. Does anybody know you are here? Alive? They…well, everyone thinks you are dead or something. The newspapers… Do you still see the players? Chuchi the Bullet? Papo, Panchi, and Tito? I have read all about you, I have all the magazines, newspaper articles, seen you on TV. Hey, terrible what happened. You were a rich man…"

Jaime turns to Stephanie and back to the man in disbelief… He whispers to her, "Are you serious? Is he for real? Stephanie shrugs her shoulders and smiles as if telling Jaime, *you are on your own here.*

Jaime turns to the man and responds, “I still am, Rolando, in more ways than one.” Stephanie is proud of Jaime’s response, and she now pays close attention to the conversation as they try to walk away to avoid any confrontation.

The man continues on even though Jaime and Stephanie are obviously not interested in a conversation, “Me too. I have been phenomenally successful thanks to Santa Barbara... Chan-go (one of the many saints/deities of the Cuban Santeria)!” Jaime frowns...and gives the man a strange look. He then asks:

“Chan-go? Really? Are you serious?”

The man keeps on, “You like Chan-go? Que suerte (Lucky you)! You practiced Santeria in Cuba, didn’t you? That is right! So, you understand. You see, I am a santero (witch doctor). I can help you...” After hearing this and with a weak smile, Jaime tries to politely move on, but Rolando trots along and persistently continues, blabbing his mouth, “I know exactly what happened to you... You should let the orishas (deities and demons) take control and give you all the revenge you need. Chan-go can help you. Jaime, come see me. I will sit with you over a spiritual consultation, and for only 400 dollars, those bad guys will know you are not going to sit on your hands and do nothing about what they did to you. Let me help!” Suddenly, fed-up Jaime comes back at him, pointing with his index finger.

“Help? You call that help?” Stephanie pulls on his arm as Jaime starts to go at the man whose eyes grow with fear as he notices Jaime is upset, but Stephanie pulls on him again, and Jaime pulls back and calms down. After a short pause, Jaime carries on, now a bit more relaxed, giving the man a stern look that lets him know he means business. “Listen, revenge is not what I want, Rolando. Being against something only weakens you. Being for something empowers you. I am going with the ‘turn the other cheek’ method. Ever heard of that? I know it is hard for you to believe a man can do this, but ‘Justice is mine,’ says the Lord... You should really read more books, maybe get out more often.”

Not fully understanding Jaime’s words, the man persists, “Yes, but...” Now giving an imploring glance at Stephanie... Rolando whispers to Jaime, "But you can afford it, can't you?" Jaime now has had it, but surprisingly he keeps his cool while responding to the man:

"Rolando, my man...can anyone afford that? Wake up! Open your eyes, you are barking up the wrong tree here! You are not going to manipulate me like you do these other poor, innocent, and desperate people here and in Cuba, I believe in a God that does not charge any amount of money for answers. I was right where you are right now not too long ago, confused, lost, and I tell you, man, stop while you are ahead, you still have time, you know. Get out of that trap and throw away all the junk you have stacked in the corner of your house, stuff they told you would help keep your enemies away, give you peace of mind and calm. Glasses of water under the bed to honor all the dead in your family, a bunch of lit-up candles inside a closet, and probably a dead chicken too. Listen, all that is going to get you is your house on fire if one of those candles tip over." Rolando frowns... And Jaime keeps on, "It is easy, my man, give your life to *Jesus* and forget about all that other mumbo jumbo. There is one way, and Santeria is not it, if it were, believe me, things would not be as they are in Cuba, but don't take my word for it. Just do your homework."

Jaime finishes his unrehearsed lecture, and Rolando is just standing there frozen, speechless for a brief moment, scared and a bit shaken up too because of the way Jaime came at him...then he suddenly snaps at Jaime: "You are crazy...you know that?" Jaime looks at him, a bit calmer now.

"Yeah, maybe... But hey, enough of that! Get out of here with all that garbage and get a life, brother! You are in America now, and all that voodoo stuff only works for the weak, the faithless, and those with low self-esteem looking for answers. Flee! Get!" Stephanie turns to Jaime and laughs at the expression on his face. They walk off.

After a few steps, Stephanie turns to Jaime. "Jaime...what was that? Where did all that come from?"

He exhales and replies to Stephanie with a nice grin on his face and almost in relief, "These people make me sick. They make a living just preying on the ignorant, on the blind and weak-minded people who are desperate for sudden changes without any effort whatsoever. People looking for a quick fix to situations they have spent an entire lifetime bringing upon themselves."

Stephanie, a little confused now, asks, "Bringing upon themselves?"

"Yes, I'll explain later," Jaime tells her.

Meanwhile, Rolando is left there bewildered and stunned as he watches Jaime and Stephanie turn their backs on him and push their groceries to their car. Stephanie looks at Jaime, impressed. "Well, well! He will never try to sell you on that stuff again. He will probably move out of the neighborhood by tomorrow too," she says.

"Good!" Jaime replies.

Jaime is hot, and Stephanie does not quite know what lit his fuse to such extreme, but she just knows he is angry. "Don't worry about that guy, Jaime, let it go." She laughs, looking back, as the man still standing back there is made fun of by others passing by and mocked by those who stopped to watch the short but loud shouting match. He turns to see the people there just staring at him, and embarrassed, he runs off behind the store, leaving his own groceries on the ground. Jaime stops and looks Stephanie dead in the eye. Then he explains:

"See, Steph, you were born here, honey, where it's different, but back home, in Cuba, it's been over five hundred years of witchcraft, sorcery, and divination based on rituals, animal sacrifices, and brainwashing, which they try to sell as just naïve cultural tradition, but it is much more serious than that. It is all part of a dying culture and tradition, but it bothers me how some people still buy all that lie and continue to live under that dark cloud. It is hard enough to find food to eat over there and to think they still pay half their miserable salaries to a santero to give them the answers they seek, it is mind-blowing. Incredible really! And still, in Cuba, I sort of understand how they could still be under that spell of desperation and doing whatever it takes under their circumstances and anguish, but here in the States, and this day and age? Come on!" Jaime concludes, and Stephanie immediately asks:

"How does that work? I don't get it, and it's always been my understanding that it has become the national religion, right?" He stops and turns to her to explain. Stephanie listens as he unloads his frustrations in an effort to make things clear for her, and he goes on even more inspired and fired up as this really bothers Jaime, it touches a nerve:

"Steph, it's simply tradition and what was once just an old religion only practiced by slaves, passed down from generation to generation, just like Thanksgiving dinner in America or football became an everyday practice there. Only these people who call themselves seers and all-knowing santeros continue to brainwash the rest, and they spook them in making them believe if they do not consult a santero before making important decisions, then bad things happen to them. They tell them they have to become spiritually cleansed in order to live a good life, a life of peace, a life of harmony, and ultimately, they talk them into becoming saints, as they call it, 'Hacerse Santos,' which, of course, comes at a price anywhere between five to twenty thousand dollars here in the US, unless they travel to Cuba to have it done there where it is much cheaper, but still awfully expensive. It isn't cheap for sure, but between what people want to believe and under all the pressure, some people just fold." Stephanie listens while Jaime clarifies, still heated and somewhat bothered and insulted by the neighbor's offer of a Santeria consultation. He keeps on, "The way it works is after they take their money, they have to go through a series of occult gatherings and rituals where they make them wear white clothes for an entire year upon their acceptance ceremonies, they can't participate in any festivities, and they can't eat certain foods as a personal sacrifice or initiation. They have to eat from a special matt on the floor too, and all this in search of a better life and some sort of enlightenment, but in all honesty, I have been told by those who live there and who have been around it all of their lives that all they are doing is making a secret pact with the dark side. All these ancient African religions are too ominous, too of-the-occult, and too secretive for me, and none of it can be good in the end.

See, the God I serve now is much bigger than any of that, and all those ancient religions tremble before the name of *Jesus*. True story, if you do not believe me, ask any of those who have crossed over, leaving Santeria behind and giving their lives to *Christ*. I only wish I could tell them all who are still involved in Santeria they can walk away from it without fear of bad things happening to them as they tell them to keep them chained. I only wish they knew they could actually break the chains and escape the bondage like their ancestors did many moons ago after arriving here from Africa. It is a choice! Slavery was abolished hundreds of years ago, but apparently, some people don't know this. And while these so-called godfathers and godmothers in the Santeria religion make their advocates believe this is a beautiful religion, pure and harmless, in all honesty, it is a shady, expensive, and deceiving technique where they make people believe they are gods themselves, adoring and worshiping rocks, stones, and sticks, doing animal sacrifice, and blood drenching rituals that are all part of the daily practice at a cost, of course. While mingling with demons and hidden deities. Come on!" Jaime concludes, almost breathless in educating Stephanie, but she still has questions, and she keeps asking away:

"Hmm? And I thought this kind of stuff was only practiced in Africa and maybe Haiti?"

Jaime moves on to reply, more relaxed now, and after a heated display of mixed emotions, he finally ends it with a calm and most convincing explanation by adding, "No, honey, the heart of Africa still beats in Cuba today, from the music to the religion and many other traditions, but in all honesty, who am I to judge? This is their choice, their lives, and their freedom to choose what they believe, and to intrude in that would be absurd. Everyone must live their own lives, and everyone must face the consequences of their actions and decisions. So, whether a person chooses to accept Jesus Christ as their Lord and Savior as I have, or they choose to believe in other religions such as Buddhism, Islam, Hinduism, in any of the many African religions or even in nothing at all, it is a personal choice as we all search for answers. I personally chose *Jesus Christ* because it makes sense to me, I feel it, I know it, but everyone can do what they choose, and that is how I feel about it, and that's the beauty of America, freedom; freedom of expression, freedom of religion, and freedom to do and be what one wants."

The next morning, Stephanie and Jaime leave the house early, and they go out for breakfast. She tells him it is a surprise, and that is all he needs to know as he continues to ask questions like a two-year-old, "Steph, where are we going again?"

"You'll see…" she tells him with a mischievous smile as they drive down the road.

It is a sunny summer morning, clear sky above. It is warm, Stephanie drives her classic convertible Mercedes-Benz, and Jaime enjoys the breeze like an honorable passenger. "Why didn't I ever get one of these? It's very James Bond of you, you know!" he comments on her classic car, and she shrugs her shoulders and smiles. Then she quickly responds:

"I thought about buying a new car at first, and the more I looked around, the more I realized they don't make cars the same anymore, so I got this from a friend who moved away, and now I can never drive a new car again. There is nothing like these babies, they just don't make them the same anymore, I repeat, but you can borrow it sometime if you'd like." He smiles back.

"This is indeed a nice car…but where are you taking me again?"

"You'll see. Gosh, you are worse than my dad when it comes to surprises," Stephanie answers with a nice smile upon her face, and Jaime becomes even more curious, frowning.

"Steph, where are we going?"

After driving a few intense minutes, about half an hour to be exact, filled with, "Where are we going? Where are you taking me?" And, of course, "Are we there yet?" They finally pull into the parking lot of a beautiful church in Miami. The parking lot is packed. Jaime's persuasive and child-like personality is one that only someone with Stephanie's soft demeanor can tolerate, one that can drive anyone crazy; however, Stephanie loves it. She smiles again. Now removing her seatbelt, she adds, "Okay, we're here!" Jaime gives her a funny look while eyeing the surroundings carefully.

"What are we doing here? Church? And you could not tell me we were going to church? Hmm!"

She peers into his eyes and adds, "Come on! I have something for you!"

They get out of the car, and Stephanie leads Jaime by the hand, who is looking slightly uncomfortable. He gets out of the car and walks beside her as they enter the church through an entrance on the side of the building. A friendly face meets them at the door, and it is none other than Jaime's old friend and now pastor of one of the largest non-denominational Christian churches in all of Miami, Pastor Ervin Oliveros. Jaime is surprised to see him, and the pastor speaks first as Jaime chokes on his own words for a moment, "Nice to see you, old friend." Then the two men hug each other with brotherly love, and Jaime whispers to his ear:

"Ervin, you're a pastor? You? Talk about a curveball… So much for destination, huh? Good for you. I am really happy for you. Change comes to us all, sooner or later, right?" The young pastor smiles.

"Who would have thought, huh? Me, a pastor? But Jaime, God has a plan of His own for us all. We may run around our entire lives like chickens with their heads cut off until the day He finally calls. We may roll the dice, but the man upstairs ultimately decides how they fall, says the Bible. I still remember the day I asked God to remove the things in my life that kept me from serving Him, and He did, now, look at me; I am a full-time pastor," Pastor Ervin replies to Jaime, smiling with even more energy.

"Yeah, tell me about it, and you have a full house too! So, what is going on here? The church is packed," Jaime asks, and Pastor Ervin stops, he looks at Jaime dead in the eye.

"They are here for you, Jaime. They are here to listen to you tell your story. Your testimony." Jaime pauses, confused, and Ervin asks as he becomes quiet all of a sudden, "Wait, what happened, Jaime? No smart remark? No quick comeback? No witty statement?" Jaime is frozen.

Jaime is mostly stunned at the fact that all these people are here to hear him speak, especially when he had no previous idea he was speaking at all, and as he contemplates a certain agony within himself and perhaps the fear of having to speak in front of such a large crowd, he is so happy to see his old friend, now a pastor. He asks, "First, I need to know this, how did you do it? I remember the old you…you were a mess, Ervin."

Ervin gives him a smirk and proceeds, "Well, you said it, Jaime, the old me! Let me tell you what happened… One day, after crying for hours and after realizing my life was just a dark and empty hole, I got on my knees, and I said, 'Lord, forgive me, I repent! I need Your mercy; I need Your grace!' And the next thing I know, I was given a second chance. You know I am telling the truth, and especially knowing the old me, it is really odd for someone like me and with my past to talk this way if it was not true. Anyway, suddenly, and thanks to my mother's nonstop prayers for my salvation, I did not feel like drinking anymore, I did not feel like hanging out with the old gang anymore, and something simply happened right there and then. I mean, it was a process in all, but with time, I suddenly became a new person altogether. Met a beautiful, God-fearing woman, I now have two amazing daughters and could not be happier with my new life. This God thing is really cool."

Jaime and Ervin hug each other in agreement and continue their chat: "Wow! Sounds familiar… I have had some interesting changes in my life too. So, Ervin, what am I doing here? Why are you making me speak in front of your congregation? I do not even know anyone here. I don't know what to say." Ervin takes a deep breath before responding…

"Jaime, just talk, you don't need to rehearse these lines. Tell them your story, the truth." Jaime agrees by bobbing his head, and Ervin guides him in. "Come on in, Jaime, there are some people inside that want to hear your story," Ervin proceeds.

"Wait, my story? What are you talking about?" Jaime asks, and his friend levels with him:

"Jaime, it is all over the papers, the news, and the internet, 'Jaime Colon, the founder of Ijaba Cigars, returns home.' Don't you read the paper? You have got to tell them, Jaime. Your story can change lives! It probably already has."

Again, Jaime is stunned, and then Stephanie looks at him, giving him a comforting smile. Pastor Ervin takes his arm and leads him inside the church and onto the church podium, where a huge congregation awaits before him. The second Jaime appears on the stage from behind the large curtains, everyone comes to their feet, and they all begin to clap, in all, about a thousand people or so, every seat inside the church is occupied.

The seemingly choreographed warm greeting lasts a few long minutes, and when the loud reception finally stops, looking slightly uncomfortable, Jaime stands at the podium all alone. He leans into the microphone, taps on it, and nervously addresses the large congregation. The church is full. "Hello! Good morning…" He pauses here for a brief moment, which seems like an eternity, then he looks back at Stephanie, who stands next to Pastor Ervin just a few feet from the podium, and he continues, "I'd like to thank the Academy…" He jokes, referring to the movie awards, to try to break the ice, and the congregation laughs. This is a congregation of his new neighbors, strangers around the community, and an audience of peers and just simply people who are glad to see him alive and well after all this time. There are many successful people in attendance among a crowd of regular churchgoers and also regular people, including known Cuban musician Willy Chirino, who will play a further role in our story. The mayor of Miami is also there, a few professional athletes, celebrities, and all sorts of folks from all different walks of life. Jaime continues, now in a more serious tone, "Seriously now, I wasn't expecting this. I do not even know where to start but thank you all for coming here today. Please forgive me if I sound like a four-year-old, but I was thrown to the wolves here this morning…no preparation whatsoever. So, I'm just winging it." The congregation laughs again as he points at Stephanie and Pastor Ervin. Jaime continues, "I think I know exactly what you would like to hear from me today, and if I notice a number of you begin to stand up and walk away, I guess I have failed, but here it goes..." He clears his throat...looks back at Stephanie and proceeds, still a little shaken and incredibly nervous, "It may seem like a lifetime ago, but it has been only a few short years since this very church helped me sponsor cigar factory workers in Nicaragua. This happened when I first decided to expand our cigar operation there. For those that do not know, I was once the face of the cigar world, and my business was incredibly popular. We produced some of the best cigars in the world. One day I spoke to a church in Nicaragua where I planted and grew our tobacco, and I asked about possibly using my cigar business to help rehabilitate ex-convicts and drug addicts in the area. I did not feel right running a successful cigar operation in a place where there was so much need, and it was only fair that we gave back; and so, we did. These were men and women who were rejects by society standards, useless individuals, according to the public eye, and I daresay most of them already knew what I am just now learning today. And it worked, they began to heal as they worked with us, finding their self-worth. Most of them learned a new trade, and it helped them with their addiction, giving them a sense of responsibility, they had lost. Others had great knowledge of the tobacco business and farming, and we benefitted from it. It was great on both sides, for them and for us. It cleaned them up, it gave them purpose, hope, and in return, we had plenty of workers there to do the work...people of all ages and all walks of life. Even kids," Jaime continues, and some of the people in the congregation look lost, confused perhaps as Jaime uses his words carefully but with conviction as he explains: "Now, I'm sure you all know by now the sordid details of my failings. So, I am not here to talk about the rise and fall of Jaime Colon. If you want that, just Google me, the pitiful story is all there thanks to modern technology. The internet!" The congregation laughs vaguely. He continues, "But what I have learned is that when you take your eyes away from your earthly possessions...your house, your car, your laptop, your home entertainment center, your wardrobe, your boat, and whatever money has bought you, whether by choice or by impulse, it really clears your head of a lot of external noise. And when it is quiet, you can finally hear. You can hear what is really going on inside…you can hear God's voice…" The congregation once again is quickly engrossed. Jaime continues, "I wanted to share with you today…what I heard." Jaime nods at Pastor Ervin. He winks at him and keeps on, "Please just cue the choir in case I run over, I tend to talk a bit…" The congregation laughs again. "I know there is a lot of confusion out there, political unrest, social injustice, the ACLU, the anti-God movement in America today, removing God from our schools, from our money and more, but I wasn't one to know anything about that, as a matter of fact, I didn't care. I, though, let people believe what they want to believe, and if they do not believe at all like I once did, that is okay too. That is their problem. Live and let die! Are you with me so far? If I am boring, you throw something at me, okay…" No laughter this time… The entire congregation is fixed on Jaime. Complete silence follows, and he now has their undivided attention, he continues, "We come here to worship God, right? Now I have thought about this a lot, some of you may come here as a habit, a Sunday thing, others come here to learn, to hear a good word of wisdom, and to feel that peace they can't find out there in the world as if God only lives inside a church, right? Well, He does not. God is everywhere, and He hears every prayer, every thought, but a church is indeed a good place to start, a place where we can learn about the love of God, and a place where not simply good people go but a refuge to those desperate for a word of wisdom and an opportunity to repent. Of course, not all churches are the same, not all pastors preach the word the way it was intended to be preached, and a church can be a place of criticism and finger-pointing too, imperfect even. Ahh, humans… Men! Why do some of us feel compelled to come here to worship God or a higher power, as some like to call it? Call it the Creator, the Almighty, or simply any of the many terms used to suddenly identify God by today, but it is only when we have a serious health or financial problem that all of a sudden, we come crawling back to God, giving Him His rightful place. Why do so many millions of people all over the world feel the overwhelming need to have God in their lives, though? Well, I am no scientist, but it is built into our DNA, into our genes. Some people call it the universal spirit, others call it God, but what it is, is *love*, and love works. All you need for it to work is to have faith. Trust in love, and it will restore you, it will guide you and empower you. Trust in God, and as you think, so it shall be. God gives us the courage to stand up to giants and still walk in peace, confidence to face any obstacle, and basically do anything we set out to do. John Lennon was right, 'All you need is love…' And I think we all know what love is, don't we? It is simple; we just have to practice it. Give it without expecting anything in return. Isn't that why we are here? To love one another, because love fills us up, it completes us. Love conquers it all, and God is love! *God* sent us His one and only son to die for our sins so that we could live! He traded places with us without our permission. It was the largest transfer of wealth to ever take place in the history of the world; however, how many people really know this? God Himself in the form of a man lived among us two thousand years ago with the sole purpose to die and with His precious blood cleanse us of our transgressions, according to the Christian faith that is, and though you have the right to believe what you want, this is my take and my faith." The congregation, now rapt, mumbles in agreement. Jaime smiles and continues, "Here is the big secret. The answers are already there, waiting inside of you. Surrender to God, yes, I said, 'God,' and give Him a shot at steering your boat, your life. We have learned to trust the world, and how has that worked out for us? We have such a hard time trusting God, and does that make any sense? What has the world really done for you?" Jaime asks…he looks around and continues, "We trust in banks giving us a miserable return on our money, our pensions and 401ks are slowly disappearing, and we still trust them. Why can't we just let go and trust God with our finances, with our lives? Senseless, right! 'How can I trust a God I cannot see?' we say. By giving God control of our lives, we do not lose it, we actually expand it. Jesus once said, 'Those who are thirsty come and drink from the fountain of life, and they'll never thirst again.' A lot of people do not quite get this, but it is all there, *He* knocks, and all we have to do is answer. Letting go is the only true control we have. Sounds crazy, I know, but it is true, I did it. I had no choice but to let go, and that is when I found a pure heart in my Lord and Savior, Jesus Christ. Even if you have never heard of Jesus or if the religion you practice does not teach about Jesus' love, it is still there for your grabbing. Take it, own it, and try it. It works. His love does not discriminate, His love does not judge."

Inside the church, it is so quiet one can hear a pin drop, except for the few who are sniffing and sobbing after being touched by the message. There is not one dry eye in the place. Jaime begins to pace from one end of the stage to the other with the microphone in his hand like a motivational speaker, he then proceeds, "And then, one day once you have surrendered your life to God, you realize, *Wow! I can see!* It is just like having an amazing new pair of reading glasses, a new clarity filled with peace, energy, abundance, creativity, and confidence. It isn't a magic pill, but a decision, one that brings knowledge without judgment, strength without fear, a love and appreciation of all life in its endless variety, and the decision I am talking about is opening that door and letting in the one who knocks. I tell you, friends, these are some pretty cool lenses I have on right now. I was once blind, but now I see." He chuckles, and Stephanie, who now sits in the front pew, her eyes full of tears, watches, beaming with love and admiration. Jaime takes a deep breath and continues, "Give it up, folks. Trust in it. When you finally walk with God, tolerance and compassion are effortless and natural. It is so simple. Enlightenment shows you that nothing can threaten your rightful place in the universe; you are now a son or daughter of God, it is your birthright, it is every essence of you. Think about it, it is not possible to not exist. Look inside yourself, what do you see? Eternity…we all sense it. We all glimpse it. Every one of us do, and it has nothing to do with race, or creed, color, or religion, but sometimes we tend to forget it, and it is easy to do as the world tries by any means necessary to keep us in the world, but we are not of the world. If anyone tells you they have never felt it, they are holding some cards up their sleeves, and that does not matter because we all know deep down inside that we are far more than just flesh and blood. We know it, we feel it, even if we screw up royally… God is there to bring us back. This I know personally." Soft tears glisten in Jaime's eyes, but he continues, "I came to America to find freedom, and I did. My wish has been fulfilled. I have also found the love of a beautiful woman I do not really deserve, and on top of that, I now have a personal relationship with my Lord and Savior, Jesus Christ. But not before falling on my face and losing everything, but not before I was ready. I was not ready for all that money and fame that magically came to me, and my actions showed it as I squandered it all, no different than a rich spoiled kid who inherits a ton of money. So, be careful what you wish for. I was overwhelmed and unprepared, I was vulnerable and inexperienced, and I suffered for it. However, I also had the experience that when I thought I lost it all, that was when I realized I had gained everything. What else can a man want aside from his salvation? If any of you do not understand this, I beg you to pray for it and be on the lookout for a knock on your door one day soon. It happens to all of us sooner or later. It is in there, in the Bible, in the book of Revelation chapter 3, verse 20."

At this, Jaime faces the congregation, and he makes eye contact with those who nod in agreement, others frown, and he keeps going after checking with Pastor Ervin to see how he is doing with time, but he pumps him up to continue and Jaime does: "You know, my old uncle who is still alive, thank God, and who was the first person to ever tell me about God in a place like communist Cuba where believing in God was prohibited and forbidden during that time, he always compared life to making a fine cigar, and I certainly can't disagree with that, and I've stolen that line many times before just to try to sound intelligent." The congregation chuckles and Jaime's face suddenly turns serious, even his tone of voice unexpectedly changes, getting the attention of everyone in attendance. There is a quick pause…then he keeps going, "But life is really a song…it's a song, and you can sing it any way you'd like. The song of our lives, it is our choice how we sing it; it is up to us, and isn't that beautiful? Isn't that a gift? Oh, it is indeed a wonderful gift, believe me. One more thing, I know some of you may be thinking, *what is wrong with this guy? Is this the same Jaime? The cigar guy we all know suddenly all religious and stuff?* But the answer is no, I am not the same guy; the change happens from within, on the outside, we still look the same, but inside... I tell you the truth, you become a brand-new person when a rebirth occurs. It has absolutely nothing to do with religion. It is all about salvation. I now know that if I am gone tomorrow, I have a glimpse of where I will be spending eternity. He (Jesus) is not finished with me yet either...there is still much work to be done for me, whatever that may be. I just know."

At this, Jaime looks around, and without a word, he tells them he is done, finished, and after a brief moment of silence, the congregation spontaneously breaks into applause, and everyone, absolutely everyone in attendance one by one begins to stand to their feet, applauding loudly. Jaime runs his hand across his face as he wipes his eyes, which are flooded with emotional tears, and with a humble smile, he bows to the congregation, and the applause seems to last forever. Stephanie walks up on the stage and hugs Jaime joyfully; others walk up and do the same, patting him on the back and congratulating him as a large group begins to crowd the stage. This expressive celebration goes on for several minutes, and when everything seems to have come to an end and as Jaime prepares to leave out the back, the congregation continues to clap in unison, asking him to return to the stage for an encore like they usually do at the music concerts. At this, Jaime is pushed back out there again. He grabs the microphone, and the crowd suddenly becomes silent again, waiting... Jaime then speaks one last time before he leaves for good, "Listen, I am as stunned as you all are. I did not prepare any of this, and if I would have done it, there is no way I could have remembered it all, so understand that spontaneous can be a good thing, but when it comes from the heart, it's all spontaneous. Now, I will end this on a quick note I think is of most importance." The audience pays close attention, and he ends with "Remember that nothing we do in life matters unless we do it with love, with conviction, with desire, and with the right intention. Love never fails, everything else will cease, everything will come to pass, but love endures. Love one another, love life, live with passion, and do for those who cannot do for themselves...and remember that faith, hope, and love, out of which love is the greatest... Practice these three principles, and you will never go wrong. I am glad I was able to share with you and to get it all out of my chest. Changing lives, it's what living is all about, and if only one single life is changed with my message here today, I am a happy man for it, and I guess I did my job. Be good, and may God bless you all. It was truly an honor sharing with you today!"

Jaime then bows to the crowd and points to the sky, giving all the glory to God. The large crowd breaks into a loud roar and applauds again, even louder than before. Jaime walks out the back, and he gives his good friend Ervin a tight hug, and the two men share a solemn smile nodding both their heads in agreement. He then joins Stephanie, who waits in the car. They leave.

Following the emotional, inspirational speech, Jaime and Stephanie drive out towards the beach. They make their way to a popular seafood restaurant Stephanie has been talking about for the last few days to have a private dinner. It is now early evening, and the place is quiet and romantic with a lantern-lit terrace overlooking the water. Jaime and Stephanie sit at a cozy, candlelit table on the breezy deck. She sits close to Jaime with her arms wrapped around his shoulders. She sighs with pleasure as she rests her head on him. It is a perfect evening. She looks away into the ocean, and she tells him, "I love the..."

Jaime suddenly jumps in and finishes her sentence, "...the smell of open water? Steph, that was your dad's favorite line anytime we were out by the water." Smiling, she gazes into his eyes. She takes his hands... Jaime is lost...

"Happy birthday, Jaime!" He smiles, surprised, as he thought she had forgotten all about his birthday, and then suddenly, a waiter approaches with a cake full of candles and begins to light them all. Several other servers and restaurant staff join in to sing "Happy Birthday" to Jaime, who blushes, looking like he is five years old. Stephanie enjoys this. The small private celebration seems to last a lifetime as Stephanie asks the members of the staff to join them for a piece of cake, and they stay and chat amiably with Jaime and Stephanie for a while.

After dinner, Stephanie and Jaime walk out to the parking lot, and upon arriving at their vehicle, Jaime opens the car door for Stephanie. Then he goes around to the driver's side. Now sitting in the car, they kiss.

"Steph, thank you, I had a great time. I really enjoyed it, and the food was great. Especially the company…you! I certainly did not expect it." He smiles and continues, "See, that right there surprised me, and I tell you, not much does anymore. I love small details." She leans closer, and placing her cheek on his, she tells him:

"I know. Happy birthday, Jaime!"

After a moment, the car pulls out of the restaurant parking lot, and instantly two other cars pull out right behind them and discreetly follow. As they drive unhurriedly towards the house, Jaime and Stephanie chat warmly, but they never notice the two cars following them all the way to the house. Arriving, they pull into the secluded drive, shut off the engine, and then she abruptly gets out of the car to help Jaime. Jaime also gets out, with his cane in hand, he looks at her…a bit staggered, and he asks, "What's wrong?" Stephanie just stands there oddly. Jaime asks again, "Steph, are you okay, honey?" She suppresses a smile right on cue when the two cars that had followed pull up into the driveway: a sports car and a midsize rental car. Jaime watches, confused, as both cars shut off their engines and turn off the headlights. The doors open, and Jaime's jaw about to drop as Chuchi and Papo get out of the sports car, and Panchi and Tito get out of the rental car. No longer boys, the four men, all wearing matching Hawaiian shirts, rush Jaime like a bunch of starving children at a busted piñata. In utter disbelief and happy beyond words, Jaime cries out with joy as they run to meet him. Stephanie laughs at the sight of the five men embracing in one big sloppy group hug.

Inside Mr. Romero's house, there is a party. Within minutes, more people begin to arrive as this whole thing had been obviously prearranged by Stephanie and the boys, and before long, the house is filled with friends, neighbors, and even strangers and all kinds of guests. There is music, dancing, food, and laughter, lots of laughter; it is a modest gathering in celebration of Jaime's surprise birthday party. A cloud of cigar smoke hovers around Jaime and the boys who stand in a circle joking, drinking, and reminiscing. The boys talk to Jaime all at once, all with cigars in hand. Doing his little shortstop dance, Tito tells Jaime, "You've missed all my major league moves, old man."

"Yeah, you blinked," Papo adds, and Tito smacks him on the back of the neck.

"Papa, all those magazine covers, they almost made you look handsome," Panchi yells in Jaime's ear. Jaime smiles and gives him a high five.

"Well, you know, Papa turned down *GQ* magazine three times," Chuchi jokes, and they all laugh, but his tone suddenly changes to serious, "You had us all worried to death...for a long time, no one knew anything about you. That was not cool. We all thought the worse." Seeing the emotion in his eyes, Jaime is nearly overcome. Panchi senses the timing is right to interrupt, and he does:

"Alright... Before you two start sobbing like a couple of little girls..." He raises his glass...and the others follow:

"To... El Pasatiempo Nacional (the national pastime) baseball, baby! And to Jaime, our mentor, our leader." Laughing, they all raise their glasses, and Jaime, who is not drinking, instead toasts with his cigar as he voices:

"And to all of us!"

The party continues, and a few hours later, as the festivities settle into a groove, Stephanie ushers Willy Chirino, the Cuban musician we saw at the church, through the crowd to meet Jaime. Jaime shakes his hand, surprised... As Willy happens to be one of Jaime's favorite Cuban performers.

"Willy! Of course! I have loved your music my whole life… You make us all proud. You are from Pinar de Rio too, no?" Willy smiles…

"Where else? Most beautiful land in all the world," Willy answers, and he gives Jaime a hug.

"It's a pleasure to meet you, Willy. We need to take a picture together." Jaime gives his cell phone to one of those in the crowd and asks that he takes their picture.

"Are you kidding me, I'm the one who has always wanted to meet you. I've kept all the newspaper articles, and I've followed your story since it hit the airwaves," Willy tells Jaime.

"You wanted to meet me? You followed my story?" Jaime surprisingly adds, and Willy, looking a little shy, replies:

"Jaime, you inspired me, you inspired all of us. As a matter of fact, I have a surprise for you, and I really hope you like it… Jaime, after reading about you in all those articles and after learning your story, I felt like I knew you, and I wrote a song, a great song." Jaime looks at Stephanie, who shrugs innocently.

"A song? What kind of song? What is the song called?" Jaime quickly asks, and Willy responds in Spanish:

"'La Canción Del Tabaco (The Cigar Song).' It is a song about your life, my friend." Immediately, Jaime's eyes water like an overflowing pool of happiness, and completely touched at hearing this, he then reaches in his pocket, and he offers Willy a cigar, one of his best cigars, which Stephanie had kept in a humidor. They break out in hearty laughter and embrace together.

"Are you kidding me? Willy Chirino wrote a song about me. I want to hear it… God bless you, brother! About me, a song? Let's go!" Willy looks at him and gives him a stare of appreciation followed by a huge grin.

"Yes, sir. Sure did. Alright, as soon as it's ready, you'll be the first one to hear it…it isn't finished yet."

"Deal!" Jaime adds, and they embrace affectionately. Stephanie watches, proud. The rest of the night slowly moves, full of fun and festivities, and as the party comes to an end, everyone begins to leave until the place is empty and dark.

The following morning, inside Mr. Jacobs's office, Stephanie and Jaime have a meeting with the old attorney, who surprisingly has a glint of amusement in his eyes. "Alright, I have some good news! You two are now officially the proud founders of the Children's Believe in Your Dreams Foundation." There is a pause. "Well, did you hear me? Steph? Mr. Colon?"

The old man watches with pleasure as Jaime and Stephanie look over a thick pile of legal paperwork, both overjoyed, and Mr. Jacobs continues on, now directing his look at Stephanie. "It's all there, just like you wanted it. Finally, a man who puts his money to good use."

"Finally, a lawyer without a fin on his back," Jaime adds. Stephanie smiles, and Mr. Jacobs replies in the most convincible manner:

"No, I have a fin too, but I have my moments. Remember, all lawyers have fins. All of them." They all laugh, and then Mr. Jacobs looks at Stephanie, and he winks. "And that other thing we talked about? Are you ready for a trip?" the old lawyer tells Stephanie, and she smiles at the timely question, Jaime frowns, clueless.

Several days later, Jaime and Stephanie land at a Nicaraguan airport. The small plane circles around the dirt runway, and moments later, it finally comes to a stop. Stephanie helps Jaime as they step down off a small plane and onto the tiny airport's dirt airfield in a rural part of Nicaragua, completely different from the times before. This is a remote area Jaime has never seen and away from everything. They unload without any bags in their hands and quickly walk inside the small, outdated terminal, which remains in ill repair after thirty years of no maintenance. They quickly come out the other end of the small terminal, and outside the passenger pickup area is a car with the engine running. A sweaty driver waits inside the vehicle. As soon as the driver spots them, he waves them down, and Jaime immediately jumps in one side of the car while a man wearing a Panama Jack hat opens the door for Stephanie, and they drive away.

It is a beautiful sunny day, and Jaime is all smiles as they are here to pick up a special group. This time it is the Colon family clan, young and old, uncle, grandmother, cousin, and all the rest, who rush forward with arms spread wide open to embrace Jaime in a tearful reunion. Jaime, in a state of disbelief, hugs them all one by one. But his eyes try to sort between the large group in looking for his old grandmother, and when he finds her, the old lady loses it. She begins to cry frantically, and he begins to laugh out loud as he runs towards her. Jaime grabs her in his arms, and he picks her up in the air, sending her flip-flops flying in the air. After a few moments of sobbing together while holding Jaime tightly around his neck, Jaime's grandmother finally speaks, "Oh my Lord, the prodigal son returns…" The old uncle agrees by nodding his head smoothly like he does everything else, but he says nothing as he smiles and blows a smoke ring in the air. Jaime, in utter surprise, weeps mildly with joy as he sees them all right in front of him. He looks at Stephanie, who has taken the time to prepare this grand surprise for him, and no words can express Jaime's feelings towards her, and she knows it. She nods her head and blows him a kiss as a sign of total understanding. She smiles, and he gets it, recognizing perfectly as this is one of those moments where a picture is worth a thousand words… Jaime takes that picture in his mind, he saves it, and he savors it. Jaime then runs to his uncle, and he gives the man a firm handshake, and they embrace in a long hug with no words. A hug that seems to last forever as neither man wants to let go.

At the Jalapa Valley region several hours later, among the lush green fields and colorful rolling mountains, the beautiful tobacco Vega is again bustling with workers. The cigar plantation has come back to life after being desolate for some time, and it is vibrant and energetic again. Inside the new cigar factory, a clean, well-lit factory is once again occupied by cigar-rollers who happily listen to the radio as they work. A few infants play in pens while their parents work. Everything operates smoothly. Everyone looks happy again, and Ijaba cigars are being cranked left and right by the joyous workers. Next to the factory and outside the cigar barn, Jaime's uncle, who is now a little frail, licks his finger and tests the wind. It is a beautiful day, and Jaime joins him out on the field. The old man speaks, "The smoking of a fine cigar is a time of contemplation, relaxation, and appreciation." Jaime smiles while staring at the old uncle, who offers him a brand-new cigar and continues, "Do you even remember what a real one tastes like, my nephew?" Jaime sneers, acknowledging the old man may be speaking correctly, and they both light up. Each blows a smoke ring in the air. The two men, who have found peace with the world, though decades apart, feel no different at this very moment. They are one and the same, linked by the cigars they enjoy at this very instant and the life they suddenly share, indulging in some of Jaime's finest.

"You were right, Tio. There was so much I needed to learn. I am sorry for always acting like a know-it-all." The old man points at Jaime, and with a grin from ear to ear, he tells him:

"I'm sorry for letting you. I should have whipped it out of you a long time ago with the belt." Hearing this, the two men laugh out loud, and then suddenly, the old uncle asks with his low rusty voice, "How does it feel, Jaime? How do you feel right now?"

Jaime takes his time, and finally, he tells him, "It feels like life being right here with you, Tio…" The old man beams at Jaime with a sparkling attitude, and Jaime kisses his cheek with much respect and affection. They hold each other for several seconds in a tight embrace, and before Jaime pulls away, the old man gives him a persuaded look that says a million words. And even though no words are exchanged between them, they understand exactly the meaning of the enduring stare. Jaime begins to grin, and the old man meets his gaze with the same familiar chuckle. They not only look alike, but at this very moment, they feel the exact same, happy, fulfilled, and proud. "Tio, thank you for everything!" says Jaime, and his uncle respectfully removes his hat, he bows and responds back to Jaime:

"You are very welcome, son. It has been an honor watching you grow and become a man!"

"You did well; you made a good man out of me," Jaime adds, and the two go inside and join the others for a family dinner that lasts forever between the storytelling and all the catching up.

After dinner, Stephanie and Jaime leave the rest of the family, and they go for a walk around the grassy riverbank outside the tobacco plantation, where dimming sunlight sparkles on a tranquil, gently flowing river as the sun is slowly coming down behind the purple rolling mountains. Under shady fruit trees, with birds singing and with only nature's own noises filling the air, Jaime and Stephanie sit on the soft grass with outstretched legs feeling numbly relaxed. He cradles her between his knees, and she has her arms wrapped around his legs, both facing the river. She reaches over and whispers in his ear, "I feel so at home here. Can we stay here, Jaime? Forever?"

Jaime looks at her, and, taking her hand with much tenderness…he replies, "Yes! Of course, we can. I know you love it here." She smiles…and then he tells her, choosing his words carefully, "Steph, I have something to tell you." Stephanie, suddenly pale, reaches his face, not liking his tone, and he explains, "Last week…at the doctor's…"

"Jaime, you said everything was fine."

"I didn't want to spoil the trip."

"Jaime, stop playing around. Tell me. What did the doctor say?" Jaime hesitates as something like this is terrible to say and probably worse to hear.

"Stephanie, the results were positive. They say it's lung cancer…in the early stages…" Stephanie, surprised, clutches her face, shock-stricken…

"Oh God!" she exclaims.

"Please, Stephanie…" Jaime tries to calm her…

"Does the family know, Jaime?" she asks, trembling, and he replies back softly:

"No…no one knows. You are the first I tell. I have been thinking a lot about this, and I'm okay with it. Ironically, but I had to tell you. I didn't want to hide it from you." With tears in her eyes, Stephanie collapses into his chest.

"Oh God… Jaime, why now? I just found you. I don't know whether to hate your cigars or…"

"Baby... Listen to me..." he interrupts, and cradling her, he continues, "Innocent housewives get clobbered by taxicabs. A Wall Street banker's heart goes when he is thirty. I've lived, and then some."

"But not with me, Jaime... Smoking is dangerous; people get lung cancer all the time, and it stinks too!" Stephanie pleads...and Jaime bargains with her:

"Look, if God wants to take me now, I've already caught a glimpse of where I'm going. So, don't be bad-mouthing my cigars, okay?" he tells her jokingly, and he smiles and kisses her. Bravely, Stephanie wipes her tears.

"Tell me, Jaime, how long did it take you to practice that little speech?"

"Not long... A week! Two!" Stephanie gazes away with forced calm at the slow-moving water, and after a moment, she asks:

"So, how long does the doctor say? How long do we have?" Jaime takes a minute to respond, and when he does, he tells her assertively. He says:

"Maybe I will live another twenty years, thirty. Who knows? The more I take care of myself, the better I will be, but, Steph, I feel good. I don't feel sick at all. He says they caught it early. Let's have faith, alright?" Jaime pauses...then he asks her, "Stand up! Would you?" Stephanie hesitates. Jaime continues, "Please?" Not taking her eyes off his face, she hesitantly climbs to her feet. Jaime crawls onto one knee and looks at her. He spills these words...while presenting a three-carat diamond ring to her, "Stephanie Romero, will you marry me?" And for one unbelievable moment, time stops here, and nothing else exists, only Stephanie and Jaime staring into each other's eyes, and it seems as if all noise around them has come to a halt. In complete silence now and with a fountain of fresh tears bursting with happiness, Stephanie collapses on top of Jaime and squeezes her arms around him.

"Yes! Yes! Of course, I will marry you..."

With the tenderness of two young lovers, they hold each other, kissing and rolling on the grass. Jaime then whispers into her ear, "Hey, Steph, the little speech took a lot longer to prepare." He smiles shyly. "I figured I'd tell you." They both start laughing and begin to kiss. Consumed with joy, they don't hear the urgent voice of the young cousin racing towards them:

"Come quickly! Hurry!" They both become startled as Jaime's young cousin suddenly tugs at their clothing, frantic and out of breath. "Hurry! Come on, let's go!"

Stephanie and Jaime run back to the cigar factory with the young cousin, where there is a large group of people waiting inside, and there, inside the cigar factory, surprisingly, work has become a party. The cigar rollers are dancing with jubilant abandon to a lively Latin song on the radio. The old uncle and grandmother are also slowly moving side by side, attempting to be dancing and nodding to the rhythm of the festive song. Everyone is dancing. The young cousin breathlessly drags Jaime and Stephanie in the door. "Listen! Jaime…listen to the song!" Jaime and Stephanie stop to try to listen to the vibrant and joyful song, hearing the words as the chorus repeatedly continues to chant:

"La Canción Del Tabaco (The Cigar Song)… La Canción Del Tabaco!" Staggering realization dawns on their faces, and Jaime rapidly exclaims:

"Is that…? Is that the song? Willy Chirinos's song?"

Stephanie quickly adds, "No, Jaime, that's your song. Your song, baby, your very own song and the song of your life."

Exultantly, Stephanie embraces Jaime, and they sway in rhythm together as the lively song continues to play. It seems to last forever, and so does the dancing as the catchy and rhythmic song comes to an end. Following the song, the DJ on the radio adds, "That right there, ladies and gentlemen, is called 'La Canción Del Tabaco (The Cigar Song)' by Willy Chirino and the most requested new song on the radio this week…rapidly moving up the charts!"

At hearing the DJ's words, every worker in the room cheers. Jaime is stunned and almost speechless as he is surrounded by rowdy, congratulatory adulation like he is the biggest hero ever. The old uncle calmly chews on what is left of his cigar with the usual grin on his face, and the fragile grandmother pats Jaime's face like he is still her little boy. The old lady then tells him, "Jaime, honey, Ijaba would be proud. You did it, son, you did it. She would be so immensely proud of you!" Jaime gives her a smile, and he glances heavenward and responds, pointing with his index finger in the air:

"I think she is, Abuela, I think she is, and by the way..." He puts his arm around Stephanie and brings her close to the old lady. "I've found her. I finally found her, Abuela." The old lady crosses herself and looks straight up to the sky.

"Thank God! It is a miracle! Now I can die happy!" Jaime and Stephanie break into laughter, and they both hug the old lady, sandwiching her between them. The old grandmother kisses Stephanie on her cheek and then turns to Jaime and kisses him. With a big grin on his face and with much deliberation, the old uncle blows a smoke ring in the air and watches it rise. His weathered old eyes, like two pools of wisdom in his wrinkled, sun-browned face, grow misty with tears of excitement. He then adds, pointing at Jaime:

"You know, every good cigar has a story, and every man writes his as he lives his life. Every day is a new chapter." Jaime looks back at the old man after puffing on his cigar in total understanding of his words; he points right back at him and blows a ring of his own. They hug and begin laughing together as joyous loud sounds of celebration cover the air... It is a party!

Across the pond, in Miami, at the Colon Playground, the same playground Jaime once dreamt of building out of an abandoned lot, it thrives. The happy sound of children playing can be heard from a distance.

It is a sunny morning in South Florida, and the playground that Jaime made possible continues to flourish as inner-city kids play on swings, slides, shoot basketballs and climb jungle gyms. The place is packed. Little children, who we recognize as the future, gleefully run through a sparkling water spray in laughter! And...not far from the park, at a local tobacco shop in Miami, a box of Ijaba Cigars is selected by an elderly customer and brought to the checkout counter.

"It's about time they brought these back. I missed them! There is nothing like these babies right here." The clerk nods his head and rings the man up, who continues to read from the lavish box like a little boy who just received his first box of baseball trading cards.

"You are lucky to have come in today, a new shipment has just arrived. We have been sold out all week, and these will be gone by tomorrow. It's our best-seller," the clerk adds, and the customer smiles at the excited clerk.

The man quickly fires back, "You know what? Give me another box just in case they disappear again. You just never know."

The clerk then adds, smiling and with a look that tells the old customer there is no chance these cigars will be gone any time soon, "Ijaba Cigars are not going anywhere, sir. They are here to stay! Darn, things are better than ever, but yes, you should take two boxes just in case."

The customer pays the clerk, and as he walks away, he stops and, looking back, he nods his head, acknowledging all the Ijaba merchandise once again hanging from wall to wall. The clerk smiles as if knowing the story behind the cigars as if knowing the story of Jaime and as if being able to see Jaime's life being portrayed before his very eyes just by staring at the fancy cigar box. One definite eye-grabbing detail about the box is the fancy gold trimming and the eloquent letters that adorn it along with the beautifully designed emblem of an African princess stamped on the box also in gold, but this isn't just a box of cigars; the box represents the struggle, the pain, the dream, and ultimately, the triumph of a man whom everyone considered a hopeless romantic fixated on one of the craziest ideas ever and what many called an impossible feat. Well, he proved them all wrong!

Now, remember that Jaime's desire to vindicate the name of his ancestor, his success, and the undeniable creation of such wonderful specimen, Ijaba Cigars, came about from wanting to fulfill another's dream and that of his ancestor, Ijaba herself, whose dream was to be free, unchained, and whose face now appears on the classic logo on the cigar box for the world to see. Yes, the picture of the young

African princess on the box is that of Ijaba, who stands out so sophisticated, so impressively printed, so present, and thanks to Jaime, she lives! She is here with him, free at last, just like he is.

Inside one of the stores, where the shelves are stocked with Ijaba Cigars, humidors, accessories, hats, T-shirts, and everything you can think of representing the fabulous product, it feels like first class once again. The flair of the once unknown brand, which became global, glows once more. Jaime's cigars, after becoming a prominent symbol in the world of fine smokes and whose name had become synonymous with perfection, are back! Realizing this, the customer smiles, he walks away and peeks back inside the store as the door closes behind him. The bells hanging from the door of the shop rattle as the gentleman finally leaves, and immediately following this, another customer enters the small tobacco shop, making the bells ring once again. Then another, and another. The man walks in. "Hello, do you guys have any Ijaba Cigars here? The clerk smiles…and replies to the man before him:

"Yes, of course, we have Ijaba Cigars. We have loads of them. How many boxes would you like, sir?"

As we pull back, behind the store, the setting sun can be seen at a distance, the City of Miami at a glance. The water around Key Biscayne…

And just like that… Many years later…

We now find ourselves on a grassy riverbank in Nicaragua. It is dusk. Beautiful mountains surround us, the sound of the water in a slow-moving river echo. An old man with a cane, with his back to us, is gazing out over the gently flowing, now familiar river. He is smoking a cigar, and the setting sun before him casts a nostalgic mood…

The voice of Jaime's uncle echoes in the air, "The tobacco plant comes from the ground, from the dust, and eventually it returns back to the dust, but in between, making a fine cigar is a complicated and fascinating process…"

"The world breaks everyone, and afterward, many are strong at the broken places."

Funny how this happens, huh? The world broke Jaime down like it so often does many, if not all of us, and he too became stronger at all his broken places afterwards. But this does not just happen to Jaime, it can happen to just about any breathing human being. The world broke him down only to build him right back up. It molded him, it instructed him, it transformed him, it broke him down into little pieces all the way down to his very core, his foundation, only to build him up the right way. It reconstructed him in a way that he could fulfill his rightful purpose, equipped with all the necessary experience to overcome. Now, when we look into our own lives, where is your miracle? I urge you to find your broken places and then acknowledge the reconstruction process that follows, making you even stronger than before. Where did your brokenness take you? Was it a coincidence that your fall may have seemed too mighty to surmount at the time, making you almost want to quit? Well, I am glad you didn't! I have concluded; the only assumption that makes any sense to me is that we are not here by accident but by intelligent design to fulfill a purpose and to leave a trail for those coming behind us. There is no way in the world that everything can ultimately fall into place so precisely, so timely, and so perfectly unless there is some kind of predestination taking place. This is my belief and my take on it, and if I am wrong, I am wrong; however, it is just too coincidental to not make me wonder. Don't you? The way everything comes back full circle in life, the way we run into people and things from the past in such dramatic ways, the way we may fall in love with a complete stranger or simply someone from way back in our lives in such an untimely fashion just makes me think, it makes me question the very core of my understanding and what we are taught since childhood. It motivates me to question the foundation of what the world teaches as we walk through it, and it brings me to one unmistakable conclusion, there has to be a God who creates, oversees, and who gives us that free will, which allows us each to make rational and irrational decisions as we navigate through life. It gives me complete evidence that we are not here by mistake. We are far too valuable and too accountable for the lives of all those who surround us to just be the casualty of some kind of mistake, an accident, and some random "boom" millions of years ago. The so-called big bang theory is total and complete speculation, a theory, and a vague attempt to remove *God*, our creator, from His rightful place as the founder and creator of our precious lives. If there were no *God* or intelligent design behind our existence, how then is it that we so often find ourselves looking for Him in times of trouble, perhaps the only time we look for Him? Why do we as humans find the necessity to reach for higher power as if knowing this to be a natural instinct? If you have never thought about it, this is the time to do so. Love conquers all, God is love, and if nothing else, when all else fails, give love a chance, give God a chance, and watch a majestic occurrence take place before your very own eyes. It happened to Jaime, it happened to me, and it will happen to you too, without a doubt, so expect it and embrace it so that you are not blindsided by it.

The sight of the beautiful river now returns the unmistakable rolling mountains in the background along with the sound of birds and nature in its endlessness and creates an unforgettable scene. We see an old man holding a cane with his left hand, leaning on it, resting all his weight on the wooden stick, which is a clear sign of his age, his back is to us. He is in deep thought… In his right hand, he holds a lit-up cigar, smoke slowly drizzles from it. Two other stogies rest in his shirt pocket. He slowly takes a puff, and as he exhales, he utters these words almost under his breath: "The hardest prison to escape from is the mind…" obviously reminiscing about his life, his past, his turmoil, and finally, his vindication.

He gazes out over the gently flowing crystalized river reminding him of heaven as described in the book of Revelation in the Bible:

"Also in front of the throne was what looked like a sea of glass, clear as crystal" (Revelation 4:6 NIV).

The old man with the cane is actually Jaime years from today, who stands by the slow-flowing river, and he now looks just like a version of his old uncle. Standing close by, an aged Stephanie smiles, and they are both at peace. She places both her hands on each side of his face and pulls him gently towards her. They kiss. They have both found heaven. Stephanie walks beside Jaime, who now holds the chewed-up cigar stub in his mouth, and she wraps her arms around his fragile body. Like two young lovebirds, they find comfort in each other's arms the rest of their days, and happiness fills their faces!

Stephanie glows with pleasure, and Jaime's face expresses pure ecstasy and contentment. They continue to walk slowly, and after a few steps, Jaime blows a smoke ring, and it gradually floats straight up into the air. He takes Stephanie by the hand, and they walk together. Jaime, who limps a bit from his right leg, moves sluggishly, but Stephanie slows her pace down to allow him to keep up with her. He looks right at Stephanie, and their eyes meet. Jaime then whispers, "Babe!"

She smiles and repeats the same word, "Babe!"

Following a warm and seductive moment of silence, they both break into laughter. After they finally stop laughing, he tells her, "Honey, this is exactly what life is, but a song, and you can sing it any which way you like!" She agrees with him by giving him what appears to be an angry frown that is followed by a beautiful smile. He understands the meaning of this, and she knows. They both know! Only they now know the powerful significance of this. Jaime then tosses what is left of the cigar into the river, and he looks up toward heaven, pointing upward with his index finger...and smiles as he mumbles: "Mission accomplished! It is done!" exclaims Jaime as he exhales yet another smoke ring in the air, his last, and he continues to smile, knowing he is now fulfilled and complete next to the love of his life. After all, how many people really get to sing their very own song the way they want?

And just like that, Jaime, along with the love of his life, carries on moving towards the setting sun until their shadows slowly disappear behind the fading bright sunlight over the mountain.

We follow the cigar stub, what is left of it, as it gently bobs along the slow-flowing river… Floating downstream, we see pieces of what a cigar stub was once continue on until it finally fades.

Where one life ends, another life begins…

"The tobacco plant comes from the ground, from the dust, and eventually it returns back to the dust…" (A sigh of relief…)

"And now these three remain: faith, hope and love, but the greatest of these is love" (1 Corinthians 13:13).

It is done!

The end

Printed in the USA
CPSIA information can be obtained
at www.ICGtesting.com
LVHW051208131223
766027LV00060B/1109